Echoes at the Abbey - a ghostly tale of love and death.

After her divorce Alison Greenways buys a dilapidated cottage in rural Sussex. She slowly uncovers the violent events that Greysmead village has held secret for nearly five hundred years and learns of the tragic love story of Mary. Although separated by five centuries, their common bond is the threat of violence from their controlling husbands. Their worlds slowly connect until past and present finally meet with terrifying consequences........but love can cross the boundaries of death.

About the author

Jan Foster-Bartlett rekindled her love for creative writing when she relocated to her maternal Grandmother's roots of rural Norfolk where she is currently working on another anthology of short stories and also the second novel about the village of Greysmead.

Other work by the same author

Norfolk tales published by Oakmagic publications 2011

Voices in the Wood and other tales Kindle edition 2013

The Black Horse Ghost and other tales Kindle edition 2015

For Kit Berry - for changing my world in a positive way

PROLOGUE

In the grey morning light the sound of laughter filled the cold dank air as drunken revellers poured out of the nightclub and onto Tower Street. In the alley alongside Cinderella's bar the air was heavy with the odour of stale urine. Within the shadows stood Billy Watson, local pimp and drug dealer. Tall and lean, arms decorated with tattoos. One announced to all how much he loved his dear old mum, the other painted with a rope of barbed wire, winding around his bicep, up across his shoulder and twisting and looping around his neck, the razor edged barbs cutting deeply into his throat…cutting deeper and deeper…and then deeper still as the blade, quick and sharp appeared from the gloom and took the last breath from Billy's sad and evil life.

A faint gasp escaped from behind the towering rubbish bins. Evie had been finishing her cigarette after making a quick buck with a punter. She held her breath and watched wide-eyed as Big Mick and Kenny stood over the body of Billy Watson.

'I think we may have ourselves some extra company Ken, don't you?' Mick muttered and indicated towards the bin.

Within seconds they had Evie by the throat, knife at the ready to sink into her soft flesh, which moments before had been caressed with passion and lust but now the only passion was a lust for death.

'I won't say nothing Mick! I won't! 'onest!' she pleaded.

Mick pulled her into the light, enjoying seeing fear in her face, the fright in her eyes.

Back in Tower Street, at the far end of the alley, a blue jeep pulled up under the street light. A woman in her mid thirties, long dark hair pulled into a ponytail, jumped out of the 4x4. She planned to seek out her husband and surprise him, give him a lift home. Try to salvage the ailing marriage. She heard a whimper and in the darkness witnessed a glimpse into hell.

Evie's mascara smudged eyes noticed the figure in the distance. She tried to raise her arm to alert the stranger. Maybe one small chance of a reprieve? But Mick and Kenny walked quickly away as the bubbling of blood from Evie's throat faded behind them.

Chapter one

She pulled the curtains across the window to hold back the darkness. She'd never known anywhere that was so devoid of light. As soon as the sun set, the view from the window vanished. Not even a tree in silhouette. It was almost as if the cottage was in a vacuum in space surrounded by blackness, but here, not even a star was visible. Alison shivered and turned on the light.

As the lamp flickered into life she thought she caught sight of a movement just under the windowsill. She turned to look. It was gone. She wrapped the fleece around her shoulders and settled down on the sofa, switching on the TV to bring some company into the place, trying to push away her uneasiness.

She had loved this cottage so much when she viewed it six months ago. It was her home. A country retreat with its four tall Georgian style windows at the front with the door in the middle, reached by a brick path from the wooden gate. It was the picture she'd always had in her mind of where she'd like to live. As a child she would draw pictures of 'her special house.' To her Mother the drawing looked like every other child's picture of a cottage. Basic and simple. To Alison it was more. It was real.

It had been after the divorce that Alison decided she would move away from London, get away from Kenny and all he stood for. Find a quiet place where she could work and relax. She had forgotten about her childhood dream cottage until the day the estate agent's listing arrived on the doormat.

She had picked up her mug of coffee and taken the envelope into the lounge of the flat, flopped down onto the sofa and flicked through the pages. Nothing at all appealed until she turned to the last property on offer. The photos leapt out at her. It was as if her childhood drawing had been copied onto the page. It was exactly the same!

Memories of feelings she'd had as a child came flooding back. She remembered the careful details she had added to her picture. She sat forward on the sofa, excitement dancing in her head as she peered closely at the photographs. There was the apple tree, the herringbone pattern of the brick path, the three chimney pots. It was all there, just as she had drawn as a child. The only thing missing was the dark shadowy figure standing just outside the fence that she had always felt compelled to draw.

After a chat with the estate agent, Alison had arranged a viewing and a few days later she left her rented flat and Mitcham behind and headed down to Sussex. She had booked a B&B overnight in a village close to where the cottage was situated. She felt elated. Life was on the up! Time for a change.

The divorce had brought her to an all time low. She couldn't get motivated with her work, one client pulled out, as he had been waiting too long for her to return his calls. She knew she had to find something to get her out of the bottomless pit of despair and sadness she had dug for herself and was uplifted that her dream cottage was a reality. And now here she was driving to Sussex so she could walk through the door that her imagination had produced all those years ago.

The sounds of Madness and 'our house' began to play on the car radio. Alison leant forward and turned up the volume, giggled and began to sing along. She was so engrossed in her excitement that the roundabout ahead arrived far quicker than Alison's reactions and she made the foolhardy decision to continue driving even though a car was in her path. The sound of the other driver's horn brought her to her senses. Heart pounding in her chest, she slowed down, waved her hand to indicate her error and managed to escape with just a gesture and angry looks from the other driver.

She took the exit from the roundabout and looked ahead for the turning for Greysmead village. It couldn't be far now. A police siren echoed behind her, she pulled aside to let it pass, then realisation hit her that the police car was pursuing her. The earlier excitement turned to concern. She shut off her engine, her mouth suddenly dry.

He walked across and peered through her open window. His steel blue eyes took in his prey in detail as he scanned the interior of her car. Her mobile was lying on the passenger seat along with an opened bag of fruit sweets. She smelt the lemony freshness of his face as he gave her a sardonic smile.

'That wasn't very clever was it Miss? Back there…at the roundabout.'

She swallowed, licked her lips, hoping her mouth would work.

'I'm so sorry. I'm trying to find Greysmead village and I lost concentration for a split second.'

There was a hint of amusement in his dark lashed eyes.

'Not on the phone were we, Miss? I see it's lying there, just next to your sweeties. Mmmm, Strawberry Delights, very nice.'

'Oh! Would you like one? Sorry... no of course you wouldn't.'

He grinned, amused at her panic. 'We'll overlook it this time. Just TRY to concentrate from now on. By the way, the turning for Greysmead is just round the next bend. Is your visit business or pleasure?'

'What?…Oh pleasure, I'm going to view a cottage nearby.' Alison picked up the agents details and began reading, 'Monkton Lane, just through the village I believe.'

The glint in his eyes disappeared, 'Monkton Lane? You sure? I thought it was all derelict down there. The hamlet's dead and gone.'

Alison felt a flutter of alarm in her stomach, looked again at the agent's details and showed it to the police officer, 'No, look. Here it is. Monkton Lane. It doesn't look that derelict to me.'

Roger Parsons decided not to get involved. She'd soon realise there was no cottage. Monkton Lane was overgrown and dead, no one would want to live there now. The place was abandoned years ago. He knew the stories about the lane.

'Drive carefully. Mind how you go Miss.' He walked back to his car, leaving Alison to start her engine and continue on her way.

Bloody man! He enjoyed seeing her squirm. No such cottage. Idiot! She leant across and grabbed a strawberry delight, popped it in her mouth and laughed when she recalled how she offered him a sweet! She grinned. He did have nice eyes.

Panic over, her happy mood returned, she took the turning towards Greysmead. As she journeyed through the village and drove past the pretty weather boarded cottages she was aware how quiet it was. Not a soul to be seen. Along the main street, opposite the village green stood the Jolly Abbot. The old timber framed pub was the choice of residence of the house martins, they swooped and dipped low through the warm April skies. Tubs of daffodils bobbed their golden bonnets in delight in the spring sunshine. Alison thought how idyllic the village looked.

She had already picked up the keys from the agents in the nearby town of Lunsford so decided to go straight to the cottage, she was too excited and impatient to check into the B&B first. She was soon driving away from the village and headed towards Monkton Lane, which according to her sat nav was fairly close by. Five minutes later Alison's blue 4x4 turned into a narrow track. The overhanging trees tapped and pinged on the roof of her jeep. Her stomach tightened with anticipation, she was going to view her cottage! She so hoped it would be as wonderful as she imagined.

She peered ahead into the gloom and switched on the headlights as she drove under a tunnel of aging, decaying trees that were encased by parasitic ivy and weeds. The bent trunks and branches were entwined with the ivy, which enveloped every inch of bark with its tendrils, as it twisted and devoured.

Alison made her way slowly in a bid to avoid great distorted fingers of wood that pushed their way through the old and crumbling tarmac. Between the gaps in the overgrown hedges she glimpsed echoes of buildings, their windows staring out blankly within the crumbling bricks. Was she on the right road? Maybe she had taken the wrong turning or maybe the police officer had been right all along. But at last the road opened out and the sunlight and sky was visible again.

A flurry of yellow butterflies danced in the breeze around the car and a buzzard, sitting on a tree stump, alighted his post and flew along the road in front of the car as if guiding her route.

Alison beamed with delight, the graveyard of trees quickly forgotten as she slowly followed her feathered guide. When the buzzard finally flew off she realised she had arrived outside her cottage.

The Darkness watched from outside the fence as she raced around the cottage, thrilled with all she found. She stood and looked across the fields that separated her from Greysmead village. The buzzard floated on the thermals high above. She watched with joy, not noticing the dark shape slither around the fence surrounding her cottage as it tried to find a way in.

The pub dining room was empty except for a dark haired bearded man who had his head buried deep into his newspaper. He grunted an unfriendly good morning to Alison as she took her seat for breakfast.

She'd driven back to the village the previous afternoon after a few hours of poking about in the cottage discovering a multitude of life: woodlice, spiders, silverfish and also the signs of mice living somewhere within the walls. The kitchen floor was littered with droppings. None of this deterred Alison, she could see past the repairs that needed to be done. There was a gem of a property beyond all the work. There were lots of old features, an amazing inglenook fireplace, even a couple of stone arched windows near the back of the cottage. Some walls were devoid of plaster and the crumbling concrete floor of the kitchen was exposed under the rotting linoleum.

All the restoration ahead would probably take months but she still had her flat in Mitcham which would be her home some of the time. When she'd arrived back to the pub she had negotiated a good rate for bed and breakfast for when she was down working on the cottage.

She'd only been at the property an hour when she had phoned the estate agent to put in an offer. The owner lived abroad so she would hopefully hear sometime that day. Her Father knew a builder who would be able to come and take a look, no doubt someone who would take a sharp intake of breath, stand there with a worried look on his face, scratch his chin and tell her just how much work was needed to get the place right. Alison grinned at the thought and picked up the breakfast menu just as a young waitress came over to her table with pad and pencil.

'Are you ready to order yet madam?' she stood poised at the ready.

Alison looked up into the face of a young girl of around eighteen or nineteen. Her hair, a multitude of colours from a bottle or three, was pulled back tightly away from her freckled face.

Alison smiled, 'Good Morning! Please call me Alison. I'm hoping I may be staying here quite a bit over the next few months. And you are?'

'Susie, madam. I'm just here mornings, I do breakfast then I go off to college. My Dad's the owner of the pub.' She stood with the pad hoping Alison wouldn't chat too much so she could get on.

'I won't keep you then,' Alison looked at the menu and placed her order.

Susie scribbled on the pad and turned to go, then hesitated, 'Excuse me madam….er ...Alison…? Hope you don't mind me asking?'

'Yes, what's that Susie?'

'Is it right, you're buying the old cottage down Monkton Lane?' she said, her face not hiding her disbelief.

'I hope so Susie, I am waiting to hear if my offer has been accepted. Why? You seem surprised.'

'It's just not somewhere us villagers go, Monkton Lane. It was deserted years ago. It's a bit creepy down there, what with the history of the place.'

'Why? What history?' Alison asked and then noticed in the doorway the figure of Jim, the landlord, arms folded, looking rather annoyed.

'Come on Susie, time's getting on. Chop chop. Ms Greenways doesn't want to listen to your silly tales now.'

Susie turned and dashed out of the room leaving Alison wanting to know more.

Chapter two

A call from the estate agents started a whirlwind of action so Alison didn't have time to think about Susie's comments. The owner had accepted Alison's offer on condition she could complete the sale quickly. Her offer had been far below the asking price and she was amazed but relieved, as the place needed a lot of cash thrown at it to get it habitable. Her Father was good as his word and arranged for the builder he knew to meet her at the cottage a week later to discuss the project and time schedule.

The white florets of clouds scuttled across the sky in the stiff breeze. The heavy showers had eased for a while and the line of tulips that edged the fence were bowing their heads mournfully with the weight of the rain. Alison's long chestnut hair danced in the wind as she stood with her back to the cottage. She looked across the fields towards Greysmead village, her waterproof secured tightly ready for the next downpour. One day she would wake to this beautiful view. She hoped the sale would go through smoothly. The house she'd owned with Kenny was sold so she was a cash buyer, so all being well in about two months she would be the owner of Orchard Cottage.

The peace was shattered by a rasping and growling sound that echoed from the undergrowth along the road. The noise got louder and then a dilapidated black transit van emerged from the ivy-strewn tunnel of Monkton Lane. Its exhaust coughed and sputtered like a hardened smoker and it billowed a black cloud in its wake.

'What the…?' Alison turned to watch as the clapped out monster came to a halt in front of the cottage.

Remnants of yellow lettering dotted along the side of the rusty black beast were the only clues to the van's previous use. The words *Farm* and *offal*

Mark got up from the well and a fragment of wood from the rotting cover broke off and plunged into the depths below. The breeze sent a shiver across his shoulders.

'Please…' the hint of a voice whispered in the air.

Mark twisted round, his face serious now as he listened.

'Please…' the voice murmured into the breeze.

He frowned. What was that?

'Mark, come and look at this,' Alison called from behind the brambles. Feeling unsettled he made his way over to her and discovered her pulling back branches of a large laurel bush.

'See this? I noticed all along the lane there are ruined buildings, it looks as if I have some in my garden too.'

Pulling back more of the branches they uncovered a crumbling stone wall.

'Wow, look at this, it looks like a stone pillar, and over here, a doorway or archway? Some wonderful carvings on this bit here.' Mark ploughed through the greenery like an explorer, finding more and more evidence of a building.

He headed into a small clearing where a worked stone column was trying to push its way up to the heavens through the branches. Alison squeezed through to join him and transfixed by their discovery, she stood in awe looking around at the stones as she realised they stood within the ruins of a religious building; a chapel or perhaps a church.

'This is just flipping amazing!' Mark grinned from ear to ear and looked at Alison who was mesmerized by all they'd found.

She looked at him, unexpectedly feeling calm and smiled, 'It sure is!'

A rumble of thunder growled in the distance and a gust of wind suddenly shook the leaves around them. Above them grey sheets laden with rain now replaced the white frothy clouds. The heavy drops began to fall and huge spheres of water splashed down.

Mark grabbed her hand, 'We best make a dash for it, it's going to get very wet out here!'

The warmth of his hand in hers felt reassuring. She gave him a sidelong glance. First time she'd felt at ease with a guy for as long as she could remember. They made their way through the brambles and back towards the house.

As they passed by the well the whispers hissed at them but the sounds were lost within the storm as the rain pounded down. The darkness swirled slowly around and came to rest onto the well cover. It had to keep the echoes of the past silent.

Alison shoved the key in the lock and they both burst into the cottage to escape the rain. Alison had her waterproof coat protecting her top half but Mark was soaked through. His wet hair was stuck firmly to his head and his now soaking tee-shirt showed off his firm muscular body to perfection.

'Don't suppose there's a nice warm bathroom with big fluffy towels I can use?' he joked. 'Blimey, it's cold in here,' he shivered and rubbed his arms.

The sky continued to empty its bulging clouds onto the already sodden ground outside. The thunder sounded close now, the crack and crash like shotgun fire echoed outside. Mark darted to the window and peered out towards his beast.

'I've got a jacket in the van, I'll just go and get it before I end up with pneumonia!' He dashed back out of the door and Alison watched him run along the path.

He seems rather nice, she grinned to herself. Not the type of builder she was expecting at all. She made a mental note to thank her Father. Nice one Dad!

She wandered about the musty smelling interior whilst she waited for Mark and tried to decide on things she'd like to do to the place, the colour schemes, the kitchen units, the floor coverings. There was so much to do.

A door or window was banging in the wind upstairs, so she carefully took the stairs, avoiding the rotting steps that she'd noticed before and headed for the noise. The top of the stairs led to a long passageway that spanned the full length of the house. It was deceptive from the outside as it was only two rooms wide but the cottage went back a long way.

The banging continued as she stepped carefully across the rotten flooring. It was probably a window hammering onto the frame. She'd best get to it before the rain came in and did any damage. She laughed. Damage! The place needed gutting, a bit of water was the least of her worries.

The grimy window at the far end of the corridor let in a feeble amount of daylight as she made her way towards the source of the noise. Her footsteps echoed in the dark passageway. The banging was coming from one of the rooms at the back. Alison stood outside the door and listened. From within the room she could hear knocking and crashing and the rain splattering onto the dusty floorboards. A flash of lightning darted across the sky, briefly illuminating the long corridor behind her. She put her hand on the door handle and slowly pushed the door open.

Silence.

It was empty, no open window, no rain pouring in. She could have sworn this was the room where the sound was coming from. She listened. No sounds, no banging. The floorboards in front of the old metal fireplace were wet and she walked over to investigate. A huge spider ran in front of her, racing across the gritty floorboards to its lair in the corner. Its web by the fireplace was a larder of dead and decaying flies and beetles. She leaned towards it, fascinated by its hoard of prey.

Without warning, a gust of soot laden air came billowing down the chimney and with it a flutter of wings. A jet-black crow, wings outstretched, started to fly close to her head.

'No! Get out!' she screamed and kept her head down as she shuffled over to the window to try to evict the bird.

It screeched and flew madly, getting closer to Alison each time it circled the room. The window was firmly shut, and no pushing and shoving seemed to budge it. She crouched low on the floor, hands over her face as the crow, incensed at being captured, flew at Alison. She felt the wings brush against her hands as she pushed them out towards the bird to try to keep it away. But it wasn't deterred. It landed on her head and she felt the claws begin to pierce the skin under her hair.

She screamed. The door flew open and Mark raced in, pushed open the window in one easy shove and the crow was gone.

'Off you go fella,' he smiled as he saw the bird regain its freedom and then knelt down beside Alison who was shaking as she curled up against the skirting board.

'It's ok now, it's gone,' he put his arm around her and she felt the warmth of his jacket against her face.

'That was just *so* scary.'

Mark pulled her to her feet. 'He was just as scared as you I expect. It's all ok now. No harm done. Still at least it alerted me to one of the many jobs that needs doing – that chimney pot needs a cover over it to stop any more birds getting in.'

Alison rubbed her head, sore from the bird's claws.

'How did you know it came in down the chimney?'

'Only place it could have come in. Come on, let's look at the place and make a plan of action.'

He was off down the hallway, notepad and tape measure in hand.

After spending the rest of the afternoon with Mark at the cottage and deciding on plans and work required they went their separate ways. She arranged to see him again before the completion date to finalise details and then the fun would begin! He estimated it would take him about two months to get everything sorted as she wanted. So if all went well it looked as if she'd be in by mid August.

The excitement was marred only by her unpleasant experience with the crow. She felt uneasy about it and wondered how Mark had managed to open the window so easily when it had been stuck hard and fast for her. He didn't seem that fazed by the whole incident and even seemed to find it amusing.

She went back to the Jolly Abbot and began to change ready for her evening meal. A hot refreshing shower made her feel more relaxed, it had been a long and exhausting day and she realised her concerns over the crow and Mark were just due to her always fearing the worst. A habit she promised herself she would try to break. She had a bit of time to kill before she went down to eat so decided to ring her Father and give him an update on the day.

Sitting back in the big easy chair in her room she put in her Father's number.

'Hi Dad! It's me.' She settled back and kicked off her shoes.

It was good to hear his daughter sounding bright and happy again. He had worried about her when she had been having such a hard time with Kenny and was relieved when the marriage finally ended. He was a bad one that Kenny, a wide boy, bit of a crook. In with some bad sorts too.

'Hello sweetheart. How goes it? All still on? Any building problems come to light?'

'No. It looks as if most things can be sorted. Mark thinks I should be able to move in by Mid August. Isn't that good? Just hope the sale goes through smoothly.'

'Excellent news. Hold on. Mark? Who's Mark? You mean Peter?'

'No Mark – the builder you arranged to see me today. Rather dishy young chap!' She recalled how he looked after he had been caught in the rain and smiled.

'No my darling. I didn't send anyone called Mark. My builder friend is called Peter.'

Alison sat up in the chair. She suddenly felt hot.

'Well who the hell was the guy I just spent the day with?'

Chapter three

'Hi, Mark here. Can't take your call. Leave a message. I'll get back to you ASAP! Cheers!'

'Mark. It's Alison Greenways…. again! Can you *please* ring me when you get this message? It is *very* important!'

For God's sake! Why wasn't he answering his phone?

She'd been trying all the previous day to get hold of him. She'd lost count of the number of messages she had left. She threw her mobile down in frustration just as Susie brought over a pot of tea.

'Morning! I hear you are leaving us today?'

Alison made a space on the table for the teapot, 'Yep, can't do anything now until the place is mine. Hopefully will be sometime in June. Then the building work starts.' She began to pour her tea, 'Just hope I can get hold of the damned builder by then!'

'Oh no. Problems?' Susie said and then noticed that another breakfast guest had surfaced and so she called over, 'Won't keep you a moment, Mr Elliot!'

He grunted, sat down and opened up his newspaper, burrowing into the pages, out of view.

Alison nodded in Mr Elliott's direction, 'He always looks a right misery.'

Susie leant forward and whispered, 'He's very odd. Always creeping out late at night in camouflage gear.'

Alison began to laugh, 'Really? Maybe he's a birdwatcher or nature watcher. I'm sure I saw him yesterday as I was driving over to the cottage, he was heading towards the field near Monkton Lane with what looked like a huge telescope case.'

'Nature watcher? More likely a perv!' Susie giggled. 'He's got shifty eyes, I don't like him, he gives me the creeps.'

Their gossiping ended when Alison's phone rang, 'Maybe that's the builder at last.' But it was her Father. She looked up at Susie, 'Sorry, I must take this.'

'That's ok,' Susie nodded and scooted over to Mr Elliot's table.

'Dad! Any joy? I still can't get hold of Mark. Have you had any luck finding out what's going on?'

She took a sip of tea and listened as her Father informed her that after a lot of phone calls he'd discovered that Peter Knight, his builder, was in hospital.

'Not good news Alison. Someone found him, he'd collapsed near his garage. He's been laid up a few days now.'

'Goodness Dad, that's terrible! What happened?' She moved her phone to her other ear to try to catch what he was saying as Mr Elliott's newspaper rustled wildly in the background.

'I assume it's a heart attack. It must have happened not long after I spoke to him last week. You know, when I arranged for him to come down and meet you? The hospital won't tell me anything except that he wasn't up to visitors.' Her Father continued, 'Hope he'll be ok. Maybe it was stress, too much work. He is in demand. In fact it was only last week I gave his name and number to a bloke I was talking to in the pub. He said was looking for a reliable builder.'

Alison became aware of eyes upon her and looked up to see that Mr Elliott was not engrossed in his newspaper for a change but was obviously listening to her phone call. As soon as he realised she'd noticed him eavesdropping he jumped up from his seat. He stood with his back to her at the buffet table and began to help himself to cereal.

'You still there love? You listening?'

Annoyed that her call was no longer private she cut it short, 'Yes Dad, you said it's probably stress. Look, I'd better go. Got to finish packing and head off. I'll keep trying to get hold of Mark. He'll have to get back to me sometime. I'll keep you posted.'

It was later that day that she pushed open the door to her flat. She'd only been away a few nights but it was enough time for her to forget how claustrophobic she felt living in her basement flat. She yearned for the countryside, the peace and fresh air.

'How did you get in?' she coaxed a huge bumblebee out of the window and shut it again quickly when the noise of the main high street above invaded her space.

Yes, it would be good to live down in Sussex, away from the traffic noise. She'd be nearer to her Dad too. He'd moved to the Sussex coast last year to live closer to his sister. Wimbledon didn't have anything for him now, only memories that were too painful when they surfaced. It had hit him hard when her Mum had died. Hit her bad too but she'd had to stay strong for her Dad, couldn't let him see she was going through a bad time of her own. Her nerves were shattered to pieces because of Kenny. She wondered how she could have ever loved him. He was evil to the core.

She thought back to the final day. The ultimatum. They'd got her to agree that she would move away from Stockwell, forget everything she knew. It was a day that was engraved in her mind and she shuddered at the memory.

He had held her head tightly, grasping her chin. Squeezing the bone between his thumb and forefinger so tightly she thought it would break. His other hand was hard across her throat. His fingernails dug into her skin and she could smell the vile stench of depravity oozing from every pore of his being.

'So Ali darlin' whatcha gonna do then?' his eyes penetrated her like a knife.

As Big Mick held her in his grasp she could see Kenny across the room cutting small chunks from an apple with his penknife and popping them into his mouth. He sat casually on their sofa as if he was watching TV, not registering in his blurry eyes that he was witnessing his wife being assaulted by his scum of a boss.

Big Mick breathed his putrid breath into her face, 'So, decision time honey!'

'Okay, Okay,' she heard herself whimper, 'you don't have to worry. I'll go! I'll forget everything. I promise.'

'You better had,' he snarled, 'otherwise we might have to help you get amnesia,' he tapped her head a couple of times hard with his fist, 'You get me drift?'

She nodded, looked back at Kenny to try to catch sight of some compassion in his eyes, but they were dead. Working for Big Mick had changed him beyond all recognition.

Mick let her go and hurled her across the room like a discarded toy.

'Come on Ken, let's get back to the club, wifey here needs to pack.' As he walked away he turned and looked at Alison, 'And you just make sure your pretty lips are sealed. We will be watching you….closely. If we find you've been within a foot of a rozzer you're dead meat.'

Kenny followed like an obedient little dog, not even looking at her.

She'd gone that day, stayed with a friend for a while and then rented the flat in Mitcham, but she knew she had to get further away. She had decided once the house was sold and the divorce was sorted she'd get out of London all together.

And now her plan was finally coming together. She'd try to spend as much time down at the Jolly Abbot as she could until she could move into the cottage. But for now she had to put up with the noise and busy streets whilst she was back in Mitcham. The only signs that she'd been away were the bags she'd thrown down on the bedroom floor yet to be unpacked, a doormat littered with junk mail and the fridge smelling of sour milk. Powdered would have to do, she couldn't be bothered to nip out now.

She frowned. The roller blind in the kitchen was open. A fragment of yellow forsythia flower from the bush that grew right outside the window had broken off and was on the windowsill. What had happened? She was certain she'd left the blind closed? Picking up the broken flower she threw it in the bin. It must have got caught up and snapped off when she closed the window. She had locked up in a hurry.

A few minutes of fishing about in the freezer revealed a cannelloni that needed to be used, so once that was in the oven she trotted off to the bathroom for a shower. Ten minutes later she was in her dressing gown, standing in front of the mirror in her bedroom, towelling her hair.

Her thoughts went back to the cottage and when she'd first gone down to view the place. Susie had implied there was something evil about Monkton Lane, said no-one from the village ventured up there. But when Alison had questioned her about it she then made out it was nothing and that she should forget it.

Alison thought back to her first glimpse of the lane, all overgrown and dark. The lane *was* shadowy and spooky. The ruins with their blank empty windows seemed to peer out from the undergrowth at her as she had driven under the dense canopy of trees and ivy. The cottage was remote too and she thought maybe it would be a bit creepy after dark. *Actually* ....very creepy.

The shrill shriek of brakes from a bus outside made her jump. She shuddered, beginning to feel uneasy. She shouldn't be daft! As for Susie and her tales, well she's young, we all have fanciful ideas at that age. But a feeling of apprehension began to edge its way into Alison's thoughts. She shivered and pulled her dressing gown more snugly around herself and began to comb her hair, tackling the knots and turned on the hair dryer. It drowned out the sounds from the road and she was lost in her thoughts for a while, blocked from the outside world by the noise of the dryer. The light had begun to fade, she turned to the window to close the curtains.

There was a flash of movement outside. A dark shadow against the glass, then it was gone. Someone was out there. Looking in at her. She hurriedly pulled the curtains across. Her heart raced as she listened for sounds outside.

The bleep of her oven timer made her jump out of her skin. Oh you stupid cow, Alison. It was probably the shadow of someone walking past on the pavement. The light play tricks in the basement flat.

As she ventured nervously from bedroom to kitchen she clicked on every light she could on route and pulled the blind down tight in the kitchen. Just as she was taking out the cannelloni there was a loud thump at the door. She let out a squeal and the pasta dropped from her hands over the floor.

There had been someone out there after all! What if it was Kenny? What should she do? Oh God, what should she do? The flat was illuminated throughout now, they'd know someone was in.

The banging at the front door started again. Louder and more persistent. She took a deep breath and stepped over the mince and pasta strewn over the floor and tiptoed towards the front door. Just as she put her eye up to spy hole, the door vibrated onto her cheek. THUMP THUMP.

She shot backwards, startled.

'You in there, Al? Your doorbell isn't working,' a familiar sounding voice shouted from outside.

She peeked out again. It was Mark. Slowly opening the door a few inches she peered out. He was standing there, grin on his face swinging a carrier bag in front of him, it smelt delicious. The aroma of vinegar on hot chips wafted towards her.

'What are you doing here, Mark?' She tried to sound annoyed but it was such a relief to see his smiling friendly face she couldn't help but feel the tension drain, 'I've been trying to get hold of you! I need an explanation.'

'Well let me in, and we can talk while I eat my fish and chips,' he beamed, 'I got some milk too, thought you'd probably need some. I'm gasping for a cuppa!'

'Come on in then. I'll just go and put some clothes on. Go through to the kitchen and make yourself useful. Put the kettle on.' As she went into the bedroom she called out to him, 'Hey. How do you know I needed milk?'

'I could smell your fridge in Croydon,' he joked back and started laughing.

She was soon sitting on the sofa. Mark had found her plates and shared out his supper.

'I couldn't believe the number of messages you'd left on my phone! You don't give up, I'll give you that.'

He had lost his phone, he explained, eventually realising it must be back at Orchard Cottage. He found it by the ruins in the garden. He'd called into the Jolly Abbot hoping to see her on his way back to his place in Croydon.

'That young girl with the funny coloured hair told me you'd checked out today, so I thought I'd pop round in person. So, what was the big panic?'

'I spoke to my Dad after you looked round the cottage with me.' She looked at his face to check his reaction, 'He tells me his builder friends name is Peter Knight.'

'Yep, that's right! Pete's in hospital, he asked me to cover his jobs for him. Didn't think I needed to bother saying anything, you didn't know him from Adam anyway.'

She dipped another chip in some ketchup ready to pop it in her mouth, 'Do you know him well?'

'You get to know lots of people in my business. He trusts my work so was happy for me to fill in.'

'What happened? Dad said he had collapsed. Was it a heart attack?'

Mark waved his hand dismissively, 'Yeah, think that's what it is. He needs to rest up for a while though, won't be working for a bit.' He took a swig of tea, 'Still you've got me now. …. I'll sort you out, no problem.'

Along Monkton Lane, the darkness swirled within the damp tendrils of air. It had been awoken from its slumbers and it snaked its way towards the cottage. It coiled itself around the fence, nudging its way through the gaps into the garden. The barriers stopping it from entering the house were firmly shut. It turned and twisted through the misty night towards the apple tree. It was patient, it could wait.

Chapter four

Alison had been looking forward to her trip back down to Greysmead. She loved late spring and always thought May was a beautiful month. It conjured up pictures in her mind of pink and white blossom on the trees and ancient woods heavy with the scent of bluebells. Childhood visits to her Granny Martin's place had left her with memories of the dawn chorus as it wafted its sweet sounds through the early morning breeze, children dancing around maypoles and the jingle of bells as Morris Dancers created merriment on the village green.

It was such a scene at Greysmead when Alison took her next trip down to the Jolly Abbot. She'd set off from Mitcham just after the rush hour and pulled up outside the pub late morning. A week of heavy rain had been replaced by clear skies and warm sunshine and the village was a flurry of activity preparing for the big May Fayre. Mrs Blackman from the Post office was walking past and stopped to speak.

'Mornin' Ms Greenways, picked a good weekend to come down.'

No doubt she was on route to pass on the news that the 'outsider' was back again. Alison smiled as she retrieved some clothes and her case from the back of the Jeep.

'Yes, I heard the fayre was something special. Thought I should come along and see for myself.'

Mrs Blackman's eyes took in every detail she could about Alison including all her luggage and clothes. She nodded towards her large case, 'I see you plan to stay more than just one night. Got time on your hands? You not working at the minute then? You never did say what it is you do.'

Alison, amazed at the front of the woman replied, 'Well, erm, I'm taking the week off. I'm self employed, web design.'

'Computers. Dot coms.' Mrs Blackman nodded before glaring at Alison's cropped trousers. 'You know we all like to make an effort for the fayre. I hope you have something nice and feminine to wear tomorrow.'

The cheek of the woman! 'Well, er….yes I do actually.'

'Look forward to seeing you at my cake stall then dearie.' And off she sped to report back to all her fellow gossipmongers who were probably congregating in the village store.

Nice to know everyone is so interested in her life! Bloody nosey cow!

Alison was soon back in her usual room above the bar at the Abbot. She'd booked in for a week. Time to get to know the village better, meet the people she would be mixing with and what better start than the annual village fayre. Although if they are all pushy old bags like Mrs Blackman it might not be that much fun after all.

The sounds of hammering on wood echoed behind the floral curtains. The village maypole had been erected and the gaily-coloured ribbons fanned out and were being secured into the grass to stop them tangling up, ready for the dancing the next day.

The sunshine reflected on the white marquee as it was hoisted into place and Jim began wheeling over some barrels. The pub would be shut tomorrow, all trade taking place outside. Alison settled back contently on her bed with a cup of tea looking out at the activity. She smiled. What a contrast to her life at the flat in London. She was looking forward to her week at Greysmead.

The house sale was progressing nicely. No chain. The cottage had belonged to an elderly couple for many years and after the husband had died, his widow had eventually gone into a nursing home. She had died within months. Probate researchers had finally located a very distant relative in the States who wasn't the least bit interested in an almost derelict cottage, they much preferred the money. So with this and Alison being a cash buyer, the sale was speeding along and it looked as if it would be hers by early June.

Alison had tried a few times to get hold of builder Mark and had eventually spoken to him a few days ago.

'Sorry Al, I'm *really* busy, trying to get things sorted so I can give you all my attention when needed.'

'Okay, that's good, but I was wondering if you would be free to pop down sometime next week? I'm heading down to the village on Friday, staying for a week. The estate agents are letting me have the key so I thought we can cost up some of the work. What do you think? You free sometime?'

The clinking of glasses echoed in the background then laughter as Mark answered vaguely. 'Hopefully I can get down sometime, yeah.' It was obvious his mind was elsewhere.

'Yes Mark, it really does sound as if you are *so* busy! Look, I'll be at the Jolly Abbot from Friday and all next week, if you can drag yourself away from the pub, just turn up!' And with that she'd cut off the call.

God, he had been a right pain from the start, she could never get hold of him when she wanted to. She hoped she was doing the right thing using him for the work. Why did she let the guy wind her up so much? Her thoughts were suddenly diverted by the sound of music from outside. The band were practising on the green by the marquee, she rushed over to the window and leant on the windowsill to delight in the sounds.

The rhythm of the trumpets and tubers whispered across the fields. The distant melodies could be heard outside Orchard Cottage. A small herd of deer were grazing by the edge of the field towards the village. As the notes of the band wafted across they raised their heads, listening to the alien sounds and then realising it was no threat continued to feed but now seemed slightly wary. They sensed there was something else in the air. Their ears twitched as a swirling film of black mist brushed past their skin. They bolted into the woodland. The haze of darkness edged its way closer to the cottage, nudging the brickwork around the windows trying to gain entry into the empty cottage.

Sunshine filtered through the window and caressed Alison's eyes until she was finally awoken from her slumbers. Slightly perturbed as to the content of her dreams, which had featured Mark quite heavily, she got herself up and ready to greet the day ahead. She picked out some linen trousers from the wardrobe and then changed her mind and put on a short cotton skirt and a sleeveless blouse. Better keep Mrs Blackman happy!

It was help yourself continental breakfast as Jim and his staff were busy outside. It wasn't long before the sound of the band drifted into the dining room beckoning her to join in the fun. She quickly finished her croissant and started to make her way out into the sunshine. The almost permanent resident, Mr Elliott, was just walking in, probably just returning from a night of bird watching.

'Hello Mr Elliott.'

'Good morning Mrs Greenways. Looks as if it's going to be a good day for the fayre.'

'Yes, indeed. Do you plan to go?'

'Not just now, had a late night last night, going to catch up on some sleep, maybe see you over there later.' He headed for the staircase to the guest rooms and then dithered for a moment as he let his mind ponder. He paused as he stood on the bottom stair and turned to speak again.

'May I just say something? Try to be careful up at Monkton Lane. It's not always a safe place to be.'

Alison was puzzled, 'What do you mean?'

'Just take care ….. especially after dark.'

'What are you talking about? Tell me, why isn't it safe?'

'I'm sorry, I shouldn't have said anything. I don't mean to worry you. Just be careful, mind your step, especially after dark.'

He turned and darted up the stairs to his room.

'But Mr Elliott….you can't just…' but he had gone.

At that moment Susie and her Dad came bounding into the pub.

'Morning! You coming outside? Things are starting up now.'

'Er, yeah ok.'

'You alright, Alison? Go and get some more glasses Susie, I'll be there in a mo'.'

Alison shook her head. 'Sorry Jim, just a bit dazed, probably nothing. Very strange, Mr Elliott. He just told me to be careful up at Monkton Lane,' she laughed nervously.

'What did he say then?'

'Oh nothing really. All a bit odd, Jim. He looked as if he'd been out all night. God knows what he gets up to.'

'Probably lack of sleep affecting him! Bloke's a nutter. Take no notice of him. He's a bit of an anorak, birdwatcher or something. Needs to get a life.' He started to go to help Susie and fetch more supplies for the marquee and hesitated, 'But you *are* sure you are happy living up there on your own? I'd have thought you could still back out. Not all signed and sealed is it?'

Susie came out from the back laden with boxes of glasses cutting the conversation short.

'Come on Dad, we need to set up.'

They left, leaving Alison feeling very unsettled. The sunshine did little to lighten her mood as she made her way over to the village green.

It was nearly lunchtime and the green was heaving with locals, tourists and people from nearby villages. The air was filled with an array of sounds. There was the ping and a huge cheer when men and boys proved their strength as the huge hammer they wielded rang the bell at the top of the gauge. The squeaky voice of Punch as he hit Judy because she allowed the dog to eat the sausages. The children yelling with delight. The brass band had been playing earlier but was now on a break as it would soon be time for the maypole dancing.

Susie looked across and noticed Alison drift past the marquee entrance.

'Susie! Come on girl. Keep your mind on it. Sergeant Parsons is waiting to be served.'

'Hey enough of the Sergeant, Jim,' Roger Parsons laughed, 'I'm off duty. Got my trumpeter hat on today. Making music rather than arrests!'

He took a huge gulp of the beer. 'I needed that! Thanks Suz. I see you are selling Mead again this year. Many takers?'

'No not really Roger. Most people stick with what they know and like.'

Roger wiped his top lip of froth. 'Shame really, it was once such a local drink hereabouts too. People forget the history of the place.'

Jim, drying some glasses said, 'Best forget some of the history of the place I'd say.'

Roger nodded and made his way across to watch the maypole dancing. His young niece, Amy, was taking part. It was a gloriously hot day and he happily noticed how he got to see a lot more female flesh when the weather was so good. His eyes rested on a fine set of legs in front of him as they headed in the same direction.

She looked familiar. He speeded up so he was walking alongside the dark haired woman who was munching on some hot food. Taking a sideways glance he realised where he'd seen her before.

'Got any strawberry sweeties today Miss?'

She turned her head to see who had spoken and frowned. Not a happy look, he could tell.

'Oh, it's you! I suppose you're going to arrest me for walking along whilst carrying a hot dog, are you?'

Alison recognised the policeman straight away from her first trip down to the village. Her terror of what problems any association with the police may bring her way and the way her stomach twisted into knots when she looked into his face sent conflicting emotions within her.

'So, Miss. You are still here then? What happened with your imaginary cottage?'

'Well yes I am, officer,' she replied haughtily. 'Actually there *is* a cottage and I am in the process of buying it. So that shows how much you know about the village.'

'That's told me!' he laughed. 'I've only been back in the area a while myself. I was born here abouts but moved away when I went off to work in London. The only thing I could recall being up the lane were derelict cottages. Oh and the old Abbey ruins of course.'

'An Abbey?' Alison almost squealed in amazement. 'We discovered some ruins right at the back of the land. Goodness, I just assumed it was an old chapel.'

'No, all monastic land up there, most of it was sold off to a landowner up in Kent somewhere. Didn't realise any of the buildings were still intact.'

Alison ate a stray piece of fried onion and licked her fingers. 'Yes, just the one right at the end of the lane, Orchard Cottage.'

He nodded. 'Ah, Ethel's old place. Didn't realise it was still standing. Oh well, good luck with it then.' He gave her a smile, 'Just be careful along that lane mind.'

'Oh not you as well! Everyone seems to be warning me about the place.'

He drained the rest of his beer. 'I was actually referring to the state of the road, be careful driving, some of those potholes and overhanging trees could do a bit of damage.'

Alison visibly relaxed. 'Phew. That's a relief. I was beginning to think something terrible was going on up there.'

As the music started for the maypole dancing Roger allowed his thoughts to glimpse back into his shuttered memories of Monkton Lane and its secrets. He hoped things didn't get stirred up again. He wasn't going to allow it to hurt his family again.

He glanced at Alison as she watched the dancing, her face alight with happiness. He didn't want to rain on her parade.

'No, you've got nothing to worry about.' He told her. He hoped he was right.

Chapter Five

'Uncle Roger, Uncle Roger! Did you see me?'

Little Amy came bursting over after performing her maypole dance with her school friends. She was a pretty little thing, curly golden locks of hair framing a sweet angelic face. She ran with a slight limp and Alison noticed a deep scar on her leg.

Roger leant down and picked up his niece, swinging her round. 'You did so well! I'm so proud of you!'

Alison could see how close he was with his sister's child. Amy giggled as he began to tickle her.

'Stop it Uncle Roger.' She laughed and bent double enjoying the attention.

'Where's your Mum then Amy?'

He scanned the maypole audience who were slowly dispersing. A blonde haired woman in her thirties emerged from the crowd, a gentle smile on her face. She watched with delight as her daughter played and laughed.

'Hi Rog. Did you see our Amy? You were brilliant sweetheart.' She squeezed her daughter's hand and looked quizzically at Alison.

'Sorry Kit, this is Alison. She is planning to live up in Monkton Lane.'

A surprised look appeared on Kit's face. 'Really? where?'

'She's buying old Ethel's place, right down the end.' He turned to Alison. 'Orchard Cottage it's called now. That's right isn't it?'

'Yes that's it. Needs a bit of work but it's not too bad really.' Alison smiled at Kit. She seemed nice, would be good to have a female friend locally of a similar age. 'So Orchard Cottage isn't its original name then. What was it called?'

'Abbot's House. It's thought it may have been part of the old Abbey. There were so many buildings up there originally. A lot of the stone has been used here in the village and over the river in Woodhurst village too.'

The maypole was now empty of dancers and they started to make their way over to the beer tent. Little Amy was holding her Uncle's hand and had been singing to herself.

She tugged at Roger's hand. 'The men don't like the villagers.'

He looked down at her and smiled. 'What men is that then Amy?'

'The men in the hoods. They hate us and want us to leave them alone.' She indicated to her ankle. 'They made me hurt my leg.'

Kit spoke sternly. 'Now Amy just stop it. You know that's not true. There was nobody there.' Exasperated she glanced across at Roger. 'Amy you know we searched for hours. There wasn't anyone else there!'

Amy began to sulk as they continued past the various stalls at the fayre. Mrs Blackman waved at them and indicated to her display of cakes. Kit called back they would buy something later, they were in need of a drink.

Laughter and the aroma of beer wafted out of the beer tent. Roger headed in to get some drinks. Amy was still in a sulk. He tried to cheer her up.

'Come on Amy, you can help me. Come and choose, what d'you fancy?'

Her reply was lost amongst the hubbub of the tent as they left Kit and Alison outside in the sunshine.

Kit sat down on the grass. 'Sorry about Amy. She'll soon snap out of it. It's just that she has a fixation that her accident was caused by some figures in hoods chasing her.'

'Yes, I noticed her ankle, poor thing. What happened?'

The heat of the sun was making everyone feeling hot and sticky. Kit wiped her brow with a tissue.

'It was last year. She'd been up in the woods by the ruins. Not that she should have been up there. I thought she was playing in the back garden.'

'So she went up there on her own? Blimey, that's a long way for a little'n to go on her own. How old is she, seven, eight?'

'Eight last month. Goodness knows why she went up there.' Kit shook her head as she remembered. 'She sneaked out through a gap in the back fence. Charlie, that's my hubby, he's fixed it now. Amy says she was running away from these 'hooded men' and she tripped. Caught her foot very badly on a rather jagged and sharp tree stump.'

'Ohhh the poor little mite.'

'Really cut her leg, damaged the ligament. You know what it's like up there, branches and rotting trees, new growth pushing through in the most bizarre places.'

'Yeah I do. Monkton Lane is almost being reclaimed by the trees.'

Alison shuffled about on the grass to get into the shade of the tent, the scorching afternoon sun was feeling unbearable on her skin.

'So who do you think these hooded men were? Just her imagination?'

'Sure of it. It was an excuse she'd made up, as she knew she shouldn't have been up there. Got a good imagination our Amy. She tells me she talks to a sad lady in our garden sometimes. I hear her whispering out there. She reads too much Harry Potter!'

Roger returned with Amy and their drinks.

'Did I hear Harry Potter mentioned Kit? You going to see the new film down in Hastings?' He plonked himself down next to Alison and handed her a glass of Cider.

'Oh can we Mum, can we?' Amy jumped up and down, spilling her orange squash.

Kit gave her brother an irritated look as she answered Amy's pleas, 'Now calm down Amy. Maybe we shall. Wait and see.' Annoyed at Roger she mouthed 'Thanks!'

Undeterred Roger came out with a suggestion 'Perhaps we can all go? You game Alison? Fancy a bit of Harry Potter?'

There was no chance for Alison to respond as at that moment a commotion started in the beer tent. Voices were raised. Roger ever on standby jumped to his feet.

'Thought it seemed a bit tense in there. Susie's fella looked blotto. Trust him to start up.'

The sound of shouting bellowed out into the summer air, glasses breaking and Susie screaming as punches were thrown.

Roger made for the tent calling back to his sister. 'I'd get out of it if I was you. I'll see you back at home.' And he went into the affray to see if he could calm the situation.

They left the bedlam behind and made their way along the village street. Suddenly a convoy of old trucks approached the green from the direction of Woodhurst village. Music blasted out from the vehicles, along with shouting and manic laughter. The sudden backfiring of an exhaust had Amy squeezing her Mum's hand tightly as they headed up the road to their timber framed home.

'Noisy boys Mummy!' She looked up to Kit seeking reassurance that all was well.

'Yes they are my love. Don't worry, we're nearly home now.'

Alison was so surprised in the sudden change in the village. 'What on earth is going on? It was so peaceful, then all hell broke loose?'

'It's Wilkinson family from Woodhurst. Normally it's okay, but now and again when they've got friends or family staying up at their smallholding they decide to come this way and cause havoc. Susie's boyfriend is one of them, they've probably come over to help him, knowing he's got into a fight.'

'Susie from the Jolly Abbot? I'm surprised Jim allows her to see someone if they're trouble. He always seems quite tough with her.'

As they marched along quickly to get to safety Kit replied, 'Yeah, most people wonder that. Jim is normally a very strict Father, but for some reason he lets her see Steve.'

A straggler appeared, a rusty pick up, it coughed and sputtered as it bounced past them and down the hill into the village. The driver, a drunken shaven headed youth shouted obscenities at them, laughed and threw his empty can out of the truck. The last remaining dregs of sticky lager sprayed the trio as it bounced down into the gutter.

'Come on, let's get inside quickly.' Kit tugged at Amy's hand, quickening her pace even more.

Alison's mouth felt dry, the heat of the sun and the panic of the situation sent her adrenaline into overtime. She had hoped feeling scared and threatened would be a thing of the past now there were some miles between her and Big Mick. So much for finding peace. The realisation hit her that wherever she went she would inevitably come across some bad sorts. It was up to her to learn to deal with it, toughen up. Easier said than done.

She followed Kit and Amy up the steps of the grassy bank that lead to their little terraced cottage. If it hadn't had been for the turmoil and fear in her stomach Alison would have delighted in the building. The white walls, which seemed to glow in the bright sunshine, were interspersed with timber framing. The small neat windows looked out across the main village street towards the post office opposite. Kit opened the honeysuckle-framed door and they entered into the calm and coolness of the fifteenth century building. The darkness and chill inside helped soothe them after the madness outside.

'Come through to the Kitchen.' Kit called to Alison who was still standing in the hallway slowly turning in a circle looking upwards at the low wooden beams, taking in the interior of Kit's home. As she continued her unhurried pirouette she turned towards the kitchen doorway and out of the darkness emerged a face – deathly white and sad.

A chill ran up her spine as she stood face to face with the ghostly female. Oh God! It had to be Amy's sad lady. Alison held her hands up to her face, eyes tightly closed, blocking out the apparition. Heart pounding, fear penetrated her whole body, ice-cold prickles formed on the back of her neck. She forced herself to look again, glancing through the gaps in her fingers. It was then she realised it wasn't a ghostly figure at all. The dark hallway was home to a rather weatherworn stone statue of an angel.

'Oh sorry Alison, you must have met our Angel.' Kit emerged into the doorway, teacloth in hand. 'Sorry! It's so dark out here, she must have given you a fright. Come and have a cuppa.'

Alison followed her into the kitchen wondering what on earth possessed someone to have such a huge statue like that in their house?

The south facing kitchen was bright and airy, the back door was flung open and the sweet smell of lily of the valley wafted in. Amy sat outside on a stone bench surrounded by the mauves and pinks of the aquilegia flowers, glass of orange squash in hand, chattering away to herself.

'She seems to have gotten over the furore already, I wish I could say I was the same. My head is spinning.' Alison sat down by the pine table and took the mug of tea that Kit passed her. 'So, a few questions are whirling around my head. Mainly -should I be concerned about these Wilkinsons? Are they likely to trouble me down Monkton Lane?' She put her hands through her

hair, pushing it away where it was sticking to her face in the heat. 'And.....
what on earth is a huge stone angel doing in your hallway?' It all seemed so
surreal.

Kit grinned. 'Okay, Wilkinson family first. Probably nothing to worry
about. It's only high days and holidays when they've had a few that they get a
bit rowdy. But they usually head off to the coast, it really is very rare they
cause trouble in the village.'

Alison sat back in the Windsor chair sipping her hot tea. 'Alright, I'll
try not to panic but I think I'll get the place alarmed when I move in just to be
sure.'

Kit offered her a biscuit. 'Look, if the village always expected trouble
at these events don't you think there would have been more of a police
presence than my off duty brother armed just with his trumpet?' She joked and
began to giggle.

Alison found she was grinning, so pleased to have found such a down
to earth, cheerful friend. Kit's laughter was so infectious that within seconds
they were both doubled-up, giggling like schoolgirls. Alison wiped her eyes
and began to hiccup, which made them burst into laughter again. In between
hiccups she managed to speak.

'You still haven't explained the bloody big angel in your hall?'

Kit took a deep breath to compose herself. 'My stomach hurts now.
Right, the angel. This cottage has been in the Parsons family for generations.
We inherited the house from our parents and with it the angel!'

'Where's it from, and why is it in the house?'

'To be honest, we're not sure of all the facts. Grandpa used to say it
came from the monastery.'

Alison leant forward onto the table, reaching for another shortcake. 'I know you said lots of the stones were used in the village when the Abbey was dissolved. I didn't realise things like that were taken too!'

'Yes, it is a bit bizarre. We've just got used to her now. My husband knows a fair bit about the whole Abbey thing. He's a real history geek. Why not stay for dinner? I doubt if there'll be food tonight at the pub so do stay and eat with us.'

Alison didn't relish the thought of going back down to the village green just yet anyway. 'Okay, that will be good. Thank you.'

'That's great. You can meet my husband Charlie. Between him and Roger they'll be able to tell you all they know about the village.' Kit stood up and put the empty mugs on the draining board. A frown momentarily touched her face as she thought of the tales they wouldn't be revealing to Alison. That was family stuff and private. She turned back to Alison and smiled. 'And perhaps Roger can tell you all he knows about the angel.'

They were suddenly aware that little Amy was standing in the doorway.

'I can tell you about the Angel. The sad lady told me. Her husband stole it because he said the hooded man made her die.'

Chapter six

Suddenly there was a gust of wind and the young blossom fluttered and swayed on the apple tree next to Orchard cottage. The delicate flowers held tightly to the branches, wanting to survive, to bear fruit. But the air was dark and thick and pulled angrily at the soft pink flowers and raped the tree of its beauty. It stood bare, battered by the gusts of evil, its bounty lost. Along the lane the air and trees were still and the rooks sat in their high branches and watched. They knew what was stirring. They could feel it. They took to the sky as one as they shouted their warnings.

The dawn chorus had woken Alison very early and she lay in her comfy bed at the Jolly Abbot savouring the beautiful sounds. She had her window ajar and listened as the birds greeted thc day. The rain from the previous day had long gone and Alison stretched her arms lazily and grinned. Rooks were calling out as they circled the woods towards Monkton Lane. She heard a couple of rifle shots. Her stomach tightened for a moment then realised it was most likely a local farmer. She'd have to adapt and get used to the ways of rural England.

She still felt a little fragile after the events of the fayre a few days earlier. The trouble that the Wilkinson family had caused had rattled her well-worn nerves. However she'd spent a pleasant evening up at Kit's place. Charlie, Kit's husband, had arrived back early that evening looking tired after working down in Hastings but after a quick shower he emerged full of life and soon everyone was in high spirits.

Alison couldn't remember the last time she'd laughed so much. Roger, who she discovered lived with his sister and family, had returned in time to eat with them, saying all was calm back at the village green. The Wilkinsons had been warned off and they'd headed back up to Woodhurst licking their wounds.

Alison still felt wary so as the evening came to a close Kit had been kindness itself and let her stay the night making up a bed on the sofa for her. Alison had been relieved not to go back to the pub that night as she worried that Susie's boyfriend would come back and start shouting and causing trouble again.

Alison had slept really well at Kit's house. The Angel statue no longer spooked her, especially when she realised the men used her as a coat stand. Charlie's jacket was hanging over one of her wings and Roger's fleece was draped over her head. No more was mentioned of Amy and her sad lady. She had clammed up after her announcement about the angel. The jollity of the evening pushed it to the back of her mind.

However thoughts of hooded men and death came flooding back to her the following morning when she had awoken on the sofa. Initially she was unsure of where she was but then looking up seeing the huge pitted oak beams she remembered she had stayed the night at Kit's.

It was a beautiful home but she found herself feeling slightly uneasy when her eyes were drawn back to the old painting over the fireplace. It was of the Abbey when it was standing in its full glory, before the ravages of time had played its part in its demise. It was an autumn scene, sun low in the sky, the stone an orangey red. The surrounding trees were gold, yellow and crimson and it looked idyllic. The structure that once stood where her cottage was now situated was at the far right of the painting.

She had wrapped the blanket around her and got up from the sofa to look more closely. It showed the ruins to the back of her cottage still intact. She surmised that the building in front would be where her cottage now stood. It looked as if it had been altered and added to dramatically over the years. The front exterior did not bear any resemblance to the house she would soon own. In the painting she saw that the one lone apple tree was once part of a large orchard. One of a mass of fruit trees that grew on the southern perimeter of the site. She then recoiled. Barely visible at the front of the painting the artist had added something extra, a dark shadowy shape standing just outside the orchard.

In her bed at the Jolly Abbot she pulled the duvet around her as she recalled the chill she'd felt when she'd looked closely at Kit's painting. She hadn't said anything to the family. What would they have thought of her? She couldn't tell them she had drawn the house many times as a child and she too had added the shadowy figure.

Kit's reaction to Amy's sad lady and hooded men tales made her think that the family had no place in their minds for anything paranormal. But Alison knew it wasn't something to be dismissed. Her thoughts took her back to when her Mother had died and she'd gone to see a medium. There had been so many things she'd never had a chance to say to her Mum, no time to say goodbye. A few friends told her she was crazy, mediums were just charlatans but she went anyway.

She'd arrived at a very ordinary looking house and had a reading with Anna-Marie, a very ordinary looking lady but there was nothing ordinary about the things she said. Anna-Marie told her she sensed Alison was open to the spirit world, that she could be a channel to the past. When she spoke of her Mother, she told her a number of uncanny facts. She came out of the reading believing even more that death isn't the end.

Outside the Jolly Abbot all was quiet except for a family of sparrows who were chattering away just out of view in the branches of the wisteria that climbed the walls of the pub. Alison got up and switched on the kettle. It was far too early to go down for breakfast.

She checked her mobile to see if Mark had tried to get in touch. It was dead, battery flat, so she plugged it into the charger. She had hoped he would have come down whilst she was staying in the village, go up to the cottage with her, there was still so much to discuss and decide. The sale was speeding along and she was getting impatient with him. She was beginning to wonder if she should find someone else to do the work. She'd discovered the other night that Kit's husband was a builder, maybe she should ditch Mark and use him? She'd certainly consider it.

She continued sipping her tea, as she planned her day. She'd arranged to go with Kit and Amy to the cinema that afternoon to see Harry Potter. Roger had said he might go too. So the morning was free to pay Orchard cottage a visit. Roger had mentioned there was a footpath over to Monkton Lane just up from Kit's house alongside the allotments. As it was such a beautiful day she decided she would take a walk in the sunshine to the cottage.

A few hours later, after a hearty breakfast, she strolled along the footpath. It was very overgrown at the start and it would have been easy to miss but Roger had drawn her a little map so she set off, allotment to one side and the woods of Monkton Lane to her left. The sun was gathering warmth and she was grateful for the dappled shade of the trees.

Once she had left the allotments behind, the path opened out into a field with open countryside to her right. The path skirted alongside the edge of the trees for a while and then would take her across the field to the end of the lane where the cottage stood. As she strode alongside the woods, the rooks started their raucous shouting and began to fly up from the trees, dipping and swirling as they circled above her.

Her eyes began to glimpse patches of blue from within the woods and a sweet scent drifted in the air. She looked at the scribbled map. If she went *into* the woods it would still lead to the lane. The lure of the bluebells were just too hard to resist.

Alison left the path and made her way across the longer grass, and headed for the canopy of beech and oak. The aroma of the woodland floor filled her senses and as she ventured cautiously further amongst the trees she entered a magical scene. The bluebells spread like a violet carpet ahead of her. The smell was intoxicating. A wren darted from a fallen tree, making a tick tick sound, annoyed to have been disturbed at its feast of insects from the rotting wood.

Alison sat on the log and took in the essence of the place. It felt very special. There was nothing to fear. She had begun to feel a little worried about the woods when she'd first had the idea that the men Amy had spoken of may have been the spirits of the monks. Now sitting here in this idyllic scene she realised it was probably youths wearing the hoodie uniform of the teenagers that frightened Amy that day, nothing more.

Reluctantly she left the bluebells and made her way across the wood in the general direction she felt would take her to Monkton Lane. The further she went the sparser the bluebells became and soon it was just leaf mould and dry earth below her feet. The wood was now devoid of bird song and she was very alone. She was sure she should get to the lane soon but all she could see ahead were more and more trees. She began to panic. Should she turn back and try to get onto the footpath again? Would she find her way?

She looked back and couldn't work out which way she had come and so on she walked. Her foot caught a stone sticking up from the ground and she nearly tripped.

She walked, a solitary figure amongst the brooding trees. The silence was loud in her ears. The trees began to look vague and unfocused. The picture ahead faded and seemed to be consumed by a grey smoky haze.

'What's that?' She held her breath as she noticed a dark shape whisper amongst the trees to her left. It flitted between the obscure trunks.

'Who's there?'

She had to keep moving. Almost feeling her way forward she stumbled on brambles as a tall tree loomed ahead, encased in ivy. As she got nearer she realised it wasn't a tree but part of the stone ruins of the Abbey buildings. Here deep in the woods amongst the swirling mist it had a menacing feel about it.

She told herself that she must be close to lane if she was near the ruins. She tried to reassure herself. Just keep going girl, you'll be fine.

As she made her way further ahead she passed more pieces of stone and evidence of buildings, now being devoured by ivy, brambles and the elements. Then in the stillness of the wood she heard a throaty growl and her stomach twisted tightly.

She hurried on ahead, almost running, avoiding tree roots and crumbling stonework as best she could. More light began to penetrate the wood, the mists lifted and the trees began to thin out. Finally she was in Monkton Lane. She ran along the track, eager to get out from under the canopy of ivy and eventually came out into sunshine with her cottage on view ahead.

She stood and took in some deep breaths and put her face up towards the sun, allowing its warmth to soothe her. The buzzard that had greeted her the first time she viewed the cottage was soaring high above the field. Feeling more relaxed she made her way towards the house. Ahead, the sun glinted onto something near the cottage, it was too dazzlingly to make out. She screwed up her eyes to try to see and held her hand to shield out the sun but whatever it was had gone.

House martins were twittering as they swirled and looped above the fields opposite and Alison watched them against the clear blue sky as they dived downwards taking their lunch as they sped through the air. She turned and started to walk up the path and it was then that she noticed the apple tree.

'Ohhh no!' She wailed. 'What has happened to my lovely tree?'

It stood amongst a carpet of leaves and blossom, its bare branches completely devoid of any growth. A large gash in the trunk oozed a reddish brown resin that was slowly edging its way down onto the floor.

She stood pondering over what could have happened when she heard an almighty splash and a shriek from somewhere nearby.

Chapter seven

Another shout echoed from along the lane. She was hesitant to follow the sounds but what if it was someone in trouble? She should go and see what it was. God, if only Mark was here. He'd lighten the situation.

The morning sun was incredibly hot as she tentatively headed towards the screams. She left her cottage behind and walked along the lane that soon petered out into a dusty, gritty track. The sharp stones pressed though the soles of her flimsy sandals with every step.

The yells up ahead were louder now but so was her heartbeat. What was she going to find? Imagination going into overdrive she finally reached the line of trees where the track bent round to the left. The howls were coming from just behind a clump of bushes and she crept over and peered through. As she made her way through the stinging nettles she finally reached the source of the noise. She laughed and watched as Mark splashed about in the river - naked. His beast of a van was parked over by the bridge.

'Yeeha!' He ran around in the cool water, jumping and splashing, unaware of his audience. The clear sparkling water let out a roar as it gushed over boulders and stones making its journey towards the coast. It flowed from Lunsford and continued south, dividing Greysmead and Woodhurst village, where it grew in size and strength, meandering and snaking around the back of the Abbey lands. This was Alison's first glimpse of the river and she was spellbound by its force and beauty. But it wasn't just the river that had her mesmerized.

'You coming in Al?' Mark had seen her and shouted above the noise of the rushing water.

'You're mad! What you doing here?' She laughed and clambered down through the long grass on the bank towards him.

Now sitting amongst the riverside vegetation he began to dry himself with his t-shirt. 'I came to see you. Thought you asked me down?'

'I did, but I'd given up on you as I've only got another few days here. I go home on Saturday.' She sat by the waters edge. It was cooler down there. Maybe she could dip her feet in the water? She began to undo her sandals.

'Watch out for the crayfish!' Mark laughed moving his fingers together like pincers.

He quickly pulled on his jeans and walked in bare feet over to where she sat splashing her toes in the crystal clear waters. As he flopped down cross-legged beside her the freshness of his skin filled her senses. He sat, bare chested. His wet shaggy hair glistened in the sunshine.

'I called into the pub and was told you were heading up here. I looked around the cottage and couldn't see your car so decided to have an impromptu swim.' He continued to try to dry himself with his sodden t-shirt. 'Jeez! Its not yet midday and it's a scorcher already!'

Alison felt her breathing quicken as his strong arms rubbed with the t-shirt over his sun-kissed shoulders and across his chest.

She finally found her voice. 'I walked up here. It must have been your van I heard rumbling and coughing! In the woods it sounded like some sort of wild animal.'

'Hey cheeky! Watch what you say about my van!' He gave her a playful slap and lost balance and fell towards her. Their bodies touched. A knot formed in the pit of her stomach as his brown arms touched her skin. She watched as a droplet of water from his dishevelled hair slowly made its way down the contours of his face. Past his dark eyes, across his cheek and onto his lips. The moment stood still as they looked at each other.

He jumped up. 'Must go to the van and get a dry tee shirt. Back in a mo'.' And he scrambled up the bank towards the bridge where his beast stood.

Mark opened the van door, looked back towards the river at Alison. Jeez, that had been a close thing. He'd nearly kissed her. No way should he go there. Business and pleasure – it didn't mix. He glanced back at her again, watched as her long dark hair caressed her shoulders. He grabbed a clean tee shirt from the back of the van and made his way back, a carrier bag in hand.

Alison sat and looked at the river, heavy after a day of rain. A grey wagtail bobbed about on the rocks and fluttered into the air catching insects. Looking up stream she glimpsed the remnants of the monastic buildings, peering out from their entombment by nature. She would clear the brambles and bushes from the ruins on her land once she owned the cottage. It seemed sad that the buildings were hidden from view.

A hint of a breeze touched Alison's face.

It would please me greatly if our Abbey could be seen again.

'Who's that?' She spoke to the whisper in the wind.

Please tell our story.

Alison jumped up and looked around. 'Who said that?'

'Who said what? You talking to yourself Al?' Mark asked as he returned to the river bank.

She shook her head. 'I don't know. I could have sworn I heard a voice…'

Mark settled down on the grass again and started to rummage in the carrier bag.

'It's funny. I thought I heard something near the ruins that day we looked round your place. Near the well. I'm sure it's just the breeze through the leaves that plays tricks with us.' He pulled out crusty rolls, pate and cherry tomatoes from his bag. 'Will you join me for lunch madam?'

She settled back down next to him and smiled. 'I knew you'd be able appease the situation. You're a good influence on me.' She placed her hand on his arm, looked at him, willing him to kiss her.

He turned his face from hers and grabbed at the rolls. 'Come on now, eat up.' He moved away slightly and began spreading the pate.

Her insides twisted. She'd thought they'd made a connection earlier. She now felt an idiot. The tell tale sting began to form behind her eyes. Would she ever get it right with men?

'Al, you not eating?' he nudged her playfully then saw that her eyes were brimming with tears. 'Hey, are you ok?'

She couldn't speak, if she did she would cry. She knew she would just cry and probably never stop. So much anger, sadness, regret. So many emotions all being held captive within her for so long, all trying to find a way out, but she wouldn't succumb to it. She had held it in check for so long. She could do it again. Push it away.

Her face held low, she shook her head, 'I'm fine…honest.' She gave him a weak smile. 'Lets have some of that food.'

'Tell me to mind my own business but you seem …'

She butted in, 'Highly strung?'

'No…I just sense you've been through a tough time. Am I right?'

No, mustn't let the tears flow.

'An Ex?' He asked, digging for information. Wanting to know her story. 'He needs his head tested to have let you go.'

She swallowed hard, tried to answer but it felt as if a great stone was lodged in her throat. She pushed the weak emotions away and allowed her anger and bitterness to take control. It was the only way to cope.

'Look, I'd rather not dwell on the past. The past few years have been absolute shit and I'd rather forget, okay?' She snapped.

Mark took another bite of his roll. 'No probs. Just know, I'm a good listener if ever you fancy talking.'

The perfume of the bluebells was intoxicating. The air was rich with the sound of birdsong as the sunlight filtered through the branches. At the base of the tree root primroses were in flower, bright as the sunshine.

John smiled. 'This wood is a place of glory where we can rejoice at Our Lords creation.'

He stood by the aging oak looking towards the fields, back to the village of his birth. She would soon be here. He lovingly laid his cloak onto the mossy woodland floor in readiness. Picking a bluebell he gently placed it on the ground. He glanced back towards the western range of the Abbey where he lived with the other lay brothers. They were working in the fields across the river and their chanting floated softly on the breeze. He was alone amongst the trees.

He saw her in the distance heading towards him. His heart missed a beat. 'Mary.' He loved the sound of her name on his lips.

They had both grown up in the village, played together as children. She was so beautiful. Then one day he had spied her sitting by the river. She had been crying. She told him she had lay with Desmond, the farrier and was with child. She looked away from his gaze when she saw the hurt and sadness in his eyes and he watched as she ran back to the village across the fields. Her braids fell from beneath her cap. Silken auburn hair he would never touch again. He had always hoped and believed she would become his woman one day.

That summer he had started his probationary time as a lay brother. After the year he was formally received as a member of the order. It was a good life for it filled every waking moment, holding at bay any thoughts of Mary. Abbot Thomas had been pleased with him, for he observed the

Cistercian disciplines and worked hard with his brothers. He began to assist brother Michael. The villagers received payment for the honey they had gathered and supplied to the Abbey. John helped Michael with the brewing and making of the mead.

John had seen her walking across the courtyard six months ago. Her arms held on tightly to her earthenware jug of honey, clutching it tightly against her breasts. Her full cheerful lips now thin and tight and her large eyes surrounded by bruises and cuts.

He knew it was wrong. Hadn't he knelt before the Abbot and swore obedience, to follow the rules of the order? But how could he not but comfort Mary?

He had eased her sadness. The grief at the loss of her child with Desmond had ripped her apart. Not that she held any love within her heart for Desmond. Not now. He had changed. Desmond was full of anger and he beat her.

She would be here soon.

No, it was not wrong to love Mary.

Alison slowly became aware of the orange glow of the streetlight as it filtered through the gap in the curtains. She pushed the duvet away, feeling hot and disorientated. Her head was fuzzy as the dream clung to her consciousness. The sweet scent of the bluebells was still strong in her nostrils and made her nauseous. She pulled an extra pillow behind her head and half sat up in bed in the darkness, taking in slow deep breaths.

It was just a dream, right? But it felt so real! Her heart continued to race as she thought back to the dream. Brother John? Had he been a monk at the Abbey? She could still feel his emotions, the love he had for Mary. A tear slid down her face onto the pillow as she thought of the circumstances that had damaged beyond repair Mary's relationship with her husband. Her thoughts went to Kenny. She had loved him long ago when he was a young happy man, full of fun. But like Desmond, he too was victim of circumstances that had changed both their lives, and filled him with hatred and bitterness.

She lay thinking about her day up at the Cottage. She'd cried off the cinema trip with Kit and Amy, she had no chance of getting there in time as she'd spent the rest of the afternoon and early evening with Mark. They'd gone back to the cottage but she had remained cool with him. They kept it business like, just discussing the work he would be doing and nothing more.

She ached when she thought of his concern for her. She would have loved to have told him everything. Keeping so much inside was eating her up.

It was no good, she couldn't sleep. She was so wound up. She sat up in bed leant across and put on the beside light. The numbers shone out from the clock, 3am.

A faint click from outside made her jump up from her bed and she peered out of the window and tried to see the street below through the wisteria. She glimpsed the figure of Mr Elliot. He was making his way silently in the direction towards Monkton Lane.

It was a warm night with a clear sky. Maybe she'd see if she could find out what he got up to. She began to get dressed.

Chapter eight

An owl made its presence known from the aging oak tree on the green as Alison made her way along the main street of the village. It was actually cooler outside than she'd realised and she wondered if to follow Mr Elliott was a good idea after all. She'd walked as far as the footpath and could make out his shadowy figure in the moonlight as he went on ahead. It was then that she heard a rustle, something was moving amongst the plants. Was that a long tail she saw disappearing in the undergrowth? A rat maybe? Before she could stop herself she let out a squeal. Ahead Mr Elliot stopped and listened. Alison leant back into the bushes, keeping motionless, hoping he wouldn't see her. A few minutes passed and he continued on his way.

Now what? Should she carry on and follow him? Then she heard it again. It was closer now. A scurrying sound under the leaves just the other side of the wire fence had Alison jumping back to the far side of the footpath. There was definitely movement coming from the allotment. Her eyes scanned and spotted something brown and small as it scampered under a plant. She stood unmoving until she was sure it had gone. The huge moon shone down and bathed the ground with an eerie white glow. It was so quiet. So still. Then the silence was broken as the tawny owl gave out its call again.

Her dream began to nudge its way to the forefront of her mind. Alison shivered. Maybe tonight wasn't the night to go walking in the woods. Who cares what Mr Elliot was up to? She'd let him get on with it. As she started to make her way back along the path to the road, the dream continued to push itself back into her thoughts.

A voice far away within her mind whispered to her.

A place of glory where we can rejoice at Our Lords creation.

The voice of Brother John! It was saying how he felt about the woods. Maybe he did exist….long ago? She could feel him close, almost as if he was part of her. She headed towards the pub, her idea to follow Mr Elliot shelved, she wanted to get back to her room.

As she turned out from the footpath she gasped. Up ahead, sitting on Kit's doorstep, she could see a hazy figure, almost glowing silver in the moonlight. The moon passed briefly behind a cloud and the figure lost its unearthly quality and she could see that it was Amy. Alison walked silently along and up the steps to Kit's front door. Amy seemingly unaware of her surroundings was in a trance like state, her lips moved gently as she whispered into the night air.

Alison crouched down beside her. 'Amy? Amy love, are you okay?'

Amy sat, her knees pulled up tightly to her chest, her arms wrapped around her legs.

She spoke softly to herself. 'Yes, I know you are. Don't be sad. I will make sure he knows.'

Amy was oblivious to Alison as she settled down on the step beside her. Alison was concerned. Maybe she was sleep walking? She'd best not wake her suddenly.

Speaking gently to her again, she touched her arm lightly 'Amy? Come on sweetheart. Let's get you home.'

Amy slowly turned and stared blankly ahead. Alison looked into her eyes but it was as if she had opened a book only to find all the pages blank. Amy's eyes were devoid of any life. Amy wasn't there. She was worried. She didn't like this. Didn't like it at all.

Amy continued to murmur faintly. 'I will tell him. He will know. I will find a way.' Then very slowly signs of Amy began to re-appear behind her big blue eyes. 'You can help the sad lady can't you?' She pleaded.

Alison took her coat and put it around Amy's cold shoulders. 'Yes sweetheart, of course I will. Let's talk about this tomorrow but for now we must get you inside. It's chilly out here – too cold to be out in your jim-jams.'

'The sad lady knows you can speak to him.'

Alison put her arms around her and rubbed at her back and arms, as she tried to warm her up. 'Is your sad lady here now? Who is it she thinks I can speak to Amy?'

'She's always here. She needs to let him know.'

'Who? Let who know?'

'Brother John. She must tell him about the baby.'

Brother John! Amy knew about Brother John? An icy chill sped deep inside her. She tried to grasp Amy's words. Her mind was spinning. The dream. Brother John.

She took in a few deep breaths, she needed to know more. 'What does the sad lady look like Amy? What colour is her hair?'

'Why, she looks sad of course! She's sad. Her hair's red. She's got very long plaits. Do you think Mummy would let me grow my hair and have a long plait?'

Every nerve in Alison's body was tingling, every cell felt charged with some sort of electric force. Amy could see Mary. Amy was sitting here on the doorstep talking to Mary. The woman from her dream. Alison had always had strong beliefs in the afterlife but it still didn't stop shivers running across her neck and shoulders at the realisation that her dream had been a message from someone long dead.

Amy sat trembling on the doorstep. Alison decided she needed to get her inside. It wasn't the time or place to have this conversation. But she'd need to find out more. She couldn't ignore this.

She stood up and rapped on the door. 'Let's get you back to bed, shall we? Perhaps we can go for a walk tomorrow, talk some more?' She knocked on the door, harder this time.

Amy grinned. 'That would be fun. Will you ask Mummy if I can have a plait?'

Alison smiled and nodded.

At last the front door opened and Roger stood bleary eyed in a pair of boxers. He rubbed his face, trying to bring himself out of his sleepy state. He spotted his niece.

'Hey, Amy! What are you doing out here?' He looked at Alison and frowned.

Alison shrugged her shoulders. 'I just found her on the doorstep, chattering away to herself.'

'No! Not to myself!' Her bottom lip quivered the beginning of a sulk. 'I told you. You know I was talking to the sad lady. You asked me about her.'

Rogers face became stern. 'Amy! Enough! There is no sad lady. Now get inside.' His steely blue eyes stared at Alison as he spoke. 'Please don't encourage her. The sooner we can stop her imaginings the better.'

'But Roger you should listen to her. I'm beginning to think there is more to it than just a child's imagination.'

Amy stood in the doorway clinging to Roger's legs. 'Uncle Roger! Uncle Roger! She is real. She is! We need to stop her being sad. Please!'

Kit appeared in the hallway. 'What's all this racket? Amy! What are doing out of bed?' She looked from Roger to Alison sensing the tension 'Well? Is someone going to tell me what's happening?'

'Its nothing sis, don't worry. It's all sorted now. Come on, let's get inside. Night Alison.' He turned and shut the door on her face.

Gob smacked Alison stood in front of the closed door. The bastard! What was his problem? She'd have to try to get to talk to Kit. See if she could get her to be a bit more open minded about Amy's sad lady. She'd go to see her tomorrow.

She tried to brush her anger at Roger's reaction aside as she made her way down the steps to head back to pub and turned for a moment to look back at Kit's house. It had been standing there for hundreds of years, its windows witness to all the happenings in Greysmead and the lives of the villagers. The moon reflected back on the leaded glass and with it a wispy shape began to form. It swirled around into an indistinct silhouette of a woman who stood in front of the door looking down at her.

'Mary.' Alison said quietly.

A slight breeze danced around the figure as it gave Alison a sad smile and then dissolved into the air.

Alison stood for some minutes willing Mary to come back but the vision was gone. She knew it must have been Mary. She sensed it. She had to speak to Kit, they had to understand Amy was really seeing an echo from the past.

Her nerves jarred, Alison rushed along and began to make her way back to the Jolly Abbot. She could make out voices up ahead and stopped in her tracks. The voices sounded angry. It was Susie and her boyfriend having a barney. Not wanting to interrupt she crossed the road and perched herself on the bench outside the post office.

Their voices carried in the air.

'Why did you have to go! You are a bloody idiot Steve!' Susie's annoyed voice half whispered in the darkness. 'You promised me!'

'Okay. Okay. I know. But it's just too tempting, a good chance to make some money Suz.'

'Money won't be much good if you get a big fine if you get caught – you fucking idiot! I thought we had something here but obviously not. You think more of your bloody family than me!' Her hushed tones getting louder now.

'Aww Susie, you know that's not true. I do love you but..'

'No buts Steve. You've got to choose. Now just piss off and leave me alone.' she stormed off heading in Alison's direction, her anger now turning to tears.

The sound of a van door slamming echoed along the street and then Steve sped by heading back towards Woodhurst.

Susie strode up the road and did a double take when she spotted Alison sitting there.

'You alright Susie?'

Susie nodded and blew her nose and sat down next to Alison. 'What on earth are you doing out at this time of night? Couldn't you sleep?'

'No, I had a strange dream and couldn't get back to sleep again. I then spotted that Mr Elliot going out on one of his moonlight jaunts and in a mad moment thought it would be a good idea to follow him!'

'You didn't? What happened?'

'Chickened out, didn't fancy walking over to Monkton Lane in the dark. Stupid really as I will be living on my own over that way soon.'

Susie pushed her rainbow hair away from her face. 'Did he come back? Mr Elliott?'

'No. I don't think so.' She looked at her watch. 'It was less than an hour ago.'

Susie sat back on the bench and took out a tin and began making a nicotine fix. 'You don't mind do you?' she asked as she lit the cigarette. She inhaled slowly and let out a long breath of smoke into the night air. 'I get so fed up with Steve. He just lets his family influence him too much. He's an idiot.'

'I heard you having a row. What's he been doing that's annoyed you so much?'

Susie drew on her cigarette again, screwing up her eyes as she decided how much to tell Alison.

'He was at college with me you know? Doing okay, then his bloody Uncle came back from God knows where and tells him he's wasting his time.'

'So did he give up college to work on the family farm?'

'Farm?' Susie laughed, 'It's just a bloody small holding really, a few pigs, chickens. Nothing much. They're all just a bunch of sponging losers and bringing my Steve down with them.' She threw the dog end down and twisted it out with force.

Alison touched Susie's hand. 'Don't just give up on him. If you feel he's worth it, keep trying Susie. Don't give up or you may lose him.'

'I DO love him but he's just changed. When he's with his Uncle he's not the bloke I knew. It frightens me. Wish I knew how I could get him away from his Uncle's grasp, he gets him involved in things just for some easy money.'

It was sounding all too familiar to Alison. Maybe she should tell her a bit about her and Kenny. Alison took in a deep breath, 'Susie, don't just leave it. Fight them. Believe me, I know.'

Susie shook her head, 'I doubt you'd say that if you knew the things his Uncle gets up to.' And she hoped Alison would never find out.

Susie had been horror struck when she had heard someone was moving up to Monkton Lane. It was too close for comfort. Steve's Uncle hadn't been too pleased when he found out. She looked at Alison and wondered how someone like her would understand the likes of Steve's family. She listened as Alison began to tell her story.

'You'd be surprised Susie. My ex, Kenny, he was once the love of my life. Everything was going well, we even talked about starting a family. But that wasn't going to happen.'

'What? Can't you have kids? Is that what broke you up?' Susie asked rolling another cigarette. She offered it to Alison who shook her head.

'No. Nothing like that. He lost his business, he tried to keep it going but it was a losing battle. It was difficult. I was still working, keeping us afloat. He felt useless, got really depressed.'

'So did he have a breakdown?'

'I suppose in a way you could call it that. He felt he had to work and took a job as a barman at a nightclub.'

'Good that he was working then,' Susie said.

'No, a very bad move. The bloke who runs the club was...still is... a bad'un. Into really dodgy dealings. Robberies, drugs, prostitutes. You name it, he's into it. My Ken got pulled into it all.'

Now she had started talking it felt cathartic spilling it all out, like seeking redemption for her association with it all. 'I tried to stop him but it was too late. He'd started using, he became dependant. On the drugs and on Mick.'

'That's the boss bloke, right? It sounds terrible.' Susie was stunned at the revelations.

'Yeah. He's an evil bastard. He took my Ken away from me, took away my happiness and I hate him for that. I could tell you tales that would make your skin crawl.' She shook herself. 'Look I really shouldn't be telling you this. My life wouldn't be worth living if they found out I was telling you stuff.'

'Hey, I wouldn't say anything. How would they find out?'

'I wouldn't put it past him. He'd find a way. Anyway, the point I am trying to make is, try to get Steve away from his Uncle's influence sooner rather than later if you think he is worth fighting for. Do it before it's too late.'

Susie gave Alison a weak smile. 'He is worth it. Thank you. I will try, I really will.'

The sky gave out a faint glow along the horizon, light was beginning to take charge over the darkness. The night was now slowly fading.

'Look, soon be sunrise. We best get back to the pub.' Alison stood up, despite her frantic night she felt good. She held out her hand to Susie. They linked arms and slowly walked back to the Abbot.

The window of the bedroom above the bench silently shut and the occupant smiled.

Chapter nine

The sound of the phone filtered through to Alison's slumbers. She had arrived back at the pub at around 5am absolutely shattered and had crawled into bed and slept the sleep of the dead. The sun was now streaming into the room and she groaned from under the duvet. Her hand reached across and she grunted down the receiver.

'Hello.'

'Sorry Alison, it's Jim. It's just that I have someone wanting to speak to you down here. They've been waiting almost an hour for you to surface.....er…are you likely to be down soon?'

'What? Who is it? Sorry Jim, didn't have much sleep last night…catching up.' She pushed the covers away and looked across at the clock. God, it was only 10.30 for Christ sake, she needed more sleep.

'You still there Alison? Shall I ask your friend to hang about?'

She sat up in bed, eyes closed to the brightness. What day was it? Must be…Wednesday. Crikey only three more days. Lots to do, suppose she'd better get up.

'Alison?'

'Yeah, sorry Jim. I'm here. Give me half an hour and I'll be down. Tel Kit I won't be too long.'

'No it's not Kit. Half an hour. I'll let him know.' And Jim rang off.

Him? Who was it then? Surely not PC Parsons, Mr Happy himself! After last night she felt even more hostile about him. Shame as underneath that armour he wears there is a dishy guy. Still, he's a copper; she'd best keep her distance anyway.

The half an hour ended up being more like an hour before she made her way down the stairs to the lobby. She put her head round the door to the bar where Jim was stacking away glasses.

'Hi Jim! Sorry for the delay. Feeling like a sloth this morning! Who is it that wants me? 'Him' you said? Who is it?'

'You'll see.' He smiled 'He's gone out the back to wait.'

She walked through the bar to the French doors that led to a small garden. Jim had it set up with tables and chairs and brightly coloured flowers in pots. She peered outside but couldn't see anyone about. Just as she was about to go back inside someone jumped out in front of her from the side of the doorway.

A huge bunch of flowers were stuck under her nose.

'I'm sorry.' He said

The flowers were lowered and she found she was looking into Mark's dark lashed eyes.

'Mark!' Surprised and confused she took a moment to compose herself.

'Don't you like them? Should I have got chocolates?'

'Like them?….I love them! Thank you.' She took them from him and breathed in their scent. 'How come you're not back home in Croydon? I thought you left yesterday afternoon?'

He grinned. 'Questions Questions! In the end I decided to stay put and find a local B&B and see you again today. I didn't like leaving it as it was.'

She played ignorant. 'What do you mean. Leaving it like what?'

'Oh come on Al, let's not play games. I know you think of me as all light hearted but I do have a serious side you know. I was aware that you were pissed off at me.'

'No I wasn't.' She lied. 'Why on earth do you say that?'

'Okay. Cards on table.' He grabbed her hand and led her over to one of the benches and they sat down. She could smell peppermint on his breath as he sat holding onto her hand as he spoke.

'There was almost a ….what shall we say? A *moment* between us up at the river yesterday and I felt you were annoyed that I didn't respond.'

Embarrassed, she tried to pull her hand away but he held it even tighter.

'Don't be like that Al. I just want to explain.'

She could feel her eyes smarting. She was so tired after so little sleep, her emotions were close to the surface. She shook her head, looked down. Couldn't look into his gorgeous eyes when he was about to tell her he wasn't interested in her or that maybe he was married.'

'I really like you Al but..'

'Yeah, right…but! Why am I not surprised there is a but!' Her tear laden eyes looked up at him.

'Oh Al! I don't want to upset you. Please hear me out. I do like you…a lot. I just worry about getting involved with you. At least while I'm working for you anyway. What if we had a big falling out just as I was half way through renewing the ceilings.... or fixing the stairs? It just wouldn't be fair.'

He put his hand up and touched her hair, let some fall through his fingers. She felt the skin on her neck tingle.

'You are gorgeous,' he said. 'But let's take it slow. At least 'til I finish the job. Just friends for now…*really* good friends?'

She nodded. A tear began to fall.

He leant across and kissed her lightly on her cheek and wiped the tear away with his lips. 'And I do mean….just for now.'

They sat in silence for a moment before he spoke again. 'Can I say something more? And please don't bite my head off.'

'Okay, what?'

'When I was asking you about your ex yesterday, you seemed to get very defensive and irritated. I just need to know that you are ready to get involved with someone else. It seems to me you still haven't put your past to bed.'

This time Alison managed to pull her hand away from his grasp. She felt angry at his assumption. Of course she hadn't put it to bed, how could she? She then recalled her chat to Susie last night, and how good it felt talking about Kenny. Letting it all out at last.

'It's not that I don't want to talk about it, it's more that I can't. It's…well it's complicated.'

She let him take her hand again. 'Al. It's only as complicated as you let it be. I really want to be your friend – be there for you.'

'OKAY, okay. Maybe I will let you in on a bit of my past. But not just now. I'm so tired, I didn't get much sleep last night and also I'm starving,' she touched her stomach as it gurgled for the second time.

'How's about we get some lunch from the bar? And spend a day together…as friends?'

She nodded. Maybe now was a turning point in her life. Time to move on.

They lingered over lunch. Mark didn't push her anymore about Kenny. They talked about the cottage and she told him how she had drawn pictures of the place as a child. He was intrigued and she found herself opening up more, telling him about the painting at Kit's place and the dark figure in the foreground.

'Maybe it's me that you drew!' he laughed, 'I'm a dark mysterious figure.'

She peered at his shaggy mane of hair and joked back, 'No – too much grey.'

The lack of sleep began to tell on her and she stifled a yawn.

'You are tired aren't you? So what stopped you sleeping?' he asked.

Should she tell him about her dream? About Amy? Would he think she was mad? Only one way to find out.

'I had a really weird dream last night,' she began as she finished her cup of coffee.

'About me I suppose!' he teased.

She carefully placed the cup back down in the saucer and sat back in the chair and looked at him, 'Do you believe in ghosts Mark?'

She lay in bed and listened to the noises of the building as it settled down for the night. The muffled sounds of voices from the bar oozed through the floorboards to her room as customers said their good nights. The chinking of the bottles echoed in the yard as Jim chucked the empties into the crates. Water pipes began to hiss and hum as Jim got himself ready for bed. The dark pitted beams above her grew indistinct as the light faded. As the night closed in around her, her mind was occupied with thoughts of Mark and the lovely day she had spent with him. She thought back to their conversation, when she told him about the events of the previous night.

He had listened intently as she had told him about her dream, and how it had suddenly become intertwined with Amy's world of visions and her sad lady. She told him how Amy had said that Mary wanted to get a message to Brother John and about Rogers's aggressive reaction to the whole thing.

Mark had not laughed at her or joked but had been genuinely interested and then told her of an incident he'd had when he'd been a young lad, still at school. He and his mates had played around with a ouija board. They'd made up cards with letters and laid them out in a circle and sat behind the carpentry workshop, fingers lightly touching the base of an old cracked glass as they asked questions.

He had thought it was just a bit of a laugh until the day his friend Mike had asked if there was a message from Archie Carter. Archie had been a local old man, Mark had explained to Alison, who had been accused of molesting a little girl.

'The police let him go. No evidence. That didn't stop the locals picking on him all the time. Goading him, making his life hell. Killed himself, was found hanging from a tree in the park. Turned out some years later that it had been her Father who'd abused her, Archie hadn't done a thing.'

'So what was your friend's question?' She'd asked him quietly, saddened by the story

'Can't recall exactly, something like how did Archie feel now that he'd killed himself and was innocent. I remember the strangest feeling ever. It started from my finger, up my arm, tingling, like an electric shock. Then the bloody glass jumped up into the air and smashed into little pieces. So yes Alison I think I do believe in ghosts.'

She thought about Mark's story as she snuggled under the duvet. She felt so sad that Archie had killed himself for something he hadn't done. She'd never asked Mark what happened to the young girl's Father. She hoped justice had prevailed. It struck her how ironic her thoughts. She was holding back information from the police and because of her, justice hasn't been done. People had died and Mick and Kenny had got away scot-free. Maybe she should confess all she knew? Her body tensed as she thought back to Mick's face up close to hers, holding her neck tightly, restricting her breathing, threatening her if she said a word. Her heart began to race as she remembered. No, she wasn't brave enough to go to the Police.

She sat up in bed and took a sip of water to try to calm herself. She could feel the panic rising as her fear of Mick surfaced again. She could hear her laboured breathing. But hang on, was it her breathing she could hear? She sat still, her ears searching the room for sounds. Her heart was certainly pounding in her chest but her breath was quite settled. The slow rhythmic sound of heavy breathing came from near the bedroom door.

Her instinct was to pull the duvet up around her tightly for protection. Her eyes gradually became acclimatised to the darkness, and the outline of furniture began to appear, grey and indistinct. Her eyes followed the contours of the shapes; the flat top of the wardrobe, the chest of drawers and then her eyes fell on a grey hazy form of a person as they stood by the door. She attempted to pull herself backwards in the bed, to reach for the light switch but she was paralysed with fear.

She tried to speak but no words would form. She sat watching the figure that stood motionless by the door. Slowly she managed to move her arm across and put on the bedside light. Her dressing gown was hanging on a hook on the back of the door. That was all it was. She had really spooked herself! She let the relief flood through her body and settled back down into her bed.

She was just dropping off to sleep when a thought jarred her awake. But who had she heard breathing? She glanced back furtively towards the door before burrowing down under the duvet, hiding herself away. Her tiredness overtook her fear and she was soon asleep.

He stood by the door watching her as she slept. His breathing was laboured, for he had travelled far. He needed to find out what had happened to his brothers and more importantly, he needed to know what had happened to Mary. The rosy tint of the bedside lamp lit Alison's sleeping form. He knew she would be able to help him.

Chapter ten

All good things must come to an end and the torrential rain that surged along the gutters and filled the drains to bursting point ended the beautiful spell of spring sunshine. The temperature had dropped drastically too and looking out of the grimy window of Orchard Cottage, Alison felt a chill envelop her body. The rain and mist encased the cottage and all she could make out in the gloom was the bare skeleton of the apple tree, now devoid of life. Mark had told her it may send out some new growth, but they were both at a loss as to what had befallen the old tree.

Mark had stayed on an extra night at his B&B and they had met up that morning for a final measure up before Alison had to take the key back the next day. He'd set off home to Croydon in his old van some hours ago, promising to keep in touch and said he would come up to Mitcham to see her on Sunday. She pulled his scruffy fleece tightly round her shoulders. She'd left her warm jacket back at the Abbot, wasn't prepared for a day in a chilly old building, so ever the hero, Mark had donated his jacket to her. It smelt of him, a mixture of wood and peppermint. She felt comforted and secure as she hugged it to her and thought back to earlier when they had met up.

He had been sitting on the bench outside the post office waiting for her as arranged. A huge grin appeared on his face and he jumped up and gave her a friendly hug. It felt good.

'Morning!' He looked up at the grey cloudy sky, 'Not a good one though, that sky is full of rain, we best get up to the cottage soon before the heavens open.'

'As you're shooting off lunch time I'll take my car too in case I want to stay up there a bit longer,' she looked up and down along the road, 'Where are you parked?'

He indicated with a flick of his head towards the post office, 'Round the back in Mrs Blackman's drive. I've been staying here. I thought I'd said? She does B&B. Not bad at all.' He lowered his voice slightly, 'She does rabbit on a bit though!'

Alison laughed, 'She rubbed me up the wrong way when I first came down. Nosey old bag!'

'Ahhh but sometimes it pays to get to know the gossips. I was asking her a bit about the history of the place. It seems the parish records are up in Lunsford, in the library.'

'And I want to know that because?'

'Looking up Mary, see if she really did exist of course you dingbat!'

She hit him playfully and grinned, 'That is a brilliant idea. I hadn't thought of that! I can go tomorrow when I take back the key.'

Feeling enthusiastic at the prospect of finding proof that Amy's sad lady really existed she was delighted when she spotted Kit and Amy heading their way. She hadn't seen her since the episode on the doorstep.

'Morning!' She sang cheerily to them.

Little Amy waved but Kit snatched Amy's hand tightly and took her across the road, away from Alison and Mark, glaring across at them as she did so.

What was going on? Totally bemused she watched as little Amy was dragged along ferociously by her Mum.

Alison called across to her, 'Kit! Wait!'

'Leave us alone!' Kit shouted back with venom, 'You've caused too much trouble as it is!'

Alison touched Mark's arm, 'I must go after her. Give me a mo'.' and she ran across the road after Kit. She managed to catch up with her and pulled at her arm to stop her speeding retreat.

'Wait Kit! Please! Tell me what I've supposed to have done.' She heard Amy give out a sob as she looked up at Alison with her tear stained face.

'See?' Kit indicated to Amy, 'You're upsetting her again. Just leave us alone. How dare you come here and fill my daughter's head with stupid ideas!'

Alison could see Kit was really angry and knew she had to put this right but was incensed that Kit was blaming her.

'Excuse me! It wasn't me that didn't keep her house locked up properly so her small child could wander wily nilly on the road at 4am in the morning! So don't go blaming me for your shortcomings lady!'

Amy was sobbing uncontrollably now, 'Mummy, Mummy. Don't tell her off. Please! The sad lady likes her.'

'Oh Amy! Just stop it!' Kit shouted, 'Just shut up about your sad lady! She ISN'T REAL!' she screamed and then broke down into floods of tears herself.

Alison put her arm around her shoulder, 'Hey, come on, it's okay. Tell me what's up. Why are you getting so het up about all of this?

Kit looked down at Amy, who was crying softly to herself now, 'I just worry about her. Alison I am SO sorry. I know it's not your fault, really I do. It's just that she's beginning to get like our Aunt Betty....and I'm scared.'

'Aunt Betty?'

'Dad's sister, she began hearing voices in her teens, said she was talking to a woman. Used to spend hours wandering about in the woods off the path near the ruins.' She retrieved a tissue from her pocket and blew her nose. 'And now Amy's starting to sound like her,' she began to sob again.

'Hey, don't cry. What happened to your Aunt?'

'She was sectioned, had to go into hospital, was there for years. It took them ages to help her. To start with, even filled with their drugs she would talk about seeing her lady. She was let out eventually; she lives down in Hastings now. Won't come back here. Refuses to come near Greysmead.'

A howl of wind down the chimney at Orchard cottage brought Alison back to the present. She had felt so sad for Kit and could understand her fears, but she was certain Amy wasn't going mad. Poor Betty. She probably had seen Mary too but no one had believed her. She did. Alison was certain there was more to this than imagination or madness. She had promised Kit that she wouldn't talk to Amy about her sad lady anymore but asked Kit to promise that when she felt ready she would meet up with her and at least listen to her theories about what was happening.

A cloud of black soot came tumbling down the chimney as another gust of wind sped across the rooftop. It was so grey outside and she began to wonder if she had viewed the cottage through rose coloured spectacles. Would she feel isolated living there? On a day like today it felt like she was so far away from the village. Alone. Was it too late to pull out?

She turned away from the window and wandered about, taking a final look around each room. Now she had become more used to the place and with Mark's builder's eye she knew that the front of the cottage was the more modern area of the house, although even this was old, probably Georgian by the style of the windows and the symmetry of the front. However towards the back it was far far older. This was the bit that must have been part of the Abbey.

When she had first seen it, she had been enchanted with its gothic arches and the huge inglenook fireplace. But today it just looked tired and worn. Her eyes were drawn to the plasterwork, the decorated coving and arched doorway, so much of it just crumbling away. The house looked as if it was dying. Maybe she should let it just die peacefully along with its memories.

A door slammed. Probably the wind. Then she heard footsteps going up the stairs. Was someone in the house with her? Another bang as a door crashed shut. She jumped. It's the wind. That's all it was. The sound of rushing water made her head towards the kitchen. The storm must have broken through and rain was getting in.

She walked into the kitchen to discover the tap pumping and coughing as it spurted out brown water into the sink, it gushed out, rising high, soon to pour over the edge. But the water supply was off? She ran over and dipped her hand into the smelly water to pull the plug before it overflowed. The water gurgled away. The flow from the tap stopped. Alison turned the tap. Nothing. There was no water in the pipes at all.

Another crash from above, then another. The wind continued to rage and whispered to her. Soft voices echoed around the room.

Pleaaasssssseeeeeeee. Please help us.

What was that? But as she listened all she could hear was the wail of the wind. The gusts were strong and the rain hammered against the windows. She shivered. Maybe it was time to head back, the light was fading and there wasn't much else she could do today.

Alison went over to the stone arched window, rubbed the dust laden glass and peered out across the land at the back of the house. Behind the trees and hidden amongst the bushes were the ruins of the Abbey. How excited she had been when she had discovered them. She had a picture in her mind of how it would be once she had tamed the wildness. Rambling roses would cascade over the crumbling bricks; wild flowers would grow in the crevices. It would be delightful and once some of the bushes were trimmed or cut away she would be able to glimpse the river that skirted along the edge of her land. Her phone rang and brought her out of her daydream. It was Mark.

'Hey Al, I just had to tell you. I popped into the library on route back to look up the records.'

'Oh! Have you found something?' She listened as he told her the parish records didn't start until 1538 – by which time the monasteries had been dissolved by old King Henry.

Her feeling of disappointment was soon quelled when Mark continued, 'But I did find some entries, right at the start...let's see...here we are. John Parsons baptised 31st October 1538 son of Desmond and Mary Parsons.

Alison squealed. 'Parsons! Wow! Kits ancestors!'

'There's more...burial 2nd November 1538. Mary Parsons wife of Desmond Parsons, a Farricr.'

'Oh my God! So do you think this is Mary – the sad lady? She must have died in childbirth. What's the betting Desmond wasn't the Father. Little Amy keeps saying Mary needs to tell John about the baby. He couldn't have known she was pregnant, I wonder why?'

Mark butted in. 'I continued looking Alison and couldn't see anything more for a bit. No mention of Desmond again, either remarrying or burial but then in 1563 a John Parsons marries a Katherine Stevens. Must be the kid once he'd grown up, so the baby must have survived.'

'Mark this is great! Thank you so much!'

'You are welcome! I have copied some other bits of information, mainly about the Abbey and its history. I can show you on Sunday.'

Her phone battery started to bleep. 'Sorry Mark, I think I'm going to lose you in a moment. Battery is flat. See you Sunday then.'

Her last words were lost as her phone rang out of steam. No worries she would head off back to the pub now. She was excited about Mark's find. The atmosphere in the cottage felt more inviting again despite the storm outside.

Feeling more positive she headed for the front door. Walking through the hall she brushed past a dusty old shelf and began to sneeze. Instinctively she shoved her hand in Mark's jacket pocket for a hanky. She pulled out an array of receipts and a couple of tissues. She shoved the receipts back into the pocket not noticing the one that fluttered down to rest in the corner.

Locking up she made her way out in the beating rain to her Jeep and headed down through the tunnel of ivy towards Greysmead. The ivy clad bushes either side of her swayed and moaned in the gusts, discarding debris over the vehicle like confetti. As she continued along the road, rivulets of muddy water began to fill the gutters. The further she journeyed the stronger the flow and soon the road was awash with water.

She knew she'd be okay, she had a 4x4. She slowed down and gingerly made her way through the increasingly rising water. The road was more like a lake ahead of her, the river must have burst its banks up by the bridge. On she went, the water beginning to seep in the foot well now. She'd be okay. Her car could cope. She didn't allow for the big dips and holes in the beaten up old track on which she drove. Suddenly one of her back wheels descended into a cavernous pothole and lowered the exhaust into the deluge of water. The engine began to struggle as water made its way up the pipe and she came to a halt.

'Bloody hell! This is all I need.' She tried the engine again but it was useless. Opening the door allowed even more dirty, muddy water to pour in onto her feet. Her trainers were sodden and the legs of her jeans soaked up the water like a wick. She had no choice but to bite the bullet and wade out into the flood. She jumped down into the water, cringing as it seeped through the denim onto her legs up to the top of her thighs.

Looking ahead she could see it was even deeper. The wind whipped the trees and branches above her into a frenzy and twigs and leaves fell down around her. There was no way out of it, she'd have to wade back leaving her car surrounded by water and sit it out at the cottage. Her legs felt like dead weights as she made her way back. The depth of the water made it hard going as she moved along, pushing each leg forward with great effort, almost losing her footing a few times as she slipped on the uneven surface of the road. She slowly eased herself along and eventually reached dry land. Shivering, she ran along the track towards her cottage, the strong wind trying to push her back. The sodden sky was throwing down torrents of rain and by the time she got back to Orchard cottage she was wet through.

She thought about attempting the footpath back but looking across at the field it was like marshland. Huge areas were covered in water. She hesitated. Should she risk it? Above the roar of the wind and rain there was a loud creaking noise and suddenly an almighty crash as one of the huge beech trees fell by the path, it toppled to the ground with huge sprays of water shooting out from the saturated grass onto which it had fallen.

Decision made, she slammed the door behind her and ran up the stairs to one of the bedrooms. She was sure she had spotted some old dustsheets up there, hopefully they may be of use to warm her up. The wind screamed through the cracks in the doors, howling like a steam train whistle. The windows continued to hold against the pounding of sharp rain that blasted against the glass.

She opened the cupboard in the back bedroom and yes, there were some old dustsheets, spattered with paint marks. She dragged them out of the cupboard, coughing as the dust they had held onto over the years floated out into the room. She wrapped them round her cold and wet body. She delved further into the cupboard and saw other discarded supplies. There were old rusted tins of paint, a few paint trays and then wedged at the back were a couple of ragged and well-worn towels. She then spotted some overalls! She pulled them out and gave them a good shake and hurriedly began to pull off her wet clothes and rubbed at her skin with the hard and brittle towels. Once she was drier, she stepped into the filthy overalls and pulled them up, securing them tightly around her. She grabbed one of the dustsheets and wrapped it around her shivering body.

She watched the daylight fade as she sat huddled up in the corner whilst the tempest failed to ease outside. She was so cold. The doors and windows rattled as each gust battered the cottage. Downstairs a door slammed. She tried to focus her mind on positive thoughts but as the light continued to weaken, the shadows of the room played tricks. As she began to fall asleep from exhaustion she was sure she saw faces at the window. They were angry, violent faces, their shouting and cursing tossed about in the wind.

The darkness hammered at the windows. It had to get to her before she found out the truth. But there was no way in. The protection that had been placed within the cottage was holding fast, keeping her safe from the evil blackness that swirled around the outside, waiting for its moment to pounce.

Chapter eleven

Alison had huddled up whilst the storm had continued to rage and as time went on her eyes had become heavy. The cold dark night had sent her voices, calling to her as she had floated between the realms of sleep and consciousness. Eventually the voices won and as she sank deeper and deeper into her slumbers the walls of the cottage began to reveal some of its secrets.

Brother John made his way across the courtyard to the Abbot's House. He had been summoned. Maybe there was a problem with the mead? It was a cold March morning. John was grateful for his cloak and shawl. He climbed the stairs to the Abbot's room. The door to the room opened and his soft footsteps slowly entered.

A kindly voice spoke. 'Come in Brother John.'

'You wanted to see me Lord Abbot?'

Abbot Thomas, a kindly man, sat looking at lay brother John. It grieved him greatly, the tales he had heard. But it was not the only thing that was playing on his tired mind. Thomas Cromwell's men had been again, questioning, investigating. He knew that the time was near and felt ill with the worry. The Abbot rubbed at his constantly aching left arm, deciding he would ask Brother Simon to suggest some herbs to soothe him, but for now he had this matter to address.

'I have been told that Mistress Parsons and yourself have become very friendly.'

'Yes my Lord. I have known Mary…Mistress Parsons since childhood. She supplies us with some of the honey for the mead making.'

'Brother Mathew tells me you meet her in the woods? Is this so?'

Brother John wringed his hands. He had to be there for her, he must try to explain to the Abbot. Mary needed him.

'She is frail my Lord. I do not wish her to journey further than she needs.'

'But she is still a young woman John. Surely the extra steps to the refectory are no hardship for her. Meeting her in the woods leads to accusations, gossip. I do not wish for stories to get out about wrong doings here.'

John bowed his head, 'No Abbot. But have not the commissioners now left us in peace?'

'They have John, but they will return. The reformers will not stop until they get their wish.' He paused and looked out of the window at the weak spring sunshine throwing golden light onto the bricks of his beloved Abbey, 'I know our days are coming to a close. We have Cromwell and his commissioners to thank for this sacrilege that is spreading the land like the pox.'

'I am sorry my Lord if you feel I have brought ill repute to God's house. I will not let it happen again.' John raised his head slightly and looked at the Abbot through his lashes. The Abbot had always been kind to him. He was a fair and good man.

'John, I know there is more to this 'friendship' with Mistress Parsons than you will say.'

John attempted to protest but Abbot Thomas held up his hand. 'No, please do not embarrass us both with lies. We both know the truth of the matter. You are to leave at first light for Coggeshall Abbey in Essex.'

John fell to his knees in front of the Abbot. 'Please, please, I beg of you. Let me stay here!' How could he leave Mary? He was all she had. Who would care for her, tend to her bruises and love her as he did? He pleaded with the Abbot through brimming eyes, 'My lord, you need to know that her husband beats her. She needs our care.'

Thomas knew the tales of Desmond the farrier. The Lord had left his heart when the couple's baby had died. He knew he struck out at his wife. But no, it was out of his hands.

'I am sorry John. That is between man and wife. The Lord will watch over her. Go now. Gather your things ready and then go and pray to our Lord for forgiveness of your sins of the flesh. Ask our Lady to protect Mistress Parsons.' He waved his hand dismissing John.

'But please my Lord…I beg you. I beg you………'

The new day began to ease its way over the horizon and Alison drifted in and out of sleep as she lay coiled up tightly in the corner of the room. John's pleads filtered through into her consciousness as she began to be aware of the stiffness of her joints. She felt disorientated, her mind was still firmly focused in the past, it was just her body that lay on the cold hard floor. She could feel the battle going on in her head as her own thoughts tried to push their way to the forefront of her mind. She was confused as she glanced around the room; images of John and the Abbot continued to flash constantly in front of her eyes like a strobe light. The bile rose in her throat as the nausea took hold. The pictures flickered brightly and the room came and went from view, spinning round in front of her as her eyes darted to and fro unable to focus. She felt sick and the contents of her bowels churned, forcing her to bend double as griping pains speared her abdomen.

She breathed slowly and deeply to push away the voices and was able to open her eyes fully as the visions faded away. Still in a half dream like state she rubbed her arms to ease her sore and aching body and stood up. A spasm went through her lower back and she held onto the windowsill to steady herself. The gales of the previous day had now died down and out of the window Alison watched the sun gain height at the back of the cottage. Its rays gently brushed the top of the ruins, sending out a glimmer of orange as the bricks soaked up its warmth.

Her mind flashed back to Abbot Thomas looking out at his Abbey in the sunshine. She could sense how much he had loved the place. She turned and leaned back against the stone window frame, seeing the room in a new light. She now knew this was once the Abbot's office. He seemed a kindly man. She could understand his actions. Poor John. He must have been heartbroken to be forced to leave. Her head began to spin again as the dream edged its way forward. Rubbing at her face with her hands she forced her brain back to the present.

What time was it? Looking at her watch she could see it was just after six. Hopefully the water level had dropped and she could then attempt to walk back. A door banged downstairs and interrupted her thoughts. That couldn't be the wind. Had she fallen asleep again? Was she dreaming? She rubbed furiously at her face and head, trying to stay in the present. Yes, she was awake and there were footsteps running up the stairs.

Whispered voices echoed into the room. 'Wait for me!'

The door to the room slowly edged open. Alison looked into the faces of Steve and Susie.

'Oh my God, it's you! You don't know how pleased I am to see you!' She found her self blubbing like a baby and rushed over to Susie to give her a huge hug.

Susie held her tightly, 'Thank Goodness you are ok. It wasn't until Steve rang me an hour ago to say he was home safely from...' She got a silencing kick from Steve. '....er..back from a night out that I found out the river had flooded over the lane. I checked and realised you weren't back.' She took off her jacket and put it around Alison's shoulders, sensing by her shaking just how cold she was. 'You been here all night?'

Alison managed a nod. 'My Jeep's flooded….in the lane.'

'Don't you worry about that, Steve's Uncle has towed it back to theirs and is getting it dried out.'

'Oh Steve, thank you so much.' Alison smiled at him through her tears.

'No worries. It'll probably stink a bit inside though!'

Back at the Jolly Abbot she received a hero's welcome from Jim. He sat her down in front of a bacon sandwich and a steaming mug of tea.

'So glad you are okay Alison. I was concerned when Suz said you were out in the storm.'

'Your daughter's boyfriend is a star Jim!' She turned and squeezed Steve's arm. 'Thank you again – so much!'

'Just glad I could help, although it was my Uncle that did the donkey work. Still it's nice to be in Susie's good books for a change!' He pulled a face at Susie who gave him a playful slap. 'I'll bring your Jeep back later this morning. We've got it parked on a hill so it should be dried out in no time.' He turned and smiled at Jim as he headed off, 'Uncle says hello by the way.'

'I'm sure he does,' Jim muttered under his breath as he topped up Alison's tea.

Steve was true to his word, the Jeep did dry out and after some coughing and spluttering it had got her to Lunsford to take back the key and then journey back to Mitcham. Steve was also right about the smell! Alison drove back with the windows wide open most of the way and one of the first things she did when she got back was get it booked in for a thorough valet.

She spent most of Saturday keeping the washing machine busy, restocking the fridge and sorting through the post and emails. She had a few new prospective customers wanting her to set up web pages and this reminded her that she needed to get organised and start advertising her services down in Sussex. She knew the internet connection was good at the cottage, the exchange was situated Monkton Lane end of the village so she would still be able to earn a crust from her web design. It would supplement the money she'd put aside from the house sale and also the tidy sum she'd received after her grandmother's death.

She had loved Granny Martin and being the only granddaughter had been very close to her. Granny had moved back down to Sussex when Grandpa had died and when she had become frail Alison's Aunt moved down to be close to her. Now that Alison's Father was also living on the Sussex coast it seemed the Martins were all heading back to the county of their forefathers. Alison was pleased that she too was going to be living in Sussex. She was sure her Grandmother would approve.

She was looking forward to moving. Orchard Cottage no longer spooked her. The dream she'd had whilst sheltering from the storm had made her feel a bond with the place and with the Abbot and Brother John. She could feel nothing evil or scary inside the cottage. But she did feel somewhat uneasy outside by the old dead apple tree and also sensed what seemed like a residue of fear lurking in the air by the ruins.

The sudden death of the old apple tree played on her mind and she sat and surfed the web to try and find reasons why a tree would die so unexpectedly. She found that a fungal disease could be the problem, so nothing spooky at all. Her imagination was obviously trying to find something more than the mundane. She began playing around on the web, searching information about Abbeys and Monks.

She sipped her coffee as she browsed a few pages about the Cistercians and their daily life and then came across a link to the Abbey at Greysmead. After reading a few paragraphs she scrolled down and the page was filled by an artist's depiction of the Abbey in autumn. It was an exact copy of the painting above Kit's fireplace. Sitting back in her chair she took in the scene. It looked beautiful in the golden light of the setting sun. Alison peered forward, nose almost touching the screen. Yes, there it was, a dark shape almost hovering by the orchard outside the Abbot's house.

She saved the picture onto her computer and began to zoom in to get a closer look. When she had the orchard area in view she enlarged it even more. The dark area was very much a wispy shape, the edges indistinct and as she zoomed in even closer she realised that it wasn't just one figure she was seeing but a combination of many, some overlapping with each other, and some floating at the outer limits of the dark form.

She recoiled as she viewed face upon face, vile faces, angry faces, sneering towards the Abbey and as they merged together they gave the impression of an ugly evil mass. Going in even closer she panned across the image of the shouting, enraged features and suddenly stopped with a start when one particular face came into view. A face that looked very familiar. A face she knew!

An owl shrieked in the woods as it watched with its razor sharp eyes the swirling force of hatred that lay in wait outside the cottage. There was strength in numbers and they were patient. They stood united seeking retribution. They hadn't completed their vengeance. It was just a matter of time and then they would find him and would make sure he was punished.

Chapter twelve

Mark was in his flat taking another look at the documents he had picked up at the library for Al. He'd had a difficult few days and had gone out for an early morning run to clear his head. The life he was leading was taking its toll. He'd not long got back and now refreshed from a shower he sat bare foot in the kitchen, huge white towel wrapped around his muscular body. Spread in front of him on the pine table was all the information he had gathered about the Abbey. He'd taken another look yesterday after Al had rung him and told him about her ordeal in the flood and the vivid dream she'd had when she'd been stuck at the cottage. But she wasn't convinced it was a just a dream and he was beginning to agree. As he picked up one sheet of paper headed. 'Abbot Thomas of Greysmead', a chill slid down the length of his spine. It was all starting to be too close to the truth.

He had felt concerned when he heard her tale about the rising waters in the lane and how she'd spent the night at the cottage, unable to get back to the pub. If it really had been ghosts of the Abbot and Brother John she had seen, at least they seemed harmless enough. It was if she encountered this other lot from Greysmead's history he'd been reading about that worried him. He was due round at her place later, he had to decide if he should give her the whole story or would it be best to keep the information back?

Mark hadn't planned on getting involved with Alison when he had first taken the job. But things had stepped up a notch or two lately. She liked him, he knew that. But was it a good idea? It might make the job more difficult if they were an item. He didn't want to hurt her. Jeez, what's the matter with you man? You don't do touchy-feely. Anyone would think you actually cared about her!

Surprisingly Alison had managed to get a good restful sleep after her shock of the face in the painting. She was spending Sunday morning lazing in bed reading the newspapers. The duvet was littered with various publications and a tray with cereal bowl and toast crumbs was perched precariously on her lap as she sipped her tea and perused the tabloids. She glanced down the page and her keen hazel eyes fell on a news item that put her into shock. The tray toppled to the floor with milk spraying the bedcovers as she pulled the paper up to her face for a closer inspection.

'Mick Brown, known locally as Big Mick, owner of Cinderella's bar and nightclub, Tower Street, Stockwell was arrested yesterday on suspicion on two counts of murder. He is being held in police custody pending further enquiries.'

Alison continued to read how Mick had been pulled in for the murder of Billy Watson, known drug dealer and Evie Morrison, a local prostitute.

Pending further enquiries? Did that mean Inspector Winter would be paying her another visit, seeing if she'd change her alibi for Kenny? And more to the point did it mean Kenny would be paying her a visit too? Shit! They must have some new evidence to pull Mick in again. Her foot located the spilt milk as she jumped out of bed in a state of panic expecting the doorbell to ring at any moment.

It wasn't long before she was up and dressed and wandering around the flat like a caged lion. What should she do? The Police were more than likely to come and ask more questions. They want to nail him. Kenny knew her address. Maybe he'll turn up. Oh God! She heard a car door slam outside and ran over to the window to peer out through the blinds. It was only her neighbour. Maybe she should get out of the flat, go and stay with friends? No, Kenny would find her! How about Mark? She'd ring him, see if she could stay down in Croydon at his place.

Mark's phone began to ring, he looked at the display. It was Al.

'Hi Mark. I know we arranged for you to come over later…would you mind if we changed the plans?'

She sounded stressed. He wasn't surprised. 'Hiya. What's up? Don't you want to see me after all?'

'Mark. I really can't say over the phone why, but…sorry if this sounds a bit full on, but can I come down to Croydon and stay at yours for a bit?'

Fuck! He wasn't expecting that! 'Croydon? Er, yeah right.. yeah. Erm.. …thing is… I've got a mate staying at the moment, might be a bit difficult. So....er... why d'you need to stay here?'

Not the response she was hoping for. 'There's a problem with my flat so I just need to move out for a bit.' She couldn't tell him why she needed to get away.

'I'm really sorry Al but I can't help. Just haven't got the room here. What will you do? Do you still want me to come over later anyway? I've got some bits about the Abbey to show you.'

'That's the last thing on my mind at the moment Mark!' She snapped back. 'Look, I've got to go.'

'But Al…..Al?' She'd gone. Hung up! Bugger! That was a close call. Bloody hell, he'd nearly blown it! That could have been difficult. He'd best get over to her place. See if he could get her to talk to him. He was sure she wouldn't be heading off that quickly.

It wasn't long before he was locking up his flat and heading down the stairwell to the main door of the building. Jeez, why did it always smell of piss down here? As he took the stairs two at a time he looked out of the filthy windows, the gloomy scene stared back at him. Stockwell - what a shit hole! A feeling of bitterness overcame him as he looked out at the grey skies. What was he doing here? Life should be better than this. He headed towards his van, he'd left it round the side of the garages last night. It wasn't any safer in than out, the door to his garage was missing anyway. As was the case for most of them in the graffiti covered block.

As he turned the corner he nearly tripped over a druggie, propped up against the wall of the garage, obviously stoned out of his head. A discarded needle at his side.

'Hey, you! Clear off!'

'Fuck off Granddad.' Came the mumbled reply.

Mark curbed his natural instinct to intervene and jumped into his van and screeched out of the car park. As he turned out of his road he left the dowdy flats behind and made his way past Victorian terraced houses, their white painted windowsills decorated with tubs of geraniums. The residents hiding in their little worlds beyond the glass, ignoring the sad and corrupt lives that were taking place just a stones throw away.

He decided he had time for a quick detour. At the traffic lights he turned into Tower Street. He'd nip in and show his face at the club, see if they'd heard from Big Mick's brief. He couldn't be held too much longer without extra evidence or witnesses. Once he'd spoken to Kenny he'd make his way to Mitcham to see the lovely Alison.

His mind went back to the day when Big Mick had suggested Alison was a threat.

'How can we be sure your missus won't spill the beans?' Mick had asked Kenny.

'Ex Missis.' mumbled Kenny, 'Naar, she won't say a thing. I'm sure she'll be sweet.'

Mick sneered, 'Well I'm not so sure. Maybe we should take her out…just in case.'

Mark had been watching from the doorway. He'd been working at Mick's club since Christmas.

'How's about we suss her out first? Get her trust. Someone from the club she doesn't know, see if she's going to keep quiet, try to tease it out of her.'

'Tease it out of her?' mocked Kenny, 'You're mental!'

'No, we don't want another stiff they can pin on us Ken. If a bit of teasing it out of her doesn't get her talking, maybe we're safe.'

As Mark parked his van around the back of the club he thought back to the wall of silence that had followed his suggestion. He had felt his stomach knot, had he crossed the line by questioning Mick's decision? He didn't want to lose this job but he sure didn't want to be party to any more killing.

Big Mick had sat mulling over Mark's words and finally the tension was broken when he had finally answered. 'D'you know I think you might have a point there Marky boy. First we'll see if we can find out what's she's up to.' He turned to Kenny, 'Didn't you say she was thinking of moving out of London? She still about round 'ere?'

'Far as I know Mick, yeah,' replied the disgruntled ex husband.

Big Mick jumped up and clapped his hands, rubbing them together. His lank greasy hair falling over his eyes, 'Yeah, let's do it. Find out where she is and then get someone to close in on her, see if she talks.'

One of Mick's long-time lackeys had set to work and found out Alison was in the first throws of buying a cottage in Sussex and was trying to get her Dad's builder to look at the place. It was decided the builder could be put temporarily out of the picture easy enough and one of Mick's boys go instead.

Mark had found himself being volunteered and it was on a wet April day that he had first set off to meet Alison at Greysmead. However he wasn't prepared for the effect she would have on his hardened heart.

Mark shook his head and banged his hand down on the steering wheel sending the memories to the back of his mind. Don't go soft man. Keep your mind on the job. He got out of the beast and pushed open the doors and strode purposefully into the club.

Meanwhile down in Mitcham Alison had been busy. Totally convinced either the police or Mick's cronies would be descending on her any minute, she knew she needed to get away. She had to keep out of the picture until the Police had released Mick. She felt let down that Mark wasn't able to help, He would have been the best bet as neither the Police or Mick's gang knew of her connection with him. He'd told her that he lived on the outskirts of Croydon so it would have been far enough away to make her feel safe. Still if he didn't want to help her out so be it.

She began to fold up an extra jacket and cram it into her bag. She'd managed to get hold of an old school friend who lived over in Oxfordshire, well out of the Met's radar. Her friend, Maria had been a bit surprised to hear from Alison after so long but having just come out of a long term relationship was happy to have a bit of company for a while. Yes, Alison could come and stay for as long as she liked.

She took a last look around the flat. It looked a mess but it could stay that way, she was in a hurry. She checked her mobile for any messages, just in case Mark had changed his mind after all. There was nothing so she turned it off, slipped it in her bag, picked up her holdall and laptop and set off for Thame.

Mark tried Alison's mobile again as he drove through Clapham. He'd got voicemail earlier. Back at the club everyone had been feeling despondent about Big Mick's arrest. Kenny wasn't about, no one seemed to know where he was. It crossed Mark's mind that Kenny may have gone after Alison. The Police would be watching him more now and probably tail him. Ken would be playing into their hands.

'Al, it's Mark. Will you pick up? I'm on my way to your place.' Maybe she'd set off for Greysmead. He'd go to her flat first, make sure Kenny hadn't done anything stupid.

He parked around the corner and sat slumped down in his seat and waited for a while and watched for any activity. It was quiet, no sign of Kenny or the Police. Confident that it was safe he made his way along her road and checking that no eyes were watching he slipped round the side. Her car was gone from the driveway. He let himself in the back door with the key he'd had cut when he had paid the flat a visit before. Last time he'd managed to get in through the kitchen window and the place had smelt of soured milk. He remembered he'd nearly given the game away when he had seen her afterwards and mentioned she needed more milk. Fortunately she hadn't twigged.

Mark glided around the flat, careful not to leave any signs of his visit. She certainly had left in a hurry. Too much of a hurry, for there on the notepad by the phone she had scribbled a name and telephone number. Maria Kipps. The code was 01844. That should be fairly easy to track down. As Mark headed off, his eyes rested on the fridge where Alison had stuck a photo of herself standing outside Orchard Cottage. Mark slowly reached his hand up to the picture, his fingers caressed her face gently before slipping the photo into his pocket. You can't hide from me my girl, Mark's coming to get you!

Chapter thirteen

Sunday night journeyed into the distance taking with it the grey and gloomy skies. A new day dawned with a promise of sunshine and warmth as Alison stretched her toes, waking up refreshed in a strange bed.

She had left London feeling stressed and wound up and as she had driven along the M40 she could still feel Big Mick's grasp as he continued to control her life. It was as if she was tethered by an umbilical cord with Mick and Kenny and they were constantly trying to feed her veins with their evil. But then as she crossed into Oxfordshire the cord snapped, pinging back towards the capital leaving her free and untied. The red kites soared above her, swirling in the skies as she completed her motorway journey, their freedom and joy a mirror of her emotions.

She'd had a fun evening with Maria, a takeaway and a few glasses of wine, and lots of giggling as they recalled their school days back in south London. Life had been so uncomplicated then.

Next morning, once Alison had dragged herself away from the cosy bed they both sat up to the breakfast bar in Maria's bright and sunny kitchen for a leisurely breakfast and continued the reminiscing of their teenage years.

'We weren't surprised when you ended up marrying Kenny you know. Do you remember that day when you saw him on the bus, on the way home from school and you managed to nab the seat next to him?'

'Do I! I don't think I breathed for the rest of the journey; he was so close to me. I couldn't believe my luck, sitting next to the gorgeous school boy who I had loved from afar for so long. He had always seemed oblivious to my existence. When he actually spoke to me when I got up to get off the bus! Wow!'

Alison thought back how simple life had been, what happened? Did it always get this difficult and painful for everyone?

'If only I'd known how it would turn out. I would have kept well away.'

Maria looked at her friend. She knew Alison and Kenny had divorced. Knew he'd turned to drink when he had lost his business but felt there was more to the pain in Alison's face than she was telling.

'Was it that bad Alison? So bad that you wish away even the good times you both had? You've never talked much about your break-up.'

'It's all water under the bridge now Maria.' Alison leant forward and started to tidy the jam and honey jars in front of her into an orderly line. She didn't meet Maria's eyes as she continued. She concentrated on the task in hand as she went on, 'Ken has done some bad things…evil things….things I'd rather forget. Unfortunately I can't. It's with me all the time, eating away like a disease,' she looked up and gave Maria a weak smile, 'But the more I talk about it, the more I'm feeding it, so it's best that I don't.' Tears slipped down her face and she wiped them roughly with the back of her hand and pulled herself upright. 'Anyway – it's you that needs support now that you and Jo have split up.'

'No need to worry on that score. I'm glad it's over. It's just company I miss, that's all.' She touched Alison's hand, 'It's good to have you here. Like old times.'

'Yeah! Too right! What's the plan…you working today?'

'On late shift at the hospital so if you fancy getting out for a bit, I'm game. How's about a bit of culture? Waddesdon Manor's not far from here, they do a good lunch and plenty of grounds to walk it off afterwards.' She looked out of the window to an eggshell blue sky, 'Too nice a day to stay here. What do you think?'

'Sounds good to me. Maybe I'll be able to get a signal on my phone, it's a bit hit and miss here. I tried ringing my Dad when I first arrived, to let him know where I was but got no reply.'

'He was probably out at the pub,' Maria said as she started to gather up the breakfast things.

'If he was I hope he wasn't over doing it. He's got a bit of a dodgy ticker now and should be looking after himself. I tried my Aunt but then remembered they are away for the weekend. I left a message, she'll pick it up when she's back from her trip and go round and tell him.'

Maria shut the dishwasher door and wiped her hands. 'Okay then, shall we get ready and head off in a mo'?'

It wasn't long before Alison was by the door, bag in hand. 'Right then Maria, stately home here we come!'

Mark was heading into Thame. He still hadn't tracked down Kenny. Mark wanted to be certain Kenny hadn't decided to take matters into his own hands to keep Alison quiet. The fact she had headed off to Oxfordshire was a good indication that she had no plans to blab. He'd left another message on her phone asking her to get in touch but had heard nothing back so with Kenny AWOL he was beginning to worry. He didn't want any more deaths.

He'd tracked down an address for Maria and followed the sat nav as it took him along the main road, past the busy market place teeming with shoppers. The Swan pub was doing a good trade with customers standing outside in the sunshine with their refreshing lunchtime drinks. He turned off just after the pub into a side road of small terraced houses with double yellow lines stretching out ahead as far as the eye could see. There was nowhere to park his van. Bugger! There was someone right behind him too. He'd have to carry on.

He managed to find himself back at the market place and parked there before he made his way on foot back towards the address. He looked around, there was no sign of Alison's car, but with the parking spaces so few and far between, it could be anywhere. He walked along and took a look into the window. No sign of life. He'd have to risk it. He rang the doorbell and sprinted along to the end of the row of houses and waited. Once satisfied no one was at home he went back to the door, checked the coast was clear and within minutes he had the door open and was in.

A quick look round the two up, two down, gave no clues to where they were. Alison had been there, the sweet tones of her perfume lingered in the house and upstairs he noticed a jacket lying on the bed that looked familiar. He wandered from the kitchen into the front room and sunk down on the well-worn sofa and began to think. They must have been gone a while, the kettle felt cold. What to do next? Deep in thought he was startled when his phone rang.

'Mark? It's Al.'

'Hey! Where are you? I've been trying to get hold of you.'

'I know that! How many messages have you left?' She laughed. She sounded okay, not stressed at all. Kenny hasn't caught up with her then. Good.

'I was just concerned, you sounded upset when I spoke to you last. I didn't know what was going on. You said trouble at your flat? What's going on Al?'

He could hear someone in the background. 'Come on Al, let's get some lunch.'

'Who's that? Where are you?'

'Don't worry – I'm fine! I'm staying with a friend, over in Thame.' He could hear her as she mumbled something to her friend before she spoke again. 'Look, why don't you come down if you're free? Maria doesn't mind.'

She gave him the address and suggested he came over and see her whilst Maria was at work that evening.

'Do you think you will find it okay?

'Don't worry – I'm sure I will.' He replied and smiled to himself.

After lingering over coffee, Al and Maria had wandered amongst the trees, linking arms as they had all those years ago as school friends. They headed over to the Victorian aviary and were doubled up with laughter. Maria was in the middle of reminding Alison about a funny incident in a maths class when Al's phone started to ring. Still laughing she took the call, it was her Aunt. Strange, she sounded out of breath?

'Alison?'

'Hello Aunty. You're back! Did you get my message? Have you told Dad, I wasn't able to…'

'Alison. Please stop…'

She sounded weird. 'What's up?…. Aunty?'

'Where are you love? Is there anyone with you?'

What is this? 'Yes, I'm out with Maria. You remember Maria from school? What's going on?'

'There's no easy way to tell you this.' Her Aunt stifled a sob. 'It's your Dad.'

'Dad? Aunty, tell me, what's happened?' The world seemed to close in and everything around her swirled out of view as her mind focused on the call. She was acutely aware of every second as time slowed down. She knew before her Aunt said them, the words that were to come.

'I'm so sorry sweetheart. I came round early this morning and found him.'

Her Aunt began to cry as she told Alison how she had let herself into her brother's home when there had been no reply. The curtains were still open, the TV blaring out. She had looked through the window and could see him, lying on the floor, his face pushed up against the settee where he had fallen.

Maria had been watching Alison's face and managed to grab her arm as her legs gave way and led her to a bench. Alison began to shiver uncontrollably and sat doubled over as she continued to talk on the phone.

'Oh Aunty! What happened?' Her head began to buzz, her brain started to feel fuzzy and disjointed. Why was she shivering on such a warm day? She couldn't take this in. Please God let it be a dream? Her Dad? Why she only saw him a few weeks ago, he was fine. She'd spoken to him the other day. No there must be some mistake. Aunty's got it wrong.

'They think it was a heart attack Alison. It must have happened yesterday afternoon. The police are here now.'

'The police?' She screamed down the phone, 'Why the bloody hell are they there? Keep them away from my Dad!' This couldn't be happening.

'Calm down sweetheart. They have to be called when this kind of thing happens. We're waiting now for….you know…for your Dad to be taken away. Your Uncle's sitting in with him.'

The huge meal she'd had at lunch time was sitting in her throat waiting to return as she began to sob down the phone. She was going to be sick. Her Dad. Lying there all night. All alone! Scared. Oh Dad! Whilst she had been with Maria laughing and joking he had been lying on the floor, needing her help. She heard an unearthly wail fill the air as she finally gave in to her grief, her world crumbling around her.

It seemed ironic that it should be such a beautiful day when a loved one is put deep into the ground, shutting out the sunlight from them forever. Mark looked across the graveside at Alison as she stood with her Aunt and watched as her Father's coffin was lowered into the earth. She was holding up okay really, compared to the mess she had been last week. God it had been such a terrible time. Seeing her like that.

He had been sitting outside the pub round the corner from Maria's house as he waited for Alison's return. He had planned on going over to see her that evening just to keep an eye on her, make sure Kenny didn't turn up and do something he'd regret. Mark had rung the club earlier that afternoon and there had still been no word from Ken but it seemed Big Mick had been released without charge so he was in no doubt that Kenny would soon re-surface. But then like a bolt out of the blue he'd had a call from Al's friend, telling him the news about Al's Dad. He offered to go over, drive Al down to her Aunts. She was in no fit state to make the journey herself, she was an absolute mess. He'd driven her down to Bexhill and handed her over to her Aunt and he watched as they crumpled together in their pain and sadness.

The week that followed was a turning point in their friendship. He knew things were changing as he held her close and she shed so many tears for her Father. It had opened the wound of her Mother's death and Mark wondered if Alison would ever re-emerge from the pool of grief in which she was drowning. He felt her pain, felt a terrible ache in his heart for her anguish.

He hadn't ventured near the club all week. His phone was clogged up with unanswered calls and messages from Mick. 'Where was he?' 'Get your arse over here NOW!' But he had ignored them. Couldn't decide where his loyalties lay anymore.

A robin hopped onto the back of a nearby gravestone, his head moving from side to side as he wondered if there were any good pickings from the disturbed earth. It began to sing a sad wistful tune waiting for everyone to go. Family and friends around the graveside began to disperse. While Alison and her Aunt were talking to the vicar, Mark walked towards the gate to wait and stood leaning against a tree by the path. A figure approached from the cemetery entrance, a swagger he recognised.

Shit! It was Kenny! He knew he'd surface eventually but not at his ex Father in law's funeral! Mark could see Alison was still talking to the vicar so rushed along the path and stopped Kenny in his tracks.

'Alright pal? Haven't seen you since Mick's arrest – where you been?'

Kenny grasped Marks arm tightly, 'Say the same about you. Mick's looking for you, he's not a 'appy bunny.'

Mark tried to calm things, 'I've been keeping an eye on things with Alison. Keeping her sweet, that's all.'

'Yeah I know…I've been watching you. Been keeping an eye on you this week. You seem a bit over friendly with my ex-missus. Too much for my liking. I'm not having it, you hear?'

Mark swallowed, you didn't cross Mick's right hand man. 'It's all part of the plan Kenny. Nothing in it, honest! If there was a time she might spill it would be now – but she's not. Mick's safe I'm sure.'

Kenny grabbed at Mark's jacket and pulled him close. Mark could see his own eyes reflected in Kenny's huge and dark pupils. He'd obviously been taking something. He needed to soothe the situation before it got out of hand, before Alison spotted them.

'It's alright Ken. Nothings going on…honest to God. I'm just trying to help Mick, that's all mate. I know you're the only bloke for her.'

Ken began to relax and let go of Mark. 'That right? Well I don't want her,' he spat on the ground, 'I remember how she looked at me. She despises me. Well not as much as I fuckin' hate her. But I'm not having you,' he poked his finger in Mark's chest, 'you....or no one else having her either. I want her to rot in hell...like her old man. Good riddance I say. He wouldn't help me, wouldn't tell me where his precious daughter was, so sod him.'

Mark took in Kenny's words, 'What do you mean he wouldn't help? Did you have something to do with his death? I thought it was a heart attack?'

Kenny grinned, 'Too much stress and agro brings on an attack don't it? Had a ring side seat, didn't I!'

Mark heard footsteps, Alison had seen them and was making her way over. Her grief very quickly had turned to anger as she screamed at Kenny.

'What are you doing here? Just leave me alone! I don't want you here.'

Kenny spat again at her feet as he turned to leave, 'Don't worry doll, I'm going... for now.'

She began to rush towards him, shouting obscenities, her claws out ready for the attack.

Mark grabbed at her, stopped her punching out at Kenny, her arms flayed around as Kenny walked away laughing. Mark held onto her tightly, his face touching her hair as he spoke gently, 'Calm down sweetheart. Kenny's not worth the hassle. He's an animal, just let it go. As long as you keep quiet he can't hurt you.'

Alison's whirring brain suddenly took in his words, 'What do you mean? What do you know about me and Ken?' She started to panic. How did he know Ken? Her eyes accusing, she said, 'Tell me Mark, what do you know?'

'Hey, nothing babe, calm down. Maria told me about your marriage break up and when this dude came along, shouting the odds I had a few words. I didn't want him causing a ruckus at your Dads funeral. He told me who he was, there's no need to stress.'

'Why did you say 'as long as you keep quiet' then?' her mind was going overtime. Did he know Kenny?

Mark took her hand, 'Look I don't know what's going on in your head but you really are barking up the wrong tree here Al. I said keep quiet because if you continued to rage at him it seemed likely he was the sort who wouldn't worry about hitting a woman, that's all I meant.' He put his arm around her shoulder and led her towards the car park, 'Come on, let's get back, everyone at the wake will be wondering where we are.'

'I'm sorry Mark, I didn't mean to go off like that. I just find it hard to know who I can trust these days, one day I'll tell you about Ken and me, but for now I'm just grateful for your support. I couldn't have got through this without you. It's good to have someone I can trust'

Mark opened the car door for her, 'That's okay babe, you can trust me hundred percent.'

As he walked round to the driver's door he glanced back at the graveyard. At the side of the newly dug earth stood a figure, watching them.

Chapter fourteen

When all the dreams and strange goings on at Orchard Cottage and Greysmead began I just knew that it was meant to be. Why else did that cottage seek me out? It had called to me as a child when I had drawn it so many times and finally it had tracked me down. I know in my heart something unearthly has done all in its power to get me to Greysmead and by doing so, has opened up my sixth sense again, and to be honest it feels good – uplifting. Like an old friend getting back in touch. I feel in need of a friend I can trust, especially after all the shit I've gone through with Kenny. Mark has been a good friend but do I <u>really</u> know him? My gut feeling tells me to be careful. For now.

I've always had a good intuition. When I was much younger I'd know about certain things before they actually happened and often felt what I called 'my vibes' when visiting certain places but then as I got older and other things seemed more important to me I soon forgot all about it. That was until Mum died.

The night she died I heard her voice as clear as day saying goodbye to me.

'Bye Alison' that's all she'd said but I knew without any doubt it was her and that she was ok. When I saw the medium, friends had thought I was crazy. What did they know! It was just uncanny how much she knew about Mum, things only I would know. And I found all the feelings from my youth resurfaced. I remember she told me I should be still and listen more as I had the ability to look through the gateway into the other world. I dismissed it at the time as mumbo jumbo but do wonder now.

Why does life have to give out good things with one hand and take from the other? I was so pleased to be buying my cottage, felt my life was on the up, was so excited and then bang, it all comes tumbling down again. God, it ripped at my heart when Dad died. I think I must have gone into shock when Aunty first rung me to tell me the news. I just couldn't comprehend it at all – my Dad? Dead? No – must be a mistake. All the way down to Bexhill in Mark's big black van, I had sat believing we would get there and Dad would be sitting on his sofa, watching the TV and wondering what on earth all the fuss was about. But no, that didn't happen. It was true. My kind and wonderful Father was no longer around. No longer there for me to ring for advice, a chat and a laugh. But I had told myself if I managed to get through that day I'd be all right, for later that evening he would speak to me, to say goodbye. Just as my Mum had done the day she'd died. It would be fine.

But his message never did come. I listened and listened, willing him to speak to me but he never did. He was gone. That was it. The end. I dreaded the funeral. Standing around that big void in the earth, slowly lowering my Dad down, deeper and deeper. But I had gotten through it, leaning on Aunty and Mark was there giving his support. And then when I had thought the worst of the day was over Kenny had turned up. The bastard! I'd gone a bit mad for a while, shouting at him, wanting to hit out, I even began to think paranoid thoughts that Mark was in league with him for a moment or two. Will I ever trust another person again?

But then everything turned good again! Mark and I got into the car and I looked across to Dad's grave, now a great big mound of earth covered with flowers and I was overcome with a feeling of pure joy. Because there he was, my Dad, standing by the grave, watching me. And I knew it was all going to be fine.

Mark felt a coldness creep down his spine as he closed the book and tucked it back into the drawer. Bloody hell! Was it really her Dad they'd seen at the graveyard? Jeez! What was he getting into here? He shivered and pushed the drawer tightly shut.

Kenny had told him that Alison used to keep a journal when they were married. What if she'd written down all she knew about the murders? While she spent so much time down at Bexhill, trying to clear her Dad's house it gave Mark ample opportunity to search around her flat. When he had first found the book tucked away in a drawer amongst Alison's jumpers he thought he had struck gold but the entries only started from when she had moved to the flat in Mitcham. Where did she keep the earlier ones? Maybe they would come to light once she moved to Monkton Lane. Mark took a final look around the flat and checked he'd not left any signs he'd been there. Now Orchard cottage was hers, Alison thought he was down in Sussex, working hard getting the place habitable so he'd best get off.

It had been a scorching July day when Alison finally received the call to say that Orchard Cottage belonged to her. It had felt good to have something positive in her life again. Mark had got busy almost immediately and said he hoped to get most of the work done during August and was sure by mid September she would be in. Since then she had been spending her days between working at home trying to keep her business afloat and at Bexhill trying to make a dent in her Father's stuff ready to sell his place.

It was after a long day at her Dad's house sifting through drawers of old papers and letters that she decided to see if a room at the Abbot was available for a few nights. She'd not been down to Greysmead for a while so it would be good to get back and see how the work was going. She was getting quite excited, September was looming closer, and it wouldn't be long before she actually lived there. It would be good to catch up with the villagers she had made friends with again, Susie and her tearaway boyfriend Steve, nosey Mrs Blackman and of course Kit, with who she still felt she needed to build bridges after the upset because of Amy.

She thought back to the copy of Kit's Abbey painting she had found on the web and the all too familiar face she was sure she could make out in the fuzzy area at the front of the orchard. She hadn't looked at anything about the Abbey since then, either on the web or the sheets of info Mark had found for her at the library. When Big Mick had been arrested everything in her life had gone crazy and then her Dad's death put all of that in the background. Now she was calmer it was time to look into its history in more detail, discover if there was something to Amy's sad lady once and for all and of course there was that face in the painting.

She began to unpack her case at the Abbot. As she glanced out to the green Al noticed Mr Elliott, as he made his way across to the pub. So he was still about. It was looking like he was a permanent fixture. She'd not spoken to him much since the day of the May Fayre. Maybe she should make the effort to chat some more, see if she could find out what he gets up to once and for all.

Mark was going to be busy at the cottage, renewing the staircase. She hoped she'd be able to catch up with him during her stay. They'd not seen quite so much of each other since the funeral. He'd said he had another job to deal with, but he'd be able to get the cottage sorted too, no problem, it just meant he'd be a bit pushed for socializing for a while. That was okay as she had enough on her plate as it was.

It was as she headed down to the bar to get a sandwich for lunch that she almost collided with Mr Elliott.

'Oh! Sorry Mr Elliot. I should look where I'm going!'

'Don't worry. No harm done. And please, call me Tom.' He held out his hand and she found herself clasping his rather wet and muddy palm. Her hand was now covered with mud, as was much of the sleeve of her shirt.

Tom fumbled for a tissue and apologized, 'I'm really so sorry. I was just going up to wash and brush up before I had some lunch. Looks like you need to as well,' he smiled and the serious looking face she had begun to expect to see from him suddenly lit up.

He seemed different to the person she had perceived him to be. His permanent frown made him appear older than his thirty-five years. Usually he was quiet and grumpy looking and always looked annoyed and she'd always felt a bit wary of him. They both headed back up the stairs to their rooms to get cleaned up and Alison found herself agreeing to have lunch with him down at the bar.

They had a nice few hours chatting over lunch and a coffee. Alison discovered that her suspicions were right and he was a keen nature lover and worked in animal welfare. Tom was keeping an eye on a badger sett along Monkton Lane. He'd been a bit worried when he'd first overheard her conversations about building work at the cottage. He was worried the badgers would get disturbed.

'Where is the sett then Tom? Is it near my cottage?'

Tom answered in hushed tones. 'If I tell you, you must promise not to make it common knowledge. I need to know I can trust you.'

Alison giggled. 'It's all a bit cloak and dagger isn't it?'

Tom suddenly had his serious face back again. 'Alison, it really IS important, believe me. There are people about who do not care one jot about these beautiful animals.'

'I'm sorry Tom. I didn't mean to laugh. I can assure you there is no way I would wish harm to any innocent creature.'

Tom sat for a moment weighing up his next move. 'Look – how about we go for a walk to Monkton Lane, I can show you and tell you a bit more about them on the way.'

As they walked along the footpath at the edge of the field Tom began to tell Alison about the wildlife and plants in the area, pointing out various flowers as they strolled along in the glorious sunshine. They headed towards the old gateposts that marked the pathway through the woods, where Alison had walked back in the spring when she had been lured by the heavenly scent of the bluebells. Was it really only three months ago? So much had happened in that time. Suddenly Alison's mind was filled with a vision of Brother John standing forlorn in the woods, staring out across the fields. His eyes seeking out Mary, hoping she would venture across with the honey to see him. The scent of the bluebells engulfed Alison's senses and she began to feel queasy.

Toms voice penetrated her thoughts. '....So that's why they are called gatekeepers. Alison? Alison? Are you okay?'

'What? Sorry.' She shook her head and smiled as she looked into his concerned eyes. 'Must be the heat that's got to me. Sorry, what were you saying?' She took a swig of water and concentrated.

'I was just pointing out that gatekeeper butterfly, also known as a hedge brown.'

Going into nature guide mode he showed her a delicate little brown butterfly sitting on the rotting gateposts, wings outstretched. Tom began to reel off lots of information but Alison could feel Brother John as he tried to take control of her thoughts and she did her best to fix her mind onto Tom's words.

'See the eyespots? They're probably....' Tom, mid way through his monolog glanced across to Alison, 'Are you sure you are okay? Come on, let's sit down over there on the logs.' He led her away from the wood and across the grass to the huge stack of logs that were the remnants of the old beech that had fallen the night Alison had been stranded in the flood.

Alison felt herself swaying, unable to focus clearly but as Tom held her arm and they headed away from the trees she slowly felt in charge of her mind again. Tom took off his hat and popped it on her head.

'There! That will help protect you bit. You're probably dehydrated. Have you had much to drink today?'

'What? Are you saying I'm drunk?' She joked and gave him a playful slap. 'You are probably right though Tom, apart from a cuppa at breakfast the only other drink I've had is that coffee with lunch.' She held her water bottle to her lips and downed the rest in one.

They sat for a while on the logs in silence, the warm air full of the smells of summer as they listened to the continuous churring of the grasshoppers and the gentle hum of the bees on the wildflowers. A skylark soared into the sky, its song fading as it eventually became a small dot amongst the soft wispy clouds that punctuated the sky above. Alison felt light hearted and happy as they stood up and continued their summer stroll.

They were unaware of the snake of darkness that was swirling around her cottage up ahead, nudging and probing. Trying to find a way in. Searching for its final victim. It coiled round and round. Tightening its grasp and then raised its head like a cobra, ready and waiting to strike out at its prey. It was patient, it could wait for as long as it needed to feed its hunger, to get its revenge.

Alison was now feeling back in control and the whispers of Mary and John had vanished from her mind. She was enjoying her walk. Tom was quite a serious man but seemed so caring about nature and animals and was delighted in having such an interested pupil.

'As we are so close to my cottage now, shall we nip in there first and I can show you around and also introduce you to Mark. You will see that the disturbance is going to be minimal to wildlife. Perhaps then you may feel you can trust me enough to show me the sett?' Alison looked at him pleadingly.

'Let's go and see inside your cottage first shall we?' Tom held her arm, still concerned that she seemed rather flushed, he didn't want her fainting on him, 'You sure you're feeling alright now?'

She felt fine, the sense of Brother John penetrating her thoughts had been left behind in the woods and they continued on their way across the grass in the afternoon heat towards her new home. Alison reached into her pocket for a hair tie and gathered up her long wavy hair into a ponytail, she welcomed the cool breeze, feeling relief as it brushed across the back of her neck and shoulders. She'd be pleased to get into the shade.

That was odd. There was no sign of Mark's van. Alison screwed up her eyes against the sunlight and shielded them with her hand as she scoured the lane for signs of Mark. He wasn't about but it looked as if there was something dark up ahead. How strange. It looked like a heavy mist was swirling around the perimeter of Orchard Cottage.

'Do you see that Tom? How weird, how can it be misty on a day like this?'

She must be feeling unwell again he thought, 'Sorry but it doesn't look misty to me Alison.'

What was happening? Why couldn't he see it? It was there, in front of them! The swirling blackness twisted around as she approached the gates and rose up to form a tall column of dark fog and then suddenly it dissolved, like a fine black powder, falling and scattering across the ground in front of the fence.

'Oh my God! Did you see that? What on earth was it?' She turned to look at Tom expecting him to be just as amazed and confused. But he was just looking at her with a worried frown. He'd seen nothing. Maybe she had sunstroke.

'Come on Alison, let's get you inside, into the shade.'

'There was something there! I saw it!' She protested as they went into the empty cottage. Empty save for the rotting corpse of a crow, alive with feasting maggots, as it lay just inside the door.

Chapter Fifteen

'Calm down, it's okay.' Tom produced a carrier bag from his pocket and deftly gathered up the dead bird, tying the top tightly. One remaining maggot danced on the floor and he quickly wiped it up with an old tissue. 'There, all cleared up,' he smiled at Alison who stood rigid by the front door watching him as he disposed of the bird.

'Why do these crows keep getting in? I had one flying around attacking my head upstairs when I first looked round the place with Mark.'

'It's actually a jackdaw, they do nest near houses and on top of chimney pots. You may find there was a nest up there. If it's open to the elements they may fall through, can't get out and then starve to death. Poor blighter.' He edged past her and put the bag outside, 'Lovely birds. Intelligent.'

'Not intelligent enough to get out again though!' she frowned. 'I can't understand it, Mark's been here recently. Look the staircase is in the throws of being replaced. So the bird wouldn't have been stuck inside trapped for that long. No, something's not right.'

She paced back and forth, wringing her hands muttering to herself. 'Something's going on. It has got to have something to do with John and Mary. But what?'

Tom was concerned. Alison seemed to be getting into a state of panic, over what? A dead bird? What was the matter with the woman? One minute she was calm and quiet and the next freaking out about a dead jackdaw. No, must just be the heat getting to her.

'Mark should have been here,' she dashed along the hallway to the back end of the house, 'Where is he anyway?' She walked faster, beginning to get angry, her voice getting louder now, 'He was supposed to be here working!' she marched into the kitchen and stopped as she looked around, 'Oh my God!'

Tom hearing her call out rushed along to see what else she'd discovered. 'Not another bird?' he said as he walked into the kitchen.

But the dead jackdaw and mist was forgotten. Alison was beaming with delight and taking in all she could see around her, 'I think I can forgive him for taking some time out. He's worked so hard! This kitchen is just stunning!'

Alison was amazed that Mark had managed to get the room finished. It looked wonderful. She'd chosen the units ages ago and had managed to get something she felt was in keeping with the style of the place. Very country kitchen with a huge sink, big dresser and an island in the middle with little drawers for herbs and good solid wood worktops. It was looking fantastic. She twirled round, clapped her hands like a little child.

'I take it you like it then?' Tom laughed. 'He does know his stuff, your man. Looks good! He must have a good team of workers.'

'No, it's just him doing most of the work.'

Tom frowned. 'Oh, I just thought he had a…? …no matter.' He shook his head, 'He's done a great job.'

'He sure has!' Why did she ever doubt Mark? He must have worked night and day to get this finished. Not much more to complete now. There was a large walk in cupboard, leading off from the kitchen, accessed through an arched doorway behind a heavy wooden door. It had been used in recent years as a walk in pantry. Still unsure what to use it for, Alison had asked Mark to leave it for now. Its crumbling floor was covered in brittle lino that cracked and broke with every footstep. Mark would have to repair and level it as he had in the kitchen. But for now it could wait.

'If the water is connected it might be an idea for you to have a drink. I think the heat got to you earlier. Do you feel okay now?'

'Good idea,' Alison headed for the sink. The newly fitted taps released a gush of clear fresh water and she leaned her head underneath and took in great mouthfuls. 'Sorry to be so uncouth,' she laughed wiping her chin, 'No cups or glasses up here yet!'

'Don't worry about that, I'm just pleased to see you looking back to normal. Why don't you fill up your water bottle before we go, we don't want you having a relapse! Are you up to showing me around now?'

Alison held her empty water bottle under the tap, 'Well, we can't get upstairs as the staircase isn't finished but I can show you around down here and then perhaps take a walk out the back?'

Tom followed Alison into the room adjacent to the kitchen. Its mullioned windows looked out across to the south, where the orchard had once stood and the room was full of the afternoon sunshine. It felt warm and bright and the lead framed panes sent out sparkling diamond patterns onto the newly painted walls. As she stood by a window, her hand softly caressed the stone that had been worked hundreds of years before.

Tom looked into her excited eyes as she turned to him and said, 'Isn't it wonderful? To think, Abbot Thomas once stood at this window.' She slid her hand across the cold carved surface again, 'He touched this stone…. looked out across the abbey land.'

'It is fantastic, I agree. So what do you know of its history?' Tom asked, infected with her enthusiasm for the place.

'Abbot Thomas was the last Abbot here, just before the dissolution. It broke his heart when Cromwell's men came and he knew the end was in sight. He loved the place so much and was such a good and fair man. The brothers loved him.'

'But that's just what you've read in books and the historian's assumptions. They can't know for sure. He may have been an ogre in reality.'

'No Tom, he was kind, I know he was,' she replied wistfully.

Tom shrugged his shoulders. He lived his life by fact and not by romantic ideas and fantasies. His down to earth approach to life had never won him many friends. He had been a quiet and studious child, rather a loner to his Mother's regret. His parent's divorce when he was eight years old had left a mark. He had witnessed the permanent sadness in his Mother's eyes after his Father had walked out. Tom had retreated into his own world to save heartbreak for himself but his soul came alive when he was dealing with animals and nature. He devoured books and knew so many facts, statistics and information about plants, birds and animals but he was a lonely man. He had found a friend in Alison for she hadn't worried about his usual grumpy, serious exterior. She had burrowed in and found snippets of the warm and caring person that usually lay hidden within.

After a quick tour of the ground floor of the cottage where Alison discovered Mark had also finished the downstairs' cloakroom and had repainted and carpeted the main sitting room ready for her to move her furniture in, they headed outside. Alison took Tom around her land, showing him the ruins. He was able to point out various wild flowers to her, suggesting which plants to save and which ones could be invasive. He was proving to be good company.

They perched on the edge of the well, the metal rivets on the broken wooden cover were hot to the touch from the intense heat of the August day. Tom rummaged in his rucksack and handed Alison a carton of juice.

'I've got a couple of cereal bars in here somewhere.' He said as he delved deeper into his bag, pulling out old crisp wrappers, used drink cartons and a couple of field guides. He piled everything up onto the edge of the well and finally found the cereal bars. They had seen better days but Alison didn't like to offend and nibbled daintily at the bar while Tom tried to get everything back in the bag.

'Oh bugger!'

Tom watched as his head torch went bouncing through the gaping hole in the wooden cover and down into the well. They heard pings and thuds as it bounced about making its way down into the bowels of the earth.

'That's the last I will see of that! The well sounds very deep. You should get this cover fixed Alison with that great hole and it's only resting on top anyway, not secured at all. Could be dodgy, would be easy to fall down there,' he said, eating his bar in two swift bites.

She nodded. 'It should be ok, I'll be careful. But yes I will get it fixed.'

'No, I'm not worried about *you*,' he replied dispassionately, 'It's animals I was talking about. What if a hedgehog drops down or someone's cat falls down the well?'

Finding his logical manner amusing she couldn't help but tease him, 'Are you going to start reciting a nursery rhyme to me now? Ding dong bell!' She started to sing and it turned into a giggle. She found his seriousness brought out the light side of her nature. He was doing her good.

Tom looked a bit confused for a moment but then cottoned on to her train of thought. Her mirth was infectious and he joined in. So they did not hear the voices of the lost souls, trapped in their subterranean world that cried out to them. The laughter blocked out the calls of despair that filtered up from the well.

'Please. Please help us. Sweet blessed Lord, will our cries ever be heard?'

As Tom and Alison set off towards the river the dark mists edged their way over and sank deep within the well, silencing the calls....for now.

After some reservations Tom agreed to show Alison the badger sett, 'It's not far from your land so best to let you know where it is so you don't disturb them.'

Once they reached the river, Tom took the path northwards towards the woods and they walked parallel to the ivy tunnel of Monkton lane. Alison hadn't been aware just how far the ivy-strewn trees had extended from the road. The towering sentinels wearing their jackets of green were on parade right up to the river bank.

Tom held up a tendril of ivy for her to duck under as they entered the cavern of trees and undergrowth. The sunlight glinted through small gaps in the canopy but for the most part the wood was immersed in darkness. The air around them was full of a sour smell drifting up from the soil.

Alison wrinkled her nose, 'Why does it smell so horrid in here? Is that the badgers?'

'No, that's the bacteria that has grown down in the soil and amongst the dead leaves,' her trusty nature guide informed her.

'It doesn't smell over the other side of the lane, where the bluebells grow. Why here?' she asked, keen to learn as much as possible.

'It's probably due to the lack of sunshine over here, it can't penetrate through the thick layer of ivy. That, combined with the river close by, means the thick clay soil gets waterlogged and that allows bacteria to form in the soil. It's that bacteria that you can smell.'

Alison continued following behind Tom through the dense woodland when he suddenly stopped.

She crashed into his back, 'Hey, you okay? Are we on the wrong path?'

Tom stood still, his mind going over some facts. He turned and put his hands onto Alison's arms, looking at her with a serious face.

'You are brilliant spotting the smell!' Alison looked bemused as he continued, 'Why didn't I notice that? Of course! Clay soils don't usually smell unless they are really waterlogged with standing water.'

Alison recalled her flooded night in the lane, 'Well we did have floods some months back.'

'Yes, yes, but it's not *now*, it's been dry. Look the top is dry,' he stamped his foot down on the ground. 'See? The other reason for the smell being released is digging. It releases the gasses that have been building up in the ground from micro organisms.'

'So someone has been digging here, is that what you are saying? Maybe they want to clear the land a bit?'

'No, I suspect something more sinister than that Alison, something more sinister indeed.'

Chapter sixteen

Tom began striding through the woodland at a rate of knots, Alison ran behind him, curtains of ivy whipping at her face.

'What is it then Tom? Digging what?' she called after him, feeling breathless as she tried to keep up.

Tom slowed his pace, suddenly remembering Alison was following. He continued walking as he called back to her, 'We're nearly there, I'll explain then.'

They emerged out of the dense woodland and Alison stopped short of a huge dip in the ground. The land then rose up into a high bank covered with cascading brambles, punctuated with enormous trees, their roots like long scrawny fingers edging their way across the ditch below.

'Wow! This is an amazing place! What was here? Is it something to do with the old iron-ore workings do you think? My friend Kit – her husband was telling me all about it some time back, he gave me a brief history lesson about the place.'

Tom, who was making his way along the ditch, shook his head and beckoned her down, 'No, something more special than that. They're not sure but there is some speculation that it's the site of an old ancient hill fort, built by Alfred the Great.'

'No! You're joking, right?'

'Not at all. There are records that one of his earthworks was built somewhere near here in the 9th century. This could be it. But the badgers claimed it long ago so it's never been excavated,' he beckoned her down, 'Come and see.'

Alison slid into the ditch and went across to where Tom was carefully examining some woody roots that overlay a gaping hole under a tree.

'Thank God,' he whispered to himself as held up some grey wiry hairs for Alison to look at. 'See, this shows they are still about.'

'Badgers?'

Tom nodded, 'See this sand? I lay it across the entrance to check for prints. Here look,' he traced out with his finger, the marks where the badger's heels had marked the sand and its other four toes out straight. 'This sett goes on a long way,' he gestured back to the path from where they had come, 'Probably half a mile that way, at a guess.'

'So what's with your worry about the digging?'

Alison stood in the ditch and leant back against the crumbling soil and roots taking a slurp of her water as Tom began to explain.

'I've been monitoring this sett for some time and heard whispers baiting might be taking place. So far haven't caught any one in the act here. I think we are safe.'

He perched himself next to her, took out a bag of crisps from his bag and started eating.

'Baiting? I've heard the term but not 100% sure what it's all about. What do they do?' Alison asked as she took a handful of the crisps Tom offered to her.

'Basically it's a case of digging the poor buggers out of the setts and more often than not using them for sport. Getting the poor blighters to fight with dogs. Badgers aren't usually aggressive creatures but when faced with a snarling dog about to rip at their throat they go out fighting. You wouldn't want to see the end result. Badger or dog.'

'Oh my God! But why do they do it, for Christ sake?'

'Either fun, but more often money. These cretins gamble large sums of money on the fights. A group were caught not that many miles away a few months ago, got a hefty fine.'

'Should have put them away and thrown away the key,' said Alison, appalled.

'They probably will go down if they get caught again. I'm glad there's no evidence here, but I mustn't get lax. You can help too. That's if you want to that is?'

They both stood up and brushed off the dirt and began to wander back. Alison linked his arm as she said, 'You can tell me on the walk back to the cottage what it is I can do.'

Alison looked at her reflection in the mirror, examining the sunburn on her shoulders. The day had been a real scorcher and there had been no respite from the penetrating heat as she and Tom had walked across the field to the cottage earlier. She would have to be more careful, remember to put on sun-cream if the hot weather continued.

The bedroom window was open but the air was still muggy, the leaves sat motionless on the trees outside, as the heat lay heavy and unyielding. The screeching of swifts echoed against the buildings of the village as they circled in the sticky evening skies, taking their fill of insects, stocking themselves up for the long trek south. The sounds of nature triggered a smile as Alison thought of her day with the reserved Mr Elliot... Tom. He really was such a serious and shy man. He brought out her extrovert nature. She had felt a real sense of achievement when she had made him laugh so much as they had sat by the well.

They had parted company at Monkton Lane. He had wanted to get back to the Jolly Abbot to pack his things before he checked out and headed off home. She wondered where it was. His home. She'd spent all afternoon with him and didn't know a thing about him. But she did now know a lot about badgers It was sickening what went on. She had Tom's mobile number and had promised him if she heard anything suspicious up near Monkton Lane, unfamiliar vehicles, dogs barking, or anything she felt might be a threat to the badger's safety she would ring him. He hoped to be back at Greysmead next month and she promised to catch up with him then.

She had stood in the sunshine watching him as he set off along the footpath back to the village. It was as she was about to head back to the cottage for one more look at Mark's handiwork when Tom stopped in his tracks and turned and ran back to her side.

His face had turned a light shade of red, 'Er, Alison? Would you mind if I took your phone number too?'

'Of course you can!' she smiled and scribbled her mobile number down onto a notebook he had produced from his pocket, 'There you are. And do keep in touch. I've had such a great afternoon, thank you.'

'Me too,' he said, 'I will see you next month then?' he held out his arm as if he was about to shake her hand, but Alison intercepted and gave him a light peck on the cheek. His face went scarlet.

'Bye Tom. See you soon.'

Embarrassed, he avoided looking at her face, as he muttered his farewells and was swiftly on his way. Minutes later a growl reverberated from the lane and Mark's van emerged in a cloud of dust. She wondered what his excuse would be for not being at the cottage all afternoon. Her stomach somersaulted as he jumped down and ran across to her.

'Hiya Babe.' She smelt a hint of mint as he kissed her lightly. 'Hope you haven't been waiting long? I just had to nip out to the DIY place, get a few bits.'

He rested his arm across her shoulder and they strolled back along the lane towards the cottage.

'So you've not been gone very long then?' Alison asked and found herself praying inwardly that he wasn't going to lie to her. But why should he? Her insides knotted. Where had these seeds of doubts come from?

'No, only been away about an hour, tops. You been in and seen the kitchen yet? Hope you like it.' He looked at her, trying to read her expression. Her face told him nothing. 'You've got nothing to say about it then?'

Why the lie? She thought as she shook her head, trying to force a smile, 'Sorry, It's so great it's just left me speechless.'

'Yeah! Knew you'd be pleased,' he kissed her forehead and they made their way inside.

Back in her room at the Abbot, Alison examined her face in the mirror. Was it her? Was she being stupid and making too much of it? She should have just told him outright that she knew he hadn't been there all day and then let him explain. She had no cause to be angry with him, the work on the cottage was going well, almost done. He must have just felt guilty for taking a long break. That's all it was. It was her inability to trust. Kenny had seen to that.

Would she ever be free from the events of her past? The snapshot of the horrific scene she had witnessed would stay with her until she died and probably for an eternity. Why hadn't she rung for help, maybe she could have saved the girl's life? Even though she had seen how low Ken had stooped she had still tried to protect him. She had done nothing except watch as Mick had stepped back, blade in hand, looking down at the body that lay at his feet. She would never forget the huge grin that had formed on his face. His evil face! The bastard! She had heard Kenny's voice, he'd said something to Mick, she couldn't make out what but they had both started to laugh. They took their laughter with them as they ran up the alley towards the back of the club. But not before Ken glanced briefly her way and for a spilt second their eyes locked before he was gone.

She wasn't sure how long she had stood there, it was long enough for her to throw up in the gutter before she gathered her wits and jumped back in the Jeep and sped off into the night. Ken had finally arrived home mid morning. The front door slammed and she heard him dart up the stairs and head straight for the shower. She continued to sit at her computer, creating the illusion of work but the only picture that filled the screen was that poor girl, reaching out towards her. When Ken finally re-emerged, he put his head around the door and looked at her through bloodshot eyes.

'Big Mick wants a word with you. Get your coat.'

Alison felt her stomach muscles tighten as she thought back. Thank God she had a good many miles between them now. How she hated Kenny. She had loved him once, so so much, unaware that such evil lay within him. There had been a time she would have tried anything to save the marriage, up until that night. How could she ever love or trust again?

But Mark wasn't Kenny, she had to try to remember that. New beginnings. They were meeting up later. Kit had asked them over for a meal. It would be good to see the family again, clear the air with them all. She just hoped Roger would be in a better mood. He was so rude to her the night of Amy's night walking.

Alison slipped the soft white camisole over her head, enjoying the coldness of the silk on her skin and selected a primrose coloured dress to wear. She began combing her hair, winding it up onto her head. It was too hot and sticky a night to wear it loose. She snatched up some hairclips from the dressing table and began securing it away from her neck. A soft breeze that began to edge its way in through the window lightly caressed the back of her neck.

Alison

A gentle voice whispered in her ear, she felt the air brush her cheek, heard the faint sound of someone's laboured breathing, close to her face.

Alison it hissed.

A ripple of shivers sped down her spine as she held her eyes tightly shut. A soft breath on her cheek whispered her name again.

Alison.

Very slowly she opened her eyes and let her gaze rest again on the mirror. She held her breath. In the reflection she could see a figure standing close to her, pale and iridescent, its face full of despair and grief as it continued to whisper to her as it leant closer still. The putrid smell of stagnant water filled her nostrils making her gag. Alison let out a gasp and the figure darted into the corner by the door behind her. Just a glimmer of movement, quick and sudden. Like a ball of shimmering light. She was aware of a tightness in her chest as she slowly turned around. She waited, stood rigid as her heart thumped against her rib cage and let her eyes rest on the light.

A faint glow, the size of a tennis ball pulsated in the corner. She was rooted to the spot, unable to take her eyes from it. She could feel its energy. Slowly it began to enlarge, getting brighter and brighter, until Alison had to shield her eyes. And then suddenly it had gone. Nothing there except a faint tinkling sound, then silence.

Alison felt her body crumple with relief as she sat back onto the bed. She could feel her heart as it rammed itself against her chest as she looked around the room. It all seemed normal. What had she just seen? A trick of the light?

The sun, now a glowing orb of red, was winding down for the day, sinking low behind the church. Maybe its light had reflected off the leaded window panes? Was that possible? She tentatively moved over to the door and her eyes scanned the floor. What had made that noise? It had sounded like something light and metallic dropping to the floor. Yes! There was something there. She could see it. She knelt down to look closer. Glinting back at her in the dark corner was a small bronze coin! She reached out to it but it was so hot to the touch that she dropped it again as it burnt her hand.

'Shit!' She ran to the bathroom and put her hand under the cold tap and let the coldness soothe her palm.

The plug secured, she filled the basin with icy cold water, dried her hands and went back into the room and knelt down to locate the coin again. It had rolled up against the skirting, half wedged into the floor board. Using the towel to protect her hand she quickly grabbed the coin and ran back into the bathroom throwing it into the basin. She watched as the water sizzled as the coin fell in.

Once it had cooled, Alison took it from the water and turned it around in her hand to examine it in detail. It was about the size of a two pence piece and similar in colour. One side had been engraved, but now was very worn and undistinguishable. Possibly battlements along the top? She wasn't sure and maybe a figure in the centre. There had been some writing around the edge but most had disappeared. She made out a few words. *grays abbatial.* The back of the coin looked as if it had been originally smooth and without decoration but two words had been scratched into the bronze with a fine spidery hand. If she was reading it correctly it looked as if it said *absolvo purgatorio.*

What did it mean? Was it to do with Brother John? She'd take this with her to Kit's, maybe someone will know what it says and maybe it will prove to Kit and Roger something is going on far beyond their world and understanding.

Chapter seventeen

Mark held his face up towards the shower letting the needle sharp jets pound his skin, he turned so he could let the cool spray ease the tightness in his shoulders and neck muscles.

Jeez that had been a close call earlier. He hadn't been sure he'd get down to the cottage in time to catch Alison but he'd just made it. He'd spent far longer than planned searching her flat for the diary. Ken had said she kept journals but surely she would have something that sensitive hidden away securely? Ken was sure it existed but would she write it down? Would someone write something like that in a diary?

'Dear diary, today I had a nice lunch with friends and in the evening saw two people murdered.'

Mark laughed to himself – no, he didn't think so!

He'd managed to convince Alison he hadn't been away too long from the cottage, and she did seem pleased with all she'd seen. He had to admit, it was looking good, the guys seemed reliable workers. He hadn't told Alison he had subbed a lot of the work out. He was needed up at the club a lot of the time so couldn't be around much but best to give her the illusion that he had done it all. Not that he couldn't put his hand to most things, apart from the leccy that was, electrics had to be all signed off and certified now. Not like the days when he had first started out.

His old Dad had run a little family business, a jack of all trades his Dad. Mark had trained at college, got a city and guilds for the plumbing and that, with some self taught chippy skills, he and Dad had made a good team. That was years ago now. Dad was long gone to the builder in the sky.

Thinking back Mark realised how much he had enjoyed that time of his life, but circumstances change. Jill hadn't been too pleased when he got involved in this new line of work. She hated most of the people he now mixed with and their usual tactics for dealing with trouble. It had only been a matter of time before they had parted company. A marriage really couldn't compete with his life and its unsociable hours and being at the beck and call of the big boss man any hour of the day.

Feeling less wound up he began to dry himself before getting ready to meet Alison up at Kit's place. He had a twinge of guilt when he thought about her. There was definitely a spark there between them and all this supernatural stuff had him fascinated. Not sure if he believed it was ghosts although that séance when he was a kid did make him think. He often wondered if evil actions left a stain on a place and sometimes it just got stirred up? Like a memory? God, he'd rather not stir up too many of his own memories, thank you very much! Best keep them in the past where they belonged. But as for Al's Monk and that kid seeing that woman? Well, all a bit tales of the bloody unexpected wasn't it? But who knows, maybe something in it? He'd uncovered a fair bit of grisly history about the Abbey that's for sure. He'd like to find out what was going on.

He checked the time and he realised he'd better get a move on or else he'll be late again! He just hoped Mrs Blackman wasn't about to catch him on his way out, she could talk for England that woman!

The sun was in its last throws of life for the day but its heat remained as the bricks of Kit's old cottage threw out its warmth like a giant storage heater.

'The garden is looking beautiful Kit.' Alison said looking relaxed as she took a sip of wine.

Inwardly she was seething. Where was Mark? He was late. She attempted to hide her angry thoughts as she smiled at Roger who was sat across from her at the garden table, looking extremely glum.

His hangdog expression revealed he still hadn't forgiven Alison about the night with Amy and her sleepwalking.

He ignored her as he spoke to Kit. 'Anything need doing in the kitchen Sis, anything I can do to stop it getting ruined?' he said to rub it in that Mark was holding up the meal.

'No it's fine Rog, honest. Charlie's in there keeping an eye on it all. There's nothing that can come to harm at all.' She smiled at Alison, feeling embarrassed and decided to go inside to her husband and leave her infuriating brother to chat with Alison.

Kit sidled up to Charlie who was mixing up salad dressing. She put her arms around his waist and kissed the back of his neck.

'It's very awkward out there Chas, the atmosphere can be cut with a knife. I really want to make up with her after my outburst but Roger's not helping matters. He's got a face like thunder.'

Charlie turned and gave her a hug. 'It will be fine, just need a bit of time and maybe a bit of wine,' he said pouring her another glass, 'and we will all be buddies again. Just try not to fly off the handle with her. Maybe it's time we addressed this problem with Amy, let's listen to what Alison's got to say.'

Trying to ignore the situation she rubbed at a splash of vinegar that he'd managed to get on his cuff, 'Messy! Can't take you anywhere!'

'Kit! Come on! You and Roger can't blot this out anymore. You know this has been going on with your family for generations, you can't keep sweeping it under the carpet. Maybe it's time to attack it head on.'

She nodded, 'You're right I know. It just frightens me that's all. Where will it all lead?'

The doorbell stopped Charlie's reply, 'That'll be Mark I expect.' He wiped his hands on a towel and went out to the hallway.

Kit took her wine and headed back into the garden where there was still no sign of a peace deal. Alison had her back to Roger and was examining the plants growing up the trellis and Rog was sitting in silence. Kit sat down next to her brother.

'Rog! Rog!' she leant over and hissed at him.

He looked back at her with angry eyes and snapped back, 'What?'

'Let's try to make an effort eh? Chas feels it time we should sort it all out, face the past at last.'

He shrugged, 'Maybe.'

A loud cheery voice echoed from the doorway, 'Hello folks!' Mark's shaggy hair was still damp at the ends and touched the collar of his crisp white shirt. His offering of a bottle of wine in his hand.

Kit stood up to greet him, about the shake his hand.

'Hi Mark! I'm Kit. I've not actually met you properly yet. How do you do?'

Mark ignored her hand and gave her a huge hug, 'Great to meet you at long last Kit!' He looked over her shoulder and caught Alison's eye and winked at her. She grinned back, the anger at his lateness snuffed out in a second.

Kit untangled herself and pulled Mark round to the table, 'This is Rog, my brother.'

Roger stood up and shook Mark's hand looking quizzically at his face, 'Don't I know you?'

'No, don't think so.'

'You look very familiar,' Roger began to scan the archives of villains he kept stored in his brain. 'Not from up Battersea way are you?'

'He's from Croydon,' cut in Alison and linked Mark's arm and gave him a kiss on the cheek.

'Stop being the detective Rog, leave the day job alone for once!' laughed Kit as Mark handed her the wine and she went back inside to help Chas.

'I'm uniformed, not a detective Sis.' Roger called after Kit. He continued to keep his brain searching. He'd remember soon enough, he was sure of it.

Mark's heart sank but continued to grin as Chas called from the doorway. 'Everyone ready to eat?'

Kit came out arms laden with plates and they all settled down in the humid evening air.

'Here's to Alison and Orchard Cottage,' Chas raised his glass and gave a smile.

A figure sat unobserved in the corner of the garden…and watched.

The evening light faded and the bricks of the cottage finally gave up their share of heat they had captured from the sun. Everyone made their way into the house and squeezed themselves into the lounge. Relaxed, full of good food and wine they all sat a while in a dreamy state. They'd left the back door open and a light breeze wafted in through the kitchen, journeying through the house and caressed the curtains as it completed its flight.

Alison sat sleepily with her head resting back against the sofa. She'd had a good evening and it felt as if she was back on track with Kit, hopefully they'd be able to rekindle their friendship. Rogers's initial coolness had thawed too and he was friendly and attentive but was still acting very oddly towards Mark. When she had been helping Kit with clearing away the dishes earlier she'd mentioned it to her.

'Seems as if Roger has forgiven me, he's talking to me again, thank goodness!' she said as she handed Kit a stack of plates to load into the dishwasher. 'But he's being quite rude to Mark, contradicting things he says all the time. Mark's not upset him has he?'

Kit slammed the dishwasher shut and dried her hands, with a glint in her eye. 'He's jealous, that's all!'

'Jealous? Of Mark? Why?'

'He thought he was in with a chance with you of course, you idiot!' Kit threw the tea towel at Al and laughed, 'He's annoyed with himself for not acting sooner!'

As Alison sat in the lounge she smiled as she recalled this revelation from Kit. She rested her head onto Mark's shoulder and thought back to her first meeting with Roger when he had stopped her when she'd nearly hit a car at the roundabout. He had made her heart flutter when she first cast her eyes on him she had to admit that. But no way was she going to get involved with a copper. Not with her secrets.

She could hear the tinkling of spoons as Chas made the coffee. Kit had just nipped upstairs to check on Amy and Roger had excused himself to take a call on his mobile.

Al sat there in a tranquil state, Mark gently caressed her hand as they sat in semi darkness. Her eyes fell upon the painting. The faces in the painting! Should she discuss it tonight? She'd touched on the subject briefly with Mark earlier, they'd decided to pour over all the info he gathered from the library tomorrow. She hadn't told him about the coin as yet, she felt for it in her pocket and rolled it around in her hand.

Chas walked in with a tray of mugs and putting it down on the table handed a mug of rich smelling coffee to Alison.

'Thanks Chas, smells good.' She hesitated briefly. 'Chas, can I ask you something?'

He handed another mug to Mark and glanced across at Al, 'Ask away!' he sat down on the arm of the sofa and blew into his hot drink before he took a tentative sip.

'Has Jim's family lived in the village for generations too, like Kit and Roger?'

Mark sat upright in the sofa and looked at Al, he knew where this was going.

Chas answered, 'As far as I know, yes. I believe his Father's side is somehow distantly related to Kit's fathers family – not sure how but I think he once told Kit that way back there is a Parsons in Jim's family history. Why do you ask?'

She wriggled forward in the seat and carefully placed her drink back down on the table. How could she say it without sounding mad? She blew out a long breath and looked at Mark, asking with her eyes should she talk about it? He nodded his head slightly, as if to say yes, go on, tell him.

'Well….' She began, 'You will probably think I'm mad but..'

'I'm sure I won't Alison, trust me,' Chas replied.

'Well, thing is, I found a copy of that painting,' she indicated with her head towards the fireplace, 'It was on the internet and I managed to enhance it and zoom in,' she jumped up and went over to the picture, pointing to the dark shadowy area, 'To this area here. And when it's magnified it looks as if it is a mass of faces, angry faces and one of them…well…it looks like a dead ringer for Jim!' There she'd said it now. They will probably laugh at her, think she's lost the plot.

'Jim? Really? Good God!' Chas exclaimed before murmuring to himself. 'A mass of angry faces. That sounds about right.'

Kit came back into the room and saw the frown on Charlie's face, 'What's up?'

Chas put his arm around her waist and pulled her close, 'It's time for some story telling I think Kit. Time to tell Alison all we know.'

Chapter Eighteen

'Where's Rog? It's his family story too,' Chas said, realising this was going to be difficult for his wife, she'd probably need her sibling for support.

'He was on the phone to the station earlier, he's had to go in,' Kit said as she sat down on the floor near the hearth, her eyes shining with unshed tears.

'Hey, it'll be okay, honey. But I think it's time to lay the ghosts to rest.' Chas sprang up from the arm of the sofa and plonked himself on the chair by the fireplace and Kit sidled over to snuggle up by his legs.

Alison and Mark sat in silence and waited. Kit blew her nose, gave them a weak smile and began the tale.

'Well, as you have seen first hand, our Amy tells us she sees a lady outside the cottage. Her 'sad lady'.'

Al nodded.

'And I've already mentioned about Dad's sister, Aunty Betty, having what was deemed at the time as mental problems, as she too saw a lady up in the woods near the ruins and would talk to her. If she wasn't mad to begin with, the pressure of having whatever was happening to her – ghostly or not – well it did drive her crazy for a while. God, it was terrible,' Kit shuddered and Chas put his hand gently on her shoulder for reassurance.

'You were quite young at the time Kit, bad memories when you are that age always seem larger than life and more intense.'

She nodded as she tried to hold back more tears, 'It was awful seeing Aunty being taken away. As Chas said I was just a kid, when it all happened. I remember so vividly Betty screaming such obscenities to Dad's parents and then to all who could hear her as they took her away. They said it was for her own safety.'

'She blamed your Grandparents for having her sectioned?' Alison asked quietly.

'Well, yes I suppose so, but at the time it was as if she was someone else. I can still hear her shouting over and over again. 'What have you done? Murderers!' over and over. It sent shivers down my spine to hear her scream like that. She doesn't recall that day at all, thank God but she remembers seeing the lady. Maybe you should go and talk to her.'

Chas leaned forward and let his fingers play with Kit's hair in an attempt to soothe her before he spoke, 'But they know most of this story Kit, it's further back, your family and the village history we need to tell them about. It all plays its part.'

'I take it you are you talking about how the village ran riot on the Abbey? And the bloodbath that followed?' Mark asked.

Alison sat upright and looked at Mark, wide eyed, 'Bloodbath?'

'He's right.' Kit replied.,'You got some info from the library at Lunsford I expect?'

Mark nodded and turned to Alison, 'I was going to tell you all about this tomorrow.'

'Well, I will tell you the story as we know it,' Kit continued, 'as it was told down the generations. It all happened at a time of great unrest in England when Thomas Cromwell, vicar general to Henry VIII, was working to get the monasteries dissolved. The Monk numbers up at the Abbey had dwindled down to less than a dozen I believe. Shortly before the Abbey finally closed, the Abbot had died very suddenly. It is said he was overwhelmed with grief that his Abbey was about to fall to Henry Tudor and his blasphemous henchmen. The story goes that he went outside to the Orchard and lay down on the grass and looked up towards the heavens, saying something like, I commit my soul into your arms.' And then he just died. Just like that. Dead!'

Alison felt a ripple of uneasiness. 'This happened outside Orchard cottage? My new home?'

'It was probably a heart attack because of the stress, nothing more than that Al,' said Chas.

'Yes, you may be right..... he was having pains the day he sent John away,' whispered Al.

Kit looked across at her, 'What? Where did you read that?'

Al shook her head, 'No, it's nothing, you tell your story first and then I can fill you in with my take on it all.'

'Okay, well story goes that after he dies, everything went down hill. Fast. No need to appoint a new Abbot as the Abbey was soon to be another victim of the reformation. No authority figure to keep the peace. The commissioner's men had been staying in the village when they had been investigating the Abbey's finances, and during this time they had turned the villagers against the monks, had carved hatred into their minds. The villagers were all fired up, it's amazing how quickly people can be stirred up, brainwashed so easily. So when she died it was their chance for revenge.'

'Who died? Do you mean Mary?'

'Best go back a little bit in time with the family history Kit?' Chas said.

'Yeah, you're right,' she looked up at her husband, 'Can I have a glass of wine first do you think? Any one else want something stronger than coffee?'

Alison shook her head, 'Not for me.'

Chas got up and brought the bottle in, they sat and reflected on the words that had been spoken so far as the gentle glug of wine filled Kit's glass.

'The tale that has been passed down throughout the family over the generations has probably been altered somewhat – a bit of Chinese whispers I should think, but I will tell you what I was told by Dad,' Kit glanced at Chas seeking reassurance and then continued the story.

'Mary grew up in the village back in the 16th century, when it was a thriving place. The Abbey would take in villagers as lay brothers, who would help work in the confines of the Abbey buildings and also on the land. Greysmead was a busy place, being so close to the Abbey and of course the river and was a tight knit little village. This house is the cottage where the blacksmith lived and he had his forge and workshop the other side of the garden wall.'

'What? Behind your garden here?'

'Yes, there used to be a stone structure, long gone now apart from a few stones but that's where he worked.'

'Desmond.' muttered Alison.

'Yes! That's right Alison. How do you….?' She waved her hand dismissively, 'No, you tell your side once I've finished, but yes, the blacksmith and farrier was Desmond, he too had grown up in the village and he and Mary were married. By all accounts they were very happy.'

Alison gasped in disbelief. Happy? She didn't think so, not with his abuse. But she kept her thoughts to herself and managed to turn the gasp into a cough.

Kit looked across at Alison before she continued. 'So, life went on, and very soon Mary found she was expecting a baby. They were so pleased but their joy turned to sadness when the baby died when it was only a few days old.' Kit took a gulp of wine and carried on, 'They comforted each other in their grief. Mary was sad to have lost the child but was happy that she at least had a good husband.'

Mark squeezed Alison's hand sensing her tension at Kit's words.

'Mary and Desmond kept bees, as did a lot of the villagers, and they would gather the honey and sell some on to the Abbey, who would use it to make the Greys Mead. It was very popular, in fact Jim's family continued to make it for a long time after the end of the Abbey, but slowly the production stopped, people were more into beer.'

'Its beginning to gain popularity again now,' Chas piped in, 'National Trust place down at Bodiam sell it. In fact Jim has recently started to produce it again now, we had some at the fete.'

'Yes.' Kit glared at Chas who, suitably chastised, smiled and kept quiet as Kit went on, 'Mary would take the honey up to the Abbey. One day, she went up with her honey, and instead of using the footpath across the fields she went through the woods. It was then that it happened.'

'What happened?'

'She was raped. By a lay brother, a village lad who had fallen on hard times and had been taken in by the monks in good faith. He was waiting in the woods, pushed her down onto the ground and the bastard forced himself upon her.'

Alison was appalled. Kit was talking about brother John. What was she saying? He didn't rape Mary! He loved her! Al felt Mark's fingers stroking hers, as he sensed her anguish at Kit's words. She felt as if she was being disloyal to John as she listened to Kit who continued her take on the events of 1538.

'Mary didn't tell anyone what had happened at first and just carried on going up to sell the honey but Desmond eventually found out and forbade Mary to leave the village. Then Mary discovered she was pregnant. Desmond was incensed and went up to confront the Abbot who assured him he would deal with the matter and see that the man would be punished. Desmond took him at his word and at first he let people of the village think the baby she was expecting was his child. By the time she was well into her pregnancy the Abbey had been dissolved and the Abbot dead. In order to keep food in their bellys for a while longer many of the monks still lived there, helping Cromwell's men with the dismantling of the buildings.'

'Desmond's anger began to fester inside him, eating away and as Mary neared her confinement date word got about the village of the rape and so when she died in childbirth the villagers wanted to seek their revenge. Over the months they had been drip-fed propaganda about the Abbey by the commissioner's men and now one of their own had suffered first hand by these evil monks. It was the fault of the lay brother that Mary was dead. It had been his child that had killed her. And so they headed up to Monkton Lane to seek retribution.'

The silence in Kit's cottage was deafening as they all sat, their minds taking in the story of Kit's ancestors.

'So, did they kill the monks? When they went on their rampage?' Al asked horrified by the story.

'The legend goes that the river flowed red for months, but obviously that's just fanciful tales. The history books tell of the villagers returning to their homes in a detached and unemotional state, their clothing soaked with blood. But no traces of any monks were ever found, dead or alive.'

'Maybe they were just injured and ran away?' Al suggested.

'They were never seen or heard of again Alison.'

'Oh my God. All that hatred up at Monkton Lane. That must be what that swirling mass of angry faces represents in the painting! The artist could sense the evil that remained. I'll change my mind, I will have that drink after all.'

It had been a long evening. The sun had long dropped from view and inside the cottage it had grown dark. The streetlight cast its shadows amongst them and unknowingly they sat amongst the ghosts of the past as Alison began to tell their story. She told them all she could recall - the vivid dream where she had witnessed John meeting Mary amongst the bluebells and the strong sense of their love, the strange vision she had witnessed at Orchard Cottage where the Abbot had sent John away and how she felt John's emotions so strongly and the vague shape of a woman that had appeared briefly near Amy when she had come across her outside that early morning.

'So I really believe that we are not talking about rape here. It was love. Mary loved John.' Alison downed the last remaining drops of the red wine and looked across at Kit who was shaking her head.

'I'm sorry but this is all nonsense!' The anger in Kit's voice was obvious. The tension in the room felt volatile. 'Why should we believe what basically is just something you have made up. Just fairy stories, dreams, imaginings?' She stood up and switched on a lamp and began to draw across the curtains, 'We got any more wine Charlie?' She sounded uptight.

'Sorry sweetheart but I think we should be having more coffee now. Have you seen the time, it's well past midnight. Maybe we should just sleep on all of this and talk some more another day?'

But Alison wasn't being dismissed that easily. 'What about Amy? Betty? Chas, you said there had been problems with the family for generations. Have other family members had visions too?' She stood up, angry now and confronted Kit, 'Have they? Why can't you believe any of it? If you can't believe me at least you should believe your own daughter?' Al put out her hand, touched Kits arm, but she shook her off and went towards the door.

'I'm going to make some coffee,' she snapped.

Chas went to follow her but turned and spoke, 'Sorry guys, she finds all of this hard. She hates the fact her ancestor may have been the ringleader of the mob that killed the monks. She needs to believe it was done for all the right reasons.' He shrugged, 'If it's any consolation, I believe you. I *have* listened to Amy's stories and I think there is a lot unresolved stuff here.'

Al flopped back down on the sofa next to Mark, 'That went well!' she laughed but inside felt like a wound up spring. The air in the room was thick with negativity and had begun to seep into all their skins as it fired up the anger within them.

'Look Al, It must be hard for Kit. I know this Desmond was a family member from centuries ago but they have always looked upon him as the good guy. It can't be easy to find out that a member of your family abused his wife and by all accounts was evil to the core. It must be hard to accept something like that.'

'Oh you can accept it! Believe me,' she retorted, her voice shrill. Mark's words had raised her hackles even more, 'Once you see the evil in someone, and witness it for yourself you believe it, I can assure you of that!'

'But Al, she *hasn't* seen it, has she? She is only going on things you say *you* have seen. It's not like actually witnessing a close family member do something really bad is it? Not like it was with you and Kenny!' He stopped. What had he said? Fuck! He got carried away in the moment. Had he blown it? Would she guess he knew?

'What's me and Kenny got to do with it?' she stared at him, face red with anger, 'What has my failed marriage got to do with bloody Desmond?' She remembered back to Ken arriving at the cemetery, Mark going over to him, telling him to leave. Would Ken have said something to Mark about what had split them up? 'What did Kenny say to you at the funeral?'

Mark grabbed her hand, think man, think. 'No Al he didn't say anything but I just assumed by his manner that maybe...maybe he used to hit you.'

'What?' She shook her head in disbelief. 'Hit me? Ken? No way! You've got it all wrong there....' Her eyes began to smart as she thought back to the couple of occasions that Big Mick had made it clear to her what would happen if she squealed on them. No, Kenny hadn't hit her with his own hands but watching his boss smack her around the face and leave her black and blue, well she supposed it was no different to him doing it himself.

Mark pulled her close to him, his arm around her shoulder and whispered light kisses onto her hair.

'Sorry Al, I didn't mean….look I just thought maybe because Desmond used to beat Mary, it made you feel….made you empathise with her …I'm sorry. I didn't mean to upset you.' He realised he *had* hit a nerve. Not really surprising though, if a man can murder in cold blood, well a bit of wife beating, he wouldn't give it a second thought. Jeez, he'd done some things in his time but hit a woman, a woman you supposedly loved? No way would he ever go down that road.

Alison pulled herself away from his hold and smiled at him through a face awash with tears, 'Hey, I'm sorry too. I didn't mean to get angry, you're right it has stirred up some personal issues for me, but that's how I want them to stay – personal. Ok?'

A voice suddenly broke into their little world. Al looked up and saw that Roger stood in the doorway. How long had he been standing there? For a split second his face flickered a slight trace of sadness.

'Sorry guys.' he held up his hands, 'Don't mean to interrupt! Sorry I had to shoot off earlier, at least I managed to get back before you left.' He looked at his watch, 'Wasn't sure if you would still be here. Chas is bringing some coffee. What's been happening?' He asked all light hearted and chirpy. 'Kit seems a bit on edge out there and you two seem to be having a bit of a domestic,' he added not hiding his amusement.

'We're fine thank you Roger. And Kit is too – we just had a slight difference of opinion regarding your ancestors.'

'Oh, I see! We are very protective of the Parsons family name Alison, but I'm willing to be open-minded. I like to give people the benefit of the doubt,' he gave a forced smile to Mark, 'I've got to in my job.'

Chas came back into the room carrying a tray of coffee, Kit followed on behind looking somewhat sheepish and sat next to Alison, leaned over and gave her a hug.

She spoke quietly to her as they made up, 'Sorry about earlier, don't know why I reacted so strongly. A life time of denial I think.'

'So does this mean you believe me?' Al asked.

Kit nodded, 'Chas has just been filling me in with a lot of Amy's tales, the ones I refuse to listen to. Her 'sad lady' stories seem to mirror a lot of what you told us.'

Chas handed round the drinks as Al pulled out a tissue from her pocket to wipe her eyes. Her fingers made contact with the coin.

'Goodness, I'd nearly forgot!' she held the coin between her thumb and index finger holding it aloft. 'This turned up in my room at the Jolly Abbot this evening. Not sure if you will believe how it turned up, it was the weirdest thing, like it just materialised in a ball of light,' she saw the looks of doubt, 'No really it did! It was really very scary. And it burnt my bloody hand,' she opened her hand to display a very nasty circular looking burn on her palm, as if she'd been marked with a branding iron.

'Hey let me see that,' Mark grabbed her hand and examined the damaged skin. 'Jeez, it's marked the skin with what looks like some lettering; it must have been red hot. That must have hurt.' He took the coin and looked at closely, 'What is it? A Roman coin do you think?'

'May I?' Charlie leant forward and Mark handed him the coin before grabbing hold of Al's hand and gently kissed the skin on her palm.

Chas went over to a desk in the corner and switched on a lamp, holding the coin under the light to examine it more closely.

''Grays Abbatial.' I think Abbatial means Abbot. So it probably says Greysmead Abbot or something like that. I've seen something similar at a museum up in London. If I am right, it's not a coin but a seal. They used it to seal documents and letters with the mark of the Abbey or Abbot.'

'And now I've got their ruddy mark on my hand! There was writing on the other side too Chas..any ideas?'

He turned the coin over and tried to decipher the spidery writing scratched into the seal. 'Absolvo…..absolve?'

Kit watched as her husband peered intently at the seal. His large stature and close-cropped hair gave most people a first impression that he was an uneducated man, especially when they heard he worked as a builder. But she never ceased to be amazed at his knowledge of so many subjects. He was good for her with his calm and gentle nature and always managed to put out her easily fired up anger.

'Absolvo - I think it can also mean release Chas,' she called across to him.

'Okay,' Chas continued to study the seal under the light. 'And the meaning of the other word I should think is quite obvious…purgatorio.'

Alison sat forward on the sofa 'Purgatory! Of course! Release from purgatory! But who? And how?'

Chapter Nineteen

Alison began to walk along the dark track, taking careful steps, mindful of the potholes beneath her feet. She could make out a figure in the distance approaching her from the ivy-clad trees. It looked like Mark. She could see his shaggy hair framing his smiling happy face....No...it wasn't Mark it was Tom! Yes, kind and caring Tom Elliot wearing a woolly hat to keep him warm from the chilly wind as he heads out to protect the badgers.

It wasn't long before Alison realised it wasn't him after all but Roger, in his police uniform, all stern and upright. Serious and responsible Roger. Unsmiling. As he walked over to her he held out handcuffs and grabbed her wrists tightly but she struggled and escaped his grasp and darted into the bushes, running between the trees. As she raced through the wood other people from the village emerged from the greenery, arms out as they tried to grab at her. Alison pushed past them and ran further into the dense undergrowth. Her own laboured breathing sounded in her ears as she ran through the forest, branches whipping at her face, as she fled. Finally she stopped and looked behind her – were they still following? There was no sign of anyone so she turned to go on her way only to find that her path was blocked. A man stood directly in front of her. There was a glimmer of recognition.

'I know you,' she said.

'Of course you do Alison. I'm your Father.'

'Dad? Is it really you?'

He nodded and smiled. 'Yes, It is me. Your Mother sent me. She wants me to tell you something. She says be careful who you trust. Not everyone is as they seem.'

She reached out to touch him before he faded away.

Dad! Dad! Don't go!' she cried.

'Al! Al! Wake up. You're having a bad dream.' Mark softly touched her shoulder, 'Alison, It's okay. You're okay,' he moved closer to her, enjoying the feel of her warm skin against his.

Her eyes fluttered open and she looked into Mark's concerned face. He gently brushed the damp strands of hair away from her cheek, a dimple appeared by the side of his mouth as he smiled at her. She'd not noticed his dimple before. Not seen him so close before tonight.

He lay on his side, resting on one elbow and continued to play with her hair. 'You were calling out. Are you okay?' he whispered.

She smiled back and stretched her legs out straight touching the base of the bed, feeling the coolness of the sheets on her toes. 'Mmmm. I'm fine. I must have been dreaming, but can't remember what. It's gone.'

'You were shouting out in your sleep.'

'Sorry. Did I wake you?' she glanced across at the clock. 5am. 'We've got a few hours yet,' she snuggled back under the sheets, turning on her side to face him as his fingers began to caress her neck and shoulders and move down to gently touch her breasts.

He edged closer to her and pulled her to him, their bodies touching. He could feel her nipples as they pressed against his chest and he kissed her softly on the lips.

'Are you going to make me call out again?' she asked quietly.

His lips touched the salty skin of her neck, 'You bet I am!'

It must have been the sound of the shower that woke Al. She lay in bed and placed the palm of her hand across to the side where Mark's body had left an indent in the mattress. It was still warm and she turned and let the scent of his skin fill her senses. She grinned.

Yesterday had been a real roller coaster of a day and it had certainly ended well. When they had left Kit's place it must have been around 2am. It had all turned out good in the end. Kit and Chas had assured her they believed her and they were going to contact Betty to see if she could go and meet her and hopefully talk with her about her experiences. Even Roger had been open minded about it all.

Mark had walked with her down the High Street to the Jolly Abbot. They'd strolled along the dark and quiet street and he took her hand in his and a spark of electricity had ignited her skin as their fingers entwined.

As they had stood under the archway at the side of the pub she rummaged in her bag for her key and began to put it in the lock.

'Here let me help you,' he pulled her round to face him, grabbed her hand and held it to his lips. They had stood there for what seemed like forever just looking into each others eyes, neither of them moving, apart from Mark's lips gently kissing the palm of her hand and then her fingers, soft and unhurried. She felt her heart begin to pound as a feeling of desire began to unfold from deep inside her.

'I think Mrs Blackman might be upset if I went back to the B&B so late, don't you?' he asked with a smile.

'I think you may be right there,' She answered as they made their way through the door and up to her room.

Al lay in bed lost in the memories of the previous night when the door to the bathroom opened and Mark emerged, steam billowing out around him.

'Morning babe,' he jumped down onto the bed and gave her a quick kiss before rubbing at his hair with a towel.

'I didn't wake you earlier, I thought you probably needed to sleep after dreaming so much.'

Al pulled herself up and leant against his damp body, 'Did I start shouting out again? I don't recall any of it!'

'You certainly started calling out again, that's for sure, but I hope you were awake at the time!' he joked as he got up and threw the wet towel at her and began to get dressed.

'You getting up already? I thought maybe....?'

'Sorry, had a call, I need to get back up to the smoke for a few days. Urgent work.'

Her heart sank, 'Oh! I had hoped we might have spent a bit more time together..now that we've ..you know.'

'I'm sorry, so did I...but can't be helped.' He began to button up his shirt.

'But what about Orchard cottage? You're half way through renewing the stairs?' she pleaded.

'Got a couple of my lads on the job, they'll finish it all off within the week. You'll probably be able to move in within a fortnight I should think.'

'I didn't realise you had people work for you? You never said.'

Distracted, Mark searched around the room for his watch. 'Didn't I? Sure I did.' Finding the watch he began to fasten it on his wrist, 'Anyway – I really must get off before I lose the job. Got to love you and leave you I'm afraid,' he leant over and kissed her lightly on the forehead before heading out the door.

Al sat up in bed in a state of astonishment as she looked at the closed door. He was gone.

'The Bastard!'

She jumped up and padded over to the window, watching as he walked up the road to Mrs Blackman's to get his van, he even didn't look up or give her a second glance. Her stomach twisted into knots. She had thought they had something. Why was she so naive. All she was to him was just a quick lay. The bastard! She flopped back in the bed and lay staring at the ceiling, feeling totally numb.

Mark got his stuff from his room at Mrs Blackman's B&B and made his way to his van. Hopefully he'd get back up to the club without too many hold ups.

'Well young man, there you are.' Mrs Blackman seemingly appeared from thin air, watering can in hand, 'I did wonder if I'd see you today.'

She doused a pot of geraniums outside the doorway and put the can down and walked over to Mark as he unlocked his van. 'I realised when you didn't come down for breakfast that you didn't use your room last night. Let me go inside and do you a credit on your bill.'

'No! No it's fine honest Mrs B,' Mark was eager to get away, didn't want to be delayed by this nosey old biddy, 'It was my choice and you couldn't have used the room. I still had all my gear in there.'

'Your evening at the Mitchell's go on into the night?' she asked.

'Who?'

'Kit and Charlie. I thought you said you were having a meal with them last night?' she probed.

'Oh yes! We did… Kit and Chas, yes.' He began to stuff his bag into the van as she twittered on.

'Ms Greenways there I suppose? Nice young lady. Moving into her cottage soon I expect?

God, doesn't she ever shut up? 'Yes, yes, she was there. Moving in soon, yes. Anyway must go,' he smiled and jumped into the driver's seat.

Mrs Blackman carried on as he tried to edge the van out of the driveway.

'Does she need any help with curtains and suchlike? I'm rather good with the sewing machine, have an eye for soft furnishings…as I expect you noticed…with your rooms decor.'

'Er…yes, very tasteful Mrs B.'

'Maybe I could go and chat with her. She still up at Kit's, your Ms Greenways?

'No, I left her in bed at the Pub, give her an hour and I'm sure she would be pleased to chat,' He smirked and waved as he headed back to London leaving Mrs Blackman to mull over the information.

So, it seems Mr Bradley stayed the night with Ms Greenways? Interesting news. She liked a bit of gossip did Mrs Blackman.

Mark had made good time and was nearing the club after his summons from Mick earlier that morning. It had been when Alison was still fast asleep that his phone had started ringing. He'd jumped out of bed and grabbed it fast before darting into the loo to take the call. Big Mick had been on the warpath.

'Where the hell you been Marky boy? We need you up here pronto. The rozzers have been sniffing about again.'

'Oh shit, I should be able to be with you in a few hours boss.'

'How d'you get on with Ken's missus and her diaries – any joy?'

'No, nothing Mick. No sign of any diaries, I think you're safe mate. She's not going to say a word. And she had ample chance to offload her woes to me last night and not a dickie bird.'

'Last *night* you say?' Mick laughed, 'Not taken our Kenny's wife to bed have we?'

'Gawd no Mick,' Mark laughed, 'Had an evening out, had a few bevies, you know how it is, but she was sweet, not a peep.'

Mick sounded amused, 'Yes Marky, I *do* know how it gets. Hey, don't you let our Ken know you've bedded his wife, he won't like that one little bit. Still if a bit of pillow talk don't get her talking…..' Mark could hear someone talking to Mick in the background and Mick's response echoed down the phone, 'No Ken, only messing mate.'

Shit, he didn't want to rile Kenny. He's not going to like it if he knew he'd slept with Al. He still thought of her as his property. He was none to happy when he saw how close he'd become to her at the funeral. Best all round if he kept his distance from now on.

Mark had crept back out into the bedroom to see that Alison was still sound asleep. Yes, best to get out of there as soon as he'd showered.

But now sitting in the van outside the club he began to be feel bad. His feelings for Al were strong and he'd just upped and left this morning after what had been a rather passionate night. And why? Just because he didn't want to upset Kenny? What's the matter with him? He'd dealt with blokes like Ken before now, no trouble and what he doesn't know won't hurt him anyway. Yeah, he'd give Al a call later, clear the air, he'd win her round.

He pushed open the door to Cinderella's. The last thing he saw was Ken's fist heading for his jaw.

Mrs Blackman was at work behind the Post Office counter. It was a busy afternoon, Ebay seemed to generate a lot more parcels to process. People moaned about the internet but she thought it was great, it was helping to keep her Post Office in business. She finished stamping up a few packages and placed them in the sack and looked up at her next customer.

'Oh Good Morning Sergeant Parsons! How are you this morning Roger?' She smiled at the good-looking young man. He'd been back living with his sister a while now. He had worked in London for the Met for a time but it was nice that he had returned to the village and his roots. His dear old Mum must be so proud of him she was sure. Mrs Blackman thought of her own daughter. Things could have been so different. Her Dorothy could have married Roger. They had been an item for a long time. If only Dorothy hadn't gone away. She sighed and reached out to take the parcel from Roger.

'Hi Mrs B. Just got this parcel to go airmail.'

She looked at the address. 'Ah, something nice for your Mother? Is she enjoying life out in Australia? Such a big move for her too, at her age.'

Roger wondered if there was anything Mrs Blackman didn't know about people in the village. He was sure she had known before them about his Mum's new boyfriend. He and Kit had been pleased his Mum had found someone new after all the years of being a widow, they just wished it hadn't have been an Aussie who had then whisked her back to his homeland. Still, David was a good bloke so he shouldn't complain.

'Yes Mrs B, she's well settled over there now. Just sending her the village parish magazine and a few bits, you know.' He handed her a ten pound note and had to stifle a yawn, he was feeling really washed out, it had been a late night.

'Oh I see you had a late night too, like that Mr Bradley, he was at your place I understand and had a pleasant evening by all accounts,' her eyes sparkled with the juicy info she had gleaned earlier and was just itching to tell someone.

'Sorry we kept our guests out so late, hope Mark didn't cause you problems coming back at that hour?'

'Oh no dear, no trouble. He didn't come back, he stayed with that Ms Greenways last night…in her room. Looked very bleary eyed this morning when he set off back to London.'

Roger felt his stomach tighten. 'Oh really? But he's gone back home now has he?'

Alison sat in the bar drinking coffee when her mobile rang. She took the call imagining it would be Mark, ringing to say sorry.

'Hi Al? It's Rog.'

'Oh hi Roger, how are you?'

'Good thanks. Bit tired after our late night though. You?'

'Yes, bit tired. Having some coffee to try to wake myself actually,' she gave an unconvincing laugh, trying to sound light and jolly, but inside she was feeling really low. Used, dirty and cheap.

'Look, I was wondering. Kit has spoken to Betty already this morning, told her about what's been going on and she is really keen to see you…so…if you are free tomorrow…do you fancy a trip down to Hastings? You and me? To see Betty, maybe have a bit of lunch on the way?'

For a split second Alison allowed a picture of Marks face to fill her mind, his dark eyes looking into hers before he began to kiss her and then she saw the bedroom door shutting as he had left so coldly that morning.

'Yes Roger, that sounds great. You just let me know what time and I'll be ready.'

Roger picked Alison up from the Abbot at 11am. It was another warm day but Alison looked cool and relaxed in her white linen trousers and shirt as she climbed into Roger's open top car. As they headed down the A21 they sat in silence, the noise from the road making conversation limited. Whilst they scooted along Alison managed to find a hair tie buried in the corner of her bag and endeavoured to capture her hair as it flew around in the blowing air currents.

Roger glanced across to her and smiled, 'Sorry!' he bellowed, 'It will get better when we turn off this road.'

True to his word as they took the turning towards Battle he eased off the speed and they made their way slowly past shops and pubs along the High Street. He pulled into a space outside an ancient irregular looking building.

'Thought we'd have a bite to eat at this place. It'll be in keeping with the day's theme – used to be home to the monks from Battle Abbey.'

'Sounds good. Wow, this is lovely!' Alison took in the old timber framed building as the aromas of delicious food wafted out to greet them.

Roger told Al over lunch as much as he could remember about Aunty Betty. How she had spent hours up in the woods as a child and told her family that she spoke to a lady who was long dead. She had become aggressive when people said they didn't believe her, that she was imagining things. Roger's Grandparents had been so worried about their daughter and it broke their hearts to see her hospitalised when she was older.

'It must have been so hard for them, to see their daughter so troubled and it must have felt like history repeating itself when Amy started having similar experiences,' Alison said.

'I think that's why we've ignored it for so long. Chas had been saying for ages we need to do something but Kit and I, we just buried our heads in the sand, hoping it would go away. It was you coming that opened it all up for us,' he reached across the table and squeezed her hand, 'I'm beginning to think you were meant to come here, you seem to be the key to help us finally unlock the past.'

Alison pulled her hand away quickly and picked up her coffee cup, 'Well, I've certainly known about Orchard Cottage since I was a child, although I didn't realise at the time that's what it was. It was just a silly childhood imagining, a house I would paint over and over again.'

Roger got out his credit card ready to settle the bill as he spoke, 'So you actually knew when you saw the estate agents photo that it was 'your' house then? The one you used to draw?'

Alison gathered up her bag and jacket and nodded, 'Yeah, it was uncanny. I do wonder if maybe I had family who lived there once, long ago, who knows? Dad's side of the family, the Martins were from Sussex so it could well be!'

'He lived in Bexhill didn't he? I was sorry to hear from Kit that he'd died recently. It must have been hard for you.'

As they headed for the door she felt her eyes begin to fill, 'Thanks. Yes it was, still is. There's still so much to sort out at his house before it gets sold too.'

Outside she allowed her eyes to avert his gaze, focussed on the High Street to allow the swell of tears to subside. She didn't want him to see her cry.

'That's hard, going through their stuff, I remember when Dad died, just little things triggered memories.' He held open the door of the car for her, 'If you ever need a hand with it all – do say.'

Why was he being so kind? She nodded, unable to speak as the lump in her throat threatened to choke her. These past few years she had felt so vulnerable, lonely even, as if everything solid and stable in her life was slowly collapsing around her. Her marriage, with Ken turning into someone she just didn't recognise anymore and their divorce and her Mum's death. It had hit her hard and then her dear Dad dying so suddenly. She felt the sting at the back of her nose as the tears fought to be released. The car glided along and she looked to her left towards the hedgerows feeling as if her heart was breaking. She surreptitiously wiped the few tears that made their way slowly down her cheeks and allowed the warmth of the day soothe her skin.

As they drove into Hastings, Roger took a sidelong look at Alison, watching her as she held her face up to the sun, as she breathed in the fresh salty air.

He wondered if she'd heard from Mark since he set off for London yesterday? She'd not mentioned him. Roger had made a few discreet enquiries with his old pals up in the Met, called in a few favours. Finally his old mate Joe at Battersea had given him a call with some info on Mark's past. He looked across at Al, looking so serene but fragile. How much did she know about Mark, and what she was getting herself into by hooking up with him? He couldn't tell her the info he had obtained, more than his job was worth, but he could watch out for her, try to keep her safe if he could.

Chapter Twenty

Amongst the ruins and crumbling stones behind Orchard Cottage a dark stream of air whispered against the dusty soil and whisked it upwards, twisting higher and higher as it began its ascent above the trees. It darted across the canopy, bruising and crushing the leaves as it forced its way towards the Cottage. Then making its way low against the ground, it pounded against bushes and tree trunks as it headed through the undergrowth. The anger and hatred burning within its inner core. It rushed along, scorching the earth, creating a path of dead grass in its wake. Its work was not complete…… but it was nearly time.

Ever restless in the air above the old orchard, the tortured soul of the Abbot wept as it watched the sweeping mass of evil circle his old home.

Alison was nearly at the cottage and could see signs of activity. Two white vans were parked across the lane and the faint sound of a radio filtered across to her on the footpath. The strains of Simple Minds filled her ears.

God, that took her back. As a kid she had grown up in a house where music filled every nook and cranny. Snippets of memories flooded her mind. Mum in the kitchen preparing the meal, radio turned up loud, a nine year old Alison standing in the doorway watching her Mother in awe, marvelling how she managed to cook and also dance around the kitchen to the music, spoon in hand. Mum smiling at her and grabbing hold of her hands and both of them dancing together, giggling around the small table, their stomachs sore from laughter. And all the while the aromas of spaghetti bolognese bubbling away setting her taste buds alight and hoping Dad would be home soon so they could eat.

From the age of five to fifteen her life had been accompanied by a soundtrack of all the best music of the eighties …and some of the worst she thought with a smile. What great memories of U2, Spandau Ballet, Simple Minds. Mum just loved Simple Minds. The radio up at Orchard cottage continued its song drifting across the fields. 'Don't you forget about me,' Jim Kerr sang.

'No Mum,' Alison said out loud as she neared the cottage, 'I won't EVER forget about you.'

She speculated what music was playing on the car radio that day. The day Mum was driving on the M25 for the very last time.

The workmen were bringing off-cuts of wood and tools out of the cottage as they loaded up the vans. She speeded up, it looked as if they were preparing to leave. One guy, in dirty grey overalls threw some bits into the van and leaned back against the fence lighting up a cigarette.

She headed towards him, 'Is Mark here today?'

She hadn't heard from him for almost a fortnight now, his phone was constantly turned off. It had suddenly dawned on her after he had upped and left that she had no idea of where he lived, how to get hold of him, she only had his mobile number.

'No darling, you still not heard from him either?' He took a drag of his cigarette looking her up and down.

'So not a word? At all?' she asked.

'Look, like I said before. He'd already paid us up front and last I 'eard was about a week ago when someone rang and said he wasn't gonna be about for a bit and to just get on and finish the work. That's all I know.'

'You've worked for him before though? Surely you have contact details? Who was the friend that rang you? Have you got his number?'

He stubbed out the cigarette on the ground, crushing it with his boot and looked up as his workmate came out of the cottage carrying a paint-spattered ladder.

'Look, he's always got in touch if he needed work doing. And no, I don't know who the woman was that rang – his missus maybe?' He shrugged his shoulders and went over to help his colleague lift some more gear into the van.

'Anyway doll,' he called over, 'It's all finished. You can move in anytime you want now.' He shut the van door and made his way back to her side and handed her a card. 'Here's me number in case you have problems with the work. But it should all be okay, we've done a good job, if I say so meself.'

Alison stood holding the grubby card and watched the vans as they headed off down the ivy tunnel of Monkton Lane. She'd been up to the cottage a number of times that week after getting back from spending a few more days down at her Father's place. She'd been sorting out what furniture to keep and what to be sold, and there was still so much paperwork, personal stuff and photos to go through. At least she had the space here at Orchard Cottage for a lot of it until she could sift through it properly. Roger had helped her with selling some of her Dad's stuff. He knew a few families locally that welcomed the cooker and freezer and a few other bits at knocked down prices. He'd been really kind and had also offered to help her move in. She had cancelled the lease on her flat and her Dad's house was now finally up for sale.

With the money she already had from her Grandmother and once her Dad's place was sold she'd have a good secure financial future. Probably wouldn't need to work again, not that she'd done much work for a long time now. She'd had clients badgering her, when would she be finishing the work for them? She couldn't fob them off forever, maybe she should hand them over to some other web designer? No, she shouldn't give up. Maybe once she'd moved in she would get motivated, she needed a distraction, a distraction from thinking about Mark.

Shutting the front door behind her she made her way through the hallway to the kitchen. This was the oldest part of the building, where the Abbot had once lived and overseen the running of the monastery. Its age was obvious by the thickness of the walls in the window recesses. The leaded glass reflected the afternoon sunlight down into the hallway, creating sparkling diamond shapes on the floor. Alison momentarily forgot her anguish over Mark and took a moment to savour the shimmering pictures that nature was giving her for free on the terracotta tiles. She bent down and picked up a piece of paper that was wedged by the wall. Builders! She wondered what other rubbish they had left behind.

The kitchen was already kitted out with the essentials so dropping the slip of paper on a worktop she filled the kettle and gazed out of the window towards the ruins. Swallows were swooping down outside, and she could hear their chattering noises as they landed on the muddy nurseries they had built under the eaves.

She grabbed a mug to make some tea and stood while it brewed and picked up the discarded paper she had retrieved from the hallway floor, playing about with it in her hands as she waited, deep in thought. She glanced at the writing. Golden Palace Chinese takeaway. Ukk! She hoped the builders hadn't eaten it here and made the bin stink with soya sauce smells. She looked again and gasped. It was for a takeaway in Stockwell. And it was Tower Street, right near the club. She looked closer and saw that it was dated February.

What was a receipt from Stockwell doing there? Oh God, had Kenny been at the cottage? Her heart began to race out of control at the thought of him, invading her space, her sanctuary. No, she was being paranoid, surely she would have noticed if someone had broken in. Who else had been here apart from her?

Susie and Steve been there the night of the flood, could it be them? Steve's family were a dodgy lot, were they involved with Big Mick? Who else? Tom Elliot? What did she really know about him? She didn't know where he lived, maybe he was from South London. Bit too much of a coincidence though wasn't it that he'd got a takeaway from a place just a stones throw from where she had witnessed a murder. Couldn't be him. Could it? She took her tea and headed back to the sitting room and sat down on one of the old garden chairs she'd put in there for now, her mind whizzing, wondering.

Mark.

Could it be Mark? He lived in Croydon, so he said. But why would he lie about that? She was just being ridiculous. Blowing things all out of proportion as usual. There was simple reason. She must have had the receipt in her own pocket, maybe it was February last year and it was Kenny's and somehow it had made its way into her jacket. Yes, that was it.

She sat back and looked out across the fields to Greysmead village and sipped her tea. There was movement in the field, she stood up and peered out and watched as two deer made their way into the woods to the south. How she loved it here! She decided she'd take Roger up on his offer and get her stuff moved in as soon as possible although it would probably have to be after the bank holiday now. She'd check with Rog when he'd be free and get a van hired ready, but maybe she could move a few little bits down from the flat before hand. Her new bed was due to be delivered in a few days so maybe she could sleep at the cottage over bank holiday weekend. There was going to be a church fete that weekend, it would give her a chance to speak to the vicar, see if he would come up and do a blessing. Let Mary and John rest in peace.

The blessing had been Kit's Aunty Betty's idea. Alison had been surprised when she had first met Betty, for some reason she had been expecting to see some frail old lady but instead a sprightly looking woman in her early sixties with short-cropped bright red hair and tatty fraying jeans opened the door to the bungalow. Her face was open and welcoming as she greeted them.

'Roger! How lovely to see you my darling boy.' She hugged him close and stepped back looking into his face, smiling. 'You are looking just as handsome as ever. The Sussex air must be doing you good, I'm so glad you've moved back home and away from London,' she grimaced, 'Terrible place…and people.'

'Err..Betty…this is Al…and…she's from London,' he laughed.

'Oh dear boy, I'm forever putting my foot in it.' She turned to Alison and looked intently at her face, 'Oh yes, yes….I can see him so clearly in your face….Oh it is wonderful…just wonderful,' she murmured before pulling Al close to her and kissing her cheeks. 'I'm sorry my dear, don't mind me, please don't take offence about London, I'm sure most of the people there are just delightful, but I feel you have Sussex running in your veins. I'm right, am I not?' she continued as she led them into a brightly decorated room at the back of the house.

Painted canvasses leant against every available wall with some half finished works stacked in a corner. An easel was positioned in front of a huge window that took up most of the south facing side, looking out towards the ocean.

'Please sit yourselves down.' She gathered up a pile of books from the shabby sofa and indicated to Al to sit, whisking up a scarf from the seat. She draped it over the easel and cleared a chair of sketchpads to allow Roger to sit too. 'I'll just get some drinks, and then,' she leant down towards Al, 'then we can talk about brother John.' She flowed out of the room leaving Alison in a state of shock.

'She's quite a character, isn't she?' she grinned at Roger and then began to take in the room, which was full of bohemian paraphernalia.

'Yes, I thought best not to warn you. It would have spoilt the effect!' he laughed.

'What are you two young people laughing at in here? It's lovely to hear the young so happy.' Betty returned to the room with a mismatch of varying size tumblers almost full to the brim. 'Here Alison, it's my own home made elderberry wine. I haven't got any wine glasses I'm afraid, broke them all when I was having one of my …'experiences.'' she fluttered her hand mid air, 'Here we are Roger. I've put some lemonade in there as I expect you are driving that wonderful sports car today?'

She sat on the arm of Roger's chair and looked across at Al. 'It really is uncanny my dear, you are so like him you know.'

Al tentatively sipped her drink, which was surprisingly delicious.

'Like who? Did you know my Father, he used to live close by in Bexhill.'

'Did he dear? No, I mean brother John. You have the same eyes, he had beautiful eyes.' She looked wistful for a moment before continuing,' Roger tells me of your experiences and I am so glad you have finally arrived. Hopefully you can resolve it all. We don't want Amy turning into a mad woman like me do we?' She began to laugh.

'We don't think you're mad Aunty Betty, you are just different!' Roger joked.

Feeling totally confused Al piped up. 'I'm sorry, but I really don't understand. Are you saying I am in some way related to Brother John?'

Betty stood up and glass in hand, glided over to her and looked at her face closely. 'My dear, of course you are. I knew you would come back sooner or later. Poor Mary needed to tell her story and now you are back they will be at peace again. It's up to you and Amy now.'

Betty began to wander around the room, arms gesticulating as she spoke, 'Of course, I can't connect with Mary very easily now – pumped full of too many drugs when I was put away – still it's opened up my other creative trait.' She indicated to the easel, 'Every cloud and all that.' She rubbed at the corner of the canvas of her current work with a paint stained rag before whirling round suddenly to face Alison, 'You dream of John I hear?'

Alison nodded.

'Well it's John's way of making contact. You are sure to have more dreams. Try to get Amy nearby when you sleep, that way Mary and John can communicate together and rest at last.'

She stood back and closed her eyes, silent for a moment and then said, 'And get your cottage blessed. The previous family at your cottage did put in some protection from the Darkness but its best to be certain, belts and braces and all that. Yes, my advice is get the vicar to do a blessing. As soon as you can.'

Alison sat with her tea thinking back to her meeting with Betty. What a wonderful lady! She had promised to keep in touch and let her know how things went with the blessing and if it helped Mary and John to finally rest in peace. Betty had been very reticent about telling Al all she knew of the circumstances of their sorrow. She implied she knew more about the events of the past than Al had discovered so far through her dreams, but Betty had told Alison that she needed to find out the full story for herself. If she revealed to Al what she felt had happened it may just be interpreted as some mad woman's imaginings but if Al came up with the same story of events, well, that would help confirm that it was the truth.

Chapter twenty one

As Alison sat wondering if the secrets behind the story of John and Mary would ever be revealed, she heard voices. Kit and Charlie were heading up the footpath. They had arranged to call over to see the cottage and also to discuss Betty's idea that Amy and Al should sleep near each other one night so Mary and John could converse from the spirit world. Kit had been very apprehensive of this idea at first but Roger had explained Betty's reasons and eventually was able to convince her it would be for the best. If it meant Amy could then get on with her life without seeing her sad lady all the time and begin to enjoy her childhood, well yes it would be worth it.

Al got up and waved across at them as they approached the gate. As she made her way out to the hall she sighed. She'd imagined that she would be sharing her first day, once all the work was complete, with Mark. Long before they'd finally slept together she had created a little fantasy about him. She'd pictured it in her mind, Mark taking her around each room, showing her the completed work and she would pretend she wasn't happy with it and then her daydream would end with him laughing and grabbing hold of her roughly and she would feel his strong arms holding her tight as she breathed in the woody smell of his skin. They would end up kissing and he would ….No! She must stop this. It sounded like a Mills and Boon novel and in the same way it was just fiction. It wasn't going to happen. He hadn't been in touch, probably wouldn't ever be in touch again. She meant nothing to him. The pain rose from the pit of her stomach and she wiped away the tears as she opened the door to Kit and Chas.

'Hello you! May we come in?' Kit beamed and gave her a quick hug before looking at her face and immediately realised things weren't quite right with her friend.

'You go and sort things out Chas whilst I just have a quick word with Al.' She nudged Chas along with a flick of her eyes towards the kitchen, mouthing at him, 'She's been crying.'

Kit put her arm round Al's shoulder and led her back into the lounge.

'What's up sweetie?'

Kit perched herself on the windowsill with Al who was blowing her nose and shaking her head. 'I'm okay, really…I just…oh I'm sorry, I'm being stupid…' She mumbled into her tissue, 'I'm not a teenager anymore, should have more sense!'

'You still not heard from the bastard then?' Kit asked angrily.

'No, not a word. The builders he employed to finish the work have headed off, they hadn't seen him or heard from him either. They said they'd had a call from a woman. She told them Mark wasn't going to be around for a while. Who was it do you think? A woman. I'm wondering now if he was married.'

Al wiped her eyes and looked at Kit, hoping to get a reasonable explanation from her, hoping she would come to Mark's defence and explain it all away in his favour.

But Kit told it how she saw it. 'You are probably right honey. He was just playing away. You did tell me you never went to his home, maybe that's the reason. Oh, come here!' she gave Al a hug as more tears began to flow.

'What an idiot I was!' Al cried.

'No – he's the idiot, for letting you go. Just you try to forget him, try to focus on this place.' she said looking around at the room, now in its full glory with eggshell blue walls, high ceilings and a wonderful view across the fields to the village.

Alison gave her a weak smile, 'I know I should but…you do know I was in love with him? And I thought he felt the same way. The bastard!' she slammed her hand down on the sill. 'He's made me so angry!'

There was a light knock at the door. 'Is it safe to come in yet?' Chas stood there with a tray of four glasses of sparkling wine and a small plate piled high with cheese straws and crisps.

'Chas thought we should toast Orchard Cottage with a drink and some nibbles,' said Kit taking a glass and passed it to Al.

'Chas! That's lovely, what a nice thought. But no need for the fourth glass, Mark still hasn't shown up.'

'No, it's not for that rat. Roger said he might pop up too, if you don't mind? He's taken Amy to her friends for us and was going to come over after.'

'Yes, no probs. Sorry the only seats are these two garden chairs at the moment. Bed's arriving Thursday, I was thinking I might go and get a few bits to bring down from my flat tomorrow so I can stay here over the weekend and then I'll take Roger up on his offer and get him to help me move the rest down after the bank holiday.' She took a sip of the wine, 'I'll be able to sort it out with him when he gets here.'

'That sounds great!' said Kit as she sat crossed legged on the newly carpeted floor. 'Perhaps you can stay at our place tonight? Save you being at the Jolly Abbot on your own. Jim's still away visiting relatives isn't he? Must be a chore for Susie having you stay there.'

'Yeah, she only booked me in as a favour; I'm the only guest! Still, Jim will be back Friday ready for the bank holiday weekend guests. But staying at yours tonight will be good, thanks.'

'Okay. That's settled then,' Kit said. 'We can pop you in the bunk below Amy, see if Aunt Betty's wacky idea has a grain of sense to it.'

'Your kitchen looks good I must say,' said Chas, munching on yet another cheese straw as he settled down next to Kit.

Kit smiling, whacked his hand! 'Hey, save some for us!'

He laughed and grabbed another one and popped it half in his mouth and she leant forward and bit off the other end. Alison felt an almighty surge of sadness in her chest. The envy cut like a knife into her heart as she watched them. They had such a good relationship, it was obvious they were very close. She thought she had something good too. Mark had been so much fun, he had brightened up her world but now that light had been snuffed out.

Kit took a sip of her drink and ran her hand across the deep pile, 'Wow, this is rather nice! What lovely thick carpet. We must get the guided tour once we've finished the drinks.'

'Well, you've really got it looking good here Al,' said Chas, as he rinsed the glasses under the tap. They had been around all of the cottage, Al delighted in showing them all the improvements and decorating.

'And this kitchen is just fab,' said Kit as she wiped down the worktop, and picked up the old receipt, about to throw it away.

'No, leave that!' Al spotted her actions before it went into the bin. 'I was going to show you that actually. It's made me wonder about Mark. It's a receipt from a place near the club, made me question if he was involved with Mick….' Her words trailed off as she realised if she told them of her doubts and the possible association with Mick, she would also have to explain further. They knew nothing of Cinderellas and Ken and Mick. She didn't want to go down that road, the past was the past and there it must stay.

'Mick? Mick who?'

Al shook her head and stuffed the receipt in her pocket. 'No, it's nothing, I'm just thinking aloud, forget it.' Thinking on her feet of a way to quickly change the subject she addressed Chas, 'I was going to ask your advice on this huge cupboard. I still haven't decided what to do with it.' She turned the key in the heavy wooden door as she spoke, 'I wasn't sure if I should use it as a walk-in pantry or utility or maybe a loo?' She switched on the light behind the arched doorway. 'Look, it's quite a big area. Maybe too big for a pantry? What do you guys think?'

They looked in and Chas rubbed his foot across the floor. 'This looks dangerous, that's what I think,' he said and took a penknife from his pocket as he knelt down and began to cut away at the crumbling lino. 'I think there's probably flagstones under this covering and here's one that is very rickety.' He pressed his hand down as the floor see-sawed below, 'You could trip up on this rotten lino, it's an accident waiting to happen. This needs sorting before you use this area Al. Do you want me to deal with it for you?'

'That would be great. What would you have to do?'

'Well first I'd have to rip up this rotten lino,' he said as he pulled at the corner. It snapped off and broke into small pieces. 'Looks like that's going to be easy then,' he laughed, 'it's gone really brittle, it's so old and most of the concrete underneath has disintegrated, so it shouldn't be too difficult to get up, look it's just crumbling away to nothing as it is.' He tugged at another area of the lino and a huge sheet came away, and with it concrete dust flew everywhere.

'Chas! Be careful! You're going to make a right mess.'

'Don't worry, it's okay,' piped in Al. 'Look, that rocking flagstone is clear now. I'll go and get a broom from out the back while you rip up the rest of the lino.'

When she got back the whole flagstone floor was revealed and Chas was trying to level the uneven stone, and began to lift it out.

'Well! well!' he stood back and placed the stone down at his feet, 'Look what we have here! An entrance to some sort of cellar!'

'A cellar?' Al rushed forward and peered down to glimpse at what seemed to be well worn stone steps that disappeared down underneath her cottage.

It wasn't long before a few more slabs were out to reveal a spiral stone stairway lined with candle sconces fixed to an aging brick wall.

'I think this is more that just a cellar, don't you?' Al grabbed a torch ready to descend.

'Hey, don't you go rushing down on your own, how do we know it's safe? What if the steps are unsound?'

'Kit! Stop worrying, it will be fine.' Alison put her foot on the first step but Chas pulled her to one side.

'Kit's right, we must be careful.' He took the torch from Al, 'we can go down, but let me go first. Do you want to stay here Kit and wait for Rog?'

'Okay, will do. Just take care you two.'

The musty air filled their nostrils as they descended the staircase that twisted to the left into a spiral around a central stone pillar. The bare brick wall to their right had no hand rail and with the uneven steps it made it difficult and slow going, they clung to the middle column in an attempt to steady themselves. Chas pushed aside great swathes of fly infested spiders webs. The torch light picked out well fed spiders running for cover after being disturbed from their slumbers. The wall became alive with long dark legs as they scampered over the dusty brick.

'Take it nice and carefully,' Chas called back to Al who followed a few steps behind, feeling glad she wasn't first in line.

As he reached the bottom he called out, 'Wow, look at this!' and nearly got knocked over as Al ran the last few steps unable to contain her excitement.

'What? What?'

Charlie laughed, her excitement infectious, 'See this? It's an undercroft. Alison, you've got a bloody crypt under your kitchen!'

Chas shone the torch into the cavernous area, the feeble circle of light flew around the roof space allowing brief glimpses of tall stone pillars rising up and fanning out into high-bricked archways. The pillars stretched into the distance like an avenue of majestic trees, beckoning the new visitors, enticing them to go further, to explore the shadowy corners beyond. Al clung onto Charlie's arm as they cautiously stepped away from the staircase. The torch revealed shadows in the walls where little side rooms sat dark and undisturbed for centuries.

A scurrying sound at their feet had Alison grabbing Charlie even tighter. Her fingers pinched at his arm, her nails digging his flesh sharply in her sudden panic.

'Hey, watch it!' he jerked away and lost his grasp of the torch. It clattered away on the floor, its light snuffed out.

They stood in the crypt, enveloped in darkness.

'Well, that was clever. We have to find our way out in the dark now, you dingbat!'

'Chas, I'm so sorry, it was that noise, it made me jump! I was scared it was rats.'

'It probably was!' he laughed as she clung on to his arm tighter still. 'Don't worry, we'll be okay. Come on, now my eyes are adjusting to the dark I can make out a hint of light over there, coming down from your kitchen. Let's go and get better equipped and come back to look around.'

As they edged their way carefully in the blackness two bright beams of light appeared.

'Hey you guys? How you doing? Blimey, it's a bit dark down here.'

Roger came down the steps followed by Kit. Roger's torch located some more sconces on the wall by the staircase entrance and Kit who had found a bunch of candles from the kitchen, carefully positioned them in place, leaving the matches and spare candles on the stone shelf below. As the candles flickered into life they were able to get a better view of the crypt and also a few rats before they quickly disappeared from sight.

'This is amazing! Come on you, lot let's explore, I feel like one of the famous five about to have an adventure.' Roger kicked out as one lone rat made a beeline for his foot, 'No, you can't be Timmy the dog!' he joked and began to make his way further along as he flicked his torch from side to side. 'Hey come and look here…'

Roger projected the beam up onto the wall.

'It's our angel!' cried Kit, 'She looks just the same. So she *did* come from here! The stories are true.'

Roger shone the torch over to the opposite wall to find stone worked corbels that mirrored the ones either side of the angel but here the gap in between was devoid of a statue, just a great gash in the wall.

'Look, here's where she probably came from,' he said, as he continued to journey further into the crypt, wielding the torch like a sword, the light swaying from side to side.

His voice echoed back to the others, 'Get over here! I've found an alcove with some sort of stone structure inside.'

They quickly made their way over to the gap in the wall and peered in. The opening led into a small brick lined room no more than eight-foot deep and probably four foot wide. Roger held up the torch and its light travelled slowly across the interior and suddenly in view was a stone table upon which lay something that made Al catch her breath. Her pulse quickened as she was suddenly aware of the void of blackness behind them; the candles were beginning to falter and were sending out strange shadows that seemed to dart around the crypt, like a restless caged animal. Chas moved in closer to the entrance of the alcove.

'It's a stone coffin,' he said, not telling them anything they hadn't already realised for themselves. But the words spoken made it seem more real somehow. Alison felt uneasy, she didn't like it, it didn't feel right being there, spying on the dead.

A shiver went up her spine and she grabbed out for Roger's hand as she spoke, 'A coffin? Are you sure Chas?'

Roger glanced her way and squeezed her hand tightly.

Chas took Kit's torch and edged his way through the small gap. He rubbed the heel of his hand across the top.

'Yep, there's some sort of engraving, looks very roughly done though, doesn't go in very deep, very amateurish.'

'What does it say? Can you tell?' questioned Al.

Chas pointed the torch down onto the top of the lid and brushed more of the dust away.

'No, think it's in Latin, but can't be sure. Needs an expert's eye on it.'

He made his way towards the back of the alcove, holding his arms up as he squeezed through the tight gap, past the coffin.

'It looks like there's a few words etched in at the far end, along the side. I'll just take a look...what the?' his cry from the shadows made them all jump.

'What is it mate?' Roger asked, 'You okay in there?'

'Yeah, just hit my foot on something…hang on?'

Chas leant down out of view behind the plinth for a moment and re-emerged holding what looked like a shepherd's hook in his hand. He grinned as he sidled out, his find held aloft.

'Looks like the famous five have found buried treasure!' he grinned.

Al felt her heart miss a beat at his words. She was frightened. Behind them the crypt lost some of its illumination as one of the candle flames finally flickered and died.

Kit took the torch from Chas so he could examine his find.

'What is it Chas? Any idea?'

They all crowded round to see the object, unaware that they were being watched from the shadows.

Al pushed the feeling of apprehension aside when she looked at the crook in detail. 'It is beautiful! Look Chas there's a picture on the flat piece within the handle. It looks very similar to the seal I found.'

Chas rubbed at the metal within the crook. 'I think you're right Al. Do you think this could be the tomb of the Abbot? Although if it is I'm surprised that it's in the crypt, I always thought they buried them up near the abbey buildings. But I'm sure I read somewhere that they used to lay the crosier on top of the coffin in the grave.'

Roger edged nearer to see, 'Crosier? What's that then?'

'Crosier or crook. The Abbot was usually presented with it when he was ordained I believe, symbol of the good shepherd and his flock and all that.' Still holding onto it tightly Chas continued, 'We best get it looked at by someone who deals with this kind of thing, don't you think?' he looked at Al.

She suddenly became aware of the smell of burning wax and realised all but one of the candles had burnt out, the thick smoke from the smouldering wicks filled the crypt and mixed with the stale musty air. She felt uneasy.

'Shouldn't we leave it on the coffin? It seems disrespectful to me to take it away.'

'I was going to take it up into the light to look at it properly. It's an important historical find. You can't just leave it here,' Chas pleaded.

Al began to sense something in the crypt, a negative feeling closing in on her. She was finding it hard to breathe, her lungs wouldn't take in any air, she was going to faint, she was sure of it. She had to get out.

'Sorry, but I want to think on it, let's leave it here on his coffin for now. We can come back down again some other time. Come on, let's go upstairs.'

The fear overwhelmed her. She made a dash for the steps, eager to escape. Once she was back up in her cottage she'd be okay, and then she'd make sure the door to the cupboard was firmly shut and then she'd keep it locked.

Chas shrugged his shoulders and placed the crosier back in the alcove, this time on top of the coffin. The shadows dispersed, panic over, the visitors were leaving.

Chapter twenty two

They had taken a stroll further along Monkton Lane, to the river. It had been Kit's idea, get a bit of fresh air after the confines of the crypt. It wouldn't have been Al's destination of choice, it harboured memories of the day she had discovered Mark skinny-dipping in the river. She pushed the memories to the back of her mind and tried to concentrate on the conversation.

They had grabbed some cold drinks from the cool box that Chas and Kit had brought up with them, also some cake and they sat by the water's edge discussing their finds. The feeling of trepidation Al had felt when Chas had taken the crosier out from the alcove had long diminished but she still felt adamant that they should leave it as they'd found it for now. Maybe she could discuss it with the vicar at the weekend, when she talked to him about the blessing.

'I was wondering about asking the vicar to bless the crypt as well. What do you think?' She looked at their faces as she took a bite of Kit's homemade fruitcake, it was soft, crumbly and delicious.

Kit nodded as she too chewed on a big wedge of cake.

Roger took a swig of the orange juice and said, 'I agree actually. It doesn't seem right taking it away.'

'But?' Chas began to chip in, keen to get the historical aspects of it all verified.

Roger held up his hand, 'Hold on, let me finish. Can't your history experts look at it down in the crypt? Anyway, I'm with Al, I think she should speak to the vicar first, get his take on it. It is a religious item after all.'

'Okay Okay, I concede defeat on this,' Chas said, always happy to keep the peace, 'but maybe you will think about getting it looked at some time Al?'

She laughed at him, as he looked at her with pleading eyes, 'Okay, I'll think about it.'

Roger looked across at her and winked before holding up the bottle to his lips to take a final swig. He'd been a real support the past couple of weeks. She'd been really spooked down in the crypt when they discovered the coffin, it would take her a while to get used to knowing that was under her house. God she was glad she'd arranged to sleep at Kit's that night. She shivered when she thought back to the dark undercroft and then the coffin illuminated by the torchlight. She'd grabbed at Roger's hand without thinking. She was scared and needed reassurance and his hand was close by. She hoped he didn't think it was anything more. He had been really kind but he wasn't Mark.

'I knew they were at it. He was all over her at her Dad's funeral.' Ken downed another whisky and banged the glass back down on the bar, nodded to the barman to fill it again, 'I went and saw him you know? Down at that bloody shit hole where she lives now. All fucking trees and fields.'

Big Mick grunted back and continued tapping figures into his calculator and half listened to Ken's ramblings.

'Told him I knew what was going on, told 'im I wasn't havin' it. But he denied it, talked me round, ended up going for a drink with him. The arsehole! Then the bastard admitted it to you!'

'You didn't have to beat the fucking shit out of him though did'yer Kenny? We don't want more stiffs on our hands do we?' Mick looked up from his projections and called across to Dave behind the bar, 'Any news on him yet Dave?'

Dave poured Ken another drink and answered, 'No boss, last thing I know is that they spotted him on the steps of the casualty dept where I left him that night and they took him in. I haven't been able to get any more info since.'

'Ain't you rung up and said you're a relative?'

'Have boss, yeah. They just say they've moved him and wouldn't say where.'

Ken finished his drink and turned his bleary eyes towards Mick, 'Well he can rot wherever he is. Bastard! Anyway, how's it going Mick? What's the verdict?'

'Now we're free to use Billy Watson's supplier, we're doing alright Kenny boy. Shame about Billy wasn't it?' he grinned.

A fresh shipment had arrived from his source yesterday, there was enough there to make a lot of people very happy, including him. With the street value of this lot, he was laughing. He'd made contact with a new dealer up west, who would probably be able to put some more respectable clients his way. Respectable! He laughed to himself. Who are they kidding? When they start stuffing their noses with this stuff it made them no different to the rest of them. They just have more easy accessible readies to support their little habits, don't they?

The first thing Alison saw was an angelic face with blonde curls peering into her eyes.

'Hello Aunty Al!' squealed Amy, half hanging down from the bunk above her. 'Are you awake now?'

She had been so excited when her Mum had told her Alison was going to sleep in her room with her. She was glad her Mum and Al had made up. The sad lady had told her that it would be all right, she knew her Mum would make friends with Alison again. Last night she had dreamt again about the sad lady, she was still looking for John but he still hadn't come to see her.

At began to stretch out her legs in the confines of the small bed and realised she'd had a great night's sleep, but unlike Betty's predictions it had been totally devoid of dreams.

'Yes, wide awake sweetheart!' Alison smiled, 'Shall we see if your Mum is awake?

Amy clambered down the ladder and jumped onto the bed with Alison, 'I expect she is...Alison?'

'What is it Amy?' At asked as she manoeuvred to get comfortable in the confines of the bottom bunk.

Amy pulled at some strands of Al's hair and began to plait it as she spoke, 'You will be coming back won't you? Mum said you are moving house.'

'Yes darling, I'm just going to London to get some of my things. I am going to live in the cottage in the lane.'

Amy, bored with her hairdressing jumped down from the bed and opened the bedroom door. She turned and looked back at Al who was now sitting on the edge of the bed as she tried to untangle Amy's attempt at plaits.

'The sad lady is pleased you are staying, she knows you will help her find John. Then it will all be alright,' Amy told her.

Before Alison set off to Mitcham to get some of her things from the flat she began to think back to the crypt and wondered how she would feel sleeping up at Orchard cottage on her own, knowing what lay under the kitchen and beyond. Amy said everything would be okay once her sad lady found John, but Al sensed the unease she felt at the cottage wasn't solely to do with John. There was something more up there, waiting and watching and it didn't feel very friendly.

She'd been so looking forward to moving in but now she wasn't so sure. She discussed her worries with Kit over breakfast.

'Why not bring your stuff down as planned and leave it up at the cottage but stay here overnight until after the weekend then? Speak to the vicar and maybe once the blessing is done you will feel happier.' Kit passed Al a knife for her toast as she went on, 'You can always get Chas to concrete it all over again, if you are that worried. I think that's what I'd do.'

'Yeah, I suppose it's an idea, although it seems wrong somehow to do that. Hiding it away again. Thanks for the offer, I'll stay here then if that's okay?'

'Of course it is, no trouble. So no dreams last night as Betty predicted then?'

Al shook her head and laughed, 'Nothing, slept like a log. You'd think after yesterday I'd have some sort of nightmares wouldn't you! But I didn't dream at all.'

'I dreamt. I dreamt about the sad lady,' announced Amy who wandered into the kitchen from the garden, 'She wants you to bring John, she needs to tell him about the baby.' She sidled up to Al who gave her half a slice of her honeyed toast.

'I know she does sweetheart. I'll see what I can do.'

Boxed memories waited to be taken to their new home. Cushions and mugs from the old place at Stockwell, the black ceramic cat with a chipped ear that Ken had bought her the year they married. They'd agreed they'd get a real cat when the time was right and then a baby or was it the other way round? Too painful to dig too deep, old wounds, starting to heal, they didn't need picking at now. New beginnings ahead. So why keep all this stuff then? Why hang onto the past?

Al grabbed a small album that contained a bunch of photos they had taken on their fourth wedding anniversary. How happy they looked. It was a trip to the New Forest with Kenny bemoaning the fact it was in the middle of nowhere. She knew he hated the countryside he had said with a laugh. He'd had fun with the head waiter, rubbing him the up the wrong way, he didn't like his sort.

Stuck up he was, said Ken. 'That's what you get in these posh hotels Al. Stuck up twats who look down their nose at you. Well I'm earning big bucks now, my money's just as good as the next man.'

And it was. He was working hard, the business was doing well. Anyone could set up as an estate agent he'd said, nothing to it. He was right. He did ok, built it up, had two branches. He may have sounded rough and ready but her Kenny, he had brains, well he did then, before the drugs and booze turned them into a mush. It was the downturn in the market that started the big fall for Ken. People weren't buying or selling, they were too worried about the economy, staying put or adding a room in the loft. When he started to feel the pinch, Ken shut down the branch on the High Street and for a while kept the smaller premises along Tower Street open. In the end it was shut more than it was open as his lunch breaks at the bar of Cinderella's soon became an afternoon session and before long he had to ditch his dream altogether, he just walked about in a drink induced dream instead.

That was when Mick began to weave his web around Ken, to pull him in, he knew he'd be useful. He gave him a job at the club. Ken had been well chuffed when he arrived home that night with the news. She'd been in bed a few hours when the front door slammed and she heard him laughing to himself as he made his way up the stairs.

'You awake Al?' he had whispered. She feigned sleep, her head hidden under the duvet. He shouted her name, 'Al, you awake? Good news, got meself a job,' he slurred as he fell about the room attempting to undress. 'Big Mick's a good bloke he is…salt of the earth, helping his mate when times are rough. On the up again now Al, you'll see.'

Her finger traced his face on the photograph. They'd gone down to the coast for the day from their New Forest hotel. Where was it now? Milford on sea, yeah that was it. Nice little place, not too touristy. She had enjoyed the break away from the hotel, it was good to get back to basics again, away from the over the top menu and the starched staff and just sit back and enjoy the scenery. She wasn't bothered like Ken about the material things in life, it was just being together that mattered.

It had been a beautiful day. They'd sat on a bench by the sea with the breeze blowing in their hair while they ate fish and chips. The sun glistened on the water and they could see the needles of the Isle of Wight in the distance. She had said to Ken how the shimmering light on the sea looked like sparkling diamonds.

'I can buy you the real thing now Al,' he replied, not understanding.

She snapped the album shut and stuffed it in the box. Time to go.

She failed to notice the space on the fridge door. The photo of her standing outside Orchard cottage was missing. She didn't know it was now crammed in a wallet, pushed to the back of a locker along with the other few items that had been found on Mark as he had lay battered and bleeding on the steps of A and E.

He knew it was daytime because his eyelids sensed the natural light as it filtered in, less harsh that the stark fluorescent lights that penetrated through to his pupils in the evenings. The noises from the ward also began to increase, doors shutting, mumbled voices but always the constant beeping beside him, he didn't mind that, it told him he was still alive.

On the few occasions he had momentarily become aware of his surroundings he had tried to open his eyes but they felt as if they were held down with weights. His throat and mouth seemed to have increased in size where they had inserted a tube to help him breathe. Although it felt uncomfortable and sore he was glad of it, even in his state he knew his lungs were unable to help him, they too needed their rest. At least he wasn't feeling pain now. He had vague memories of his journey through the dark streets of South London that night. He'd thought at first he'd been in an ambulance but realised it wasn't the case when his body began to be thrown around the back of the van like a carcass of meat as the driver sped along, taking corners too fast. His already broken body cried out as he rolled around amongst the debris in the back of the van, the streets lights strobing in through the windows as he crashed and bounced against the metal panels and doors until everything went black.

He was vaguely aware of a female voice echoing into his stagnant brain.

'A visitor for you Mr Bradley,' he felt her soft fingers touch his arm, checking one of the tubes that infiltrated his body. 'Just a few minutes, he is very weak,' she said quietly.

'Can he hear me?'

She shook her head, 'He's been unconscious over two weeks now. But it's always worth talking, hearing a familiar voice can sometimes help. I'll be back shortly,' she smiled and left the room.

The voice of the visitor filtered through to Mark's consciousness. Snippets of words, some meaningless, some having some glimmer of familiarity. What was being said? He tried to shift his brain into action. It was too hard. He was so tired.

The door to his room gently shut as his visitor left. They would come back and try again. They owed him that much.

Chapter twenty three

Jim hoped his cousin would stick to her promise. Now back from his trip to Somerset he felt a little less stressed. Jess and her husband had been looking at investment ideas and Jim's visit had been to persuade them of the virtues of putting some of their cash into the pub. They'd be sleeping partners at first but were considering moving back to Sussex within a year or so to have more of an active role.

However they didn't know that some of the money they'd promised was earmarked by Jim to pay off his gambling debts. Once the Pub coffers were full again by the end of summer Jim was sure he'd have enough to smooth it over so they'd be none the wiser. It was a gamble he knew, but he was experienced with that wasn't he? He knew all about odds. It was a pity he didn't remember the odds were usually against him.

Susie was feeling quite positive about the venture, unaware of the under hand dealings her Father had planned. She'd been wondering how her Dad would cope once she left college so if cousin Jess did move back to the village it would take the pressure off her. Susie didn't plan on working at the pub full time when her studies finished that was for sure! She picked up a tray and went into the dinning room where their regular, Tom Elliot was buried in the newspaper whilst finishing his coffee. He was staying for the week, having arrived the day before and already had been spotted the previous evening taking part in his usual habit of heading off across the fields at dusk.

Susie noticed a headline on the front page of the tabloid he was reading. Not his usual choice of newspaper but he'd left it too late and it was all Mrs Blackman had to offer. He had to make do with news of sex, drugs and scandal.

'Sorry to interrupt Mr Elliott but may I be cheeky and have a look at your paper when you've finished please?' she asked.

Tom's serious face came into view above the newsprint and he actually smiled. He'd mellowed since his last visit and seemed more approachable.

'Something catch your eye? Something about a celebrity no doubt?' he grinned.

'Donna Peters?'

'No Sorry,' he shook his head, 'don't know the name.'

'Lead singer with the band Dark Wish – heavy metal?' She said as he looked at a complete loss. 'I thought I noticed a headline about a close call she'd had with drugs. Just wondered what happened?'

He fumbled with the paper and scanned the pages for the news item. He was out of touch with today's music scene that was for sure, although thinking back was he ever in touch with it? He found the article and read a few lines for Susie.

'Seems she was found unconscious in her hotel room last week, but says she is beginning to make a good recovery.'

'Was it drugs then?' asked Susie, as she gathered some of the condiments from nearby tables now that breakfast was over.

He nodded, 'It reads 'they found cocaine in her room, which after analysis was found to be cut with other substances. One being Chloropromazine.'' He looked up at Susie, 'Seems to be some sort of tranquilliser.' He continued to scan the paragraph, 'She was on beta blockers to help with anxiety, been taking too higher dose if the levels in her system was anything to go by, so with this other drug her blood pressure fell like a lead balloon.'

'Poor Donna, how terrible.'

'Yes it is Susie but don't forget it was her choice to take the drugs. Says here she is co-operating with police to help them trace the source. They say it looks like a new supplier to the area.' He flicked the paper shut and handed it to her, 'Here you are, read it for yourself. I'm going to go and get some fresh air now,' he said as he pushed back his chair, ready to leave. 'Susie? I haven't seen Mrs Greenways come down for breakfast yet? She'd told me she was staying this week.'

'She was, but has now decided to stay with the Mitchell's until she moves into her new home. I think she said she was going to the church fete this afternoon.'

'Okay, thanks Susie. I'll probably catch up with her there.'

Susie smiled and popped the paper under her arm as she carried plates through to the kitchen. She'd read it later with a cuppa. She thought about Mr Elliot's words. He was right. It had been Donna's choice, but it still wasn't a very nice thing to happen. Maybe she had been under pressure by the people she mixed with to take the drugs. People do get pulled into taking part in things they don't always want to do. Look at Steve. His family get him into some dodgy dealings sometimes, thank God it had never been drugs. Since her chat that night with Alison, she'd spoken to him about her fears and he was starting to take more notice of her now and not get pulled into his family's illegal schemes so much.

Outside summer continued its reign over the South East. There was lots of speculation when the spell of hot weather would ease, so far apart from a few days of deluge earlier in the year it had been an ice-cream salesman's dream with wall-to-wall sunshine day after day. The usually lush and well tended village green was now devoid of any grass apart from a few straw coloured strands and some scorched weeds. With the water table so low, the reservoir levels were depleting and everyone had been asked to do their bit in conserving water, hosepipes were banned and car washes shut and now everything seemed to be covered with a fine layer of brown dust.

Tom took a slow stroll in the direction of the church. The bells filled the air with their chimes, calling out for the pews to be filled. They could toll all they wanted, he wouldn't be attending. Lost any faith he had a long time ago. Lost faith when he began to witness so much suffering in the animal kingdom at the hands of the so-called civilised human race.

There was a steady stream of parishioners making their way through the lych gate, disappearing from view behind the yew bushes to re-appear at the door of the church.

'Tom! Tom!'

He turned to see Alison as she dashed towards him, running the last few metres to catch up.

'So glad I've seen you,' she said, sounding out of breath, 'I did try to ring you last night to let you know I was about but didn't have a signal at Kit's.' She linked arms with him and continued walking along.

'Susie told me you were staying with the Mitchell's, would that be your friend Kit?'

She nodded, 'Yes, Kit and Chas and their little girl Amy. I'm sleeping in with her, in the bunk bed!'

'So why are you staying there if it's so cramped? You usually stay at the pub, although I would have thought your place was ready by now?'

She squeezed his arm and smiled, 'It's a long story! I'll tell you after the service,' as they continued along he found himself being guided under the lych gate and into the church.

They edged their way into one of the pews near the back, the locals turned to see if they recognised the new worshippers. Mrs Blackman sitting near the front gave a little wave and made a mental note that Al was now with yet another man! It's that Mr Elliott. She hadn't seen that nice Mr Bradley since he'd left the B&B some weeks ago. She'd have to see if she could find out what was going on. Maybe she'd try to catch Ms Greenways after the service for a friendly natter. She had to stay neighbourly, didn't she?

However she didn't get a chance, for when she left the church Alison was deep in conversation with Reverend Mahoney. Mrs Blackman tried to catch her eye but apart from a polite smile her way, Ms Greenways continued to discuss something with the vicar, something that looked quite serious if his face was anything to go by. Mrs Blackman looked around trying to spot Mr Elliot, he was the one that was always creeping about near the woods at dusk. Looked like a birdwatcher to her. Bit of a loner. She surmised by his manner and clothes that he was probably a bit of a mummy's boy. Not the sort she'd had thought Ms Greenways would go for, especially after that Mr Bradley. Even she'd been smitten by his charming smile and good looks.

Unaware that his personality was being picked to shreds by the village gossip, Tom had wandered around the churchyard, whilst he waited for Al. At the back of the church there was a large field, left to grow wild which was something he approved of as it was a haven for wildlife, flowers and insects. As he edged his way through the long grass towards an old elder tree he could hear a wren shouting out its alarm call. Not wishing to disturb it, he headed back towards the front porch where Alison was shaking hands with the vicar.

'I'll see you Wednesday then. And thank you again for your kind donation,' Rev Mahoney said as he turned and headed to the vicarage to make final preparations for the fete and maybe test another of his wife's cakes.

Alison stood and waited for Tom. She looked more relaxed than she had earlier.

'So are you going to tell me all or will I have to treat you to lunch before you spill the beans?' he asked feeling at ease with her now. When he had first met up with her in the fields earlier that summer he had been awkward and shy but since then they'd had a number of friendly phone conversations. She had been keen to find out more about the badger charity and was keen to help and wanted to do her bit to make sure the sett near her property stayed undisturbed. Tom knew she was romantically involved with the builder who had worked on her cottage, so had no illusions that she wasn't being anything more than just friendly. He didn't mind, in fact knowing that made it easier for him, no need to suffer the embarrassment of rejection.

They had a quick bite to eat in the tearoom just along from the post office. It wasn't usually open on a Sunday but was making the most of the extra visitors to the village for the church fete that afternoon. Al had arranged to meet Kit, Chas and Amy there later so until then she filled Tom in with the recent events. She could tell by his face that he thought the whole Mary and John story was beyond his scientific and down to earth take on life. He didn't mock or argue with her, he just sat quietly listening and nodding but made no comment. But when she began to talk about the crypt he became animated. He sat upright in his chair; his eyes began to light up with excitement as she told the story of the dark under croft and the eventual discovery of the tomb.

'So there we are. I'm living in a house with a coffin! The vicar has agreed to come and do a blessing on the house as Betty suggested but he is also going to go down into the crypt and perform a service.'

'Will you leave the coffin down there? Will it bother you?' Tom asked as he wondered how to steer the conversation away from the coffin without seeming rude as he wanted to be able to ask the question that was running through his mind.

'Rev Mahoney is going to speak to the Bishop. Maybe have a burial up in the churchyard. He thought the crosier would probably end up in a museum,' Al said.

Tom shuffled in his seat, looking like an excited schoolboy, 'Would I be able to go down into the crypt do you think?'

'Well yes of course. If that's what you would like. Come to the service on Wednesday.'

He frowned, 'Well...er...it's not really my thing to be honest. But I was hoping to go down and see if there was any evidence of red-armed bats? There's a lot of bat activity in the woods and it's possible they may be roosting there.'

'Red-armed Bats?' she grinned.

'Yes, red-armed! Old Sussex name for Natterers bat, on account of its pinkish limbs. I rescued a few recently up near Hartfield, they'd been attacked by cats, poor things had severe rips to their wings. The hospital at Forest Row sorted them out though.'

'Hospital?'

'Sussex Bat hospital. Wonderful woman there does all she can for them. Someone has to look out for them!'

'Okay!' she laughed, convinced of his conviction to help any creature he could, 'we can go and look for bats.'

The door to the tearoom opened and Amy skipped in.

'Are you coming to the fete Alison? It will be starting soon. I'm going to take part in the egg and spoon race!' She turned and looked at Tom, 'Hello! You are the wood man aren't you? Mary says you keep guard over the woods to try to keep bad people away.'

Tom smiled, 'Your Mary is right, I do go in the woods. I watch the birds and animals. I don't think there are any bad people there though,' he looked at Al, his eyebrows raised in question.

'No, I don't think there are bad people there Amy. Where's your Mum?' Al asked just as the door opened and Chas and Kit made their way in. Al could see Roger was following closely behind but had stopped outside to chat to somebody. Kit and Chas kissed Alison's cheeks and turned and smiled at Tom.

Kit held out her hand, 'Hello there, it's Tom isn't it? We haven't met but Al has spoken of you,' she shook his hand as Chas added.

'And we've seen you heading up the footpath for your nature watching.'

Tom's eyes narrowed, he wondered if Al had said anything about the Sett. He had told her to keep it quiet for now.

Al realised his concern as he looked at her and said, 'Yes, I've told them how you love nature and how you've been able to tell me about all the different birds that are in the woods and the plants as well. I didn't know until meeting Tom that there were so many types of wild flowers!'

'And still lots more to learn,' Tom replied as he went off to settle the bill.

A few moments later the tearoom door opened and Roger walked in, 'Hi folks, all set for the fete? I can hear the punch and Judy setting up and getting in some practice Amy. Mr Punch is calling out his usual phrase.'

'That's the way to do it,' shouted Amy, Al and Chas in unison and they laughed.

Roger looked across and noticed Tom at the counter and wandered over as Al chatted to Kit and Chas.

Roger slapped his hand on Tom's shoulder. Tom jumped but then seeing who it was, smiled and said, 'Roger! Nice to see you! How you doing?'

'Good thanks mate. How about you? Still keeping your eyes peeled?' He tapped the side of his nose and grinned.

Tom laughed as he took his change and headed back, 'I'm having a peaceful afternoon today, going to the fete with Alison over there. She's bought a cottage up Monkton Lane and they're her friends, Kit and Chas. Do you know them?'

'Know them! I sure do! Kit's my sister!'

'No! really?'

Roger nodded, 'Yep! And I've known Alison since the day she viewed the cottage, must be last March or maybe April?' He smiled as they made their way to the door where the rest of the gang waited.

Tom was momentarily taken aback, 'Oh, I didn't realise, you live in this village? I've never bumped into you when I've been here, although I suppose I do keep rather odd hours usually!'

Kit, one ear listening to their conversation chipped in, 'Do you two know each other then?'

Roger nodded, 'Yes we do, don't we Tom? You could say we've had a few dealings with each other in the past.'

Alison frowned. She suddenly had a vague memory edge its way to the forefront of her mind. Her Dad...in the wood? Was it a dream? Yes, he had been warning her. What did he say? Not everyone were as they seemed. That was it! She looked hard at Tom. What dealings had he had with Roger? What had he been doing?

Chapter twenty four

'So how do you two know each other? Al asked as they all made their way to the field behind the church.

Roger looked at Tom, 'It's alright, we can trust my family. You okay for me to tell them?'

Tom nodded, 'Al knows already, so as long as it stays between us?'

Al knows? What was Tom talking about? She didn't know anything about Tom's dealings with Roger.

'What am I supposed to know?' she asked angrily.

'Badgers Al. You know about the badgers,' Tom said and then proceeded to reveal that he worked for an animal charity that the police consulted if they needed advice when they came across suspected badger baiting. He'd helped Roger on a couple of occasions and happily they had managed to get convictions.

'So it's badgers you are checking on in the woods!' said Chas, 'Top man! If there's anything we can do just say the word. I would love to be able to see them. Any chance we can come up with you one night?' he asked as they headed for the far end of the field where the Punch and Judy was taking place.

'Thanks for the offer of help,' Tom said, 'much appreciated. I'll let you know but for now the whereabouts of the sett is best kept quiet, there's been an increase in baiting recently, so don't want to risk alerting the scum to this sett too.'

The sound of children squealing revealed that the Punch and Judy was about to start. Amy had run on ahead so Kit made her way over to sit with her whilst the others dispersed for a while to see what prizes were on offer at the various stalls and try out the Vicar's wife's home baked cakes.

Later that afternoon the men decided to try their hand at the tug of war and Kit went over to watch but Alison was feeling the heat and decided to settle down under one of the trees along the edge of the field. The long angular branches of the ancient oak acted as a giant parasol and shadowed her from the glare of the afternoon sun. She slumped down, glad to be off her feet, she felt exhausted and was pleased to be in the cool.

Amy came running over with two ice creams and sat next to her, 'Mummy sent me over with an ice cream for you,' she handed Al a vanilla cone.

'Thank you honey, this looks nice. Don't you want to see your Dad and Uncle Roger in the tug of war?'

Amy licked on her 99 and pulled out the chocolate flake and began eating it separately, 'No, I don't like the tug of war that much. They just shout and groan and then fall over!' she giggled.

They both rested their backs against the tree trunk and ate their ice creams. The sounds of laughter and shouts echoed across from the fete.

'This tree must be very old,' said Al looking up through its branches.

'Do you think it is as old as the days when the sad lady lived here?' Amy asked as she licked the ice cream as it dripped onto her fingers. She gazed up into the canopy with Al.

'Mmmm, not sure,' Al answered sleepily. The leaves above had a hypnotic effect as they rustled gently to and fro in the light breeze and she stifled a yawn.

'I know trees can be as old as the Stuart Kings,' said Amy, 'was that before or after the King who shut down the Abbey when the sad lady lived here? Do you know?'

'Tudors and Stuarts. Let me see. If my memory serves me right the Tudors were first. So how come you know about old trees and the Stuarts? I'm impressed!'

Al smiled as Amy popped the last piece of chocolate flake in her mouth.

'Terrible Tudors,' said Amy in a deep singsong voice. 'Dad and me, we watch Horrible Histories on the TV. It's fun. It once said about a Stuart King, Charles II I think it was, who hid in an old oak tree and they said the tree was still alive even now!'

'That programme sounds good. Wish I had learnt history in that way when I was your age,' murmured Al, slowly drifting off to sleep as the leaves on the branches swayed rhythmically above. She found it difficult to keep her eyes open.

'They sing lots of funny songs too,' Amy continued and began to sing softly a little song to herself.

The sound of Amy's voice as she sang about the Tudors slowly faded and disappeared, as Al's eyes became heavier. The flickering sunlight through the leaves shone orange and red behind her eyelids and the gentle coo of a wood pigeon finally sent her into a deep sleep.

The woods looked overgrown to John as he walked across the fields towards the village. He saw her standing by the house, waiting for him. Just as he knew she would be. She looked so beautiful with the sunshine on her auburn hair. She was smiling.

'I knew you would come back. I need to speak to you,' she said.

He smelt musty, of the woodland floor, as he took her in his arms and held her close.

'Mary. I've waited so long for this moment. I have been back before. You know that the Abbot sent me away to an Abbey far into the county of Essex? I obeyed him but as soon as the King took the Abbey from the brothers I made my way back with great haste to see you. But I found that you had gone.'

'I do know you returned but I was unable to speak to you. I did see you from afar. I did know you came back for me,' she said as she looked into his eyes and touched his cheek and traced his lips with her fingers.

'The villagers said your husband, Desmond the farrier, had gone away and that you were no longer living in Greysmead village. So where were you? Where were you that you could see me but not speak?'

'Sit with me John. I will tell you.' They settled down together on a tree trunk that lay close to the path. John held Mary's hand tightly.

'John, first I must tell you I never stopped loving you.'

He kissed her hand, 'Nor I, you.'

'When the Abbot sent you away I found I was with child.'

He gasped and looked into her eyes.

'Yes, I was expecting your child. A boy. He was born in late October. A healthy child, an easy birth. My husband, he knew what I had done. He knew the child was not his and whilst the child grew in my belly his anger lay hidden deep within him but finally when my time came his fury burst out with great force.'

John held her hand tightly. He was scared to hear what Mary was about to tell him.

'Desmond's Mother helped me. She could see the red fury that raged in her son's veins and feared for the child's life so she took the babe away. I did not wish to be parted from my son but I knew he would be safer away from Desmond. I made her promise she would name the child John. She gathered him up as soon as he had taken his first feed, wrapped him in a warm blanket and took him from me. It tore at my very soul to have my son taken from me so soon. It was as if my heart had been ripped out. Desmond's Mother sped out the back of the cottage with my baby, she did not wish to be seen by the villagers for they favoured Desmond to me. He had blackened my name and told them you had taken me unwillingly.'

'Desmond's Mother said that once the child had been blessed by the church she would take him to her sister at Northiam who would care for him and maybe one day, Desmond would accept the child and love him.'

'What happened to our child? Did he survive?'

'Yes, he did. Desmond's Mother had him baptised with the name John, he was a good strong lad and kind…like his father,' she smiled at John, her eyes glistening with tears, 'He was told the truth of his parentage when he was a man and so returned to his home village. Desmond had long since died, a sad pitiful creature at the end – too much mead and pent up bitterness was his taker.'

'So you were able to watch over our son when he returned?'

She nodded, 'He married a local girl and so our line continues. I felt such joy seeing him again, for the only memories I held were of him as a new born. His sweet smell as he took to my breast that one time was something I hold within me to this day. How I yearned for more.'

'Could you not have gone with him to Northiam?' John asked.

Mary's head fell to her chest and she sighed, 'As soon as Desmond knew I was ready to bring our child into the world he had taken himself off to his workshop. He vented his anger through his work. The constant hammering echoed in my head all the time I lay with the spasms surging through my body. But his anger was as red hot as the fire in his forge and he came to me after he saw his Mother pass by his workshop with the babe.'

'He came in to me, my womb still swollen, my limbs sore and tired. I was weak and as I lay he looked at me with evil in his eyes. He told me I was a whore and just as Nan Bullen had fooled King Harry, I too had seduced him by witchcraft. The hatred in his eyes, I could see it filled him to the core. He said Good King Harry had taken the Queen's life with a sword for her adultery but that was too good for me. I pleaded for mercy but he spat in my face and turned to go from the room. He stood in the doorway for a few moments and suddenly turned and stood over me. I felt his rough calloused hands grasp my neck tightly. My throat was pressed closed. I could take no breath. And he held his hands around my neck until he was satisfied my life had gone.'

John felt the salt touch his lips as the tears flowed down his cheeks, 'I should have stayed. If I had stayed I could have protected you.'

Mary held his hand, 'Hush hush. We are together now and no pain will we ever feel again. I knew you would come back. I did not allow myself to be taken into the light. I had to wait for you. I called to you when you returned to the village. I tried to let you know about our son but you could not hear me but now we can be with each other for all time.'

They clasped each other tightly, at last together again in death.

A skylark began to ascend from the field behind them, singing with joy as it rose into the heavens and the higher it climbed, the fainter the figures sitting together on the tree truck became and as the skylark's song reached a crescendo and it fell to earth, they disappeared from view.

Alison opened her eyes. Her head had slumped to one side as she had slept and she could feel the muscles of her neck complain as she moved. The song of the skylark whispered in her head as she slowly became aware of her surrounding again. Her heart raced, she could feel it as it pumped the blood around her head, the shock of witnessing Mary's account of her murder had sent her system into overdrive. She felt nauseous as she tried to gather her thoughts and attempted to get up. Her mouth was dry, she needed to get some water. The field spun as she attempted to stand and she put out her hand to the rough bark of the oak to steady herself. She couldn't lift her head without the world becoming a merry-go-round, she clung onto the tree for dear life, bent double. Unable to move, she kept her eyes firmly shut.

'Alison! Are you all right?' a voice called out to her, 'Alison?' They were getting closer. She felt an arm around her shoulder; the fresh smell of lemons filled her nostrils. Just before she collapsed completely she realised it was Roger who had come to her rescue.

Later that evening back at Kit's place, Alison was half lying on their sofa, sipping water and trying to get a grip on reality. The dream had penetrated her head so solidly that she found it difficult to sweep it away and become one hundred percent in the present. Being at Kit's house wasn't really helping, she was in the room where she knew Mary had been murdered. Pictures of the events flashed in her mind. She had been unable to verbalise what she had dreamt to Kit or Roger. They thought she was suffering from mild sunstroke.

Kit popped her head around the door, 'How you feeling now? Do you want some more water?'

Panic suddenly overwhelmed her, 'I must get away. Please, can you help me get to my house?' She tried to move from the sofa but the room began to sway.

'Hey, careful. You're in no fit state to be on your own. Don't you think you will be best staying here?' Kit pumped up some cushions behind her head and rubbed Al's hand comfortingly.

'I must go. It was Desmond. Please Kit, I cannot stay here!' she cried in desperation.

'Look if you are that determined to go to your house at least let one of us stay up there with you. How about I see if Roger will go up there with you tonight?'

Al tried to nod her head in agreement but the room began to spin again.

'Yes please,' she whispered.

Kit tapped her hand, 'Ok, I'll go get him, he's just outside with Chas and Amy. I'll be back in a moment.'

The sun was now low in the sky and out in the garden Amy and Roger were watering the pots. Kit smiled when she saw the determined little face on Amy as she lifted the heavy can over to the plants at the back of the house.

'You're doing a grand job there Amy, thank you.'

'Who's Nan Bullen Mummy? Do you know?' asked Amy as she began to trickle some water onto the fuchsias.

'Nan Bullen? I don't know honey. Why do you ask?'

'Nan Bullen? That was the name for Ann Boleyn, King Henry's second wife,' called out Chas.

'The sad lady was telling John that her husband said she was like her, that's all.'

Roger put down his watering can and went over to Amy and Kit.

'Amy. When did your sad lady say this? Did you dream about her today?' he looked up at Kit, 'It may be that Al's not suffering from sunstroke after all, maybe John and Mary came to her in a dream like Betty predicted. Betty said it could be powerful.'

'I did see John and the sad lady Uncle Roger, when I fell asleep under the tree with Alison. The sad lady was talking to John. She said her husband spat at her! That's not nice is it? I made myself wake up then, I didn't like what he was saying so I went and played on the merry go round instead.'

'Alison's asking to go up to her cottage Rog. She looks terrible, says she's got to get out of here. I said maybe you'd stay with her up there tonight. I don't want her being on her own.'

Roger began to tap a number into his phone and nodded, 'Yep, that's fine with me. You and Chas get her into the car and I'll be out in a moment. I'll just ring Betty, see what she can suggest.'

Betty had felt sure that the influence of the dream would wear off in time and two hours later, now she was up at Orchard cottage, Alison was feeling back to normal again. She still didn't feel able to discuss what she had discovered though, every time she thought back to her dream it tried again to take over her mind. Betty felt it would slowly release its grip and had asked that Alison ring her when she was happy to talk about it. She knew from her own dreams and visions what information Al most likely had discovered about Mary's life...and death. She hoped that John now knew the full story and that their souls could rest in peace at last.

Roger had told Betty about the crypt and how they had found the coffin and how scared Al had felt down there, how she had become rather panic stricken. Betty had promised she would send some crystals and herbs for Alison to place around the cottage for extra protection.

Roger pushed open the lounge door with his foot, holding two mugs of tea and balancing a packet of biscuits under his arm.

'Here we are my lady,' he joked, 'tea is served!'

Al was sitting on the floor, it was more comfortable than the garden chairs. She'd be glad to get her furniture up there after the weekend. Roger had agreed to help her move the things on Tuesday when he had finished his early shift. They could then get the van back the following day after the blessing.

'You really don't have to stay over night you know. I'm fine now really.' She opened the packet of biscuits as she looked up at Roger who was stood at the window gazing out across the fields.

He turned and smiled down at her, 'Kit would never forgive me if I abandoned you! Anyway, I've brought my sleeping bag up with me now so you're stuck with me I'm afraid!' He took a sip of his tea and turned again to look out of the window, 'It's odd, have you noticed how the lights from the village seem muted somehow, as if they are being viewed through a mist or fog?'

Al stood up next to him, 'Yes, I see what you mean. It's funny you should say that as I remember when I walked up here one day with Tom. I was sure I saw a swirling black cloud, like a thick fog next to the cottage, it was most bizarre – almost like a big swarm of insects.'

'Maybe that's all it was, and maybe it's just a cloud of mossies over the fields that I can see.'

'Could be but I think it's more than that. Tom didn't see it when I pointed out, I think he thought I was mad!'

'Good bloke Tom. Straight as a die, but so down to earth he's almost horizontal! You'd never have him believe anything he hadn't seen for himself.'

Al laughed, 'Still you seemed that way to me that night I caught Amy outside. You were rather rude to me I seem to recall! Amy and her sad lady, you wouldn't have any of it. What has changed your opinion on it all so much may I ask?'

She sat back down on the floor and he sat down cross-legged next to her.

'The night I shut the door in your face? Yeah sorry about that!' he laughed. 'Well, here's a thing. Confession time. I looked out of the window after I sent you off with a flea in your ear, felt a bit bad about it to be honest and I saw, or think I saw, just for a moment mind, a faint figure of a woman standing on the grass bank. Gave me a start I can tell you and then she just vanished! You probably think I'm the crazy one now!'

'No, not crazy. That was Mary. I also saw her that night. I'm glad you did too and that you believe me.'

'Yes I do. Perhaps when you are ready, you can tell me about what happened today? Do you know, I'm so glad that we have finally become friends. We didn't get off to a very good start did we?' He nudged her playfully with his shoulder and almost spilt his tea.

'No, that's true. I was driving a bit erratically wasn't I!'

'Hey don't admit to the crime, I might still arrest you!' he joked.

A slight feeling of apprehension crossed her mind, the remnants of the past and her life with Kenny. She wondered if the police would ever nail Mick and Ken for the murders? It was still possible the police would want to talk to her again. Does Roger know of her past she wondered? He probably had access to files and databases, maybe he'd looked up her name on his computer? She'd still be careful that's for sure. If Mick got wind that she was mixing with the police he'd be down on her she had no doubt of that.

'So, may I ask, any news from your builder friend?'

Her heart began thumping just at the thought of Mark. She shook her head and sipped her tea.

She still has feelings for him, Roger thought. Should he tell her what he knew about him? No, she'll forget him in time.

'Maybe you're best out of it. Sounds as if you had a lucky escape there,' he said.

'Yeah, maybe you're right,' she jumped up. 'Right,' she said, changing the subject, 'let's decide what room you're sleeping in. Do you want to be down here or upstairs? This carpet is very thick in here so might be most comfy.'

'I think I'd prefer upstairs if there's a room I can use?'

'Yes, you can have the room at the back. Go on up, I'll just check everything's off in the kitchen.'

Roger gathered up his sleeping bag and swung a holdall over his shoulder and went up the stairs. He made his way along the upstairs corridor, past the bathroom and the other rooms and into the back bedroom. He glanced out of the window but it was pitch black, no moon tonight, strange he could see no stars either, maybe the weather was turning? After a final look he pulled the curtains across, tugged off his trainers and threw his overnight bag into the corner. As he opened out his sleeping bag he could hear Al down below in the kitchen running the tap and the tinkle of crockery, cupboard doors being opened and closed. He'd nip into the bathroom before she came up.

He pushed at the bathroom door. It was shut tight. Must be a dodgy catch. He pushed down again on the handle, rattling it up and down and nearly fell forward as the door suddenly opened inwards.

'What are you doing? I won't be long!' Al was standing in there, dressing gown wrapped tightly around her, toothbrush in hand, looking rather annoyed.

But surely she was downstairs? 'Alison? What are you doing in…?' he began just as a loud crash echoed from the kitchen.

Chapter twenty five

'What the heck was that?' Al roughly wiped away the toothpaste from her lips and darted down the stairs behind Roger as he clambered down two steps at a time to investigate.

God what was going on? He was sure he'd heard Al down there just now, it had given him a right bloody fright when she opened the bathroom door. Once Roger was outside the kitchen he stopped. The door was closed and he could still hear noises from inside. Somebody or something was in there moving around. Al stood behind him and he felt the softness of her dressing gown through his thin shirt as she edged up against him for reassurance. Her heart was going frantic in her chest and he could feel the rushing beats hammering across from her body onto his spine. The smell of the minty toothpaste on her breath filled his nostrils as she tiptoed up and whispered into his ear.

'Don't you think we should arm ourselves with something? Shall I get the poker from the dining room, just in case?'

He nodded, turned to her and put a finger to his lips. They didn't want to let the intruder know they were on to him.

Roger started to worry. What if it was the arsehole that Mark was mixed up with? Maybe he'd come down to Sussex trying to find him? He had a right reputation. Roger wasn't sure he felt confident tackling him alone. They didn't call him Big Mick for nothing. His thoughts quickly flitted back to the moment at hand as the sounds of glass shattering onto the slate floor continued, one after the other in quick succession. There was a crash as another cupboard door slammed shut. While the constant barrage of destruction continued, Roger felt a tap on his shoulder as Al handed him a heavy metal poker. He let out a long breath, trying to slow his heart that echoed in his ears as the adrenaline rushed through his system. He swallowed, ran his tongue over his teeth; they were sticking to the inside of his dry mouth as his body prepared for the attack.

'Okay,' he hissed at Al, 'I'm going to open the door really slowly, see if I can glimpse in first, see who I am dealing with.'

Her warm lips were close to his ear as she answered, 'Be careful, the door's a bit stiff.'

It bloody well would be wouldn't it! He thought as he put his hand up to the door and very very slowly began to turn the handle.

Stay calm.

He gave the door a gentle push and it allowed a small gap to appear. In that split second of looking into the unlit kitchen Roger witnessed a hazy figure over by the cupboards, it turned as it heard the door open and glanced over and spotted Roger. In a flash it ran to the right, out of view. There was a loud thud and then all went quiet.

Roger tilted his head back and whispered to Al who was edged up close behind him, 'He's gone out of sight, towards the door of the big cupboard, the one that leads down to the crypt.'

'Well he can't get in there, I've locked it and the key's up in my bag,' Alison hissed back.

'You okay if I go for it then?' Roger asked, as his now clammy hand gripped tightly onto the poker.

'Okay, but be careful.'

'Where's the light switch?' Roger whispered back.

'Just to the left of the door.'

He nodded. Roger pushed hard at the kitchen door and it flew open to the right, there was a loud crash as it banged up against the edge of a kitchen cupboard. His fingers scrambled over the light switches and flicked them all on. His reflection jumped back at him from the glass of the kitchen window opposite, making him uneasy for a second. There were no blinds at the window and it was pitch black outside. The dark night combined with the fog hid whatever may be skulking out there from his view - but they would be able to see him.

He jumped forward into the kitchen and stood, poker held rigid in front of him as he scanned the kitchen. It was empty. Darting forward he pulled the door shut to check no one was hiding behind.

'Well Al I think we have had the invisible man visiting tonight.'

Al put her head around the door and looked slowly from the left. Her eyes took in every inch of the room. All the kitchen cupboard doors were flung open and the worktops piled high with the contents. Who ever had been there had emptied all of the units. Her eyes rested for a moment on the sink, the tap was running, the plastic bowl was full and was now cascading over into the basin.

Roger put his hand on her shoulder reassuringly, 'I can't see where they could have gone. Can you?'

She shook her head, 'Not really no, the only place would be the crypt cupboard, but as I said that is locked.'

'I best just double check that it is,' he handed her the poker. 'You okay to stand guard just in case?'

She nodded.

Roger put his hand on the metal ring handle, turned it and leant against the thick wooden door with his shoulder. It opened.

He sprang forward and spun around in the empty cupboard. His heart quickened its pace as he leant over and picked up the corner of the thick mat that lay over the entrance to the crypt. Al stood by his side holding on tightly to the poker with both hands as he deftly flicked the rug away. The flagstone entrance underneath was still secure in place; there was no sign of any disturbance. Where on earth had he gone?

Fear stroked against Alison's flesh with its icy touch. 'I don't like this Roger.'

He shut the cupboard door and glanced around the kitchen again, 'To be honest nor do I.'

'What did you actually see, did you make out any detail at all?' Al asked as she made her way across to the sink to turn off the tap. Suddenly she called out in pain, she looked down and saw that her bare feet were treading on a thick layer of broken glass and crockery. Fragments of wine glasses lay in huge shards on the kitchen floor, cutting into the soles of her feet.

'Roger!' She looked down at a river of jagged pieces of smashed plates and cups and razor thin needles of broken glass that spread out in all directions forming a barrier around her. Her feet punctured and stabbed, began to bleed. Holding the tears at bay she leant against the worktop, allowing it take some of her weight, to ease the pressure from the cuts on her feet.

'Hang on Al.' His socked feet would be cut to ribbons if he tried to get across to her. Quick, think, what could he use? He looked around the kitchen, his eyes darted past the old wooden cupboard door. Yes! He could use the thick rug covering the flagstone! Within seconds he had it rolled out over the broken glass and he'd managed to make his way to her, sweeping her up in his arms and rushed up the stairs to the bathroom.

'I'll just pop you on the loo seat while I fill up the bath with some water.' He grabbed a towel and put it on the floor underneath her bleeding feet. 'Okay, let me take a look. We may have to get you to the hospital you know. How you feeling?' He propped himself on the edge of the bath and gently rested her foot onto his knee. She winced as he carefully pulled a sharp piece of china from her heel. 'Sorry! Have you got any tweezers here?' he asked.

'Yes, in my makeup bag. Over there on the shelf below the mirror.'

He gently placed her foot back down on the now blood stained towel and began to hunt amongst the mascara and eye shadow without success and ended up empting the contents onto the bathroom floor.

'Here we are! Got them!' Her foot back on his knee, he began the delicate task of taking out the fine needles of glass embedded in the sole of her foot.

'I really don't understand how I managed to get so far without noticing. I mean, how could I have walked across it without being aware of it all? Ouch!'

'Sorry. Okay, it's all out now.... I think. Lets look at the other foot,' he lifted it onto his lap. 'There only seems to be one cut on this one, there got it!' He held a sharp needle of glass in the tweezers to show her, 'To be honest I think you got away lightly. God knows how.'

Alison twisted herself around and with Roger's help slowly dipped her feet into the bath, a cloud of blood swirled around in the water, 'God, that stings!'

'I think it's best we get them looked at properly Al. Just to be sure. I can't be certain if there's more in there or not. I wouldn't want to risk it. I'll just go get my shoes then I'll get you down to the car.'

'Can you get my handbag from my bedroom too? It's got the keys in there.'

'Will do. I won't be a second,' Roger said leaving Al in the bathroom.

Now alone, the shock of what had happened hit her. She began to sob as the tears she'd held back finally won their battle with her emotions. Her feet had started to throb, she looked down and saw the wispy ribbons of blood in the water. Panic took hold and she began to shake uncontrollably, her teeth chattering together. Moments later she felt Roger lift her up, and hold her close. She wrapped her arms around his neck and let him carry her back down the stairs, out to the car ready to head off to the hospital. Out and away from Orchard cottage.

He heard the front door slam shut. She'd gone. His anger grew. His wife had lain within another man. The whore! She needed to be punished. She'd regret her actions. He would make sure of that. He left his hiding place and went back outside. Within minutes he had disappeared from view into the whirling black fog that weaved its way around the cottage.

Al and Roger returned to the cottage on the Monday afternoon, but not before sitting for hours watching Sunday night become Monday morning as they waited to be seen down at Hastings A&E. She had finally had her feet checked out and the wounds dressed. The bleeding had made the injuries look worse than they were and armed with some spare dressings and antibiotics she was free to leave. Roger wheeled her out into the dark night air, and tucked her dressing gown tightly round her legs, which made her laugh.

'Good to see you smiling again!' he said as he pushed the wheelchair out to the car park. He helped her into the passenger seat and checked the time on his watch. 'It's nearly 5am Al, what do you want to do? Where do you want to go now? Back to Kit's?'

'I was wondering how early Betty is likely to be up and about as she's only down the road from here, isn't she? How about we drive down to the sea front for a bit and then give her an early call? Do you think she'd mind?'

'I was thinking the same thing actually. To be honest, knowing her she's probably awake but let's give it a but longer eh? She might have some ideas about tonight's events.'

They arrived at the promenade and drove eastwards. Roger slowed down near the little all night café on the seafront. He knew the owner. It was a regular haunt when he was on nights, it kept him topped up with tea and with gossip, always good to have local knowledge in his job. He parked up and nipped across the road.

'Gary! How's it going mate?'

Gary, making the most of the lack of customers was washing the floor, singing along to a sad romantic song on the radio. His rather large beer belly swayed from side to side in unison with the mop. He looked up at the sound of Roger's voice and broke out into a big smile, 'Rog! How goes it? You on duty mate?'

Roger shook his head, 'No, not today. I just wondered if a friend and I could sit in here for an hour, just to watch the sea and drink your tea? We need to kill some time.'

'No probs at all. I'll get a brew going.'

He hid his look of surprise as Roger carried Al into the cafe, decked out in her fluffy pink dressing gown and white bandaged feet.

'This is Alison,' said Roger as he positioned Al by the window so they could watch the gentle waves down on the foreshore.

She smiled up at Gary, 'Hello! Sorry to barge in on you, we've just spent an age at the hospital. It would be nice to just unwind for a bit,' she pointed at her feet, 'I cut myself on some glass!'

'You just make yourselves at home. I'll bring over some tea and then leave you in peace.'

'So any more thoughts on who or what you saw tonight Roger?' Al asked as she sipped the steaming hot tea.

He shook his head, 'The more I think about it, the more I'm sure it wasn't your average intruder.'

Al nodded, 'Nor me. I take it you mean spirits? Ghosts?'

Roger stretched back in his chair and yawed. It had been a long night. 'Oh I don't know Al,' he sighed, 'even after all that's happened lately I still find it hard to get my head around anything supernatural. There's always been feelings about Monkton Lane, all the legends and tales about the villagers and the monks have stirred up stories over the years of spooky goings on. Bad spirits lingering near the ruins. That's why as kids we never went up there much, apart from when we played dare.'

'So did you think the lane was haunted even as a kid?'

There was a hint of sadness behind Roger's steel blue eyes, 'My ex girlfriend used to live along the lane. Mrs Blackman's daughter.'

'Really? You went out with her daughter? And Mrs B used to live at Orchard cottage? I didn't know that.'

'No, not your cottage, their place wasn't far along the lane, about five minutes from the bridge.'

'Well, I never knew she lived up there, she never said. So did your ex see any spooks?'

Roger, elbows on table, rested his chin on his hands and smiled, 'She did tell me some stories about things she'd seen. If they were true I don't know. She probably made out she was scared so I'd give her a cuddle. And it worked!' he laughed.

Al smiled. She wondered what had happened to her. Why she was an ex.

As the first glimmer of sunlight began to make its self visible they headed along to see Betty. Roger had rung her from the café and as he suspected she was already up and about and sounded concerned to hear what had happened.

'Come in my dears, come in. Oh you poor lambs, that's it Rog, carry Alison through to the back. I've made space for her on the sofa.'

She sat quietly as they told her of the events at the cottage. When they had finished their tale she sat for a moment and closed her eyes, deep in thought before suddenly looking intently at Alison.

'I know you don't feel happy yet to talk about your dream of Mary and John. I do realise these things feel very powerful and you can feel out of control, so all I will ask for now is…are Mary and John together now?'

'Yes, they are. They deserve so much to be together, they were, still are, so much in love.'

Betty nodded and picked up a large wooden box from behind a stack of unfinished canvasses propped against the wall. She began to delve inside, her hands pulled out various boxes and packets. Alison looked across at Roger who smiled and shrugged as they waited to see what Betty had in store for them.

'Now my dear, these are the items I was going to pop in the post to you tomorrow, but you best take them with you now.'

She produced a couple of muslin bags from the box and began to fill them with dried leaves and small berries, then as an after thought popped a brownish shiny stone in too.

'Here Rog, take these for Al please. Now Alison I want you to hang these bags by the exterior doors. There's juniper and elderberries and some angelica root, all good for protection, plus some bronzite, it will repel negativity.' The bags now full, Betty passed them to Roger as she continued, 'Now, the crypt. Roger said you felt unhappy down there. Did it feel evil to you or just sad?'

'I'm not sure really, maybe not evil, I just felt as if I was being watched.'

'Good, good,' she muttered and began to pick out some small dark stones from her box. She held out her hand, her palm full, 'These Alison are black obsidian stones, place them on window ledges, corners of rooms, maybe pop some in the bags too. These crystals will help to protect the boundaries of the house.'

'But, they are black? I thought you said I needed crystals? I found loads of stones like these about the place when I first moved in.' Alison took one from Betty's hand and began rolling the smooth stone in her palm, finding it comforting. 'So they were there to keep bad spirits away, is that what you are saying? I chuckcd them away!'

'I should have guessed as much. I knew Ethel had laid lots of protection at the cottage long ago, when she lived there, they had no trouble at all from the Darkness, it stayed outside, couldn't get in. No wonder you had problems last night, you'd enraged Desmond I expect,' said Betty as she continued to sort through some more stones for Al.

'So you think it was this guy from 500 years ago who opened cupboards?' asked Roger shaking his head, 'I can get my head around spirits, but spirits being able to do physical things? Are you sure Betty? Seems a bit…'

'Crazy? Is that what you were going to say Roger? Did you find anyone? Did you see where they went? No!' She indicated to Al's feet, 'But you can see the damage they have done. I am certain that Desmond found a way into the house. With the blessing from the vicar and these crystals I'm sure soon all will be well again inside the house.'

'Betty? You said Ethel didn't have trouble from the Darkness, it stayed outside. What did you mean – the Darkness?' Alison asked.

'Why my dear, surely you have seen the dark mist that rises and swirls around the cottage? It is the remnants of the evil that once raged against the Abbey, the villagers, led by Desmond were fired up into a mad fury and murdered the monks in cold blood but unable to find their true quarry – Brother John, they continue to wait so they can seek their revenge.'

Chapter twenty six

Al looked out of the window as she filled the kettle and mulled over Betty's words. Outside the cottage it looked so peaceful as the fading sun teased her with snatched glimpses of the sunset bathed ruins amongst the trees. No sign of evil swirling mists tonight. Should she take what Betty said with a pinch of salt? Betty definitely was rather…what should she say…eccentric? However, Alison's throbbing foot reminded her that something strange had happened in the cottage the night before. She flinched as she hobbled over to the fridge to get some milk.

'Hey, what are you doing? You were supposed to be resting your foot!' Roger's voice interrupted her thoughts about Desmond and his revenge as he led her to one of the kitchen stools and he began to make the tea.

'How's the foot feeling now anyway? Any better?' he asked as he found a couple of mugs that hadn't been smashed in the previous night's events.

'Yes, it's not too bad really. I'll live,' she smiled.

'What do you want to do about tomorrow? You still happy to get your furniture and stuff down here? I'm sure Kit and Chas will lend a hand too.'

She nodded, 'Yes, I'm not going to let what happened last night frighten me off. I've put out all the crystals and stones that Betty gave me, you've added extra door locks so if we are dealing with physical or spiritual intruders we've got both sides covered.'

'I hope you will agree to stay back at Kit's until after the blessing though?' Roger asked, feeling concerned about leaving her at the cottage on her own overnight.

She nodded towards the big heavy door that led to the crypt, 'It's crazy but it's the coffin down there that spooks me the most. Mad I know, as the

Abbot was a good man and I'm sure wouldn't wish me any harm but I've just got a sense of ....I don't know..dread? or anger? Not sure really but it made me feel as if I was a trespasser down there.'

'Well come back to ours tonight then, we'll go get your gear tomorrow afternoon when I've finished my shift and then once the blessing on Wednesday has been done you might feel happier.'

Al didn't want to be pushed out of her own home but agreed staying at Kit's for a few more nights was the best option. She watched Roger as he sipped his tea. He had been so kind and supportive to her, so had Kit and Chas. They felt more like family than friends now. It was good to have them around, they'd helped her cope with the sadness she was keeping bottled inside her.

She so missed her Dad, dare not think about him too much otherwise she'd cry and probably never stop. His house was now under offer, and she'd nearly finished going through his things. So many memories of her childhood flooded her mind when she was there as she sifted through his drawers and cupboards. She'd recently found a batch of letters he had written to her Mum when he had worked abroad on and off for a few years back in the eighties. She had sat and read them all one afternoon with tears spilling down her face. She had lost herself for a few hours as she glimpsed into her parent's loving relationship. Would she ever have closeness with someone like they'd had? She thought back to that last night with Mark. An ache lay heavy in the pit of her stomach, What had she done wrong? Where was he? She really needed him right now.

The door to the ward swung open as the visitor arrived, eyes flicking from side to side, seeking him out.

Mark was making a very slow recovery. He no longer had a machine to assist his breathing as his lungs, although weak, now managed on their own.

Moments of consciousness were limited. Nurses were grey shadows that flashed across his vague field of vision. The sounds of the ward were muffled as his brain struggled to interpret all he heard. But there had been one noise he had recognised just a few moments ago. Nurse Atkinson had been taking his blood pressure, the touch of her hands on his arm had brought him momentarily out of his dark world. A world without clarity or substance. In that small lucid moment a blackbird began to sing just outside the ward window. A joyous, liquid melody. A memory registered in his shattered and wounded brain. Bird song, a sound he remembered hearing the morning he had woken up next to Alison.

Jeez Al. I'm so sorry.

Nurse Atkinson made a note of the blood pressure reading and began to tidy his pillows. His eyes were watering again. She took a tissue and wiped the tear that had slowly made its way down his face.

A voice interrupted her, 'How is he? He's off the ventilator, that must be a good sign.'

'Yes, he's breathing by himself now. Doctor,s hopeful,' the nurse answered.

'Has he woken up yet? Do you know if… if his brain…is it okay?'

Nurse Atkinson smiled kindly at the visitor and shook her head, 'I'm sorry, he's not out of the woods yet. It's early days.' As she began to leave she said, 'Talk to him. It's always worth talking to him, he may hear you.'

A faint rumble could be heard as the tea trolley was wheeled along as it headed for the wards. Coughs and grunts echoed from along the corridor as patients that were able, sat up and made themselves ready for the mid morning ritual of a warm drink and biscuit. No such ceremony for Mark as he lay still whilst his visitor continued to talk to him, hoping some of the words would be heard.

The sunlight shot its rays through the gap in the curtains and slowly filtered through into Alison's slumbers. She blinked, open her eyes, the glare of the sun made her squint and she turned on her side and snuggled under the covers for a while longer. Her eyes caught sight of the clock. 2pm! What? She sat up quickly and swept her hands through her hair. Had she really slept that long?

It wasn't surprising really, it had been a mad and busy few days. Roger and Chas had helped her move her stuff down on Tuesday and yesterday had been a very emotional day when the vicar came down to perform the blessing. His soft voice had murmured words to cleanse and bless the cottage. He'd taken it all very seriously and had gone from room to room with his holy water and swaying a silver vessel with its burning incense, the smell of which still lingered.

Somehow he had managed to obtain the Bishop's agreement to take the Abbot's coffin away and it was now stored somewhere safely with the church authorities ready for its burial in the churchyard.

An archaeologist, Alex Meyer, from the local council had also come along to attend the service down in the crypt before the Abbot's remains were removed. When everyone had begun to disperse she had hung back to talk to Al and had taken a look at the seal and crosier.

'Would you mind if I took them away today for analysis and to record my findings?' Alex had asked Alison as she examined the seal closely, slightly perturbed by the roughly scratched words on the back.

'Yes of course you can. I was hoping they might eventually be able to be kept at the museum in town?'

'Yes, I would think so,' Alex had replied vaguely, her thoughts still taken up with the seal, as she continued to make out the wording on the back.

'So where was it you said you found this?' she looked up at Al with a serious frown on her bespectacled face.

'It was just lying by the skirting board,' Al told her, letting her believe it was on the floor in the cottage. How could she tell the truth – that it appeared in ball of light when she was in her room at the pub! She'd never believe that. Best keep that fact quiet.

'Have you read the scratched writing on the back? I wonder who put that there?' Alex's eyes went back to the seal as she read, 'Absolvo purgatorio….release purgatory. I wonder who is asking that?'

'I wish I knew,' Alison had replied, 'If I knew I would do all I could to help them.'

Alison wondered if she would ever know the answer as she slipped out from under the covers and carefully slid on some sandals, her cut foot complained slightly at the pressure. She pulled open the curtains, the muslin bag of herbs and stones swayed on the curtain rail above and she savoured the view outside for a few moments. Today she felt as if she could conquer anything that came her way. The house really did feel tranquil and at peace since yesterday's blessing and last night she had slept so well. Roger had wanted to stay with her. Just in case, he had said.

'In case of what? I'll be fine now, honest!' she had told him as he stood at the door about to leave.

He held her arms and looked intently into her eyes, 'If you are sure?'

'Yes! Now go!' she laughed.

He had leant forward and given her a light kiss on the cheek, 'Okay. Okay! I'm going.'

She smiled at her memories as she stood at the window. She was glad he wasn't pushing for more. Just friends. That's all she could cope with. A sudden flicker of sunlight alerted her to movement along the lane. She tried to peer out and see what or who it was, without success, but then the doorbell sounded.

Oh goodness, who can that be? She wasn't even dressed! She quickly pulled on her jeans and a t-shirt and made her way down the stairs.

The doorbell rang again.

'Okay Okay, I'm on my way. Keep your hair on!'

She opened the door to find Tom decked out in his camouflage trousers, laden with rucksack, tripod and small telescope, binoculars around his neck and a plant spilling compost that she just managed to catch before it fell onto the floor.

'Oh thanks Alison. It was for you anyway!' he laughed, 'It's a welcome to your new home present.' He stood on the doorstep looking decidedly awkward.

'Thank you!' she grinned, 'You better come in.'

Tom followed her as she made her way through to the kitchen and popped the plant by the sink.

'It's Myrtle, I had a read up, you plant it outside to protect the house.'

'Well thanks Tom,' she touched his hand, 'I didn't think you believed in all that? Mmm, a nice smell,' she said, sniffing at the rich green leaves.

'No I don't, but I know you do, so thought it might help. You don't mind me calling over, do you? Roger said you'd moved in Tuesday and as I leave tomorrow I hoped I could get to see you before I went.'

Alison began laughing, 'So were you keen to come and see me or was it my crypt?'

'Am I that transparent? I'm sorry. I did want to see you too.'

'Don't worry, I'm only messing Tom.' Al opened the fridge and looked at the near empty shelves, 'Look, I have only just woken up, it's been a pretty full on couple of days and now I'm starving. Have you eaten yet?'

He shook his head, 'No, I was going to have this. I bought it at Mrs Blackman's shop.' He rummaged in his rucksack and held up a limp and forlorn looking sandwich.

'Ukk! How's about I cook us a mushroom omelette and then we can go and have a look for these bats of yours.'

They re-emerged from the undercroft later that evening after their wildlife expedition. They had journeyed a little further into the crypt than Al had before and Tom told her he could see signs of bat activity. She had looked up into the roof space of the under croft expecting to see lots of little dark creatures hanging upside down.

'No, not all bats do that. The Natterer bat crawls into small gaps to roost and also when they hibernate. There are lots of crevices up there for them to squeeze into. Just wish I knew how they were getting in down here.'

'It is a mystery. There's no obvious sign of an exit is there?' Al replied, hoping they weren't going to venture further into the bowels of the crypt.

They'd discovered that two small alcoves hidden away in the dark were actually archways leading off in opposite directions, they had no idea how far they went, but it looked as if the tunnels went a lot further than just under the cottage. The strong and rather disgusting smell that Tom had informed her was from the bats droppings, soon became very over powering and Tom had reluctantly agreed with Al that they call it a day.

They sat later that evening discussing their findings over a plate of cheese on toast. Al made a mental note to go to the supermarket the next day. Tom had helped her finish off what little food she had brought with her. Not that she minded, she enjoyed his company, albeit somewhat serious at times. But he did make her realise that she had a strong desire to get more involved in animal welfare and was planning on asking him if she could help, perhaps do some volunteering.

Tom cut his knife into the melted cheese and said, 'I was thinking maybe I could go back down one night, when the bats had gone out to feed, so not to disturb them, have a look deeper into the crypt. See if I can locate the entrance.'

'So when are you likely to be back at Greysmead again? I thought you said they hibernate over the winter, will you be back before that?'

He nodded, waving his knife as he finished chewing, 'Mmmm, yep. I was thinking of coming back next week actually. I've got to go and monitor a sett up near Tunbridge Wells but I'm a little concerned about your sett. A bit of suspicious activity over the past week, think I want to keep a closer eye.'

'Really?' Al raised her eyebrows, 'What kind of things?'

'Nothing concrete, just a few vehicles hanging about that I don't recognise, nothing much to go on, just got a feel for it.' He rested his knife and fork and sat back, 'Thanks Al. That was great. I was thinking, perhaps when I come back we can arrange that you, Chas & Kit can come up and watch the badgers one night?'

'Oh yes please! I'd love to see them. I was also thinking about asking you about me helping more. Be some sort of volunteer?' She took their plates over to the sink and switched on the kettle, 'Coffee?'

He nodded, 'If you are serious, they always need people up at the sanctuary. Perhaps you could help out there? I'll take you along to meet them sometime.'

'Great! I'd like that.' She brought over the coffees and sat back down on the kitchen stool next to him, 'I'm a little concerned about what you've said about this sett though. Vehicles hanging about? Tell me more, maybe it's just someone I know. Can you give me anymore info?'

Tom grabbed his rucksack and pulled out a ring binder, 'I keep a record in here. Let's have a look.' He opened up the file and it was full with pages and pages of photographs. 'I usually click at anything I feel looks a bit dodgy. Always handy to have a record, just in case. Now let me see.' He began flicking through the sheets, 'These are too early on in the year, we need to look at the more recent ones.'

'Hey, hold on! Stop a minute,' Al put her hand out onto the sheets, 'Go back a few pages will you?'

He flicked back the pages in the file slowly and Al suddenly called out.

'Stop! There it is. Let me see,' she grabbed the file and studied the photograph. 'When did you take that?'

'This one? I think it must have been around June. Or late May maybe?'

'So was it taken up in the woods? Up near here?' Alison frowned.

'Yes, just up in Monkton Lane. I remember it quite well. I'd been in the woods at the Sett and was about to head back to the pub when I heard voices. Angry - sounded like they were arguing. One of them had quite a coarse voice. Both Londoners. I was worried they might disturb the badgers. As I got nearer I managed to get a couple of furtive shots of them, just in case they were up to no good.'

'Did you hear what they were arguing about?' Al asked.

'No not really, anyhow the row didn't go on for long, they soon began laughing and one of them said about going for a pint.'

'Are you sure? So do you think they were friends?'

'Oh yes, I remember thinking that I hoped they weren't going to the Jolly Abbot for a drink as they were really loud and uncouth. Then that one,' Tom pointed at the photograph, 'he suggested they go back to Stockwell to the club, so I was quite relieved as I was looking forward to going back to the pub for a quiet drink myself.'

Alison's rapid heart sounded in her ears, pounding away at the realisation of the meaning of Tom's words. She couldn't get her head round it. Could it be true?

'Alison. Are you ok? You've gone very pale.'

He'd betrayed her. He didn't care for her at all. It was all one big joke to him.

'Alison?' Tom said again, 'Do you know these men?'

'Yes I think I do…' She rubbed her fingers on her brow, her head spinning with the revelation, 'I'm sorry Tom I've got a terrible migraine. Do you mind if we call it a day?'

A brief feeling of rejection was replaced with compassion when he saw her discomfort and Tom jumped up and gathered up his things.

'No, no, that's fine. No problem. Have you got anything to take for it?' He began sorting through a pocket in his rucksack, 'I've got some tablets in here I think.'

'No, don't worry, I've got some.'

His kindness touched her wounded heart. With her eyes now pools of unshed tears they headed for the front door.

Ever practical Tom said, 'Must have been the cheese that brought it on Alison. Drink plenty of water,' he made to go and then turned and gave her a quick hug. 'Take care. I'll see you next week,' he mumbled shyly into her ear before he quickly pulled himself away, embarrassed by his own show of affection.

'See you next week, yes.'

She closed the door to the world and her hand flew to her mouth as she tried to stifle the sobs that began to form in her throat.

'Oh God, I can't believe it! Oh Mark. I loved you,' she wailed and ran up the stairs to the bathroom as her food made a play to return and made her retch.

She slumped by the loo, her face awash with tears, feeling as if her heart had been smashed into a thousand pieces.

God what a fool she'd been. Taken in by his charm. Her suspicions had been right, that's where the receipt she had found had come from. It had been his. He must have worked for Mick after all. She was just one big game to them. 'Let's see if Kenny's wife will fall for him. Let's have a laugh.'

Mark must have been sent to keep an eye on her, make sure they were safe. Make sure she didn't talk to the police. Well maybe it was time she did. Maybe she should turn this around and stop being the victim. She had the upper hand. She could tell the police all she knew. Mick and his cronies couldn't get to her down here. Her mind suddenly flashed her a reminder. Because he had worked on the place, Mark had a key to Orchard Cottage. Shit! Maybe it had been him who got in the other night!

Chapter twenty seven

The following morning Al sat at the breakfast bar and aimlessly pushed around the cornflakes in a bowl, feeling unable to eat. A sparrow was happily chirping on the window ledge outside hoping for some titbits, oblivious to the sadness that filled every cell of Al's body. Her stomach felt tight with the anguish of seeing Tom's photo of Mark and Kenny and the knowledge they were in league together. Mark wasn't the innocent builder after all. Not the knight in shining armour who had stepped into the breech when the man her Dad had recommended had suddenly been taken ill.

Oh God, no! Her stomach muscles tightened their grip at the thought. Hadn't her Dad's builder been found lying unconscious outside his garage? What if he hadn't had a heart attack? Had Big Mick arranged a little accident so Mark could step in and keep an eye on her? She should try to get hold of the builder, try to find out what happened. What was his name? Peter? Peter what? She couldn't remember and she could no longer ask her Dad.

Anger took hold and she slammed the cereal bowl onto the draining board. The spoon jumped out and flew down into the sink, clanging loudly against the porcelain, making the sparrow outside fly off in fright. Determined that she wasn't going to allow yet another man wreck her life, she took a final swig of the black coffee and forced herself to head down to Bexhill to do food shopping, not that she felt like eating ever again.

Her eyes were puffy from spending most of the night in a fitful sleep. Every time she had woken, tears had trickled down her face as she thought over all the good times she had spent with Mark. She desperately tried to think of innocent reasons why he'd be out with Kenny up in the woods, seemingly all matey, but all scenarios led to him working for Big Mick and to her being a complete fool.

In the small hours of the night it had dawned on her how so alone in the world she was. There she was, rattling around on her own at Orchard Cottage. Her dream cottage. It was more like a nightmare cottage. The day she had come to view the house her life had been on the up. She was escaping from London and Kenny, a new home, new village. Her Dad had still been alive. And now…what had she got? A cottage that had housed a body in the cellar, possible evil spirits lurking outside and a romance that failed within a few months of it starting, which then turned out to be no romance at all, just a big joke by a bunch of sick and evil thugs.

She had thought long and hard about going to the police about the murders and giving a witness statement but she didn't think she had the emotional strength to deal with it all. She'd have to go to court, have to see Mick and Kenny again and then most probably Mark. It was only her word against theirs, they'd find a way to knock her down in flames. No, she would say nothing.

She'd been relieved when she'd remembered that Mark didn't have a key after all. She'd recalled that the workmen Mark had put in place around the time he went missing had given the key back the day they finished the work. Anyhow, Roger had added extra locks so the cottage was secure. It was unlikely Mark had broken in that night after all. She'd been mad to think he would have done something that destructive. But did she know him at all? Did he ever have any feelings for her? She thought he had, he'd been very convincing in her bed. Her heart sank when she thought back to that night.

She sat in the supermarket car park with fresh tears on her face. Pull yourself together woman! Wiping her nose, she checked herself in the mirror. Oh my God, what a mess. Her eyes had almost disappeared; they were so swollen from so many spent tears. Come on Al, you can get over this, she told herself and jumped out of the car.

She was leaning on her trolley, letting it take the weight from her throbbing foot, as she tried to decide what butter to buy when she realised someone had been calling her name.

'Alison! Alison! Wait up!'

She turned to see her Aunt and Uncle heading her way.

'Hello! What are you both doing here? I thought you were still away in France?' she said as she tried to keep upbeat and cheery, didn't want her Aunt Norma to worry about her. 'When did you get back?' she asked, feeling so relieved to see that they'd finally returned from visiting their son and new grandson across the channel.

Norma had been concerned about leaving Alison to deal with her Father's estate but when their first grandchild had been born, Alison convinced them she'd be okay and the doting grandparents headed off for an extended trip to France.

Norma gave her a hug, 'We got back yesterday morning, thought we best pop into town for some shopping. Has that gorgeous hunk Mark finished your place yet? Have you moved in?' she said and then saw the look on Al's face, 'Hey, are you alright Ally sweetheart? You look terrible!'

'Thanks!' Al gave a watery smile, eyes brimming, 'Yes I'm fine.'

Her Uncle Joe came across from one of the displays and slung some bags of vegetables into their trolley.

'Hello there my love. How you holding up?' he smiled, and seeing Al's eyes filling with tears pulled her to him. His huge arms felt comforting and secure and Al felt like a little girl again as he held her close and said quietly, 'It'll get easier, you'll see.'

She nodded, unable to speak.

'Oh Ally, oh lovie, don't cry.' Norma held Al's hand, her own eyes spilling over. 'Your Dad wouldn't want you to be so upset. Come on sweetheart, don't cry.' Norma pushed the trolley towards her husband. 'Joe, would you mind finishing off here?' She turned to Al, 'Have you got a list, you got much to buy? Your Uncle Joe can get it for you, can't you Joe? Why don't you come back to ours for lunch.'

Al shook her head, 'I'll be alright. You've only just got back from time away, you don't want to be messing with lunch guests.'

'Guests? You're not a guest. You're family and you look as if you need us. Come on, you and me, we can go back in your car. Joe?' she turned to her husband, 'Can you just get some essentials for Al? You know, milk, bread, veg…' she looked at Al, 'Anything in particular you need?'

Al shook her head, 'Anything really. I've got nothing in at home at all. I seem to have run out of everything.'

'You're okay with that Joe? We'll see you back home.'

He nodded. Best not to argue with Norma when she was on a mission.

'Look at her, she's worn out poor lamb,' Norma said to her husband as she pulled the door to the lounge shut leaving Al sleeping on their sofa as they went into the kitchen and cleared away the dishes.

When Al had arrived back at her Aunt Norma's house earlier she had spent a few hours opening her heart, telling her about Mark. She filled her Aunt in on everything that had happened with him, how they had taken it slowly at first. How understanding he'd been, how funny and loving.

'I know lovie, he seemed such a kind young man that day I first met him when he brought you back from Maria's, when your poor Dad had just passed away,' Norma said patting Al's hand and handing her another tissue, 'So what went wrong do you think?'

Al wasn't sure how much to tell. If she told her Aunt about Tom's photo of Kenny and Mark in the woods, how she now realised that Mark was a con man, and worked for Big Mick, how could she explain that? They didn't know the true extent of why she split up with Kenny. They knew he was a rogue but was blissfully unaware of just how evil he was. In the end she said she had discovered Mark had betrayed her with someone else. Let her Aunt think he was two-timing her.

It was later, over lunch when Al was feeling slightly less weepy that she began to tell them about the cottage and her new life up at Greysmead. She told them about all the various villagers, Mrs Blackman the nosey Postmistress, Susie and Steve, and then began to tell them about the Mitchell family.

'They really are a lovely family. Kit and her husband Chas are so nice and have helped me out a lot. They feel more like family than friends to be honest,' Al said as she took another mouthful of curry, realising just how hungry she was.

'It's nice you've made friends,' said her Aunt, 'I'm glad you've settled in well. We'll have to come up and see it now it's all finished. I was telling your cousin Simon about it all, he said again how strange it was how everything has gone round full circle.'

Al looked up, 'What do you mean, full circle?'

'I don't think we had a chance to tell Al at the time, Norma. It was just before her Dad died,' butted in Uncle Joe.

'Tell me what?'

'Well,' her Aunt began, 'You know Simon started researching the family history?'

Al nodded, 'Yeah, he was looking into Granny Martin's line wasn't he?'

'That's right, well her maiden name was Collins and Simon tracked the family right back to…when was it Joe? 1500's wasn't it?'

'Something like that Norm. We've got it all on the computer, we'll give you a copy later,' he said.

'Gosh, that's rather impressive! He's done well. So why the full circle?' Al asked again.

'Seems the family used to live in that village of yours, you've really gone back to the family roots. Isn't that strange, that you'd be drawn back there.'

Al nodded as she finished her meal. So maybe Aunt Betty had been right about her link to Brother John! She kept quiet, her Aunt and Uncle wouldn't be open to all the happenings at Greysmead but to Al this new information explained the pull the place had on her.

The following morning, after a good nights sleep in her Aunt's spare room, Al loaded up her Jeep with all the shopping her Uncle had bought for her.

'I can't thank you enough for the meal and for getting all this shopping for me,' she said, loading the last carrier bag in the back and grabbed her purse from her handbag. 'You never said how much I owe you.'

'Put that away Ally, it's on us, call it a house warming gift!' Norma laughed. 'Come here,' she pulled Al to her and gave her a hug. Al felt the tears begin to form. 'Hey don't start that again!' Norma joked, 'Still we can use those tears to water the garden!'

'We couldn't believe how many plants we'd lost in this drought whilst we've been away. It's peeing down over in France! Typical!' said Joe as he pushed the Jeep door shut.

Al began to drive off and waved as Norma called out, 'We'll speak to you tomorrow, arrange to come up and see you soon.'

Al arrived back at the cottage feeling a bit brighter. She found sharing some of her troubles with her Aunt had helped, got it into perspective a bit. Norma had reminded Al that Mark had been the first man she'd been with since the break with Kenny, which to be honest had still been raw and painful. Maybe she'd fallen for Mark on the rebound. She'd try to push the good memories of him away, he was a scumbag that was all she needed to remember. So the next week she put all her attention into the cottage, any negative thoughts she immediately banished from her mind. The cottage had a feeling of peace and harmony again since the blessing. There had been a few occasions when Al thought she heard fragments of words floating up from the under croft below, soft gentle sounds, like religious chanting. She pushed the whispered voices to the back of her mind and kept the door to the cupboard that led down to the crypt firmly locked.

September soon arrived and with it an early dose of autumn. The hot still summer suddenly turned into grey days with spells of drizzly rain that chilled to the bone. The mist clung to the spider's webs as they spread across the hedgerows like lace curtains glimmering in the scant daylight.

Al had a call from Tom, he told her he planned on visiting Greysmead the following weekend and suggested a trip up to see the badgers with Kit and Chas. She thought it was a great idea and would get hold of the Mitchells to arrange it. She hadn't seen Kit or Roger since her return from her Aunt's, they'd all been busy. Roger had been away on a course and Kit was getting Amy ready for the start of the new school year.

Al decided she'd pop out see Kit later and tell her about the badger watch and suggest they make an evening of it, all come back to Orchard cottage afterwards for a meal. Alison slid the phone back into its cradle by the window and smiled as she watched an industrious squirrel helping himself to the rosehips along the front fence before scampering across to the footpath to bury his booty in his skilfully dug larder.

She'd have to get some more bits in for her larder too. Uncle Joe had been sweet when she'd been down at Bexhill and had bought her some groceries, it had been enough to keep her fed and watered for a while but not enough to feed a badger watching party. Feeling excited at the thought of her first dinner guests she headed along to the dining room. It would be great to have a dinner party in there at last.

She loved the old room with its stone mullioned windows and huge inglenook fireplace. She'd bought a huge replica tapestry from a shop near Battle to hang on one of the walls. It added to the room's old flavour with its muted greens and red threads depicting a scene of castles and knights. Only days before, her latest acquisition had arrived, an exquisite Elizabethan style oak sideboard she'd ordered some months before from a Kent company specialising in reproduction furniture. She was delighted with her purchase and couldn't wait to have everyone there so she could show it off.

An icy chill touched her neck and she shivered, it was certainly getting cold at the far end of the cottage. The thick stone walls were great in the summer, they kept it cool inside when the sun was beating down but now were showing their flaw. It was decidedly chilly in there, the radiators didn't seem to take the edge of the cold. She looked across at the fireplace. Of course! She could have a log fire when she has her visitors! Would she have to get it swept first? Al ducked her head under the long oak beam and stood up inside the fireplace. The aroma of wood smoke and soot filled her lungs. Looking upwards, the brick lined interior looked relatively clean but it bent round at an angle so she couldn't see what state it was in. Not that she would have a clue if it needed sweeping or not. Maybe she should check with Kit, she had an open fire, maybe she knew someone who could sweep it for her.

Inside the fireplace it was at least half a metre wider each side than the exterior surround and it occurred to Al that it would be a good place to hide. Could this be where the intruder hid that night? But if so, how would they have got from the kitchen to the dining room? Al began to look closely at the bricks and tried to find a secret doorway, maybe there was a passageway through to the crypt cupboard. They had things like that in old houses didn't they? It was as she was running her hands across the interior that she noticed that high up, about full arms length there was a shelf cut into the wall.

Her injured foot complained as she stood on tiptoes and her fingers flayed out over the shelf as she attempted to discover if it stored anything interesting. The rough stone scuffed at her skin as her fingertips rubbed across years of gritty brick dust. She reached her fingers further inwards, slowly edging in as far as she was able, stretching up higher, her tightened leg muscles crying out as she pushed them to full capacity. She felt their relief as she quickly pulled her hand away when she made contact with something cold. It had felt like metal.

Unable to reach up high enough, she rushed and got a stool from the kitchen and climbed up higher inside the chimney so she could peer onto the shelf. There she discovered a tin, its red painted lid was now faded through age and it had a thick covering of dust and grit. Excited at her find, Al carefully lifted it from its hiding place and noticed that it concealed another object almost hidden from view. There was something wedged at the back of the shelf, wrapped in brown sacking. Putting the tin on the floor she reached back in and pulled at the item, tugging at the canvas, which was now rotting and falling apart with age. A hole in the sacking had got caught on a metal hook imbedded on the shelf and she had to wrench at it to try to get it free. It didn't budge at first but then one final yank and the canvas material and its secret store suddenly flew out at Al's face and two eye sockets stared blindly towards her.

Alison screamed.

Chapter twenty eight

The mummified cat had gazed blankly at Al as she gingerly picked it up from where it had fallen in the hearth. She bundled it in the rubbish bag she'd grabbed from the kitchen.

Her lips turned downwards with disgust as she tied up the bag and deposited the leathery deceased feline outside into the bin before she headed down to the village to meet up with Kit. As she shut the door behind her and made her way up the lane she was unaware of the whispers that filled the cottage, grating harsh voices floated around, pleased that at last they had gained entry. They would wait for her to return, now that she had opened the door to them, they could complete their work.

'God, it was disgusting! How the poor creature got onto the shelf and died is beyond me,' Al said as she sat over lunch with Kit in the restaurant at the Abbot.

'That sounds horrible. I wonder how long it had been trapped in there? Maybe it was ill, they say cats hide away to die.'

'Mmm, possibly… actually thinking about it, that theory wouldn't work. It was wrapped in a hessian bag. Someone must have put it there. Evil bastards!' Al's strength of feeling at the thought of the cat being ill-treated made her even more resolved to get involved in helping at the animal sanctuary.

'There certainly are some horrible people about. Did you look in the tin you said you'd found?' Kit asked as she waved to attract Jim's attention to get the bill.

'Yes I did. It was full of an assortment of items, there were similar stones to the ones Betty gave me, a silver crucifix, other bits and pieces that to me looked like good luck type charms and a little corked bottle tied up with string.'

'Sounds like a Mary Poppin's song!' laughed Kit, 'Still now we know what an evil arse Desmond was, sounds like you need all the protection you can get.' She beckoned again to Jim, 'What's the matter with him today? He seems to be in a world of his own.'

Susie rushed through from the kitchen with a tray of food for an elderly couple seated by the window and Al managed to nab her as she went past.

'Susie, sorry to trouble you love, but we're after the bill. We can't get your Dad's attention. Is he okay?' Al asked.

'Yes Suz, he seems a bit distracted. Everything alright?' Kit chipped in.

'Sorry, I'll get you the bill in a jiffy,' Susie answered, looking harassed, 'and sorry about Dad, he's just a bit disappointed that's all. His cousin was planning on joining him in the business, becoming a partner, but has changed her mind,' Susie told them, 'I was surprised at Dads reaction. He really shouted at her down the phone, he seems really stressed out about it.'

'Everything's going okay with the Pub though isn't it? I wouldn't have thought you'd have a problem financially,' said Kit looking around the packed eating area, 'You always do a good trade.'

Susie shook her head, 'No, it's all fine as far as I know. Sorry, got to get this food over to the table. Be back shortly.'

It was later, back at Kit's place that they expressed their worries to Chas who had arrived back early from a job down at Seddlescombe. He sat with them, drinking his coffee as they speculated about Jim and the Jolly Abbot.

'Hope he's not in trouble. That pub has been in his family for donkey's years. It would be a shame if he had to sell up and it got into the hands of an outsider.' Chas said and looked at Al, her eyebrows raised at his faux pas. 'Opps, sorry Al, no offence to you!' he laughed.

Al delved into her bag and pulled out an envelope she'd picked up from the post office earlier.

'Well… actually…' she grinned taking out the CD that her Uncle had posted to her. 'In my hand here I have details that apparently shows I'm not really an outsider after all!'

While Chas switched on his computer so they could all look over the information on the CD, she filled them in about her cousin and how he had researched her Gran's family. They all sat together on the sofa, Chas in the middle with the laptop perched on his knee. He opened the document and they began reading.

After a few minutes of quiet as they studied the information Al exclaimed, 'Oh my goodness. Do you see that? This is just amazing!'

Kit's finger pointed at the family tree on the screen, 'So your ancestor is this Thomas Collins?'

'Yep,' Al nodded, 'my Granny, Dad's Mum, well her maiden name was Collins, this is her line.'

'So this Thomas Collins married a Matilda Parsons and you think she is part of my family?' Kit grinned, feeling as excited as Alison and leaned across closer to peer at the screen on her husband's lap.

'Blimey, your cousin's done well piecing all this together,' Chas said.

'Do you remember?' Al asked excitedly, 'Mark got a load of info from the library about the Abbey, we also had details of some of the parish records,' she indicated to the tree on the screen, 'Look, this Matilda's line goes right back to John Parsons, he was the little baby born to Mary and fathered by Brother John.'

'So let me get this right,' asked Kit, 'Does this mean Desmond Parsons wasn't really my blood relative?'

'That's right. The only baby Desmond ever fathered died when it was very young.'

'So this John Parsons was the baby that Mary had just before she was killed?' Kit said.

'That's right. He was Brother John's child.'

'But the baby was given the surname Parsons? For appearances sake I assume. And when he grew up and got married, one of his descendants went on to marry into your Collins family?' She looked at Al who nodded in agreement, 'And Roger and I, we descend from this John Parsons too?'

'Yep! Got it in one!' said Chas, 'Which also means your maiden name by rights isn't really Parsons!'

'What is it then?' Kit frowned.

'God knows! Don't think we know the last name of Brother John do we? Anyway doesn't matter after all this time, does it?'

'I'm glad to know I'm not descended from Desmond, that's for sure. We'll have to fill Roger in on all this when he gets back.' Kit looked at her watch, 'He shouldn't be long now, depends on the London traffic I expect.'

'London? I thought he'd finished his course up there?' asked Al.

'Yes he has, but he's been seconded back to the Met for a while, back at Battersea where he used to work. There's some big operation going on, they are trying to nail some slime ball who is supplying dodgy drugs. They are sure it's someone he had dealings with in the past so they wanted his input into the investigation.'

'I think I read about a big drug operation in the paper. That female singer, Donna Peters, she nearly died after taking some coke and has now vowed to help the police nail the supplier.'

'Yeah, it's probably the same thing. Rog can't tell us too much but reading between the lines they've been trying to get this bloke for years for lots of things but he always seems to come up smelling of roses.'

'Well wish Roger luck from me!' said Al as she gathered up her things, 'I'll catch him some other time but must get back and ring my Aunt and Uncle and let them know I got the CD and the amazing news that you and I are distantly related.' she laughed and hugged Kit as she headed out.

'I'll let Roger know everything and also tell him about the badger watch and meal at the weekend,' Kit said as they made their way to the door with Al, 'but I'm not sure if he will be free. I can't keep tabs on his shifts these days, they seem to be constantly changing.'

Chas stood at the door with his arms looped round his wife's waist, 'Still won't be that long before we won't know what he's up to at all!'

Al frowned, 'Why's that? Is he going away?' she asked, aware of a pang of dismay at the thought.

'Roger move away from Sussex? I don't think so!' Kit laughed, 'He only moved in with us when he joined the Sussex Police, he's looking at getting a place of his own. Think he's looking down by the coast, Hastings way.'

'Glad he'll still be about, he's been a good friend. Tell him about the meal will you? I'll get back to you when I know what time Tom wants us up in the woods on Saturday,' Al said and headed back to the cottage.

Alison could hear the voices as she made her way up the path. She stood and listened. Was it coming from inside or round the back of the cottage? She wasn't sure. She had passed Jim up at the turning into Monkton Lane. He seemed to be having some sort of heated discussion with Steve's Uncle. She had hooted at them, they had been blocking her way but they turned and made off into the woods without giving her a second glance. Could it be them she could hear?

She strained her ears to catch the sounds but the air was silent again. There was a sudden gust of wind and the rooks in a nearby tree headed for the skies making a loud and noisy furore as they swept into the air, circling above the cottage. They flew around in the wind, shouting and croaking as they looped above the cottage, calling words of warning to Alison that she failed to comprehend.

As soon as Al went into the kitchen it hit her. A rancid smell filled her nostrils and made her gag. She rushed to open the back door and stood looking out towards the ruins taking in gulps of fresh air, as she debated where the odour could be coming from. She suspected it was the crypt but was uneasy about going down there on her own.

Then she heard the voices again. What on earth was it? She was now certain it was coming from inside, from behind the big wooden door that led to the undercroft. She held her hand up to her nose and mouth to shield her from the smell and tentatively went back into the kitchen. The voices from the crypt were clearer now.

The soft gentle tones of chanting edged their way through the cupboard door into the kitchen. It wasn't frightening and Al found herself surprised at this. It was soothing and she smiled as she listened to the beautiful voices of the monks. The effect of the chanting seemed to counteract the terrible stench in the room, almost smother it, banish it. Al stood mesmerised as the chanting continued to fill the kitchen.

'Stop it, you dirty immoral monks,' a coarse voice suddenly hissed close to her ear.

She broke from her reverie and jumped.

'Who's that?' she looked around, the kitchen was empty, the chanting now lessened in volume and the disgusting odour had become stronger again. She then felt the grasp of fingers on her shoulders. A smell of stale beer filled her nostrils as words hissed in her ears.

'Bring me John,' it whispered as the strong hands made their way up to her throat.

Her arms flew up to protect herself, to pull the hands away but the only thing her fingers made contact with was her own neck. There were no other hands there but still she felt his palms, pressing harder as his thumb pushed onto her windpipe.

Then the rasping voice spoke again, 'John must pay for Mary's death. You know where he is.' The hand jerked at her throat tighter, restricting her breathing.

'He's gone, John has gone,' she half whispered, her heart racing with fear.

'You lie!' the harsh voice replied.

'Please listen to me.' she felt the hands tighten their grip on her throat, 'He has gone. He went into the light with Mary.'

The smell of decomposing flesh filled her lungs as she struggled to breath. She felt his hands grasp her neck, harder and firmer.

'I loved Mary and that monk took her from me. Do you know how that feels? Do you? I married for life. Until death we do part,' he said, as his putrid breath wafted across her face. But the smell didn't reach her senses. There was buzzing in her head now, the room faded from view. Her lungs were almost empty, her chest tight, the few remnants of air gurgled up through her constricted airways.

This is it. This is the end. She was too tired to fight. A rainbow of colours filled Al's senses, strange abstract patterns zigzagged in her mind as the spectrum of shades began the dance of death in her brain as it began to shut down.

In the distant recesses of her mind a familiar voice pushed its way forward.

'Come on. Al! Wake up! Come on, breath woman!'

The swirling colours slowed down their ballet in her mind and began to take more form as her lungs welcomed the new life that was breathed into them.

Al's eyes began to seek out shapes in the blackness that now appeared behind her lids as they slowly flickered open. Gradually the room and Rogers's worried face came into view as he knelt across her, breathing precious life into her lungs.

He leant back and smiled as he saw her eyes lock onto his. 'Welcome back'

'Are you sure you don't want me to get the doctor?' Roger asked a few hours later as he continued to gently massage her feet.

Al shook her head and sipped some more water. It was just nice sitting there on the sofa, her legs stretched out on Roger's knees. Her throat felt bruised and sore but there was no visible sign of the assault. No marks or redness.

Roger had told her that when he had arrived he had found her unconscious on the floor. Her hands had been grasped tightly around her own neck.

'So you think I tried to strangle myself?' she had said, angered at his words. But he quickly soothed her and told her he didn't think that at all. He knew forces, evil forces beyond his comprehension were the reason for her collapse. He too had heard the rasping voice whisper in his ear as he had given her the kiss of life. A voice had hissed the words, 'Just as you helped John take Mary from me, you will see how it feels to lose the one you love.'

Roger and Al continued to sit silently in the lounge, both thinking about the events of the previous few hours.

Roger looked across at her and smiled, 'I'm just glad I got back home when I did. Kit had started gabbling on, all excited about the family history as soon as I got in. Then she mentioned the mummified cat you had found and thrown away in the bin. I knew I had to get up here straight away.'

'But why? What was so important about the dead cat?' Al asked.

'When we were down at Betty's do you recall she was saying how the house already had some protection? Well when you were in the loo she had explained to me that she knew Ethel, you know, the old girl who used to live there? Well Ethel had told Betty about the cat. It seems it had been there years, in the fireplace, along with the tin of amulets and stuff to protect the place.'

'But I didn't throw away the tin, it was only the cat, and anyway, how can a dead cat protect the house from evil?' she said.

'Betty told me it's something that's been done for hundreds of years. It's the intent of the thing that matters. If the evil forces believe it's going to keep them away, it will. So Desmond's spirit must have seen you throw the cat away and knew he was able to attack you. I'm glad it's nice and peaceful here again now that I've taken old Felix out of the bin and put him back on his shelf.'

'I'm so grateful to you Roger, for everything, thank you so much.' her eyes began to fill as the trauma of the recent events finally hit her, 'You saved my life. If it wasn't for you I'd be dead.'

Suddenly a picture appeared in her mind. A young woman in an alleyway, her young life swiftly taken from her with the blade of a knife. Her pleading eyes crying out to Al, as she took her last breath. Help me, they said. Help me. If she had acted straight away would the young girl still be alive? There was nothing she could do now to bring her back that she knew. But there *was* something she could do for her.

'Roger? Can I ask you to do one more thing for me?'

He smiled, 'Of course. What would you like? Cup of tea?'

She shook her head, 'No. Will you go with me to the Police station? I want to make a statement.'

'A statement? I don't think we can arrest your ghost!' he laughed not realising how serious she was.

'No, not this ghost. But there is a ghost I want to lay to rest. It's something that I've been carrying with me for some years. I want to give a witness statement about a murder that took place in Stockwell a few years ago. I think it's time the bastards paid.'

Chapter twenty nine

Alison spent the next few hours opening her heart to Roger. She told him everything, starting with her romance with Kenny, how happy they had been when they'd first married when she had been blind to his need to prove himself all the time. She had gradually realised he always wanted to show how well he was doing in the world, he needed an outward show of wealth and achievement and was addicted to financial success. She slowly accepted it was just his way, but when things went downhill with the business and he hooked up with big Mick his addiction changed. Drink, then drugs, then violence. Kenny looked up to Mick, here was a man who had done well for himself, albeit by sick and violent means, letting nothing and no one stand in his way. Mick could do no wrong in Kenny's bleary drug glazed eyes.

It was beginning to get dark as the afternoon faded into dusk. As Alison bared her soul, Roger said nothing while she shared her dark secrets with him. The waning light dulled the colours in the room giving it a sepia like quality. He felt he was sitting in an old photograph of the past as Al continued to share with him her memories.

He glanced over to the window and was aware of the fog as it lapped against the glass, trying to ease its way inside. Desmond was still out there with all his village cronies trapped in the swirling darkness. It struck Roger how over the mists of time things never change. Desmond had managed to get the villagers to blindly follow him and join in with his violence. Desmond's anger fed his desire for revenge, his need to kill his wife's lover. Just as Kenny had tried to kill Mark.

He'd have to go and visit Mark again soon. See if there was any change. The nurse had told him to keep talking, said it might filter through. He'll have a bit to tell him next time, that's for sure with all the recent events.

Roger wondered how Mark would feel knowing that Al had decided to talk to the police about Kenny and Mick. With his injuries he should think he'd be happy they'd get what's coming to them.

He looked across at Al as she wiped her eyes and began to tell Roger about the night Mick had threatened her. There had been moments recently when Roger thought he should tell Al all he knew about Mark, but seeing her get so upset was hard enough, it would only add to her pain. No, best to keep it to himself. He wouldn't gain anything at the moment by telling her. He was unaware she knew something. She hadn't yet told him about Tom's photo of Mark and Kenny and her suspicions that they were connected. She'd decided to hold that back for now.

It was when Al had finished her confession that Roger had turned to her, taken hold of her hand and squeezed it gently. He knew there were some things she needed to be told.

'You've been so brave Al. How you have coped all this time, keeping all that inside is beyond me,' he said quietly.

She let out a sob, 'Brave? I'm not brave. I'm a coward. I should have said something before now. I've left it far too long.'

'But you were scared. Mick had threatened you. You don't take his threats lightly that's for sure.'

'Have you come across him Rog? When you worked in London? You sound as if you know him,' Al asked. She watched as he leant forward, his arms rested on his thighs, hands clasped together tightly.

The room, now only lit by the outside light, its feeble bulb filtered in a warm yellow glow on Roger's silhouette as he spoke. 'I need to tell you something. Yes, I do know of Big Mick, I had dealings a few years ago, that's why I'm back up working with the Met for a while. Working on this new operation.'

'The thing with the drugs? Al asked.

He nodded, 'Yes, we know the dealer got the supplies from Mick. We are holding out to try and find out from where they were originally sourced. Try to get the main supplier.'

'I see,' she said and began to wonder if she'd been duped. 'So tell me, did you know of my links with Mick and Ken before I just poured out my life history?'

Roger sat back and half turned to face her, grabbed her hand tightly, 'Please don't be annoyed.' Al pulled her hand away. 'Al, please. Yes, I did know you were Kenny's ex. I also knew that it was likely you may have been giving him an alibi for the murders.'

'You knew!' she shouted and stood up to flick on the light. It revealed her tear-streaked face, her cheeks were glowing as her anger grew, realising his betrayal. 'Why didn't you say anything? What is this? Why am I such a mug? So were you befriending me, hoping I'll finally squeal?' He could see the fire burning in her eyes as she raised her voice, 'I suppose you are happy now.'

Roger stood up and took hold of her arms, not allowing her to break free.

'Alison, you have got to believe me, it was nothing like that at all. I didn't know at first, but yes, I have known for a while. But all I wanted to do was protect you. I know what Big Mick is like, I know he is likely to want to see you taken out of the picture.' His voice began to get louder, as he tried to make her see he could be trusted, 'There was no way I was going to put any pressure on you.' He released the hold on her and gently pushed back a strand of hair from her face as he looked into her eyes, 'For God's sake woman, don't you realise that I care about you. I want to look after you.'

He watched as a tear slowly trickled down her cheek. He tenderly wiped it away as his eyes kept their hold on hers. As he waited to see who would win.

She shook her head, 'I'm sorry Roger. There are so many trust issues, I can't help it, what with…' Another tear spilled over as she thought about Mark and the small seed of hope that she had clung onto since he had gone. The crazy idea that maybe she'd been wrong about him and he would come back. That he did love her after all. A weak smile appeared on her face and she allowed Roger to pull her close and she rested her face against the lemon scent of his neck. He silently whispered into her hair that he loved her, knowing that he had lost.

Early the next morning they set off for London to the police station at Battersea where Roger was due to start his shift. He had spent the night in Al's spare room. He felt sure the cottage was now safe for Al, but he knew Desmond was still loitering outside. He didn't want to risk it. So that morning he'd rushed back to Kit's to get changed and called back to pick up Al who had been waiting nervously, pacing the lounge like a caged lion, although not feeling as brave. The doubts she'd been plagued with most of the night were beginning to resurface.

She hadn't slept well at all. Her neck was still very sore and she had tried to get comfortable but every few minutes she had to adjust her pillows to no avail, she was still aware of the tenderness of her throat. There was a vague circle of blue and mauve on her neck as the bruising began to appear. Unable to lie down without feeling as if she was choking, she had sat propped up for the rest of night. Initially her mind busied itself with thoughts of the possible consequences of giving the witness statement. At Orchard Cottage she was dealing with the unknown, an unseen evil but after tomorrow she may have real physical danger at the door if Mick gets to her.

Roger had told her that because of the current drugs operation they would probably have to sit on her information. But once they had nailed the main drug dealer they would pull in Mick and Kenny for the murders. She'd become worried, knowing Mick would still be at large but Roger assured her that Mick wouldn't know that she'd spoken to the police, at least not until after he was banged up. She would be fine. Don't worry, he had told her and looked at her with his ice blue eyes.

Sleep didn't arrive for hours as she mulled everything around in her head. She knew she'd only have to say the word and Roger would be changing their relationship into something other than just friends. She couldn't go there. She wasn't saying that she didn't find him attractive. She had thought he was gorgeous from the first time she'd seen him. And after the initial coolness between them, which had been mainly her fault due to her fear of the Police, in time that had thawed. He obviously cared for her and worried about her. Yesterday he'd saved her life - well you didn't get more attentive than that did you? She did feel at ease in his company and she valued his friendship, they got on so well, she didn't want to spoil that. But he wasn't Mark.

She sat in the car with her stomach tight, feeling uneasy the nearer to London they travelled. Her neck was still painful and with the bruising more pronounced she'd covered her throat with a silk scarf, the light material felt soothing as it touched her skin. They stopped at traffic lights and around them the people rushed along, heads down as they made their way to work. No time for niceties for them, no smiles and chats as they passed each other in the street. She was glad she now lived away from the anonymous face of London.

Two teenagers ran across the road just as the amber flashed, light on their feet and light of hand as they snatched at a handbag from a woman on the crossing. She clung on tightly and hurled abuse at them. Roger jumped out of the car and the lads sped off, shouting obscenities as they disappeared into the distance empty handed.

'I'm getting really nervous now Rog,' she said as the car drove past Clapham Common.

'You're bound to be nervous. It's a good thing you are doing though Al, don't forget that.'

She turned her head to look at him and felt the painful stretch in her neck, a reminder of what might have been. She could have been dead if it hadn't been for Roger saving her yesterday. Guilt sat heavy in the pit of her stomach, could she have saved Evie in the last moments of her life? Roger had told her it was unlikely there was anything she could have done for the girl, but it didn't stop her feeling as she did. At least she would see Mick and Ken pay.

At the station the detective had been very kind. Al had been worried they were going to give her a hard time as she had withheld information from the police. He took his time, allowed her to tell him at her own pace what she had seen. He threw a few questions at her, but nothing she couldn't deal with. She told the truth and within a couple of hours was back at the main desk waiting for Roger to arrange for someone to drive her back home.

She sat on the hard plastic seat in the waiting room. An elderly woman waddled in to report her cat missing, the desk sergeant was sympathetic and was taking her details when Roger emerged from the back room.

'Sorry for the delay Al, I'll be with you in a jiffy. You okay?' He sat down next to her, 'I would drop you back myself but I'm needed here I'm afraid. We'll get you back home no problems, just waiting on Bert the driver to get back from a drop off and then he will take you back to Greysmead.'

'Unless I stay here and go back with you when your shift finishes?' Al asked.

He frowned and touched her shoulder, 'I'm going to be hours yet. You'd be bored silly and anyway I never know these days what time I will finish. It's all a bit unknown. One reason why I plan on getting my own place as soon as. It's not fair on Chas and Kit being disturbed all hours.'

'I was thinking about that actually,' Al began but got interrupted when a door to her right opened and a scruffy man in his fifties emerged.

'Alright Sergeant?' the man grinned a toothless smile at the desk sergeant, 'I will bid you farewell! Thanks for the room. Very nice and comfy, breakfast was a bit shit though,' he cackled as he made his way to the door. His eyes took in Al as she sat with Roger, 'I wouldn't let him get too close to you darling. You'll not like the smell!'

'Shut up Johnny, just go before we arrest you again,' Rog replied light heartedly.

Johnny laughed and made pig-snorting noises as he went out through the door.

Al smiled, amused by the down and out and his banter, blissfully unaware how that one chance meeting would trigger a chain of events that would ultimately end in a death.

Chapter Thirty

Alison put all of her attention that week into preparing for the Saturday badger watch, and pushed any negative thoughts of Big Mick and Desmond to a far corner of her mind, sealing the door tightly. When Tom rang he had suggested they have a fairly light meal late Saturday afternoon and then they could head up to the woods around 8 o'clock.

'Al, we don't want to be feeling too full when we are crouching down on the ground. So don't go mad and do a banquet will you!'

'Don't worry, I'm no Nigella!' she joked back.

'Nigella? ' he asked, perplexed.

'Don't worry,' Al laughed realising TV chefs were unlikely to be on Tom's viewing schedule, 'I'll do something light. Okay. See you around 4ish?'

Al decided to get salmon fillets from the fishmonger. She waited in line by the little white van that arrived every Friday morning in the village. It parked up outside the Jolly Abbot for an hour or so. Al had spotted Mrs Blackman ahead in the queue and hoped the village gossip wouldn't notice her. She was bound to detect the bruising on her throat and make some sort of comment.

The vicar's wife, Mrs Mahoney, stood directly in front of Alison and she made small talk as they waited. Al was aware of a raised voice coming from inside the pub. She tried to keep her mind on the subject in hand but not finding flower arranging very riveting her ears couldn't help but home in on Jim's words. He was obviously on the phone and it sounded as if he was pleading his case with someone.

'Can't you get someone else to do it? I will get it for you, I will. Please, just give me a bit more time.'

Al smiled at Mrs Mahoney who had just finished enthusing about the display Mrs Blackman had arranged in the church at the weekend.

'So do you think you would be interested in joining the rota?'

'Pardon?' Al's thoughts were brought back to the conversation, 'Rota?'

'The flower rota. Would you have time to help do you think?' the vicar's wife asked.

There was a moments silence as Al tried to work out how to politely decline but fortunately her response was over shadowed by a loud stream of obscenities that bellowed forth from the open window behind them.

'The fucking bastard! Bollocks to them all!'

'Well really!' muttered the disgusted Mrs Mahoney who took her turn with the fishmonger.

Jim realised he could be heard and slammed the window shut leaving Al to wonder on the cause of his anger.

Mrs Blackman caught her eye, 'Hello there Ms Greenways. Don't see much of you down in the village. How you settling in up at old Ethel's place then?'

Al noticed her eyes flick down to her neck where some flecks of yellow and green bruising were slightly visible above the scarf.

'Yes, getting on fine thank you,' Al answered, about to take her place at the van.

'That Desmond giving you much trouble is he?'

The fishmonger, about to take Al's order, waited as she addressed Mrs Blackman, 'Sorry? What did you just say?'

'Old Desmond. He gave Ethel a bit of a song and dance for a while. I assumed he'd been up to his old tricks again, seeing as your neck's in a sorry state,' Mrs Blackman said as she turned and began to walk away.

The fishmonger eager to set off to his next port of call badgered Al for her order.

Al called out after Mrs Blackman, 'Hang on a moment will you. Please.'

Al bought her fish and dashed after the busy body as she headed back towards the post office, 'Please tell me about Ethel and Desmond. I really would like to hear more.'

Mrs Blackman smiled, pleased that Al had taken the bait, 'Of course dear, come in and have a chat over a cuppa.'

They sat in the conservatory at one of the dining tables Mrs Blackman used for her bed and breakfast. 'So I take it you have had a visit then?' asked Mrs Blackman as she poured out a cup of tea for Al.

Al nodded, 'I was stupid enough to throw out some of the crystals and bits that Ethel had placed in the house and yes, he came a calling the other night.' she pulled her scarf away to show the full extent of the bruising.

'Ohh, that does look nasty. He tried it on with Ethel too, when she first moved in, her neck was a rainbow of colours for weeks. She soon got rid of him from the house when she put back that manky old cat that her hubby had thrown out. Didn't realise you see, did they? You got everything back in place now?'

'Yes, Roger's Aunt Betty gave me lots of things to put around the cottage.'

Mrs Blackman stirred her tea and said, 'Poor old Betty, the ghosts of this village got too much for her to cope with. Could never manage to block them out, poor love. You seen her lately?'

'Yes, Roger took me down to see her fairly recently. She's been really helpful. Gave me lots of stones and herbs to help protect the house. So tell me, did Ethel talk much about the spirits up there? Did you witness anything yourself?'

'Ohh yes dearie I did. All us old Greysmead residents, we saw things when we were young. When we were growing up, we knew how it lingered up in Monkton Lane.'

'So hasn't anyone been able to get rid of it, help the spirits find peace and move on? Surely the clergy must have been brought in to help, if it's been going on all this time?'

'They've tried. Ethel got the house blessed and placed her stones around the place and all the other paraphernalia. That worked a treat, but it's outside the cottage that's the trouble. The Darkness that's what us old villagers call it. Well, the Darkness, it just doesn't know it's time to move on, does it? You know the story I expect? Kit's probably filled you in? With the monks and all? God rest their innocent souls.'

Al nodded, deciding not to tell Mrs Blackman about the new twist to the story of poor Mary's murder that had been gleaned from her dream from Brother John. 'So no one knows how to help the Darkness rest and find peace? Surely there must be something that can be done.'

'Maybe you will find a way dearie, you've got a young head on your shoulders and with this internet nowadays. You said you work with computers? Well maybe there's one of these dot coms that has the answer, maybe someone out there on this world web malarkey knows the answer. I certainly don't I'm afraid.'

She started to clear away the teacups and Al got up ready to go as Mrs Blackman said, 'We've always thought the only thing that would rid us of the Darkness is if it gets what it's been waiting for - that lay monk who raped Desmond's wife. And that's unlikely isn't it? He's already dead and gone.'

Mrs Blackman watched as Al made her way across the road and knock at the Mitchell's house. Probably going to see that Kit. Mrs Blackman was glad she had a chance to speak to Ms Greenways, get an update on the goings on up at Monkton Lane. She liked to know what was happening, keep her finger on the pulse. After her chat with Al she had a feeling it was nearing the time, the time for redemption. She casually lifted up Al's teacup, swirled it round a few times before turning it over onto the saucer. Her eyes homed in on the patterns the tea leaves left behind. Yes, it looked as if an end was in sight. What a pity someone will have to lose their life in the process.

'Your neck is looking colourful! How you feeling now?' Kit asked as they went through to the kitchen.

Kit knew all about Desmond's attack on her. Alison had gone straight to see Kit from the police station and had filled her in on everything that had happened including all she'd told Roger about her life with Kenny.

'I'm feeling a lot better now thanks,' Al said as she glanced at the headlines in the local newspaper that was lying on the table. There was a hazy photograph of two men with terriers. They'd been arrested over at a nearby village after being caught digging at a badger sett. Al made a mental note to talk to Tom again the next evening about volunteering.

Cuppa?' Kit asked

'No thanks, just had one at Mrs Blackman's!' she laughed.

'Oh no, poor you. Get the third degree did you?'

'Actually she told me something interesting.'

Kit raised her eyebrows, 'Okay - what have you found out from old nosey?'

'Ethel had a similar thing happen to her when she first moved into the cottage. Mrs B spotted my bruised throat and put two and two together.'

'Well I never. It's all getting rather worrying to me. Are you sure you are happy up there on your own?' she shivered, 'I bloody wouldn't be, I've always been wary of Monkton Lane ever since I was a child. Dorothy Blackman used to frighten us with tales of spooks. Sorry don't mean to scare you,' she gave Al a hug as she realised her words had hit on something.

'Yes, Roger mentioned her. He said she had told him some spooky tales. But really, it does feel okay in the cottage now but I did have an idea. You know Roger is thinking of moving out from here so he can give you and Chas a bit more space and not disturb you as he comes and goes at all hours?'

'Yeeeees,' Kit felt she knew where it was going and felt inwardly quite pleased.

'I was going to suggest to him moving in with me up there, see if he fancied sharing. He'd be my lodger, I've got plenty of room, it would just be for a while, until everything settles down that is…what?...what?' she looked at Kit's grinning face, 'What's up with you?'

Kit laughed and shook her head, 'Nothing! I just think the lady protests too much!'

'You think Rog and me? No, we're just mates that's all,' Al tried to convince Kit, 'I had hoped to have spoken to him about it before now, but he's been so busy. Can he make it tomorrow night? I did text him but not heard back.'

Kit told Al that Roger was very heavily involved with the current police operation. All Kit knew was that the police thought they were closing in on their quarry so it was unlikely he'd be free. He'd not been home for days, he'd been staying with a workmate up near the station. Al was disappointed, she would have liked him to have been there. She had thought back a number of times about the evening they had spent up at Orchard cottage together, how at ease they had been with each other. It would be good to spend more time with him.

Al left Kit's and started to stroll along the footpath back to Monkton Lane. A light drizzle had begun to fill the air and she pulled the hood of her jacket over her hair and stepped up her pace hoping to get back before the rain became heavier. The wind began to pick up and she started to worry if the badger watch the following evening would get cancelled if the weather continued to worsen. Black clouds began to scud across the sky at a rate of knots and she continued to march along as the gusts of wind caught onto her hood.

She rushed along as the rain began to fall more heavily, great drops pounded down onto the track, within minutes they were falling as hailstones that bounced onto the soil and stung at her face as the storm began its attack. She kept her head low and focused on the ground in front of her to try and stop the blustery air blowing the hail and rain into her face. Thunder rumbled close by and Al began to run the last few metres. She rushed breathless towards the gate of the cottage and the roar of thunder filled the air again as she closed the door behind her.

She had just put the fish in the fridge and was drying the wet tendrils of her hair with a towel when there was a knock at the door. Maybe Tom had come up a day early, probably going to cancel the watch due to the weather. Smiling, she made her way along the hallway but within seconds her head began to spin as she opened the door and saw her visitor standing there, one arm resting on the frame.

'Morning Al! Jeez what rotten weather eh?'

Time stopped, her heart crashed against her chest. In those few moments so many emotions flooded her senses. Joy followed swiftly by anger but then fear took hold when she recalled the photo. Mark and Kenny were friends. Maybe Kenny was with him? Did they know she had given a statement to the police? Is that why he was here? Had he come to make her keep quiet?

Her eyes took in his face, now thin and gaunt, skin pale and translucent. His head of thick hair was now cropped short and revealed a large angry scar that ran above his dark eyes and across the top of his skull. Finally concern overruled the fear and she found her voice.

'Mark! What's happened to you?'

The smile she remembered appeared on his face, but no longer lighting up his eyes, now they just mirrored his pain and sadness.

'Aren't you going to ask me in then Al? It's a bit wet out here.'

The rain thundered heavily onto the path behind him as he waited unprotected from the elements, clad in just a fleece, t-shirt and jeans.

Would she be safe alone with him in the house? Her heart rammed at her chest, pounding with a mixture of alarm and elation at seeing him again.

'Okay, come in,' she gestured to him to follow her through to the kitchen. He walked slowly, obviously finding it painful, limping slightly as he made his way down the hall. The blood pumped in her ears as the shock of seeing him sent her system into overdrive.

Mark sat carefully down onto one of the kitchen stools, 'Don't mind if I perch here? My legs can't take my weight for too long at the moment. Not that I'm very weighty at present I know!'

'You best give me your fleece, I'll hang it over the radiator, try to dry it off.' It was a struggle for him, he winced as he pulled his arms from the sleeves.   She could see how thin he had become, the once broad chest was almost concave, the skin on his arms hung loose over the bone. Whatever had happened? He looked terrible. Still wary, Al kept her distance and stayed close to the back door, an escape route if needed.

'Do you want a drink?' She flicked the switch on the kettle, wondered what he would say, how he would explain.

The rain hammered at the glass behind her, as the leaden sky continued its rampage. A sudden flash of lightning gave a brief burst of light to the darkened kitchen giving Mark's skeletal figure a sinister glow.

'Al, I don't want a drink and I can't stay long. I just felt I owed you an explanation. You need to know, *I* need you to know.'

Al stood the other side of the breakfast bar, she began to feel dizzy. He had stirred up so many emotions.

'Okay, explain away. Explain why you never told me you knew Kenny, explain how you know of the club in Stockwell,' her voice began to get stronger as her anger erupted, 'And perhaps you can explain why you left me that morning and have never been in touch with me since.'

His eyes reflected his sorrow as he answered, 'Al, I can explain. Please hear me out.'

'This better be good,' she said but suddenly felt a pang of remorse, as it was obvious he was in pain.

'Yes, I do know Kenny *and* Mick,' his breathing was laboured as he continued, 'but it's not what you think. I couldn't tell you before. For your own safety, and mine too.'

'What do you mean?'

He indicated to his wounded body with his hands, 'Why do you think I'm in such a state?'

'I don't know, you tell me.'

'Kenny wasn't happy when he found out that you and me - found out we'd slept together,' he began to cough as his airways struggled.

'What?' she cried, 'Kenny did this to you because we slept together! Are you serious?'

He nodded as he continued to cough. She watched as he wiped his mouth with a tissue and slipped it back into his pocket but not before she spotted a hint of blood.

'Oh my God!' her hands went to her face, 'I'm so sorry Mark, I didn't realise.'

'How could you know? The hospital have done all they can for me. Still look a mess though don't I?' he laughed and then began another fit of wheezing.

'You sure I can't get you a drink?'

He shook his head, waved his hand dismissively, 'No, I'm fine. Look Al, you need to know that I wasn't working *with* Kenny and Mick. I was working against them. I'm a copper.'

She clung onto the worktop, momentarily taken aback, 'The police? But what…? I'm sorry I don't understand?'

'I was working undercover at the club. We've suspected Mick of having links with a big drug ring for some time. I was working there to see if we could track down who his supplier was, then Mick volunteered me to come and shadow you. Make sure you weren't going to talk to the cops about the murders. What could I do? I couldn't argue. I didn't realise I was going to complicate matters and fall in love with you.'

Al found it hard to cope with his revelations. Was it true? Or was he spinning her a line? Surely Roger would have known? Wasn't he working on the drug operation too?

Her heart raced, 'How do I know you are telling the truth? What's happened with the under cover work now then? Does Mick now know you're a copper?'

He shook his head, 'They don't know where I am. They dumped me on the steps of the hospital the night Ken half killed me, the police moved me to somewhere else, somewhere safe so Mick couldn't find me. Ask your mate Roger, he knows.'

'Roger? Roger knew all of this?' God it just gets better and better. How will she ever know who to believe again?

'Don't be angry with him Al. He didn't say anything, he didn't want to put you in danger. If you'd tried to see me in hospital and it turned out Mick was still having you watched you would have led him to me. We both would have had it,' he told her as he fidgeted on the stool trying without success to get comfortable. His face betrayed the pain he was feeling. 'Roger was only protecting you sweetheart.'

'Don't sweetheart me! I'm truly sorry Kenny did this to you but how do you think I felt when I never heard from you again? Surely if you cared for me enough you would have got a message to me somehow, there must have been some way to let me know you were okay.' Her head felt tight, so many emotions raced around.

'I did care, *do* care but Al, I was bloody unconscious. I couldn't tell you! Roger wanted to. He knew how you were feeling, how sad you were about the whole situation.'

'How do you know that? Did he tell you?' she asked.

He nodded, 'He did actually. He came to visit me in hospital a number of times. In my hazy world I heard some of the things he said. He tried to keep me posted on what was happening in your life. The blessing, the crypt,' he inclined his head toward the door, 'Jeez what a find eh?' he smiled. 'And that bloody mummified cat! God, you couldn't write stuff like that could you! Crazy old life you've been living since I've been gone!' he laughed and started to cough again. 'Sorry. Bloody lungs!'

But Al saw a slight spark of the old Mark come through as he spoke. Relief filled her heart, he did care for her, and he wasn't in league with Kenny. He was back! She would care for him, look after him, get him well again.

She moved towards him as he sat and tried to control his breathing, 'I can help you now Mark. You can stay here. I can get you well again.'

She stood close to him, breathed in the aroma of wood and peppermint that always seemed to ooze from his skin. His eyes met hers and she saw the regret.

'I'm sorry Al but I can't do that. I've come to say goodbye. Working undercover comes with its drawbacks. It's the risk we take. The big boss wants to see me. Will probably move me on now.'

'But you can't go! Stay here with me,' she reached out to his hands, so thin, no flesh to speak of, 'Mark, you need rest, you can't go anywhere.'

He touched her cheek and smiled, 'I'm sorry honey but I must do as the boss says. He's dealt with this situation before, he knows what's best. This time next month I'll probably have a new name, a new life somewhere else. It's just the way it goes.'

Al felt the light touch of his lips on hers as he leant forward and he kissed her gently. He stood up and drew her to him, held her close. God, he had dreamt of this moment when he was lying in the hospital bed. How he had longed to touch her again. She felt his hands on her back, gently pushing her closer to him as his face nestled into her hair. His bony frame felt so fragile against her body.

He pulled away, 'I really have to go. I'm so sorry. Be happy Al.'

He became blurred as her eyes overflowed with tears as he walked away. She watched from the door as he made his way painfully along the path and out onto the road. The rain continued to pound down but he made no effort to rush to escape the deluge as he slowly headed towards the ivy tunnel of Monkton Lane.

His figure shone out against the black trees as it was lit by a flash from the skies and then he disappeared from view. She heard the rumble of his van in the distance. He was gone.

She had sat kneeling up against the back of the sofa, her face pressed against the glass as she looked out at the rain, willing him to change his mind and come back. Her eyes were focused only on Monkton Lane waiting for the headlights of his van to appear. Time went by, she was cold, but she continued to wait. The wind was unrelenting with its assault on the cottage as it whistled through the gaps in the door. The rain splattered against the window, but Al's eyes couldn't see it, her gaze was fixed further away, towards the ivy tunnel. Waiting.

She was finally brought back to the moment as her stomach gurgled. She hadn't eaten since that morning. She couldn't see the clock, but she'd been sitting there for hours, it was getting dark. Her legs complained as she moved, and she carefully stretched them out and twisted herself around on the chair and sat back. She felt numb to the core. She rubbed at her feet and they slowly began to tingle as the blood started to flow freely at last.

She made her way along the hallway into the kitchen and opened the fridge. The light illuminated her face as her hand grabbed at a mini cheese, and she popped it in her mouth. Her stomach cramped as it was finally given something to quell the emptiness. She stared vacantly at the shelves, unable to concentrate and slammed the fridge door shut and turned towards the bread bin. She'd have toast. She stopped as she glanced over at the radiator.

The earthy smell filled her nostrils as she buried her head deep into the fleece, savouring the odours. It smelt of him. Peppermint, aftershave, wood. Pushing her arms through the sleeves she pulled it tightly around her cold and numb body and gradually she sunk down onto the floor next to the radiator and finally allowed herself to cry.

The liquid gold melody of a blackbird eventually worked its way into Alison's head. For a brief moment she took pleasure in hearing the beautiful song, rarely heard now that summer was at a close. But then the memories of the previous day returned and snapped the happiness away. She struggled to get out of bed, aching after having sat slumped against the radiator on the slate floor until she had finally dragged herself up the stairs. She had no more tears to shed. She decided to concentrate on the fact that Mark did care for her after all and the despondency she had felt after seeing him leave was pushed aside and was replaced by a determination to track him down.

She dialled Roger's number. He would know. He could help her. But his mobile was switched off, she cancelled the call without leaving a message. She rang Kit.

The phone rang for a long time but then she heard a sleepy voice, 'Hello? Alison? Is that you? Is everything alright?'

She forgot the niceties, 'Kit, is Roger there?

'He's still working in London, staying up there for a while,' Kit wondered what was wrong. Al sounded decidedly strange. 'Al? What's up? It's 6.30 in the morning!'

'Is it? Oh God, I'm sorry! Oh Kit. Mark was here!'

'Mark?' Kit's heart sank, 'What did the rat want after all this time?'

'I thought he didn't care…but he does! But I really need to speak to Roger. When will he be back?'

Kit didn't like the sound of Alison. What had happened? Why did she need Roger? Chas came from the bedroom, looking bleary eyed.

'It's Al,' she mouthed to her husband, 'Something's not right. I'm going up there.' She spoke again into the phone, 'Alison, I'll be there in a jiff.'

A few hours later after a bowl of porridge and hot drink Al started to thaw out. Kit had been concerned when she had first opened the door to her. Al's eyes had been swollen and puffy from the tears she had shed the previous night but now after a shower and some food she was starting to look a little better. Kit had listened as Al had told her all the things she had kept back about Mark, about her suspicions that he was working for Mick and finally Tom's incriminating photo.

'Why didn't you tell us? If what Mark told you yesterday is true, Roger would have been able to put you straight before now.'

Kit wondered at her brother's reasons for not telling Al. Had it just been to keep her safe from this big Mick or did he have his own personal agenda?

She squeezed Al hand, 'Look honey, don't get your hopes up too high. Mark's life is going to be in danger if Mick finds out he's a cop so I can understand why he's going to be given a new identity. Maybe it's for the best.'

Al pulled her hand away, 'But I must try. Please let me contact Roger, he will help me get a message to Mark, so I can see if I can try to stop him leaving.'

'I'm sorry Al but Roger made it clear we are not to contact him while things are hotting up with this drugs operation.'

'But can't we leave a message for him at the station? Ask him to get in touch?' Al pleaded.

Kit shook her head, 'I really don't want to do anything to put him at risk,' she saw the desperation in Al's eyes and added, 'but I promise I will tell him as soon as I hear from him.'

Kit decided it was time to get Al's mind on something else, 'Now come on,' she stood up, hands on hips, ready for action, 'Let's sort out what we are doing later for this meal,' she glanced out at the black sky, 'Although looking out there I'd say the badger watch will be off, don't you?' Her ears picked out a vague sound as it wafted gently into the room, 'Sounds like the breeze is picking up again too.'

The gentle whispers pushed their way up from the crypt and through the old wooden door the hushed cries of despair floated around the kitchen. The voices were lost, they were trapped and needed help but their strength was waning, they had waited so long.

'Placere nos liberum. Please set us free, we beg of you,' they whispered.

Al shivered and hugged Mark's fleece tightly around her for comfort as she was suddenly overwhelmed with a feeling of claustrophobia.

'Kit, I know it's pretty grim out there but I really need to get some fresh air. I'm going to go for a walk, clear the cobwebs away.'

'Okay, if that's what you want to do, I'll come with you.'

The whispers continued to echo around the room, *'Help us,'* they cried but their strength was gone, their voices lost.

Al began to sense their pain, their entrapment and her heart begin to race as she felt the panic rise from the pit of her stomach. The walls of the cottage suddenly felt that they were closing in, a fear of being trapped took hold. She had to get out. 'Okay. I'll go get my waterproof. But I really must get out of here.'

Kit frowned. Al looked pale. She waited in the kitchen whilst Al charged upstairs to get her boots and coat. Kit sat in silence, just the hushed whispers from the hidden voices stroked at her face, trying to get her attention.

A tapping at the window drew her gaze out to the garden. The long branches of an elder bush caught in the breeze and a bare twig whipped rhythmically against the glass. Aunt Betty had once told her that elder trees planted by the house would keep the devil away but burn the wood at your peril. Maybe old Ethel had planted it when she lived at the cottage to help keep Desmond at bay.

Kit stood up and stretched, it had been a fraught morning so far, she could do with getting some more sleep. She yawned as she thought of her bed, left prematurely that morning after Al had rung her at the crack of dawn. Her eyes took in the dark sky, heavy with rain. A slight movement over by the ruins caught her attention and she peered through the window trying to make out what she had seen. In the murky grey light it was difficult to work out what it had been, at first glance it had looked like someone standing amongst the ruins, watching the cottage. But now whatever it was had gone. She leant closer, and pressed her face up to the glass and stared out into the gloom. Suddenly she leapt back as a face appeared inches away on the other side of the glass looking back at her.

Chapter thirty two

The face peered through the glass and looked at Kit. The mouth contorted into a grotesque shape, it screwed up its eyes before grinning inanely.

Kit's mouth widened into a huge smile and then she began to laugh.

'Chas! You fool! What are you doing here?' she located the key and let her husband in the back door and gave him a playful slap, 'You could have given me a heart attack!'

He gave her a hug and laughed, 'Sorry, just couldn't resist it when I saw you peering out of the window, your nose pressed up at the glass like that! What were you looking at that was so riveting?'

She leant and kissed him on the nose, feeling so grateful to have such a good man in her life. The tiredness she had felt earlier vanished, he always lifted her spirits, always managed to make her laugh. Aside from Amy he was the most precious thing in her life.

'I thought I saw a figure standing over by the ruins, I was trying to make out who it was, I didn't realise it was you.'

'Over at the ruins? No, It wasn't me. I've just walked round from the front of the house. I tried the doorbell but it didn't seem to be working.' He leant on the window sill and looked out into the misty garden, 'Someone over by the ruins you say? Shall I go and look?'

She shook her head, 'No, it was probably nothing. I couldn't be sure. So, what brings you up here, I've only been gone a few hours, can't you cope without me?' she teased him and gave him another kiss.

'Now then you two!' Al walked into the kitchen decked out in waterproof jacket, 'Enough of that!' she joked, 'Hiya Chas. So you couldn't be apart from your wife for a just a couple of hours!' she smiled but Chas could see it was superficial, there was a sadness behind her eyes.

'Actually it was you I came to see. Is it okay if Amy comes along for the meal later?'

Kit looked at her husband in surprise, 'But I thought she was going over to Melissa's for a sleep over?'

'Melissa's been taken ill, so it's been cancelled. Roger will have to get back to work soon so he won't be able to watch her so we would just have to bring her along, I know we are eating early…if that's okay Al?'

Al's eyes suddenly gained a glimmer of light, 'Roger? He's back?'

She frowned at Kit who shook her head, 'I didn't know. When did he turn up Chas?'

'He popped home about an hour ago to get some fresh clothes but will be heading back to London after lunch.'

Al frantically zipped up her jacket, 'Sorry Kit but can we shelve the walk and get over to your place now? I need to see him.' She grabbed her car keys and didn't wait for an answer as she headed for the door.

Roger headed down the stairs with a couple of clean shirts draped over his arm when he heard the key in the lock as Kit and Chas arrived home with Alison in tow. He knew from Chas that Al had rung at the crack of dawn sounding really upset so Kit had gone up to see her. He hoped Al was going to be okay, he was concerned about her, didn't like the thought of her alone up there with Desmond and his cronies loitering about outside. When he'd last been up at her place he had sensed their dark presence still lingering outside Orchard Cottage. He had felt it getting stronger, felt its negative energy in the dark mists that swirled around the outside of the building.

He'd always been aware of it up there, even as a kid. He recalled evenings as a youngster spent with his friends as they perched on the crumbling stone bridge that arched over the river. They'd head up there after school, having illicit smokes and the odd can of drink, ducking down if a car came along on its way to Woodhurst village. Monkton Lane hadn't been as overgrown then. The ivy hadn't yet taken it in its grasp. The village kids used to dare each other to walk along the lane towards the woods. The girls would run back squealing, scared of their own shadows.

There had been a few other cottages along the track as well as Ethel's old place at the far end. Mrs Blackman and her daughter Dorothy lived in the first cottage. As they all sat by the river at dusk Dorothy would delight in frightening them with tales of spooky happenings along the lane. Most of which she exaggerated for amusing effect but when it was just her and Roger together she'd talk more seriously about the strange things she had seen in the woods after dark. She told him about the whispers she would hear along the empty lane and how her Mother would sprinkle salt around the boundaries of their property to keep them safe.

Just like his Aunt Betty, Mrs Blackman was in tune with the other world and knew how to keep it at bay. She probably would have been the village wise woman in days gone by, she knew all about herbs and potions and would dabble with tarot cards and tea leaf readings. Not that she was able to predict her daughter's future. She had been upset when the romance between Roger and Dorothy had ended. Roger knew Mrs Blackman had it all mapped out in her mind, that he and Dorothy would marry and settle down in Greysmead but it wasn't to be.

By the time they had all left school, the cottages had become more and more run down and in need of repair and eventually all the inhabitants except Ethel moved down into the village. Mrs Blackman took over the post office and after Uni, Dorothy had secured herself a teaching post at a school in Hastings. But she had bigger ideas for herself than spending the rest of her days living at Greysmead. She decided to broaden her horizons and found a teaching post overseas.

Although Mrs Blackman was nice enough to him now, Roger was sure she still blamed him that her daughter was now living her life so far away. It hadn't been his fault, he didn't want her to leave either but Dorothy was a strong willed woman, she wouldn't be told what to do. A bit like Al, he thought. He had tried to persuade her to move back to the village but she was determined to stay on her own up at Orchard cottage, even after all that had happened there.

Roger had spoken to Betty after Al's frightening encounter with Desmond. She had been horror struck when she found out about Al's narrow escape. She had confirmed to Roger that the mummified cat was vital, it was the one thing they should make sure was always kept in the house at all costs. The rest of the protection, crystals, amulets and blessing were just belts and braces

Betty had sounded worried, 'You can't under estimate the power of the evil that resides in Monkton Lane. If you set it free to roam the cottage, who knows what will happen. Look after Alison, won't you Roger. She is very precious.'

'I know Betty. I will. I'll make sure she is watched over, don't fret.'

He wished he didn't have to be away so much, but things were really hotting up at the station. Hopefully it wouldn't be long now. With Mark in hospital it had taken some doing but they had managed to get someone else working at the club undercover. If the next drop happened on the day their insider predicted they would be able to nail the main supplier. Then they could concentrate on pulling in Big Mick and Kenny for the murders. The thought of going to court must be hanging over Al. No wonder she was looking so stressed.

She rushed over to him as soon as she came through the door.

'Roger! I really need your help,' she grabbed his arm and pulled him into the sitting room, her eyes brimming with tears.

He sat her down on the sofa and turned to face her as he settled down beside her.

'Hey, come on, tell me...what's up?'

'It's Mark! He came to see me yesterday,' she half sobbed, so relieved to be able to see Roger, maybe he could stop Mark before he left for good.

'Really? He's out of hospital now? Thank God he's recovered,' Roger said. 'Did he tell you about Kenny and what he did to him?'

Al nodded, 'He told me everything, is it true? Is he really with the police?'

Roger was amazed the hospital had discharged Mark. He'd still been in a bad way last time he visited him. Still, Mark was a fighter, Roger was pleased he had recovered from his injuries. He looked at Al and sensed the strength of her feelings for Mark. God, he'd been so selfish. He should have told her the truth, he'd been unfair keeping it from her. No way would she ever see him as more than a friend, it was Mark she wanted to be with.

He smiled at Alison, 'Yes, he is with the police. I didn't realise he was out of hospital. I'm so glad he's okay. I'm sorry I didn't tell you all about it Al. I thought I was doing the best thing, keeping you both safe.'

'It's alright, I understand. Mark explained all that but Roger you must help me get a message to him. He's gone. Said he won't be back, that he was going to be given a new identity.'

Roger frowned, 'Are they sending him away? Is that what he said?' He was surprised that his guv had deemed it necessary to give him a new ID. Did they really think he was at risk from Mick? Maybe it had been decided before they knew Al had given her statement. It was likely they'd now re-consider. If they didn't get Mick for the drugs they'd certainly be able to nail him for the murders.

Roger held her hand and watched as the tears spilled over onto her checks as she spoke, 'He said that he had to go and see the big boss and it was likely he'd be sent away. Please Roger, can you try to get a message to him. Try to stop him going.'

He nodded, 'Now you've given a statement it's likely he may be able to stay put. Look Al, I can't promise anything but I'll make some enquiries, try to get hold of him. But it won't be easy.'

'Oh Roger thank you! Thank you so much,' she sobbed as he pulled her close. Roger felt a wrench in his heart as he held her while she cried with relief knowing that she might see Mark again. For a second he had a fleeting thought. The outcome was in his hands. He didn't have to try contact Mark, did he? He could tell Al it was too late. No. He couldn't do that to her. He loved her but he had to let her go.

'I'll see what I can do Al. I'll do all I can to find out what's happening with Mark. I'm not going to be able to contact you for a while. When I go back it's going to be very risky. It looks as if we are closing in. I will call you with news as soon as I can. I promise.'

Al popped another bottle of wine into the fridge, happy that everything was in order for the evening. The early mist had turned into a persistent drizzle and with it had brought a drop in temperature. She'd lit the fire in the dining room when she had returned from Kit's place. The room felt cosy as the flickering flames danced around the logs. The aroma of burning apple wood filled the air. Her ears picked out the faint gentle sound of chanting that whispered its way up from the crypt. The soft sweet voices were her constant companions now and they gave her a feeling of peace.

She took a glass of juice into the sitting room as she waited for her guests, feeling as if a weight had been lifted from her shoulders. She knew Roger would do all he could to get a message to Mark. All she could do now was wait. She would try to push her sadness to one side and enjoy having good friends around her.

Tom had rung earlier to say the badger watch was now probably a no go due to the rain but was keen to come up anyway. She knew he was hoping to get down in the crypt again. He was determined to find out how the bats were finding their way in. She grinned thinking about him and his addictive enthusiasm.

She spotted the headlights of Kit's car as it emerged from the ivy tunnel. They had seen no sun at all the whole day. It had been gloomy and depressing but Al's mood was lifted when she spotted Amy in the back of the car. She was a well-behaved and good-natured little girl. Al had spent a lot of time with her since moving to the village and although her maternal instincts had been non-existent, Amy certainly made Al reconsider her ideas. She was, however, perturbed to see that as soon as Amy alighted from the car she began to scream. Al watched as Kit grabbed Amy's arm, tugging at her, as she dragged her towards the garden gate.

'No! Please Mummy, don't make me go through the dark clouds. They are in there! Please Mummy!' she cried as she resisted her Mother's tugs.

'What's the matter with Amy?' Al asked as she dashed down the path, 'Has something scared her?'

Amy's eyes looked at Alison, her bottom lip quivered, 'Aunty Alison, I can see horrid things. I'm really frightened.'

'Where are they? What can you see?' Al knelt down beside Amy and put her arm around her waist.

'It's dark, like a curtain. Your house isn't there anymore,' Amy sobbed, looking wide eyed at Al.

'That's just the fog Amy, it's nothing to be scared of,' Al said but felt the back of her neck tingle. Deep down she knew it was more than just fog that had frightened the little girl.

'Your house is hidden by the darkness. It's all black and whirly Aunty Alison, like lots of big snakes and there are eyes looking out at me…and horrid mouths,' she put her hands over her face to block out the vision.

'Okay, enough of this Amy,' Kit said sternly, 'Your imagination is going into overdrive now.' A recollection of Kit's own childhood momentarily rose to the surface, a memory of running scared for her life back to the bridge, to the safety of her brother and his friends. She had never gone back down Monkton Lane alone or after dark for many years. The only way she could cope with the evil she had seen that night was to close the door on it. Forget it. Her way to deal with Amy's sensitivity was to deny it. She had hoped Amy had finished with her visions now that Mary and Brother John were reunited.

'Amy, it is just the fog, that's all it is.'

'But I can't see Alison's house Mummy,' Amy pleaded.

Chas made his way over from the car as Al stood up and spoke quietly to Kit. 'Both Roger and I have noticed that the fog around the house is getting thicker. Aunt Betty talked to me about the darkness – the evil that still lingers from Desmond and the villagers. Maybe Amy can sense it more than us? She used to see Mary, didn't she? Please don't be hard on her.'

'What's happening guys? You alright sweetie?' Chas squatted down to Amy's height and with a tissue gently wiped the tears from her cheeks. His heart burst with love as he looked at his daughter. Her blonde hair was damp from the drizzle and tendrils of curls clung to her cheeks, framing her angelic face, 'What's made my princess so upset?'

'Alison's house has gone! The fog has taken it away!' She grabbed her Father's hand, 'I'm scared Daddy!'

'She can see more than just the fog. I think she must be able to see what Betty called the darkness. She's really freaked out by it,' said Al.

'Well we can't stand out in this weather for much longer. We'll either have to go inside or go home Amy,' Kit announced, not letting on just how apprehensive she felt. She couldn't let Amy see how scared she was.

A gentle purr of a vehicle echoed from the ivy tunnel and Tom's little car trundled up and parked behind Chas. The six-foot form of Tom disentangled himself from his tiny car and he rummaged in the boot. It wasn't long before his beaming smile appeared from within his bushy dark beard.

'Rotten day for it!' he said, oblivious of their fraught faces, 'What are you all doing hanging about out here?' and he strode over to the gate. He was weighed down with a box laden with bottles of wine, binoculars, bat detector, torches and laptop all of which were adorned with a scraggy bunch of flowers for Al that he picked up at a garage as an after thought. He headed down the path and pushed at the door with his bottom and called back to the others as they hovered by the gate.

'You going to hang out in the rain all day?'

They had watched with amazement as he walked along the path, with each step he had taken the fog had parted. It then dispersed and melted away into the drizzle.

Amy giggled, her terror forgotten and skipped up the path. She turned to her parents and grinned, 'He made them go away! He must be a wizard! Tom's a wizard!' she yelled and skipped happily towards the cottage.

Chapter thirty three

On his arrival Tom had handed over a couple of bottles of red wine.

'Hope these will do,' he screwed his nose up whilst he perused the label before passing them to Al, 'I did wonder at one point if I'd have any drink to bring along after Jim's attitude when I asked to buy them!'

'Jim? Is he playing up again?' Al asked as she read the label, 'Mmm this is great Tom, thank you.'

'Playing up? You can say that again. What's the matter with the man? He's normally so friendly and I used to enjoy staying at the Abbot but not any more.'

'Well you're stuck with him or old nosey Mrs Blackman's B&B, I know who I'd prefer!' laughed Chas, 'So anyway - what was up with him?'

'I asked him if I could buy a couple of bottles of wine and do you know what he said? 'I'm not a fucking off-licence you know!''

'Tom! Watch what you say,' Kit inclined her head towards Amy.

'Ohh sorry Kit, I forgot!' he gave an embarrassed smile.

'Jim's not been himself for ages,' said Al, 'I heard him ranting to someone on the phone yesterday when I was queuing at the fish van.'

'Yeah, you're right, he always seems angry these days. Must be the company he keeps,' said Tom, 'When I've been up in the woods checking on the sett I have seen him recently with that lot from Woodhurst village, they seem a rough sort.'

'The Wilkinson family? Yes they are,' Chas agreed.

'Still, young Steve's not too bad. You know? Susie's boyfriend? He's a Wilkinson,' Al chipped in as she opened the wine, 'Anyway Tom, I take it Jim must have relented and sold you a couple of bottles after all,' she took a sip, 'and very nice it is too!'

A few hours later the wine was now finished and the plates were empty. The wind outside had grown stronger, sending a blast of air down the chimney. The dying flames received a reprieve and danced around the logs enjoying their new spurt of life. Rain thundered down and splattered against the window in the gusting winds but it felt cosy and peaceful in the dining room. Alison felt content after a good meal and a few glasses of wine and reluctantly got up and wedged some more logs onto the fire.

She smiled as she looked across at Tom's flowers that sat on her new sideboard, they were already looking forlorn as they hung limply over the edge of the vase. She heard Amy giggle as Tom kept the sleepy girl amused with his tales of the badgers and other creatures of the woods. Al knew he was itching to get down into the crypt but was being patient and answered Amy's questions as best he could. The only one he couldn't answer was when she asked him how he had managed to make the evil fog move away. He hadn't seen any fog, he had told her, just drizzle and mist and certainly nothing evil.

Tom wasn't affected by anything that wasn't of this world. Which is why Al hadn't mentioned to him about her near death experience with Desmond or that she could hear the faint voices of the monks emanating from the crypt. She knew he would pass it all off with a reasonable explanation. Earlier when they were gathered in the kitchen, Chas had said that he thought he could vaguely make out the whispered chanting from the crypt. Tom had been amused at his suggestion that it was the spirits of the monks.

'Monks?' he laughed, 'But they've been dead and gone donkeys years! No, it's probably the wind finding its way in.' His mind mulled this over as he then aired his thoughts, 'Actually it could be blowing in through the gap where the bats are coming in, would be a good night to check it out. It might help me locate them.'

'Ok mate. We can take a look down there later. I can seek out the monks and you can find your bats.' Chas slapped his hand on Tom's shoulder and joked, 'That way we both get out of helping with the washing up!'

Al had overheard as she carried the dishes of vegetables through to the dining room, 'Washing up will wait. If you go bat hunting I'm coming too!'

Now some hours later she wondered if she'd have the energy to trek down in the crypt, maybe she would let the men go on an expedition on their own. She gathered up some of the plates ready to load in the dishwasher.

Kit, deep in conversation with Chas looked up.

'You doing that now?' she stood up and picked up a few dirty dishes from the table, 'I'll come and give you a hand.'

In the kitchen as Kit passed the plates she said, 'I was just saying to Chas, I might go home shortly, go back with Amy. I'm feeling really zonked out. Do you mind?'

'So soon? It's only just half past seven. You are both welcome to stay longer you know.'

'Chas will stay, he's keen to get a look in the crypt again, but no, I think I'll take Amy back.'

After goodbye hugs all round from Amy, they waved them off as Kit drove her young daughter home. The men turned towards the kitchen as soon as Al had closed the front door, eager to make their way down into the undercroft.

'We all ready to go?' Tom asked with head torch in position as he felt in his box for his bat detector, 'Oh bugger!'

'What's up?' Chas peered over to see what had given Tom cause for concern.

'The bat detector was left switched on. I wonder if the batteries will last out.' He fiddled with some controls, 'Hope it's not upset the residents down below. It's been outputting recordings of their echolocation for the past few hours.'

'Do you think that's what I heard earlier when I thought I heard chanting?' asked Chas.

Tom shook his head and smiled as he retrieved new batteries from a bag, 'No, it's unlikely you'd be able to hear that. Humans normally hear up to 20 kHz but Natterers output at over 35. It's this little gadget that helps me make out their calls when I set it to replay at a slower speed.'

'So was it on when you first arrived?' Chas asked as he begun to form a theory in his mind. He wondered if this had been the cause of the darkness dispersing. Maybe this gadget was the weapon they needed against the loitering fog.

'Yep! Still, I've got some more batteries now,' Tom looked up and smiled, 'Are we ready? They normally head off out about an hour after sunset,' he glanced at his watch, 'It's nearly eight now, so hopefully we will be down there in time.'

They cautiously made their way down the winding steps. It was the first time Al had been down in the crypt since her last visit with Tom. She had kept the great wooden door firmly locked ever since. She was sure the monks were down there somewhere. Maybe it was the monks that needed her help. Perhaps they had sent her the coin with the message? *absolvo purgatorio*. Release from purgatory. After being killed by Desmond maybe they were still waiting for a Christian burial? But if they were down in the crypt – where? Would they find them this evening? Al was certain she could make out their soft voices echoing against the bricks as they headed down into the dark towards the split in the tunnels at the end of the undercroft. The division of the tunnels was as far as any of them had ventured before and her stomach somersaulted, partly with excitement but also with fear.

'Okay folks, time to turn off the torches, we are close to where I saw them roosting before. Let's just hang about herc for a minute and see if we get any action.'

Turning off the torches was the last thing Al wanted to do. Whispered cries began to surround her, whirling round and round, circling her, no escape.

Help us. Please help us.

The air became thick with their despair. The chanting had stopped and her head was now filled with whispers of anguish and torment as they scratched at her mind for attention.

'Al? You need to turn your torch off,' Tom snapped.

'Okay, Okay!' The walls disappeared and she was in a void as the blackness surrounded her, 'How are we going to see them Tom? I can't see a bloody thing here!'

Chas sensed her panic and he reached out his hand and felt her squeeze it tightly, 'You alright Al? Don't worry, hang onto me.'

'Can you hear them Chas? I can hear the monks.'

'I can hear something, but I think it's just the wind. It's certainly blowing in from somewhere. Can't you feel it?'

Al tightened her grip on his hand, 'Yes I can…but…oh God...this is horrible Chas. I hate not being able to see.'

'Take a few deep breaths. Try not to panic. Don't forget you can turn your torch on anytime.'

'Keep close to me both of you,' Tom's calm voice said from the blackness up ahead. 'Here you are Al. Look through these. Night vision bins.'

Al reached out and held them up to her eyes. The infrared binoculars gave her an element of vision again. The panic subsided. She glimpsed a bat fluttering out from its hiding place and along the tunnel.

'Wow! This is amazing! Look, there goes one now!'

'They must have started heading out! Can I look again Al, I need to see what direction they're going.'

'The one I saw headed down the tunnel over to the right,' said Al not wanting to part with her only source of sight.

Tom took back the binoculars and Al edged herself up close to Chas and said quietly, 'I hope we can put the torches on soon Chas, I don't like this. I feel vulnerable not being able to see.'

'I know, hopefully not long now,' Chas reassured her but he too, felt as if the walls were closing in. The air felt damp and musty and the smell of droppings from the bats was becoming overpowering. He'd be pleased to get back up to the cottage.

'I think you're right Al,' said Tom, 'they are going to the right hand tunnel. Shall we make our way along there and see if we can find their exit point?'

'Can we use our torches yet? I don't fancy walking far in pitch black?'

Tom passed her a small torch, 'Here, use this, but point it to the floor.' A thin beam of red light trickled down onto her feet as they carefully made their way towards the spilt of the two tunnels. Al felt the bats brush past her head and she clung onto Chas as they took tentative steps forward into the dark abyss. All the while the hushed voices seeped into her mind.

Help us.

Tom strode on in front, holding up the night vision binoculars to catch sight of one or two bats as they headed through the tunnel.

'I can really feel the fresh air coming in,' Tom hissed back to them, 'I don't think it can be far now. I can see them heading up higher. Hey, this is great, more of them now! Here, take a look!'

They took it in turns to watch as the bats fluttered along the tunnel and up into the gloom above before they disappeared from sight.

A short time elapsed and then Tom announced to a relieved Al and Chas, 'I think that's the last of them, we can turn our main torches on now.'

The bricks of the tunnel suddenly emerged from the dark emptiness that had been their world for the past ten minutes. It had felt like ten hours to Alison. Their lights revealed that they were standing at the end of the passageway, a semi circular brick wall blocked their way. They were unable to continue further. Tom's torch scanned the wall, skimming across the surface for signs of an opening. As the shaft of light neared the top it hit on a gentle stream of water that trickled slowly down from a mass of spidery roots that protruded through the ancient bricks.

'Look!' Tom directed the light above, his head tilted back, 'There's a huge gash just above those roots, must be at least a metre wide, they must be heading out up there. I wonder where outside this can be?'

Chas rubbed his hands across the dusty bricks, 'It's circular. Do you know what? I think this could be the old well! It's definitely in the right direction.'

'You're right! And I know there's a great hole in the cover. Yep, I think that's it Chas. They're getting in through the well. Can I take a look outside in the morning Al, see if I can catch sight of them, they usually return an hour or two before sun up?'

'Yes, of course you can. But don't expect me to join you at that hour!'

They headed back towards the main undercroft. As they approached the split where the other tunnel headed off the left Chas said, 'Seems a shame to be here and not check out where this way leads, don't you think?'

Apprehensive they would end up getting lost in a maze of passageways Al said, 'As long as we can use our torches I'm happy to take a look, but only if it's not too far. I don't want to end up walking for miles.'

Ten minutes on and the passageway continued its trail under the earth. Al flicked the torch around the walls as they carried on deeper down into the tunnel. The bricks had now been replaced with natural rock, and the beam picked out veins of white stone weaved within the walls like ribbons of satin.

'Look at that. Isn't it beautiful?' Al moved her torch higher and a few areas of crystallised rock sparkled in the light, 'What is it? Any idea?'

Tom peered up, 'The white stone looks like Gypsum to me. They still mine it locally I believe, they use it to make plasterboard.'

'I assume the monks must have gleaned their supplies from here,' Chas said.

Al rubbed her hand over the soft stone, 'Monks? Why would they need it?'

'I remember reading in the blurb about the Abbey. It was used to make something called gesso, a sort of primer I suppose. It acted as a base before they painted their illuminated letters,' Chas told her.

'How lovely!'

'Actually I believe gypsum is sometimes added to the water when they made mead too,' Tom added.

'Yes, that's right,' Chas said, 'I think Jim has been using it in the mead he brews.'

'So the monks may have taken it from here? Wow, to think all of this is under the Abbey ruins!'

As they continued, the air gradually began to feel less oppressive and underfoot it became softer as the gritty floor made way for soil, slightly damp and muddy in places. Thin rivulets of water dribbled from the bare rock. Al looked down at her feet, the bottom of her trousers were becoming wet.

'Well, we have been walking twenty minutes now and it just seems to be going on and on. What do you think guys? Five more minutes and then head back if we don't reach anything?'

Tom shone the torch along the tunnel as it veered round to the right, 'I think we must be close to the river now. Can you smell the freshness? And I think I can hear the rain.'

Al listened, 'Yes, you're right. Sounds like it's tipping it down.'

As they followed the path round the bend they found that the tunnel opened up into a massive cave.

'Look at this, you could have a party here! It's huge!' Al spun her torch around revealing a high roofed room, 'I think I've spotted the way out to the woods and river over there.'

She made her way over to an opening, but found that it was barred by high metal railings, 'It's padlocked up. It makes it feel like we are in a prison!'

Chas lifted up the lock and heavy chain, 'The lock's not rusted up, looks like it's been used recently. This place puts me in mind of the hellfire caves over at Wycombe. There were some dodgy characters who used to meet up there centuries ago!' Chas shuddered.

'Looks as if some dodgy characters meet up here too Chas,' Tom scuffed his foot at something lying on the ground, 'There's been people here for sure. And not that long ago.'

Al was suddenly aware of the shadows in the cave, dark corners where someone could still be hiding. She dashed over to Tom.

'What is it you've discovered?'

'Look here. The floor is littered with cigarette butts and empty beer cans but more worrying are those marks near the middle of the cave,' Tom told her, 'If I'm not mistaken those stains on the ground look like blood to me.'

Chapter thirty four

Chas crouched down and looked at the blood tinged soil.

'I don't like the look of that, I wonder what's been going on here?'

Tom knelt next to him and picked at some grey hairs that he spotted on the gritty floor, rubbing them between his thumb and index finger.

'The bastards!' His eyes filled with tears. He really couldn't comprehend the mentality of people. Why? What on earth was wrong with them?

'What is it Tom?' Al placed her hand on his arm and looked intently into his eyes. She could see he was deeply upset, 'What have you found?'

He held out his hand. She watched as the wiry fur on his palm floated in the breeze and fell gently to the ground.

'Badger fur Al. They've been using this area for fighting. The bastards!' he screamed and banged his fist again the wall of the cave, 'God, when I get my hands on the scum!' An empty beer can flew across the floor as he kicked out, his anger at boiling point.

'Fighting? You mean you think they've been using this spot for fighting the badgers? Are you sure?'

Tom paced around the floor of the cave trying to keep his rage in control. The anger was searing through his veins.

'As sure as I can be. It has all the hallmarks of a fighting ring.' He knelt down and pulled at a metal ring that protruded slightly from the floor. It was rammed in solidly, no way he could remove it with his bare hands. 'They sometimes chain the poor sods to this, makes it easier for the dogs to do their work.' His hand gripped tightly around the ring, his knuckles white as he continued to pull madly at the metal hook to no avail.

'So it's not even a fair fight then. What do they get out of it? Seeing innocent creatures mauled to death?' Al knelt beside Tom and gently took his hand away from the metal ring. She called across at Chas who was now examining the gates, 'Is there anyway we could block it up Chas? Stop them from coming in do you think?'

'I was just wondering that Al. I've got some steel sheets back at the yard, they're from a building job I did for the council. I could fix them against the gate, that would stop the buggers getting in.'

Tom stood up, ' No! We don't want to do that!'

'But we don't want them getting in surely?'

'As long as they don't know we are onto them we can do our own baiting - catch them at it. I'll get in touch with the police wildlife officer, fill him in on what's happening, I can keep a close eye until then.'

'I don't like the thought of this all being open access to Al's place though Tom.'

'Nor me. I wonder if you could block it off further up inside the tunnel perhaps, up inside enough that they wouldn't notice. It will give Al some peace of mind. I doubt if they will be back immediately though. Takes them a time to set up the next one.'

'I'll get onto sorting this out first thing in the morning Al,' Chas said, 'Block this passageway off. Come on, let's get out of here.'

He kept his breathing in check as he stood in the shadows. He thought he had heard voices earlier and at first just assumed it was the irritating monks again. He always heard their whispered cries when he was here. But then the intruders had made their way past his hiding place, their torch beams not giving him away. He stood tight up against the rock in a small gap along the passageway up from the cave, safely out of sight. He'd be unlucky if he was caught. His ears strained to listen but they were too far away; the voices too muffled to catch their words. But he knew. He knew what they would have found and the assumptions they would have made. He had an idea. It wasn't the best solution but he was tired. He couldn't carry on as he was. At least it would put an end to it all.

Their voices became louder as they made their way back along the tunnel towards the undercroft, walking past his hiding place, unaware of his presence. Once their voices faded into the distance he sneaked his way to the cave. He double-checked the coast was clear before heading over to the gate. The key turned easily in the padlock. He disappeared into the night.

Back in the kitchen, Chas and Al were sitting drinking coffee. Tom had sped off, he wanted to get a report to the police as soon as he could and make a plan of action.

Al warmed her hands on the mug. It had felt cold in the cottage as they walked back through the oak door into the kitchen. Smouldering remnants of glowing logs was all that remained of the fire in the dining room. She had tweaked up the heating thermostat in the hall and hoped it would warm up soon and had pulled on Mark's fleece, wrapping the oversized jacket around her. It felt comforting, as if he was there with her, protecting her from evil.

'So, are you okay for me to come back in the morning and fix some metal sheets along the passage?' Chas looked at Al and wondered if she would be happy staying there that night alone.

'That'll be good Chas, thanks. I doubt if they would come this far, and the door is pretty heavy and secure but it would make me feel happier if it was blocked off.'

Chas nodded and sipped his coffee. They sat in silence for a few minutes, the sound of the freezer cutting in broke them from their thoughts.

'I wonder where that opening is located? I'm sure if the villagers knew it was there it would be common knowledge. The kids of the village would be on it like a shot, a great place to play but I don't remember Kit ever mentioning it. I'll ask her when I get back,' he looked at his watch, 'talking of which I best make tracks soon.' He stood up and put his mug under the tap and washed the last dregs of coffee away and glanced across noticing the box on the worktop.

'Looks like Tom's left his stuff here.' He went across and started to look inside, 'He'd thrown his torches and gear in here when we first got back and he dashed to the loo. He must have forgotten about it when he headed off, he was in that much of a rage, he was like a man possessed!'

'Perhaps you can take it back with you and drop it off at the pub tomorrow for him?' Al yawned and watched as he pulled out Tom's night vision binoculars and then the bat detector.

'I had a few ideas about this,' he told Al as he examined the object and fiddled with the switches, 'Tom said it could play back the bat echoes at their output or at a frequency we can hear.' he continued to play around with buttons with no success.

Al offered out her hand, 'Shall I have a look?' she took it from Chas and twisted the gadget around trying to locate the on button, 'That's nice!' she smiled.

'What's nice?'

'The maker's name, look. It's called the 'The Angel Echo locator.''

Chas laughed, 'That makes the bats sound rather prettier than they look! I always think they are ugly little things.'

There was beep from the gadget as Al finally sussed out how to switch it on.

'Well done Al, that sounds like you've got it working. If you can manage to work out how to play back the recording at bat frequency, you know, how Tom had it playing by mistake when he first arrived, then I'd like to try something out.'

'Okkkaaaay…that sounds intriguing.' Al fiddled some more, the clicking sounds of the bats suddenly stopped but the unit was still running.' Al passed it back to Chas, 'Here, I think that's it. So, what do you have in mind?'

'First, let's see if the fog has come back outside.'

Chas headed for the front door, bat detector in hand. Al followed close behind. What on earth was Chas up to? She had no idea where this was leading at all. What had the bat detector got to do with the Darkness?

The door swung open, the air was thick with the swirling mists. Nothing was visible outside. A slight shiver of apprehension came across Chas when he realised he was going to have to walk home across the fields as Kit had taken the car back earlier. Still, if his plan worked maybe it would be okay.

'Right, let me see if my theory is correct,' he hesitantly stepped down onto the path and slowly made his way towards the gate. The heavy dark fog around him began to clear, he felt like Moses and the red sea as the dark clouds of evil dispersed, circling swiftly above and then it just disappeared into the night sky.

He turned and smiled at Alison, 'I think I have discovered the tool to rid you of Desmond and the Darkness! How good is that?'

Al grinned from ear to ear, 'Chas! That is amazing! It just disappeared. Pop – off it went! How does it work do you think – any ideas?'

He shook his head, 'Beyond me. Must be the frequency of the bat echoes and the way it's transmitted. Old Desmond and his cronies obviously aren't too keen!'

She grinned, 'This is brilliant! All these years and finally we know how to send the Darkness packing! Okay, only temporary I know but it's a start.'

'For now! I was thinking Al. Maybe we could set up something by the door to constantly send out the signals? That may work.'

'That would be wonderful. Do you think we could? Oh Chas, I'll have to tell ole nosey Mrs Blackman about this. She was only saying when I had tea with her yesterday that nothing can rid the area of the darkness!'

'Mrs B? You had tea with her? I'm amazed she gave you the time of day…'

'Awwww she seems alright, why do you say that?'

'I just didn't think she'd be too keen on you, yet another woman who is friends with her Roger,' Chas laughed.

'Her Roger?' Al frowned, 'Sorry I don't...'

'I'm only messing. Roger had a romance with her daughter, way back. Kit tells me that Mrs B blames him that she went away. They split up when Dorothy wanted to move abroad to work. Kit has this mad idea that Mrs B sends anyone sniffing around Rog packing as she is hoping Roger will get back with Dorothy and she will return to Greysmead to live. I can't see it myself, it was years ago now.'

'Well, I'm not 'sniffing around' Roger. I'm no threat! Don't know why you think I would be!' Al snapped.

'No, of course not. Only joking,' Chas smiled when he saw he'd hit on a nerve. Best to change the subject. 'Anyway, this bat detector, perhaps you should hang onto this up here for now? I can pretend to Tom I left it behind by mistake, you can use it for a while and then maybe buy one if you think it's working. I can help you fix up by the door if you'd like me to.'

'That's a great idea Chas, thanks,' she smiled at him, her claws now retracted. 'You've been great.' She tried to stifle a yawn, she'd not had a great deal of sleep since Mark's visit and it was catching up on her. 'So tomorrow? You'll come over and fix up that barrier? Sure you don't mind?'

'No, that's no trouble Al,' he touched her arm lightly and handed the detector back to her, 'Here take this, I'll just nip in and fetch Tom's box of things and head off.'

A few moments later he was heading across the footpath towards the village. The orange glow of the village streetlights filtered through the benign mists that gently caressed the fields. The rain had finally stopped and the air smelt fresh with the rich scent of wet earth. Al felt a surge of contentment as she watched Chas head towards Greysmead. The bat detector gave her a feeling of power and control. She looked at the small device in her hand and read again the maker's name. She smiled. Echoes from an Angel were protecting her.

She pulled Mark's fleece tighter, and as she did so it released the aroma of peppermint. It soothed her, reminded her, making him feel close. She closed her eyes momentarily and could almost feel him standing beside her, kissing her neck. Her stomach twisted with excitement. Maybe Roger had managed to track him down by now, hopefully it wouldn't be long before he came back. She prayed she would hear from him soon.

Roger finished his coffee and started to sift through the CCTV footage again. There had to be something there. WPC Ellis came into the room and sat next to him. She'd recently transferred over from a station north of the river and when she heard what had happened to Mark she had volunteered to help Roger. She had worked with Mark some years ago and Roger wondered if they'd once had a bit of a thing going as she had been quite upset when she first heard the news that he had gone.

'There must be something here showing them chucking him into a vehicle,' he said, feeling frustrated. He'd been looking at hours of footage with no luck.

'So the hospital's CCTV didn't show up anything? No proof? Nothing to pin it on Big Mick's lot?' she asked.

'No, an ambulance was in front of the doorway. The pictures show the steps of A&E empty, then two frames later we see Mark lying there, out cold.' He stretched his arms back behind his head, 'There must be something! I'm going to look at one more and then call it a day.' He clicked on the folder labelled Cinderella's. Roger watched, almost on autopilot but his alert brain was ready to spot anything at all that looked suspicious. Suddenly he re-wound a section and played it again.

'Shit! I don't believe it!' he clicked to look at the date of the file, 'Fucking hell!' He felt sick.

'What? Have you found something?'

Roger replayed the scene again, 'I have, but nothing to help us to either nail the bastards who gave Mark the beating or anything to do with drugs supplies. This is something else.' He jumped up, 'I'm just going to have a word with the Guv.'

She nodded. So what had he seen? She saw it was footage from only three days ago. She played the film and watched as a burly doorman stood on the steps of Cinderella's, as he talked to an old scruffy down and out. The doorman turned and called to someone inside. A few moments later Big Mick appeared and the tramp could be seen speaking to him. Mick looked angry and grabbed at the old man who nodded his head. Mick let him go and said something to the doorman and then swiftly headed back inside. WPC Ellis watched as the doorman took some notes from his wallet and handed them to the tramp who then happily headed off, but not before looking straight up at the CCTV camera, kissing the money and giving a toothless smile.

She knew that face. It was only recently he'd spent a night in the cells. It was that old toe rag Johnny.

Chapter thirty five

Chas headed into the Abbot the morning after the underground expedition. The pub seemed deserted when he arrived.

'Hello! Anyone about?'

The dining room was empty, most of the breakfast tables cleared, save for a few spent coffee cups and toast crumbs. Chas had hoped he'd catch Tom at breakfast but he could hear the chink of cutlery from the kitchen as Susie and staff busily cleared the way ready for the lunchtime sitting. He wondered if Tom was back up in his room or had he already headed off? He hadn't noticed his car outside but he may have parked round the back.

He decided not to disturb Susie and headed back outside, towards the archway that led through the cobbled courtyard to the car park beyond. He would check and see if Tom's car was still there. He glanced up at the pub sign as it creaked in the wind. It was looking worse for wear. The Abbot didn't look that jolly anymore. The breeze eased as Chas stepped through into the sheltered courtyard that had once been the first port of call for travellers. A place where they would leave their horses to be taken to the stables overnight. The stables were long gone, pulled down and now in their place was the tarmac car park.

As Chas crossed the courtyard he heard a noise from behind the door that led off to the cellar. Something heavy was being dragged along. An uttering of swear words drifted out from behind the door before it suddenly swung open. It was Jim, looking extremely hot and flustered. He did a double take when he spotted Chas.

'Hello Charlie mate,' he said, his face red and damp, 'Why are you lurking out there?' He rubbed his forearm across his brow, wiped away the sweat, took out a tin from his pocket and began to roll himself a cigarette. He leant against the wall, one leg bent back, foot held flat against the bricks as he deftly crafted his nicotine fix.

'Just heading to the car park – looking for Tom Elliott. You look a bit hot Jim, you need a hand with anything?'

'No, you're alright. Just moving some of the mead ready for bottling. Mrs B is going to stock some on the shelves of the shop. Got me some labels made up too.'

'Are you sticking with the original name?'

Jim screwed up his eyes as he drew deeply on his roll-up, 'Yeah, Greys Mead. That's how the village got its name after the mead of the Greyfriars so I thought I best stick with it.'

'It's good to know the village mead is back in production Jim. I bet the old Abbot would be pleased to know the old tradition is back up and running again.'

'I don't give a toss what the bloody monks think of it to be honest Chas. All I want it to do is sell, so I can make some money.'

'Do you still make it to the old recipe?'

'Yep. The one Mrs Blackman has,' Jim dragged hard on his cigarette, 'Said it had been handed down her family from one of the monks. Hah! Don't believe that, do you?'

'It's possible. We've got stuff at home that was ransacked from the Abbey after the...you know... '

'After the villagers went on the rampage you mean? Yeah, there's a couple of bits in the pub too,' he shrugged his shoulders, 'Yeah, maybe it is from the monks then. Maybe it will eventually shut the buggers up if I make it how they like it!'

'What do you mean? I didn't think you believed in all the ghostly tales about the Abbey?'

'No, I don't usually but lately I keep thinking I'm hearing them when I've been up the lane getting the gypsum for the mead. The monk's recipe calls for it to be added to the water – softens it I think. Don't know if it's worth the hassle. But Mrs B was adamant I kept to the recipe if I was going to call it Greys Mead.'

Chas began to probe, 'Ahhh yes, I remember you telling me you added gypsum, so where do you get yours then? Up the lane you said?'

Jim's eyes flicked from side to side, not looking directly at Chas as he answered, 'There's a rocky crevice up near the river, in what was once Mrs Blackman's back garden. I get it from there when I'm up that way.'

Chas was poised to ask more, see if Jim had any knowledge of the badger fighting when Susie appeared from the archway, tea towel in hand.

'Dad…Dad…phone.' Seeing Chas she smiled and came closer, 'Dad, a call for you. Hiya Charlie. How's you?'

Chas nodded and smiled.

'Who is it Suz?' Jim said, 'Can't it wait?'

'They said it was urgent.'

'Sorry Chas. Catch you again soon.' He went over to the door from where he had emerged and locked it before making his way across the cobbles. He turned and called back to Chas, '…And by the way, Tom Elliott went out early this morning, said he'd be back this afternoon.'

Susie stayed in the courtyard, wringing the tea towel around in her hands. 'Does Dad seem okay to you Charlie?'

He could see the worry in her eyes. He took in her bright red hair, her dark made up eyes. She always came across as a strong young woman, able to look after herself. But behind all that makeup and way out clothes she was still a young girl, she couldn't yet be 20 but all her teenage years she'd had a lot to contend with on her young shoulders. Ever since her Mother had left she'd been there supporting her Dad. Chas felt a pang of concern for her.

'Yes Suz, I have noticed he has seemed a little stressed lately. Any idea what's wrong?'

She chewed her lower lip, her hands still squeezing at the tea towel.

'Not really no. He says everything's okay but he is always going off on one over nothing. Trouble is I'm wanting to tell him something but not sure what to do. How to get him at the right moment. Chas? You'd watch out for him wouldn't you if I wasn't around?'

'Of course I would but why d'you say that? Where you planning on going?'

She leant against the wall and Chas smiled inwardly. How like her Father she was, same mannerisms, same tough exterior.

'You know my Steve?' she began, 'Well he's really straightened himself out. He got pulled in with a bad lot for a while but he's good again now. He's got a job. Starts next month.'

'That's great Susie!'

'Yeah, trouble is it's down in Somerset. Working for a friend of Dad's cousin who lives down there. We'd both be going.' She bit her lip again and her face began to flush as her eyes filled, 'I SO want to go but how do I tell Dad? How can I leave him? I'm worried he might be caught up with the same people that brought Steve down for a while,' a tear trickled down her cheek and she roughly brushed it away.

'Doing what Suz? What do you think he's caught up with?' Charlie's brain ticked over. He said he was collecting gypsum from Monkton Lane. Surely Jim wouldn't get involved with badger fighting?

She shook her head, 'I really don't know for sure but at a guess it's Steve's Uncle, he's into a lot of dodgy stuff, so it could be anything. It was him on the phone for Dad just now. What shall I do Chas?' She let the tears flow freely as she cried to Chas in desperation, 'What can I do?'

Later that day Chas was about to head back home. He'd spent a few hours at Al's where he'd managed to block the way to the cave with steel sheets bolted to the rock. His thoughts dwelled on Susie and how he could help her. He'd told her he'd get Kit to have a chat with her, help her talk it through, try to decide how to broach the subject with Jim.

'I've just got a bit of tidying left to do down there, but it's all secure. I'll pop back in a few days if that's okay,' he called to Al as he drove off.

'No problems. Thanks again Chas,' she stood at the gate smiling, the Darkness suppressed with the bat detector in her hand.

He waved his hand out of the car window as he headed along the lane and hit the gloom of the ivy tunnel. It was a dark damp day and even though it was only three o'clock he needed his headlights as he carefully drove around the potholes and avoided the sinewy snakes of roots that protruded from the crumbling tarmac. He hadn't travelled far when he spotted Tom's car parked up alongside a gap in the undergrowth so he pulled up behind him and walked up to the driver's door. Tom was sitting in his car eating a sandwich. He hurriedly finished chewing and put down the window.

'Hello Charlie! You just finished your barrier work in the tunnel?' He opened the door and slowly manoeuvred his lanky legs out of the car, stood up and stretched his arms, arching his back, 'I think it's time I changed my car. I got this one as it's economical on fuel but there really isn't much leg room!' he grinned and leant in to retrieve the rest of his sandwich.

'Have you been back to the pub yet? Did you get your stuff okay? I left it with Susie at the Abbot.'

Tom nodded as he finished another mouthful of sandwich, 'Yes, thanks for that. But the bat detector doesn't seem to be there. I was just popping up to Al's to see if she still had it but got sidetracked when I saw this opening. I just wondered if it leads to the cave entrance.'

'Sorry Tom. I will come clean, Al does still have your bat detector.'

He wondered how could he explain something so bizarre to this logical man? Chas proceeded to explain to Tom about all the happenings at Orchard Cottage as best he could, the glass on the floor, the chanting of the monks, the attempted strangulation and the dark fog and his detectors ability to clear it, at which point Tom interrupted him.

'Sorry Chas, but I really can't believe anything you have told me is to do with spooks, there really must be a reasonable explanation for it.'

'Like what?'

'Well, what if the badger baiters don't like the fact Al is living up here, maybe they are worried their game will be blown…which it has…what if they are just trying to frighten her off?'

'What? All that for a bit of badger baiting. I can't see that,' Chas wasn't convinced.

'It's not just the fun of seeing animals mauled to death Chas, bets are placed on these fights, vast sums of money are won and lost. It's a big money making game for some of the arseholes who run it. It's more than likely that a majority of badgers being caught locally aren't fighting here. They're probably being sold on to some gambling den in London.'

Chas looked at Tom, he knew a little about the activity, mainly from what he had read, but he'd assumed the fighting was just for their sick laughs, didn't realise money was involved.

'So how much money we talking about here?'

'God! They sell on the badgers they catch…four hundred…five hundred quid. Then the gambling, well it could be thousands of pounds!' Tom shook his head, even after all these years he found it hard to comprehend, 'So you see why I wonder if they are just trying to scare Al off, they won't be very nice people. They're probably into lots of other underhand dealings too.'

'I really didn't realise. You're right, everything that's happened. Frightening Al, yep it's plausible but I'm not totally convinced. It doesn't explain a lot of stuff that's happened.' He thought back to Amy and her visions of the sad lady but he knew Tom wouldn't believe it. He wouldn't even try, 'Yeah Tom, you are probably right.'

Tom laughed, 'Let Al keep the detector if it makes her feel safer. Just believing it's actually doing something will probably help her. Some people like having lucky charms, our Al likes a bat detector!'

Chas laughed along with him but inside had a gut feeling that it wasn't all as clear-cut as Tom imagined. 'Anyway Tom, did you get to see the wildlife officer? Did you report our findings? What's the plan?'

He wondered if he should tell Tom about Jim and the gypsum. Was Jim involved with more than collecting minerals from the area? He'll keep his suspicions to himself for now. He would really like to talk it over with Roger. Hopefully the drugs operation would get sorted soon and he'd be back.

Roger walked into the room. On his second attempt, he'd finally managed to get to speak to the Guv about the film footage he'd spotted earlier. His cheeks had two pinpricks of red, the only sign visible of his rage. He was usually a calm man and it took a lot to upset him. He wasn't someone who showed his anger but when it affected his family and loved ones – well that was an exception.

Carly Ellis took her eyes from the screen and watched as he came in and sat down, 'Well? What did he say?'

Roger shook his head, 'Not a lot. He's going to get someone down there, someone to keep an eye on her place in case any of Mick's cronies turn up.'

'So this friend of yours, she's Kenny Greenways ex? She's the one who finally came clean with the witness statement?'

He nodded, 'Yeah, and I know it makes sense to wait before we pull them in. It would jeopardise this big operation. They are small fry in comparison to the main source of the drugs.'

'Too right. It's beginning to look like it will be a huge hit if we get them. So do you think Johnny knows Kenny's ex has spilled to us?'

Rogers's stomach twisted with anguish at the thought that due to him he may have put Al in danger.

'Johnny saw her talking to me, when he left the station that morning. God! I didn't know he had connections with Big Mick!'

His hands went to his face and he rubbed at his eyes. He felt wrecked. He had been viewing the footage all day long and this was the end result. That little shit Johnny had recognised Al, had blabbed to Mick that he saw her at the station. That *must* be it. What else would he be telling him? Should he ring her? Warn her? No, he told himself, she would panic; probably push her over the edge after all she's been through. She'd blame him for making her give the statement. Did he make her? No, it was her idea, but she'd probably not see it like that. She'd hate him. He couldn't have that.

He gave Carly a weak smile, 'I'm heading off for some shuteye now. Catch you first thing. Hopefully by then we'll have definite news on when the drop is happening.' He sighed, hopefully then all this hanging around and waiting will end and he could get back to Greysmead and see Alison.

They knew their strength was being sapped. Every time the echoes rushed at them they felt their power being drained. They watched from a distance until it was safe to return and then slowly they slithered through the air, spiralling down and eventually coiling themselves around the building again, keeping it in their grasp. It wouldn't be long now. They had to act soon. They needed feeding to replenish their strength and now anyone would do.

As the lamp flickered into life she thought she caught sight of a movement just under the windowsill. She turned to look and it was gone. Mark's fleece wrapped around her, she settled down and turned on the TV to bring some company into the place, to try to push away her uneasiness until finally, bleary eyed she made her way up to bed.

Maybe it would be soon that she would get news about Mark. She remembered his face, his laugh, his kiss. She only had to nestle her face into his fleece and she could smell him. The wondrous aroma of wood and peppermint lingered within the material allowing her to imagine him by her side, the strength of feeling so strong, it was as if he was there when she closed her eyes. The fine hairs on her arms rose slightly as she imagined him brushing his fingers along their length and up to her shoulder and neck.

She undressed and carefully hung his fleece over the back of the chair and slipped under the quilt. Eyes focused on the ceiling she relaxed as her body gradually sunk down into the mattress and she thought of him. Her eyelids became heavier as she drifted off to sleep. The room was quiet except for Al's gentle breathing. Mark's fleece was lit softly in the moonlight that filtered in through the gap in the curtains. There was movement. A presence, light and soft as gossamer, floated silently across the room and sunk down onto the chair. As it gently came to rest, the fleece slipped slightly on the wooden backrest. A sleeve moved. The arm began to swing, rocking from side to side like a pendulum, back and fro, lightly at first then faster and higher until it suddenly dropped and hung still.

She dreamt of her Father again, he was standing the other side of the barrier in the tunnels that had been erected a few days before. He was calling to her.

'Be careful Alison,' he cried in anguish and banged his fist against the metal sheet in despair unable to get to her.

'I'm okay Daddy,' she murmured in her sleep, 'The barrier will protect me, it will stop them getting to me. Don't worry I'm safe.'

'No!' he screamed, 'You will be trapped! Be careful my darling.'

There was a second voice. Someone else was behind the barrier with her Father. Who was it? She was sure she recognised the voice. Who was it? What were they saying?

The familiar voice whispered to her, 'Listen to the Monks Al. They will be your guide.'

But her Father cried out and thumped his hand loudly against the metal, 'Alison!' he called and still the banging continued. Thud, Thud. Hammering. Louder and louder.

Her eyes opened as she woke with a start and sat up in bed, her heart racing in her chest, her mouth dry. She looked across at the clock. 11pm. She'd only been asleep a short time. The room glowed silver in the moonlight. And still the banging continued.

Loud insistent thuds echoed up the stairs and then she heard the voice. 'Alison…Alison,' as a voice called to her from the floor below.

Chapter thirty six

At 9 pm that same night Cinderella's was a hive of activity. It was an hour before the club would open. A couple of barman were busy re-stocking the mixers and emptying the dishwasher, checking that the glasses were sparkling. Big Mick had high standards.

He clicked his fingers, calling his most trusted henchmen into the inner sanctum. They followed him obediently into his back room. Mick sat regally on his throne, as they waited to hear his declaration.

Mick's eyes scanned his tribe through half closed eyes, 'It seems the rozzers are hell bent on pinning the murder of Billy Watson on me.'

Murmurs were heard around the room, 'Bastards!'

'What about Evie? They trying to get you for that an'all?' the doorman asked.

Mick slammed his fist down hard on the table, 'Forget Evie! She is the least of my worries. She was just a tart,' his raised voice ricocheted around the room, 'but yeah, they do think I slit her throat,' he looked across at Kenny, 'And now we have word that your ex missus has spoken to the fifth, telling them all she knows.'

The room fell silent, eyes switched to Kenny to see where his loyalties lay. The chink of glasses echoed through from the bar as Mick leant back in his chair and lifted his arms high giving a full stretch before bringing them down behind his head. 'Well, I've been thinking. It might be best we take a visit to Sussex.'

Kenny's usual dull eyes momentarily displayed a slight notion of regret. Mick stood up, and grabbed his jacket, 'I think it's time we gave wifey her final visit Kenny boy. Come on.'

As they walked towards the door they were unaware their words had been overheard. He had been careful. He had stayed hidden from view. He needed to act quickly so turned and sped off as fast as he could to Greysmead.

'Alison,' he called and continued to bang at the door. Mick and Kenny were not long behind him. He had to alert her, 'Alison, open the door!'

At last, to his relief the door opened. She stood there, her face flushed, eyes bright. His fleece was wrapped around her shoulders. A pink nightdress clung tightly to her thighs making him swell with desire for her. If only it was possible, he sighed.

'Mark! Oh my God! It's you – you've come back! I knew you would,' her face alight with happiness. Her eyes met his and for that spilt second they were the only two people in the world. She knew in her heart he loved her. He had come back.

Mark rushed in and slammed the door behind him. She went forward to touch him, hug him, but he rushed past her in a flurry of activity.

'Mark! What's the matter? What's happened?'

She ran behind him, followed him into the kitchen. She wanted to hold him, feel his arms around her but he seemed hell bent on unlocking the wooden door to the undercroft. She could see that the spark in his eyes had returned.

He turned to look at her, 'Al, I'm sorry but there is no time to explain fully. Big Mick and Ken are on their way - and they want you dead.'

His words winded her, 'What?' her mind was a whirlwind, 'How do you know? Are you sure? Oh Mark! Do they know…do they know I told the police?'

He nodded as he knelt and pulled aside the rug that covered the trapdoor to the crypt and lifted the hatch.

'Al, I'm sorry I can't tell you more. There really is no time. You must trust me,' he looked at her and nodded, 'You do trust me don't you?'

'Of course I do. Tell me what I must do,' she went to touch him but he kept his distance.

'You must get away Al. Go down into the crypt. Go and hide. I will lock it up before they get here, hopefully they won't find the trapdoor. Go on,' he indicated to the steps, 'Get down there – fast! GO ON!' he shouted at her. He knew Mick could arrive any moment and there was something he needed to do first.

'But what about you? They'll hurt you. Aren't you coming down with me? You can't stay here Mark.'

'I'll be okay. I'll make sure I'm out of sight by the time they get here. Don't worry I've got a plan.' He pressed his hand firmly on her back and pushed her down towards the opening, 'They'll be here soon. Please Al, just get down there.'

She was crying now. He hated seeing her so upset, hated shouting at her but he had to try to stop Mick. This was the only way. He pushed the trap door shut.

The void of black hit her. He hadn't given her a chance to prepare. She didn't even have a torch. She felt in the pockets of the fleece and her hands touched on something cold, but her hopes were short-lived. It was the bat detector. That would be of no use to help her see. Her feet carefully felt each step down as she placed her palms flat against the wall and slowly descended the spiral stone staircase. She knew there was a candle sconce at the base of the steps and remembered she had left matches there when she first came down into the crypt. If only she could find them. Her feet continued their tentative descent, one foot slowly down, then the other, her hands pressed tightly against the wall. Her tightened stomach muscles loosened slightly as her foot finally touched the bottom. She breathed out long and slow, realising she had been holding her breath.

Her mind rushed with so many thoughts. Ken and Mick wanted to kill her! If she was to survive this she had to be quiet. If they heard a noise they'd try to seek her out. They'd pull the place apart to find her. She knew Big Mick. He always got what he wanted. But what about Mark? Her stomach tightened again. Where could he hide? If they found him, he was dead.

She began to sob, her lips contorted as her emotions took hold. She felt the nausea rise in her throat and held her hand tightly against her mouth to hold back her cries. She had to stay calm. Think Al, think. Where were the matches? She slowed her breathing and tried to stay as composed as possible and thought back to her first visit to the crypt, pictured it in her mind. She was certain they were on the shelf by the candle. She had to find the candle.

Blinking in the darkness she placed her hand against the bricks and slowly and methodically scanned every inch alongside the stairway with her palms. It had to be there. Her hands suddenly hit on the metal bracket of the candleholder. Thank God! Her fingers felt along the ridge in the bricks and eventually touched upon the box of matches. Her hand tightened around them, scared they would fall. Her hands shook as she opened the box and took out a match, carefully pushing the box tightly shut before striking. The flame burst into life, illuminating the crypt. As Al stretched up and put a light to the candle, a dark figure stepped unseen into the gloom.

Along the high street the side door of the bed and breakfast opened. Mrs Blackman went outside to investigate a noise. She'd heard the sound of a car engine and she thought she'd heard voices. Bobby, her huge bruiser of a cat wasn't in. It was a good excuse to go out and see what was happening. She did so like to know what was going on.

'Bobby! Bobby! Are you there?' Her torchlight shone out onto the grass bank outside Kit's home. A vague shadow lingered for a moment outside the front door of the house and seemed to head toward the footpath. Was there someone there? Mrs Blackman began to make her way across the road.

'Bobby, is that you?' She swung the torch again. It picked out the flower tubs under the windows. Was there something near the pots? She couldn't quite make out if there was anything there or was it just a trick of the light? The moon appeared from behind a solitary cloud and lit up the road allowing her to watch the broad figure of a man as he headed up the path towards Monkton Lane.

That was funny. It wasn't anyone she recognised. Surely no one would be visiting Mrs Greenways at this time of night. Her mind went back to the tealeaf reading. It had been worrying. She stood for a moment in the moonlight wondering if she should knock at Kit's. Let her know about the man. It might be wise. Or was she being silly? It was as she was about to press the doorbell that a hand came from behind and pressed firmly against her face. She felt hot breath against her ear.

'No you don't, you old bag.'

She struggled to breathe. His hand smelt of stale urine and the stench penetrated her nostrils as he held his hand tightly over her mouth and nose. She tried to call for help, but a low mumble was all she managed before his other hand slipped the cold steel into her chest. She felt the warmth of her own blood as it pumped out of the wound before she fell to the ground.

She vaguely heard the gruff voice of the large man on the footpath, 'Kenny, what are you up to? Come on. Hurry up.'

Kenny hissed back in the darkness to his companion, 'Doing nothing Mick, just coming.'

His vacant eyes swept across the bleeding body at his feet. Did he do that? Confused he took in his surroundings and then realised he had a blood stained knife in his hand. He slipped it under his coat and went after Mick. Best get away. He didn't know who she was, didn't care.

The grassy bank cushioned her back as she stared up at the night sky. She felt calm as she watched the stars glittering above her. The moon bathed her in its silver light and she smiled as the glowing ball turned into the face of her daughter Dorothy looking kindly down at her. There was a rushing sound in her ears and everything went dark.

Mark locked the wooden door and went to hang the key on the hook. He stopped and looked at it and frowned. His eyes looked round the kitchen and fell upon the deep fat fryer. He opened it up and tossed the key inside and grinned.

He knew he didn't have long now. Time was tight. In the dining room he ducked under the fireplace and reached up to the shelf.

Sod it, it was too high!

He grabbed a dining chair and managed to manoeuvre it in place and he leant in and pulled out the canvass bag. Gotcha my beauty. He smiled and threw it down on the floor and reached back in and took out the tin of amulets and charms.

He gathered up his booty after replacing the chair and scanned the room. Satisfied he'd left no clues of his visit he slipped out of the back door and headed towards the river. He stopped for a moment and looked back at the cottage, his face looking up at the sky, watching the wisps of dark mists gradually sinking lower towards the house.

'Yeah! That's it! Come on you fuckers! Come on down! Do your worst!' He laughed, 'Mick won't know what's bloody hit him!' He scooted past the ruins and disappeared under the trees. He had to get his cache as far away from the cottage as he could.

Desmond and the darkness sensed the boundaries had been unlocked. They could replenish their strength at last! The dark fog circled Orchard cottage, round and round, faster and faster and slithered its way in through the gap below the door until it had choked the house with its evil presence.

'Look, there it is, that's her cottage, I remember it from that day I came up to check that bastard wasn't getting too friendly with her.'

'Turns out he was though eh Kenny boy!' Mick laughed, 'And a fucking copper too! I pissed myself when I found out! Your missus shagged by the filth and you gave him a right hiding! What a laugh!'

'He had you fooled though didn't he Mick? He worked for you for months without you realising.'

Mick turned round to Ken, his face close. Ken could see the whites of his eyes shining in the moonlight.

'You just shut it. Let's concentrate on the job in hand okay?' Mick snarled.

Ken knew he had over stepped the line and continued to follow Mick along the footpath. He had a twinge of remorse about the old woman he'd knifed. But he didn't want to take any chances. They'd parked the car far down the little lane by the church, it was well out of sight there. They didn't want the car being seen anywhere near Al's place, just in case. Shame the old biddy was out looking for her bloody cat just as they were heading up to Al's. Still she was ancient, probably would have popped her clogs soon anyway.

They walked silently through the gate and along the path of the cottage and Ken deftly slipped the lock with the blade, still stained with Mrs Blackman's blood. Mick put his fingers to his lips. He could hear noises inside. He'd had thought the lovely Mrs Greenways would have been tucked up in bed by now. It wasn't going to be as straightforward forward as he hoped.

Big Mick's hand pushed at the door and it swung open slowly and they stepped inside. The house was in darkness but it wasn't just devoid of light. A thick fog filled the hallway and swirled around in great sweeping circles. The smell of sulphur and decay filled the air. Mick and Kenny were rooted to the spot, unable to move. Fear was their jailor. They watched as distorted faces appeared momentarily in the thick clouds that whirled around them. The faces came and went, flying around within the thick, foul smelling fog, the mouths moving, screaming and shouting obscenities. Hands, bony with putrid weeping sores flayed out to them, grabbing at Mick and Ken's faces, long yellow fingernails scraped at their skin. Razor sharp, they stabbed at their neck, probed at their flesh.

And then one face loomed out to them, it lacked flesh apart from rotting ribbons of skin hanging from what were once its cheeks. Maggots crawled amongst the eyeballs that hung loosely from the sockets. It opened it mouth and screeched. The front door slammed shut behind Mick and Kenny and their screams echoed around the cottage as they became absorbed by the darkness.

Chapter thirty seven

Abbot Thomas stood in the shadows and watched the young woman. He was aware that she carried the bloodline of lay brother John. John had been a good man, but weak, unable to resist his desire for the woman named Mary. Thomas did feel sorrow for his own actions against John, he regretted treating him badly by sending him away. Things may have ended so differently if he had been allowed to stay at Greysmead. He knew that now.

He sighed. He was tired. His worldly body may have been taken away from his beloved Abbey but his spirit remained and would do so until his brother's souls could rest in peace. He would not rest, could not rest, until they too had found their rightful place in heaven. He hoped he had the strength to help guide the young woman to his brothers and in doing so keep her safe also. He could sense the evil above, knew it had taken a firmer grip on the house. His house. He had to do all he could.

Relieved that she now had light, Al sat on the bottom stone step and wondered what to do next. Should she move further into the crypt just in case Mick did find the trapdoor and try to get to her? Mark said he had a plan. What was he going to do? When would he be back to let her out? *Would he be back?* Oh God! What if Mick kills him, no-one would know where she was! Her heart hammered in her chest and the panic began to rise as the full impact of the situation hit her. She was trapped in the undercroft, the trapdoor shut, door locked and even if she could get out, Mick and Kenny were up there, waiting for her. Wanting her dead.

The distant voices of the monks momentarily helped calm her panic. She'd become used to hearing their constant chanting in the background, their voices were soft and calming to her ears. She sat on the step as the beautiful sounds reached out and touched her soul, caressed her skin like gentle kisses. Then the voices became louder, no longer just a hint of sound, the singing was slowly gaining strength. But it wasn't loud enough to drown out the commotion that suddenly exploded from above. Al nearly lost her grip on the candle as wailing and screeching from the cottage made her jump up from the step. Wild and savage cries of anger and rage echoed down from the house. After a moment of quiet the air became thick with horrific screams that reverberated around the building, resonating through every brick and stone. Then there was silence.

Al moved quickly, her blood rushed madly through her veins as the living nightmare unfolded. She had to find a way out. The cries from above had not been of this world. Desmond and the evil Darkness must have found a way in. Her hand went to the bat detector. Her angel protector. Whatever had happened up in the cottage she knew she had to try to get as far from the trap door as she could. Gathering up the spare candles, Al began to make her way further into the undercroft, hoping there was a means of escape.

The candle flame danced as she held it aloft and headed deeper into her underground prison. She had no idea how she would get out. Now that Chas had put up the barrier, her way to the cave was barred. She then remembered her dream. Her Father had been warning her from the other side of the steel sheet, warning her that she would be trapped. He had been right. But there had been another voice. What had they said? She racked her memory, tried to recall. So much had happened in those few hours since waking.

The voice came back to her, 'Let the monks guide you!'

The monks! That was it. She would follow their voices. She made her way deeper into the undercroft.

Mark had watched from the edge of the river as the huge cloud of evil had slowly made its way down through the moonlit sky towards the cottage. He hoped he'd done the right thing. The river had its offerings now. No going back. He prayed it wouldn't make things worse but there was nothing else he could have done.

He knew that the big Boss had wanted to move him on as soon as he'd said goodbye to his hospital bed. He was so grateful he'd been allowed to hang on abit longer, was able to keep a watchful eye over Al. He'd kept at a distance, he hadn't wanted her to get ideas that he'd be staying around, but he had been able to watch and listen and be ready to step in if needed.

As he sat on the riverbank he thought back to the day that Al had caught him skinny-dipping. He grinned. They had nearly kissed but he had held back. He had been trying to protect her. Didn't want her getting hurt. Jeez, he must have had a sixth sense of the future for he wasn't usually one to hold back with women, undercover cop or not. But Al had been different. She could have been the one. If he had his time again he would have kissed her that day for sure. If only he could kiss her now.

Overwhelmed with sadness he watched as the canvas sacking that floated in the river became entangled with the overhanging branches and the mummified cat edged its way out of its bag and drifted slowly away down stream. It was off on its final journey to the ocean.

He stood up. It was time he was off too. He made his way into the wood and disappeared from sight just as a scream filled the night air.

Susie stopped talking for a moment and listened.

'Did you hear that? It sounded like screaming?'

Jim shook his head, he needed to get this sorted before he headed out.

'No, probably a fox. Look Suz, I appreciate you feel stifled here and you want to be with Steve when he starts his job, but please can you hang on just a few more weeks. Just til we know what's happening.'

'Happening with what?' she asked, her voice raised now, 'We know what is happening, I am moving to Somerset and you are staying here looking after your pub and probably shouting at everyone just as you have been this past few months.'

'Shouting? Of course I'm shouting. This business is going down the pan Susie. I am at my wits end. You don't know the half of it!'

'Well tell me then. Tell me what's wrong. Don't keep me in the dark Dad. Maybe I can help?'

Jim checked his watch, 'Sorry, I really have got to go, I've arranged to meet someone and don't want to be late.'

'But Dad, we haven't finished. Where are you going? Who are you meeting at this time of night?'

But Jim had already walked out of the door.

Outside in the cool night air he stood for a few moments to allow his racing heart to ease. That had come as a bolt from the blue, Susie moving away. He hoped he could keep her from leaving until he knew his own fate. He felt in his pocket for his tobacco and realised he'd left his phone back inside. Sod it! He'd pop back in a minute. He'd just make up a fag, give it time for Suz to go up to bed out of the way, he couldn't hack anymore from her tonight.

He began rolling a cigarette, was about to light it when he heard a moan coming from along the road. Whimpering. Was it an animal in pain, injured? He best go and see. He laughed at the irony of it – tonight of all nights.

He strolled up the road and checked his watch again. It was later than he realised. Maybe he'd have to leave the animal, he needed to be there in time otherwise they might suspect something was amiss.

He almost trod on her. It was only because she started moaning again that he realised she was there.

'Mrs B! What's happened?'

Jim knelt down beside her and was shocked to see blood. Her dressing gown was soaked, all sticky and red. Gently he pulled her clothing apart slightly to reveal the wound under her rib cage. He felt her forehead, her skin was clammy. She was barely conscious and was mumbling incoherently. Jim ripped off his jacket and then his t-shirt, folded it tightly and pressed it hard against the wound.

The feeling of the pressure on her chest registered with Mrs Blackman and her eyes opened briefly.

'Jim…Jim.' she mumbled faintly, 'Get Kit.'

'Hold on there Mrs B, just hold on. You're going be okay, you hear me?' He moved her hand across and onto the T-shirt, 'Try to hold this on, hard if you can, there's a girl,' and then he jumped up, banged his fist against Kit's door, 'Kit! Chas! Need some help down here!' he shouted, 'Anyone, please help, we need an ambulance!' He thumped at the door, leaning hard against the doorbell as he looked down at Mrs Blackman, 'Stay awake Mrs B, you're going to be fine.'

Bleary-eyed Chas opened the door, 'What's going on?'

Behind him, Kit ran down the stairs, tying up her dressing gown and pushed past her husband. She saw Mrs Blackman lying on the bank, her hand flew to her mouth, 'Oh my God! Quick Chas, get an ambulance.'

Jim knelt again beside Mrs Blackman and pressed the wad of clothing down onto the knife wound and called back to Chas, 'Tell them to be quick, she's lost a lot of blood.'

'Shall we bring her inside?' Kit asked as she knelt down beside Jim.

He shook his head, 'No, best not move her. Have you got a blanket or something we can put over her, keep her warm?'

She nodded and darted back inside, a few seconds later was out again. She laid the blanket carefully over Mrs Blackman, whose eyes fluttered open again and looked up at Kit and she tried to speak.

'No, don't talk, you need to keep your strength. The ambulance will be here soon,' Kit squeezed her hand gently. Okay, she was a nosey old biddy but had a heart of gold. She mustn't die. 'Who on earth would do such a thing Jim? This is terrible.'

Mrs Blackman murmured again, 'Kenny. Gone to Mrs Greenway's.'

Kit edged nearer, 'Sorry? What are you saying Mrs B?'

Jim pulled at Kit's arm, 'No, don't make her talk Kit. She's too weak.'

'I know Jim, but this could be important. I think she knows something,' she leant across and looked down at Mrs Blackman again, gently stroked her brow and smiled, 'Do you know who did it? Is that what you are saying?'

Mrs Blackman's lips were dry, it was difficult to speak, but she had to let Kit know. She had to find the strength, 'Large man called him Kenny,' her throat felt constricted, she swallowed and tried again, 'Gone to Mrs Greenways. You must help her.'

Alison's ex husband! Sounds like he was here at Greysmead with that evil bloke Mick, 'Don't worry Mrs B. We'll get help. We'll make sure Alison is safe.'

She jumped up and called to Chas, 'Charlie, tell the Police to be quick. They've come to get Alison.'

The sound of the ambulance could be heard in the distance. Jim held Mrs Blackman's hand, and hoped they wouldn't be too late.

Alison pulled the fleece tightly around her, it felt much colder than usual in the crypt. Icy cold. Her legs, covered in just a light nightdress, felt numb. She bent down and rubbed them briskly with her free hand, trying to get the circulation going. She best keep moving.

It was probably just her imagination, her nerves were tight, but it felt as if someone was walking closely behind her. Soft footsteps sounded on the floor directly at her back. She twisted around quickly.

'Who is it? Who's there?' Her pulse racing, she strained her eyes in the dim light. No one there, but the candle cast so many shadows it was hard to be sure. At least she had the candlelight. It didn't bear thinking about being trapped there in total darkness. The candle was getting low, she'd have to light another soon. What if she was still trapped down there when the last of the candles had gone? She had to find a way out. Just had to!

The singing became louder, strong and clear. She reached the spilt in the tunnels. The monk's voices seemed to be coming from the right hand tunnel, towards the well. Was there a way out along there? She hesitated. It was unlikely. She knew that Charlie had now blocked up the left tunnel that went to the cave, but it was worth a look to check it was really secure, just in case she could force it open. It wasn't far along that she came face to face with the flat steel sheet. She pressed hard against it with her shoulder, pushing with all her strength. But no way would she ever get that down, Chas had certainly done a good job. It was bolted well into the brick all around the edge.

A pair of steps had been left leaning against the bricks with dusty overalls hanging over one of the rungs. She nearly tripped as her feet hit against a few of his tools he had left lying on the floor. She crouched to see if there was anything of use, a torch maybe? But all she found was a few screwdrivers and a pair of cutters, big and sturdy, like industrial secateurs.

Her hopes of a way out dashed, she turned and made her way back and up towards the well, hoping there was something they had missed when they were there before. The Monks continued to sing, louder and clearer the nearer she was to the well. She had lit the second candle and once that was gone would have just one more left. She began to panic at the thought of being there alone in the dark. As she reached the far end of the tunnel the circular brick wall of the well blocked her way. Al checked and rechecked, her hands feeling along the bricks but there was no way round. It was a dead end.

Up in the house the evil darkness had been replenished and had gained strength. It snaked around the cottage, coiling and weaving it way along the hallway, through to the kitchen and then slipped easily under the great wooden door. Circling around the cupboard, filling the enclosed space with its putrid smell before edging its way under the rug, through the gap around the trap door and down into the undercroft. It spiralled around, and began its attack on the crypt. The strong smell of decomposing flesh filled the air.

The beautiful voices of the Monks started again, singing so loud now that their chants vibrated through the wall. She slumped down on the floor and began to cry. The tears came slowly at first, trickles slipping down her cheeks but soon she was sobbing, great wracking sobs tearing at her chest. She really didn't know what to do. Her nose began to run and she fumbled in her pocket to see if there was a tissue. Her hand touched upon the bat detector again. Bats! Of course!

She sat up, wiped her sleeve across her face and stood up, holding the candle high so she could see the opening where the bats flew in. It was a big enough gap to get through and maybe once inside she could climb up somehow? It was worth a try.

Her hopes rekindled she dashed back as quickly as she could to fetch the ladder. It was a struggle to carry with one hand, she needed the other to hold the candle but somehow she managed. Opened out and leant against the bricks the ladder almost reached the hole in the wall, just falling short about a foot or two, but there were thick tree roots poking through, maybe she could climb up on them. But what could she do about light? She wouldn't be able to climb inside with a candle. Was there anyway she could do it by feel? She had to try, there was no other way.

Candle in one hand, she climbed up the rungs to the top. With her free hand Al grabbed at the roots and tugged them slightly. They seemed pretty solid and thick. Dripping some wax onto a flat area of vegetation to her left she managed to secure the candle, albeit somewhat precariously. It flickered slightly as the flame touched the tendrils of ivy above and she waited, holding her breath to see if it would survive. It stayed alight.

Al grabbed at a thick rope of root to her right and pulled herself up, climbing higher, using tree roots and huge swathes of ivy as foot holds. All the while the chanting continued, even louder now, their voices seemingly coming from inside the well.

She stopped for a moment in her ascent as the candle flame, now almost burnt down, wavered slightly. Please don't let it go out yet. One final push and she was level with the huge gash in the bricks. It looked lighter inside than she had dared hope and realised that shafts of moonlight were seeping down through the hole in the cover, giving her a small measure of help. She had expected to look into a huge void, below and above but the well was a mass of tangled roots and thick tendrils of ivy, some of which seemed to reach up quite high. Huge stones and boulders, rocks and rubble, were piled high over the far side. If only the moon would stay out she may be able to see enough to climb up the roots and stones.

A thick branch of ivy that criss-crossed the gap in the bricks barred her way through, she tried but no way could she push it aside. She was stuck. But then she remembered the cutters. They would probably get through that. Manoeuvring back down the ivy and root rock face she gingerly stepped down the ladder and left the remnants of the candle burning up near the gap, lit the final candle and made her way back to get the bolt cutters.

She glanced back towards the undercroft as she reached the split in the tunnels and wrinkled her nose as an unpleasant smell reached her nostrils. A vague movement caught her attention but she dismissed it as shadows from the candlelight. Once she had grabbed the cutters and dragged them back to the well she placed the candle on the ground and proceeded to climb back up the ladder, carrying the heavy tool. To her relief they snipped through the root as if it was paper and she leant in and managed to clear the way.

She hesitated for a moment, daring herself to go through the gap and try to climb up. She looked over her shoulder, back to the tunnel below, debating if she should just wait to be rescued than risk climbing into the well, falling and never being found. The candle's flame beside her began to falter. She knew it wouldn't be long before she would be plunged into darkness.

She leant further into the gap with the giant secateurs and snipped at one last piece of vegetation and noticed something glinting in the moonlight in front of her. The ivy was rough and sharp as she felt in with her hand to retrieve the object and finally her fingers met with the cold metal of the head torch that Tom had dropped so many months before. Al couldn't believe her luck. Would it still work? The glass cover was cracked but she slipped the switch across and the light beamed out. In utter relief she slipped it onto her head.

There was movement below as the unpleasant odour, much stronger now, began to creep up from the floor of the tunnel. The candle on the floor was suddenly snuffed out and as she sat perched on the edge of the opening, the nauseating smell of sulphur and decay filled her nostrils making her gag. She watched in horror as the wispy tendrils of fog began to wind their way along the tunnel, getting thicker as the black smog filled the area, dark and rancid, moaning and wailing and slowly working its way up towards her.

Chapter thirty eight

Alison froze as the Darkness edged its way higher, fingers of black mist clung to the bricks and began to crawl up the wall towards her. She felt her heart crashing with great thuds against her chest and all the while the monk's rich voices echoed behind her as she perched on the gaping hole that opened up into the well.

Then out of the chaos a voice, light as a feather, 'Your Angel will protect you.'

'Oh my God, of course! The echo detector!'

Al grabbed at the angel bat detector that sat deep in her pocket and frantically attempted to switch it on. Her hands numb with the cold, the detector fell from her fingers into the cut vegetation in the cavity behind her.

'Oh no!' Al screamed and leant inside pushing her hand amongst the mass of cut roots and branches. Her legs, blue with the cold, dangled down on the outside of the hole as she balanced across the opening and edged her way head first through the gap. Wriggling her fingers to try to gain life into her frozen veins she plunged her hand deep into the vegetation. The sharp edges of the debris tore at her arm, scratching and cutting into her unfeeling flesh. She could see the detector wedged against a clump of ivy, she just had to reach a little bit further and it would be in her grasp.

She was suddenly aware of pressure on her feet as they became locked in the grip of the dark mists that swirled ever upwards. Fingers of evil lapped at her skin, entwining her ankles, wrapping itself round and round, tighter and tighter, as it bound her feet together. She could hear the cries of rage and anger that were locked within the black mists, trapped souls imprisoned by their own wrong doings. As she lay across the brick ledge the Darkness attempted to pull her back down. From within the black fog, long bony hands struck out at Al's legs, grasping tightly, digging yellow talons into her flesh. She held on tightly but could feel herself being pulled, felt her grasp loosen. She mustn't give up now. She had to fight it. Hold fast. She could do it. She had to.

The stench from the Darkness filled her lungs and she felt the scant contents of her stomach try to rise up. Holding on fiercely to a large tree root she managed to twist around onto her back and pulled herself upright, she held her hand out, her angel echo locator aimed at her feet. As the machine started its onslaught, the silent voices of the bats battered against the molecules of the fog, penetrating deep within. It uncurled and let go its grip on her feet and retreated down to the floor of the tunnel.

She continued her bombardment of echoes at the putrid smelling fumes and it fled further back, deep into the undercroft, as it tried to escape the attack. It had nowhere to go, it could no longer float easily into the sky as it did when it was outside the cottage. Now everyway was barred as the angel echoes bounced from wall to ceiling, spitting echoes deep within the Darkness, penetrating every atom, breaking down the evil.

Al positioned the detector on the edge of the bricks, leaving it to fire its soundless shouts of destruction as she wriggled through the gap and cautiously crawled over the roots and headed for the pile of boulders at the far side.

Roger was just dropping off to sleep when his phone rang. He'd leave it, he was bushed. His eyes felt gritty where he had been looking at the computer screen for too long. He hoped their insider at Mick's would know when the goods were being dropped soon so they could go in and make the hit. He hated all this waiting around and he really wanted to get back to Greysmead now, especially when Al might be in danger.

His phone beeped, the caller had left a voice message, but it began ringing again. He reached across and squinted at the screen. It was Kit. He'd told her not to get in touch unless in an emergency. Shit, it must be about Al. Was she okay? He pulled himself up and leant back against the headboard and took the call.

'Kit? What is it? What's happened? Is she alright?'

'She's been stabbed Roger. The ambulance have just taken her, but it's not looking good,' Kit sobbed down the phone, 'I'm sorry to ring you but didn't know what to do.'

'Al? Been stabbed, when? Do you know anymore?' Roger jumped out of bed and switched the phone over to speaker phone as he rushed to get dressed.

'No, not Al, it's Mrs Blackman. Stabbed outside our house. But she said Kenny and Big Mick are heading up to Al's. And Susie said she heard screaming from there. Oh Roger what shall we do? The police are in the house talking to Chas, asking him questions. Jim's gone missing too!'

'Mrs B? Oh no! Are they going up to Al's? They must get up there fast, there's no knowing what Mick will do to her! Where does Jim fit in with all this?' he looked around for his keys, pushing newspapers aside, they had to be there somewhere. He finally grabbed them from under his dirty socks and picked up his jacket.

'It was Jim that found Mrs B,' Kit told him, 'As soon as the ambulance arrived he was off. Oh Roger, what shall I do? Shall I head up to Al's?'

'NO!' he shouted, 'Stay where you are. I'm coming down,' sod what the Guv says, he couldn't stay in London with this going on, 'Kit, give the plods there my number, get them to ring me in five minutes, I'll fill them in on my way down, try to persuade them they need to get up there as soon as. Don't worry sis, it'll be ok.'

He hoped he was right.

Jim dashed up the lane towards Woodhurst Bridge. He was running really late now. He'd headed off just as the ambulance had appeared. He had run back to the pub to get a clean shirt. Hearing him come in, Susie had put her head round her bedroom door and looked aghast at his bloody hands.

She pattered over the landing to him, 'Dad! What on earth have you done?'

'Nothing Suz, I'm okay. It's Mrs B, I found her lying on the grass bank, she's been stabbed. Ambulance has just arrived.'

'Oh my God! Stabbed? Are you sure?' she pulled the landing curtains aside, the blue flashing light of the ambulance rushed past and stopped at Kit's, 'I better go out and see if I can help.'

She hurried back into her room and pulled on a pair of jeans. Jim was standing in the bathroom doorway drying his hands when she came back out onto the landing, pulling a sweatshirt over her head.

'You coming back down Dad? I suppose the police will want to speak to you?'

'You go on ahead Suz, I'll follow you.'

Susie ran down the stairs and headed towards Kit's. A few minutes later Jim made his way out of the side door and darted across the road. He slipped by without being seen. As he reached the bridge he saw the silhouette of a figure against the moonlit sky standing back from the road.

Steve's Uncle stepped out, carrying a large spade, 'You took your time Jimbo, thought you were going to cry off,' he shoved the spade into Jim's hand, 'Come on, we've got some digging out to do.' He whistled under his breath and two more figures appeared from the trees with terriers at their heels. Jim followed as they made their way into the woods towards the badger sett.

Above the sound of the chanting, Al could make out the wails of despair from the crypt as the Darkness slowly disintegrated under the force of the sound waves. It was time to get away, she didn't know how long the batteries of the echo detector would last.

In the well shaft an enormous root had plunged its way through the brick on the opposite side. It had spread itself out and created a bridge of entwined tendrils across to the gap from the tunnel. Legs astride Al pushed herself towards the rubble, hoping she would be able to clamber up to safety. The moonlight glistened down as she slowly made her way across. Below her was a tangle of roots that over the years had made the well their home.

Half way across, a small gap in the network of vegetation gave Al a view down into the dank dark base of the well. The head torch beam shone into the chasm beneath that until then had been hidden from view by the undergrowth of roots but there in the centre she only had to lose her balance and she would plunge down with nothing to break her fall. She had to keep calm, she had to get across. If only she could feel her fingers and hands, they were numb, she was so cold. It was difficult to get a grip on the roots. Unaware of the scratches and cuts on her legs as the rough and gnarled roots dug into her cold skin, she slid across the nature made bridge.

Finally she was close to the boulders and rubble. Not long now and she could clamber up to the top. But she was now close enough to discover that she had been wrong. The rocks revealed their secret to her. They had been lying patiently in the well for hundreds of years waiting for this moment. For they weren't made of stone but of bone. The boulders she had glimpsed from the far side of the well were skulls, some broken and smashed. Eye sockets stared blankly at her. Jawbones and teeth grinned inanely. Arm bones, legs, hands and rib cages all jumbled together and piled high in a great mound that had sat there for almost 500 years. She had reached the final resting place of the massacred monks.

The officers at Kit's had called for back up after speaking with Roger. He'd put them in the picture as he had sped down from London. They now knew who they were dealing with and Roger just hoped they would get to Al in time. As he raced down to Greysmead the two officers headed out of the village towards Monkton Lane. They turned off just before Woodhurst Bridge unaware of the figures armed with spades and terriers making their way deep into the wood. The headlights of the police car flashed across the tree trunks as the dark figures stooped below the rotting branches heading towards their prey. They paused and waited. The car continued. They were safe. A tawny owl cried out from the canopy above and relying on its keen senses flew away. It didn't want to witness the carnage to come.

Chas felt the cold night air cut into his lungs as he dashed up the footpath. His breath rasped in his chest as he pushed himself to keep on running. He had to get up there, he couldn't just sit at home and wait. The police had no concept of what they may have to face. He'd left Kit and Susie waiting at the house. He had glanced back as they stood in the doorway and watched him go. The amber light in the hallway shone out around them and he could see the worry and fear etched on their faces. In the background he glimpsed the stone angel, its face serene as it continued to silently witness events as they unfolded through the centuries.

As Chas turned the corner by the allotments and began to run along the footpath he wished he had a guardian angel with him tonight. They could all use some angels looking after them. Susie had told him about the screams she had heard earlier, seemingly coming from Monkton Lane.

The air above the cottage looked still and calm in the moonlight, no sign of the black mists tonight. But he had no doubt they would be lurking somewhere. He hoped Al had her Angel echo detector with her. It may not keep her safe from Mick but at least she could have a chance against Desmond. It felt as if the gates of hell had suddenly sprung open in the village. God what a nightmare. Poor Mrs Blackman. It wasn't looking good.

As Chas continued his breathless dash across the fields, headlights shone out up ahead as the police car emerged from the ivy tunnel and skidded to a halt outside Orchard Cottage. As the moon lit up the scene, Chas watched from the footpath. The front door of Al's place was already open and the two officers stepped inside. Chas picked up speed and willed himself to carry on even though his chest felt tight as he struggled to catch his breath. He didn't have far to run now.

Above the badger sett the bird glided silently on its broad wings. Tom caught sight of the owl in silhouette against the shimmering night sky before it disappeared deeper into the wood. Tom began to lose the feeling in his toes but he couldn't move. He had to sit tight. Camouflaged by netting and an assortment of greenery he sat buried down in the ditch near the badger sett. The only giveaway of his presence was his breath as it hit the cool night air in soft wisps.

He'd had a call from the police wildlife officer earlier that day, they'd had a tip off hinting that there was planned activity that evening. He had been expecting police backup but so far no one had shown. He'd hidden himself well, but wasn't sure if he should sit tight. He would be no match on his own against a gang of thugs who were hell bent on digging out the badgers. If the police didn't show he'd be an idiot to intervene alone. He couldn't bear the thought of having to sit and watch, but it was either that or risk injury himself.

Bloody hell! Where were the old bill? Should he head off and get away out of ear shot before the scum turned up? He could then ring the station, find out what was causing the delay.

Voices. Voices getting nearer. If he was to get away it was now or never. As quietly as he could manage he raised himself up very slowly, pulling off the netting and letting the leaves and vegetation that had been his lair fall to the ground. He pushed himself up and out from the ditch. As his hand reached back down to get his rucksack there was a rustle of leaves behind him. He felt the crack in his skull as something heavy came down onto his head.

Chapter thirty nine

Chas stood for a moment at the gate as he tried to catch his breath. His lungs screamed at him and he leant forward, hands resting on knees as he gasped for air after his sprint up the footpath. Wiping his damp forehead with his sleeve he tried to judge what to do. Should he go in? The cottage was silent as he made his way up the path and put his hand onto the front door. It swung open. All the lights were ablaze but the cottage was very quiet. He crept in and cautiously looked into the sitting room. Nothing seemed amiss in there.

Treading lightly along the hallway, Chas edged his way carefully around the door to the dining room. The heady aroma of beeswax polish from the dark wood furniture filled the room. It looked tranquil as the pendulum of the old timepiece swayed hypnotically. The house felt as if it was at peace, he no longer had the sense of foreboding that he had always had when at the cottage before.

He was puzzled. It was so quiet. Where were the police? Where was Big Mick? And Al? Where was she? He headed into the kitchen and was suddenly aware of the smell. It put him in mind of the local rubbish tip, rotting vegetables and meat long past their sell by date. He looked under the sink, the bin was empty and smelt fresh. No, the smell was coming from behind the cupboard door, from the undercroft.

The heavy wooden door was ajar and he peered round to discover the entrance to the crypt was open and the disgusting stench wafted up from there. He stood at the top of the steps for a moment. What should he do? It was then he heard sounds of life. Voices down by the foot of the stairs and then the click click of metal on stone as one of the police officers made his way up and his head came into view.

Seeing Chas he spoke sternly, 'What are you doing here sir? I'm sorry but you can't go down there,' he grabbed at Charlie's arm and led him back into the kitchen.

'But what's happened? Have you found Mick and Kenny…and Al? Is she alright?'

'I'm sorry Mr Mitchell, but we have to wait until CID get here. I can't let you down to the crypt, to be honest you probably wouldn't want to go down there. I'm afraid there have been a number of fatalities this evening.'

'What? Dead? Who? Who have you found? Please, you must tell me? Is Alison…is she ok?'

'Please sit down sir. As far as we are aware Mrs Greenways is not amongst the fatalities we have discovered.'

'As far as you aware? How can you not know? Either it's her or it's not!' Chas rushed towards the door again, but the officer slammed it shut and stood to bar Charlie's way.

'I am sorry sir but that's all I can tell you for now. We will have more information once SOCO and CID get here.'

Down in the crypt the remaining police officer tied a handkerchief over his face, covering his nose and mouth to try to keep out the smell of decomposing flesh. What on earth had happened down there? He sat on the bottom step, unable to venture further, he didn't want to destroy any vital evidence. He swung the strong beam from his torch across the floor of the undercroft and gagged again as it picked out numerous corpses, mostly in a stage of advanced decomposition, plus mounds of thick dust that were once human beings, the powdery remnants interspersed with fragments of bone. Long thin bony fingers and jawbones sat amongst the debris. How many dead here? So many of them must have been dead for God knows how long. How did they get there? Were they looking at some sort of grave robbing ploy that went horribly wrong?

He allowed his torch to fall upon the remaining two victims. Recent deaths for sure. The giant of a man lay on his back, eyes still open as he gazed horror stuck ahead. Although now devoid of life, the absolute fear in his eyes was unmistakable. Next to him, curled up into a foetus position was the other man. The terror the man had suffered as his life had ended was there for all to see.

The officer shook his head. It was beyond him what had gone on. And unless she was amongst the pile of bones and dust there was no sign of Mrs Greenways.

It was as Alison had come upon the skeletons of the monks that she was aware that the chanting had suddenly ceased. They no longer needed to make themselves known. They had been found. At last they would be able to rest in peace. Abbot Thomas hung back in the shadows and smiled. He had known the woman would be the one to put things right.

Al glanced up, the shaft of moonlight above enticed her with a view of freedom. There was nothing for it, she'd have to use the skeletons as a way out. She'd have to put aside any feeling of respect for the dead and clamber up over them. If she didn't she would be joining the pile of the dead herself. Looking up, her eyes followed the mountain of bones. It fell short by a few feet from the great gaping hole in the well cover but she could make out ribbons of ivy poking down, some thick as rope, almost touching her. It wouldn't be easy and she was absolutely shattered. She'd used the last ounce of energy getting across the well.

A feeling of despair overwhelmed her. Behind her eyes she felt the familiar sting as the tears waited, ready to fall. She just couldn't do it. She was so tired. She had got this far and now this. If only she wasn't so cold. She'd lose her grip for sure, she couldn't feel her hands anymore. They were so numb they had stopped hurting.

It was as the tears pricked at her eyes that she felt the heat. She sat astride the huge root by the edge of the bones and felt herself become encompassed by a huge cloak of warmth. Heaviness pressed against her and she could feel a heartbeat against her back, warm arms stretched around her, hugged her close and rubbed at her chilled limbs. The warmth filled her veins, bringing her body the energy she desired. Her frozen skin gradually felt the life filter back as an unseen samaritan held her close.

She didn't know what or who it was, but she knew it was benevolent and without harm.

'Thank you,' she whispered, 'thank you.'

She leant forward and rested her hand onto one of the skulls and gently stroked the unseeing face. It felt so delicate. It would surely break when she climbed up. Her hand caressed the bones.

'I'm so sorry. Once this nightmare is over I will get you out. I promise.'

The ivy kept her secure as she clambered over the monks, and they didn't shatter, as she had feared. She pulled herself up using the ivy rope for extra support and was soon above the skeletons and near to the entrance. Just a bit further and she would be there. The wet ivy slipped through her hands and she nearly lost her grip but she pushed her feet against the wall of the well and twisted another hanging tendril around her wrist. Nearly there. She reached through the gap and her hands clung onto the side of the well as she made the final push and squeezed her cold and tired body through the broken cover. She fell out onto the grass and it was only then that she allowed herself to cry.

Roger stopped briefly at Kit's before heading up to Monkton Lane. The police tape hung limply as it cornered off the area where Mrs Blackman had been stabbed. Uniformed officers milled around and the sound of mumbled voices on police radios echoed in the night air. Roger went across to speak to Bryan, one of his Sussex Police colleagues who had just finished talking to the Vicar, one of a vast number of villagers who had congregated outside Kit's house, all keen to share their grief at the news. All saddened that Mrs Blackman had lost her fight.

'Alright Bryan? Any news from Orchard Cottage?' Roger asked and spotting Kit in the doorway, looked across at her and gave her a comforting smile.

'CID are on their way. There's been fatalities up there,' Bryan told Roger in a hushed voice.

Roger swallowed hard. He had to keep calm and professional otherwise they wouldn't let him get involved.

'Do you know who?' He prayed to himself. Please God, don't let him say Alison. His wait for an answer seemed to hang in the air for an age.

'Looks as if this Big Mick and Kenny you've been dealing with up in the smoke have copped it. Not sure who the others are.'

'Others?' Rogers said loudly. Faces in the crowd turned to look, wondering what else was amiss. 'Sorry Bryan,' Roger continued softly, 'How many more? Any idea who?'

Bryan shook his head, 'Sorry mate, no idea. But all a bit odd, they weren't recent deaths by what I hear.' Bryan squeezed Roger's shoulder comfortingly, 'You best get up there, they need as many of us on the case as they can. We already had to delay a callout from the wildlife crew. There was a tip off about some action up near the bridge…possible baiting…don't know if anyone's managed to deal with that yet.'

'Ok Bryan, thanks. Catch you later,' Roger began to squeeze past the crowd and towards Kit as she ran towards her brother and held him close.

'Oh Roger, it's so terrible,' she sobbed. 'Poor Mrs Blackman. What had she done to them? It's so unfair.'

'I know. Life is unfair sis. Has anyone tried to get hold of Dorothy, do you know?'

Kit blew her nose and shook her head, 'No, I don't think so. The woman officer who was about earlier was going to look you out first. I told her of your connection with the family. She wanted to check if you wanted to be the one to break the news to Dorothy?'

'Thanks Kit, I think I probably would. If you see the WPC get her to hang on and speak to me first, but I must get up to Monkton Lane now. Is Chas still up there?'

Kit's face was awash with tears as she replied, 'Yes. He rang me to say he was okay, but couldn't tell me anything. I'm worried about him, what if this Mick is still up there? I'm so scared Rog.'

'It's okay, don't worry. I'll see if I can get him back here with you. No sign of Jim?'

Kit shook her head and wiped away more tears, 'Susie's inside watching Amy for me but she's worried sick.'

Roger pulled Kit towards him again and held her tight. He felt her body shake as she began to cry again. 'Ssshhhhh, it's okay. I must go now. Must get up there.'

He jumped back into his car and sped up towards Monkton Lane wondering what he would find.

Alison allowed herself a few moments of self-pity, as she lay exhausted on the grass by the side of the well. She pulled off the head torch and looked up at the stars, relieved to be out of her underground hell. There was no sign of the dark mists. It felt so tranquil. Maybe the echo locater had done its worst and eradicated the darkness for good. An owl skimmed the top of the moonlit ruins beside her and disappeared from sight. She best get out of sight too, she didn't want to come across Mick and Kenny if they were prowling about trying to find her.

Her best plan would be to head towards the river and then make her way to the village through the woods. That way she had a better chance of not being spotted. She still had to be careful, they could be anywhere. She ducked down amongst the ruins and darted across the grass and amongst the shrubs towards the riverbank. She stopped. There had been a noise behind her, it sounded like a twig snapping. Maybe Mick was following her? She crouched low and waited. She felt her heart race as she squatted amongst the brambles hoping she wouldn't be spotted but then heard the familiar snuffling sound of a muntjac as he began to feast on a crop of mushrooms nearby.

Relieved, Al smiled and continued towards the river, she ran low across the field, using the bushes as cover. The sounds of soft gurgling water reached her ears and she stopped a few moments to get her breath. The gently flowing river looked beautiful in the moonlight as its circle of silver reflected in the rippling waters. It was as she was watching the reflected moon change shape in the currents that she spotted the tin. It was wedged up against a small tree by the river's edge. She grabbed and held onto the trunk and slid down the sandy bank and reached out. It was the tin from the fireplace. What was it doing by the river? It was empty, no sign of the crystals or amulets. Who would have done such a thing?

Is this why the Darkness had penetrated the crypt? Someone had taken out the protection, letting hell break loose? But who would do that? Mark?

Could it have been Mark? Had that been his plan to try to hold back Mick and Kenny? The idiot! Didn't he realise he had put her life at risk?

She knelt by the river and placed the tin on the ground and frowned. What had happened to him? Why hadn't Mark been waiting for her? Maybe he was hiding out of sight in the woods, waiting for a chance to go back to the house and let her out of the crypt or had Mick…had Mick killed him? Her heart missed a beat. God, it didn't bear thinking about. She stroked the arm of his fleece and nestled her nose into the material, trying to remember him…smell him...feel him close. She wished he was there with her now and prayed he was safe.

The outline of the trees loomed out in the moonlight as she followed the river's path into the woods. As the river snaked in through the trees, it became hidden from view amongst the dense undergrowth. She waited for a moment to try to let her eyes adjust as she stepped under the dark canopy.

The noises of the forest were all around her. She could hear moths fluttering amongst the honeysuckle, the scurrying of mice under the woodland floor as they rustled in the leaves by her feet. The moonlight couldn't penetrate the thick vegetation above and it was hard going. It was difficult to see anything ahead but Al didn't want to use the torch and alert Mick and Kenny of her whereabouts.

She trod carefully, almost tripping as she tried to avoid broken tree stumps and fallen branches as she continued to follow the flow of the river towards Woodhurst Bridge from where she would head down to the village. The river, now bordered by a tangle of shrubs and twisted trees, gurgled peacefully a few feet away but Alison had a feeling of unease as she stepped silently along the muddy path. The noises of the woodland creatures unnerved her. The rustle of leaves and branches echoed out from all directions. An owl screeched in the distance.

She turned to look behind her. She couldn't shake off the feeling that someone was following her. She stepped up her pace and began to run, darting in-between the trees, her heart pounding in her chest. She willed herself to keep going.

She stopped short when she heard the dogs. They were close by. Breathing hard she leant against a tree and listened. Voices. Shouting. Whoever it was they were close by. Was it Mark and the police? Had they come to find her? Or was it Mick?

She cautiously headed off the path and followed the sound of the voices. The dogs continued to bark, the harsh sound penetrated into the wood. She was getting closer and could make out snatches of conversation. She crouched down and peered through the vegetation and found herself looking into the entrance of the cave.

The padlocked gates were swung open, pushing aside the thick shrubs that normally hid them from view and she could see a couple of men. Steve's Uncle was inside, smoking a cigarette. Standing by the entrance with a couple of terriers was another man. He was holding a shotgun. Al gasped and stooped lower into the undergrowth.

'Where the hell have they got to with the rest of the gear? We need to get over to the sett and get the dogs down,' Steve's Uncle said and threw his cigarette end onto the ground.

'What are we going to do with him?' Shotgun man nodded his head, indicating into the cave.

'Just leave the interfering twat there. He can't get away can he?' he began to laugh.

Al edged her way over slightly. She held her breath. She was breathing so hard she was sure they'd hear. She peered through the leaves and looked deep within the cave. There was someone chained to the huge metal ring.

Whoever it was they were unconscious. She strained her eyes to see. It was Tom!

Chapter forty

Roger strode purposefully into Orchard Cottage and headed straight for the kitchen.

'Hello Charlie. You alright?'

Chas was standing by the sink, looking very uptight. His face lit up when he saw Roger.

'Thank goodness you are here. They won't let me down there. They don't know if Al is dead or alive but they haven't fully searched the crypt. They've said they're waiting for CID.'

'Is that right? Have you not searched further into the undercroft yet?' Roger addressed the young officer. He couldn't believe they were just sitting about. Al could be injured down there for Christ sakes!

'We were instructed to leave it until SOCO got here. It's a right bloody state down there.'

Roger pushed past him and opened the heavy oak door, 'Sorry mate but I can't sit about up here when we may have someone injured down there,' he turned to Chas, 'You coming with me?'

'You bet your life!' Chas beamed and they pushed passed the bemused rookie and ran down the stone steps.

Constable Malcolm Bailey was sitting at the base of the stairs. He'd seen some sights during his career in the force but this was probably the most horrific. With the handkerchief still close to his face he had kept the torch shining on the bodies. Some were just bone, some no more than dust but a few still had ribbons of decaying flesh hanging from them. An eyeball hanging limping from a socket seemed to follow his gaze, he didn't like it down there on his own. He jumped up in surprise when Roger and Chas came bounding down the steps behind him.

'Hey, where do you think you are going?' he did a double take when he saw his colleague, 'Roger? What you doing back? You know you can't go in there!'

'You try stopping us!' Roger snatched at Malcolm's torch and jumped down the last two steps into the crypt with Chas close to his heels.

Roger shone the torch across the floor, taking in the full impact of the horror the beam of light revealed to him. He found it hard to take in all he was seeing. It was as if a graveyard had been dug up and the decomposing bodies had been thrown out of their coffins onto the floor. The smell was overpowering and with one hand held over his nose he pulled with the other at Charlie's arm, who had stopped to look in disbelief at the corpses and skeletons that littered the place.

'Come on Chas, get a grip man,' Roger tugged at Charlie again and then stopped short as his torch picked out the bodies of Mick and Kenny. He whistled under his breath, 'Fucking hell! What on earth happened here tonight?'

Roger called back to Malcolm who was now left in growing darkness, 'Don't worry. I take full responsibility for going against orders. Go back up into the kitchen and wait. CID will be here soon.'

'No way, I'm coming with you!' and Malcolm dashed over to join the posse.

They rushed along the crypt, flicking the torch beam from side to side in hope that they would find that Al was hiding in one of the alcoves. As they made their way to the split in the tunnels, Chas filled Roger in about the cave and how he had barred up the passageway.

'So there's no way she would have got out from down here. She must still be in the house Roger. Unless she got away before those thugs got here.'

Roger listened as he continued to check every nook and cranny, 'Okay Chas, but I want to look down here anyway.' He continued to shine the torch around the walls as they headed deeper into the undercroft, 'Let's look near the well first shall we?' Roger said as they reached the t-junction.

'Hey! It's my ladder! I left it down here the other day,' Chas shouted as they came to the steps propped against the circular wall of the well. He looked at Roger as he directed the torch beam upwards, 'Are you thinking what I'm thinking Rog?'

Roger nodded, 'I certainly am!' he handed Chas the torch and began to climb upwards, 'Keep the light on me if you can Chas. Thanks mate.'

As he reached the top of the ladder he called back down, 'I'll have to climb the next bit, the roots look pretty tough so should hold my weight. Can you try to keep the beam steady and point where I'm climbing?'

'Sure thing Rog.'

Chas held the torch towards Roger and guided him where to place his feet with the beam. Within minutes Roger was on the ledge.

'You see anything?' Malcolm called up.

Roger's voice echoed down as he put his head into the opening.

'The well's a mass of vegetation and rubble. She could have climbed up. Although it would have been tough, but if she was that scared, she probably would've risked it.'

'No sign of her now?'

'No, nothing. But hang on, what's this?' Rogers's hand fell upon the angel echo detector. He slipped it into his pocket and shouted down, 'I've found something. I'm on my way back.' He made his way cautiously down the rungs, 'I think we should go outside to the opening of the well. Might be worth getting a strong light and rope ladder too, take a look down inside, make sure she hasn't fallen and injured herself.'

Malcolm nodded, 'Good idea. Let's head back and I'll get some help.'

Roger took the object from his pocket, 'I found this lying on the ledge. Any idea what it is guys?'

Chas shone the torch at Rogers' hand, 'It's the echo locater! That proves she must have been up there and it explains the carnage down here. I bet you'll find when tests are done on those remains they will be from the time when old Desmond was around. Come on, let's get outside, I'll fill you in on the way.'

Al watched as Steve's Uncle kicked at the unmoving body of Tom as he lay on the dirt floor. A thick chain clasped around Tom's ankle fixed him to the metal hook imbedded into the ground.

Steve's Uncle's stubby legs kicked again and he laughed, 'He's still out cold!'

Shotgun man wandered inside, 'What are we going to do with him? Once we're done up here? He'll go to the police.'

'He's got no proof it was us. We can dump him once we have our goods safely bagged up. Or we can leave him here to rot!' his lips curled into a grin as his manic laughter filled the air.

Al felt a wave of panic overwhelm her. She couldn't believe what she saw. She knew from what Tom had told her that the badger baiters went to great lengths to get what they wanted. But this? To have injured Tom, knocked him out! She had to get help and fast. Where was Mark? She couldn't understand it, surely he'll be looking for her?

Sharp stones and pieces of grit dug into her bare knees as she crawled away across the forest floor. She couldn't let Steve's Uncle spot her. She had to get help. As soon as she was out of sight she jumped up and began to run blindly through the woods. She tripped and stumbled, crying out as she fell to her knees. She listened and waited. Had they heard her? But the only sound was her heart as it pounded in her ears. As soon as she felt it was safe, she got up and carried on running.

In her panic she headed deeper into the wood, the ancient trees sent their bent and distorted branches down onto the ground and barred her way, luring her down twisting paths until she had no idea which direction to turn.

She reached a fork in the path. Her heart raced in her chest as her eyes darted from side to side. Which path should she take? She made her way to the left and had brief glimpses of the moonlight as it filtered down through the thinning canopy. Maybe she was nearing the road?

A twig snapped and the sound of footsteps on fallen leaves. Al stood tight up against a tree, her blood racing in her veins. She watched as a beam of light followed closely by a dark figure emerged from the trees. Thank God! She was safe! She jumped out onto the path in front of him.

'Jim! Am I relieved to see you! I so need your help!'

'Alison?' he looked at her in disbelief and glanced behind him furtively before hissing at her, 'What are you doing here? Quick. You must get back to the village.'

'We need to get the police. I've just found Tom. He's unconscious.'

Jim looked behind him again and dropped the spade that he carried to the ground. He grabbed her arm aggressively and shoved her towards a large bush.

'Keep out of sight!'

'But Jim!' she protested just as a red-faced man appeared, shotgun slung over his shoulder.

'What's going on Jimbo? Who have we got here then?' he pressed his face close to Al and grinned at her with huge tombstone teeth. She tried to back away but he pinched at her chin tightly.

Jim's worried gaze left Alison and he turned to the stocky man, 'Found her wandering, I'll just point her in the direction of the road…'

'No you won't Jimbo. She's coming with us.' he said and dragged Al back towards the cave.

Malcolm climbed out of the well and rolled up the rope ladder.

'There's no sign of her down there Roger. She must have managed to get out and headed back to the village.'

Roger turned off the bright halogen beam that had been directed down into the shaft of the well to illuminate Malcolm.

'Well at least we know she's not trapped down there,' Roger said, 'You better go and let forensics know about the skeletons. Bloody hell, that lot's going to keep them busy for some time!'

'I couldn't believe it when I saw them. I thought I was going to fall off the ladder when I swung down and had a face grinning at me,' Malcolm laughed it off. He wouldn't admit it to Roger that coming face to face with the skulls as he had climbed down the ladder had been very unnerving, 'I wonder how they got down there and who they were?'

'My guess is they're the monks who were murdered. It has always been a bit of a legend, never really knew how true it was. Mad villagers playing vigilante and a lot of innocents killed but there had never been any sign of the bodies. Looks like they were right under our noses all along.'

'So much for sleepy little villages eh?' Malcolm said as he turned to make his way back to Orchard Cottage.

Roger gave him a friendly slap on the back, 'Thanks for all your help Malc. Sorry you ended up getting a bollocking because of me. I'm going to head off towards the woods now, see if I can find her.'

'Why don't you hang on Roger? You're in enough shit with the Guv as it is. CID told us there's a party on its way to help with the search. They should be here soon.'

Malcolm wasn't happy that Roger planned to go off alone. CID had arrived just as Roger, Chas and Malcolm had emerged from their earlier visit to the crypt and had not been too pleased that they had ventured into the undercroft without authorisation. Malcolm had stood submissively as he was reprimanded for allowing Roger into the crime scene. Charlie had been duly escorted back to the village after Roger received a blasting from his boss for letting a member of the public get involved.

SOCO and the police surgeon were now down in the undercroft but every indication so far was that Mick and Kenny had died of natural causes. It was looking as if the other remains were of people who had been dead for centuries. It was a mystery as to how they had got there. The remains were being bagged up. It was hoped that the forensic anthropologists would be able to give them some answers.

Roger flicked on his torch. He needed to make a start. He couldn't wait. Al could be hiding out in the woods, thinking Mick was still on her trail. He hoped the tip off about the badger baiting had been wrong, he didn't want her meeting up with that scum. He headed to the river path hoping he'd be able to find her.

Tom began to groan, Al pointed her torchlight close to his face. His hand came up and shielded his eyes.

'Bloody hell! Turn it down can't you!'

She moved it away quickly, 'Tom! Thank goodness you're awake! Are you alright?' she whispered.

He sat up slowly, rubbing his huge bear like hands over his head, 'God, my head!' he winced as his hand touched the area on his skull where he had been hit. He looked at his fingers and licked them, 'Oh sod it! I'm bleeding!'

Al shone the light again, directed at his head, 'It doesn't look too bad.' she dabbed at it with a tissue.

Tom blinked and took in his surroundings. They were on the floor of the cave, the metal gates were now padlocked shut and bushes and ivy outside hid the entrance from view. Tom's eyes rested on his ankle and the chain that secured him to the metal ring. A second chain ran across the dirt floor and was clasped around Alison's leg.

'Do they really think they can get away with this? Surely they know they'll have to let us go and then we'll go to the cops. Idiots!' he looked at Al, feeling guilty that she'd got caught up in his war.

'How did you end up here Al?'

She slumped down, exhaustion finally taking over, 'It's a long story but I was up in the woods trying to get away from my ex who is out to get me.'

Tom had been trying to chip away at the ground around the ring with part of the chain. He stopped what he was doing and looked up, 'What? He's come up to Greysmead after you?'

She nodded, 'Yep and his animal of a boss. They came looking for me. I've no idea where they are now, they could still be back at the house waiting for me,' she shuddered, 'Or they could be up here in the woods.'

'But it wasn't them that put us here was it?' he asked as he continued to dig away at the soil, 'I didn't see who hit me over the head. I assumed it was the baiters. Do you know who it is? Did you recognise any of them Al?'

'I did. You'll never believe me when I tell you. I feel sickened by it. Jim is part of it! Jim from the Abbot!'

Tom shook his head and moaned, 'God! That hurts!' he brought his hand up and rested it briefly over the cut, 'I must admit I did have my suspicions about Jim. He'd been acting really odd lately and I'd seen him a number of times up near the woods talking to that lot from Woodhurst. And then when Chas told me Jim put gypsum in the mead it linked him to this cave.'

'Of course! I hadn't thought of that. And you're right, another of the men is from Woodhurst, it's Steve's Uncle. He seemed like the ringleader to me. And I don't think they are going to be bringing back badgers to the cave for fighting tonight. He began to laugh and told me not to wait up for him. He said they would be heading off to sell what they harvest.'

'They're going to sell the poor buggers then, they can get good money for them from gambling dens in London,' Tom told her.

'The Uncle came across as being unhinged. He's a horrible man!' she shivered, 'What's the matter with me, I seem to find evil thugs wherever I go.'

Tom saw her mouth tremble as she held back tears. He couldn't help himself, he reached out and held her hand, 'So you got caught up with all this trying to escape your ex?' he asked.

Al nodded.

'They actually turned up at your place? Your ex and this other bloke? Did they threaten you?' Tom felt concern for Al. She looked done in. It was then it struck him how cold her hand felt. She only had a nightdress on under the fleece. What on earth was she doing running about in the woods at night in her nightdress?

He began to take off one of his many layers and covered Al with his jacket, 'Here, warm yourself up. You must be frozen! So tell me again what happened, were you in bed when they broke in? And how on earth did you manage to get away from them?'

Al shook her head, 'No, they didn't break in, to be honest I didn't actually see them.'

Tom began to feel worried as Al continued, 'But I knew they wanted to kill me so I went down into the crypt. I got away by climbing out of the well.'

Her face took on a faraway look as her mind went back to the moment that Mark had arrived. She had been dreaming when his crashing at the door had woken her. He had warned her that Mick and Ken were on their way and then shoved her down into the crypt. She had believed him. She was beginning to wonder now. There was something about it all that kept niggling at her; she couldn't put her finger on it but something wasn't quite right. Should she have trusted him after all? He said he wanted to help her, if so where was he now? She glanced at Tom and smiled. He was looking at her intently, a worried frown on his face.

He moved to get more comfortable and shuffled closer to her, 'Are you sure you are okay Al?'

He was concerned about her. Her story sounded rather far fetched. Had she been sleepwalking? Or had the cold got to her? Maybe hypothermia was setting in? That can make people drift off into a sleepy state. Al had said she climbed out of the well? He really didn't believe that!

She snuggled closer, his warmth radiating across to her chilled bones, 'What's going to happen to us Tom? Do you think Steve's Uncle is going to hurt us?'

An owl screeched in the distance as she waited for his reassurance. Tom was about to speak when he suddenly held his finger to his lips. He waited and strained his ears. He was sure he'd heard something.

'What is it?' she whispered, scared that it might be Big Mick.

The sound of a dog barking in the distance echoed through the trees.

'They're a long way off Tom, sounds like they are still up at the Sett.'

Tom shook his head, a finger still held on his lips. Then they both heard it. Crunching of stones and crackle of leaves as somebody walked amongst the trees and made their way closer to where they were held captive.

Al looked at Tom, 'What shall we do?' she hissed, 'Should we call out, let whoever it is know we are here? We don't know who it is. Tom I'm scared!'

Chapter forty one

The last of the straw had been stuffed down all visible exits, giving no way out for the unsuspecting badgers down in their sett. It was now time to get the dogs in. The terrier man knelt down and fixed the transmitter collar to one of his excited wiry haired helpers.

'Go on boy, down you go,' the dog wriggled down into the hole and sped underground in a bid to locate their quarry.

Jim watched from the edge of the ditch. He felt sick. He used to love being up at the old fort. King Alfred's ditch the kids from the village used to call it. So many good memories but now he hated being there. He despised what Steve's Uncle was doing to the badgers. But he had no choice but to go along with it. What else could he do? Jim wished he hadn't been so weak. If only he could have curbed his habit, but the buzz when he won made him gamble even more. But by the end of last year he always left the casino with empty pockets.

He knew he shouldn't have risked his business for his addiction, he knew that, but there was nothing he could do about it now except try to dig himself out of the mess. He was doing that – literally. Steve's Uncle had helped bail him out, loaned him money - money he was having difficulty paying back, especially with the interest. Jim's loan grew bigger each hour. So it was agreed that the interest became jobs instead of hard cash, jobs that were always outside the law. Tonight it was to dig out the badgers ready to sell them on to the gambling dens in London. Ironic that he was helping fuel some other sad bastard's gambling addiction.

Terrier man called him over, the transmitter was indicating where he needed to dig. Jim reluctantly made his way over to the sett. This was the third time he played a part in a dig. He hated it. Last time they had the fight take place in the cave. Chained the beast to the ground, broke its jaw to make it easier for the dogs. It was sick. He'd had enough. Tonight was going to be the end, but the police hadn't shown. He'd given the tip off, thought they'd get caught in the act. But Jim hadn't accounted for the madness that had happened down in the village. The police had enough on their plates without having to worry about badgers. Jim put the spade to the ground and began to dig.

Tom and Al waited in complete darkness on the floor of the cave as the footsteps became louder. The gates rattled as the padlock was tugged.

'Over here! Think I've found something,' a voice called out into the wood.

Tom's hand curled around Al's fingers and squeezed her hand as they sat in silence.

A man's voice shouted, 'There are gates here, padlocked up. Anyone got any cutters?'

The beam from his torch darted from left and right behind the veil of leaves and ivy. More footsteps headed closer, running this time. There was a breathless response, 'Here, will these do?'

There was the sharp sound of metal snapping. Tom's hand squeezed Al's hand tighter. The light from the torch became brighter as the vegetation was pushed aside. The gates swung open with a clang, followed by the crunch of feet on the dirt floor. The beam from the torch finally hit upon the two people tightly huddled together in the middle of the cave, bound to a metal ring with thick metal chains. They slowly peeled themselves apart and with trepidation looked to see who had broken into their prison.

'Alison Greenways?' asked the police officer as he knelt down and gently placed his hand on her shoulder, 'You've had a lot of people worried about you.'

He called his colleague across who deftly cut through the chains and released the prisoners from their shackles. Their legs felt weak as they attempted to stand up.

'And you are sir?' the officer asked Tom, who had crouched down again quickly as the blood had rushed from his head.

'Tom…Tom Elliot. Sorry, got up too fast. Still feeling a bit woozy where they bashed me over the head.'

'Take your time sir. We have requested an ambulance, they shouldn't be long. Do you both feel able to walk?' he looked at Al with a kind smile and saw she was crying. His eyes glanced across the cuts and scratches on her legs and arms and called a woman officer over to look after her.

Tom forced himself to his feet again, he couldn't let them cart him off in an ambulance, 'Is anyone heading over to the sett? It was the baiters that locked us in, they are planning on digging out the badgers. That's why I was knocked out. It was while I was waiting for you lot.'

Tom felt his anger rise, annoyed that the police hadn't been there to help him earlier. If they had come as requested he wouldn't be in the situation he was.

He raised his voice as he continued, 'For pete's sake, why didn't you turn up to help me earlier?'

'Calm down Mr Elliot. We did have a log of your request but I'm afraid our resources were required for some other incidents in the village.'

'What incidents? What's happened?' Al asked.

'I'm afraid there has been some fatalities.'

'Where? Who?'

'One down in the village,' the officer looked at Al and hesitated a moment before he continued, 'and also at your cottage Mrs Greenways.'

Al began to feel woozy. Her thoughts went to Mark. Was it him? Was he dead? She had doubted him, felt angry with him that he hadn't turned up to help her. What if all this time he had been lying dead in her cottage! Her head began to spin.

'Come and sit down Mrs Greenways,' the WPC's voice sounded strange. The voices around her began to lose form and sound distorted. She couldn't think straight. There was rushing in her ears. The woman officer had her arm around her and guided her down onto the floor just as Al passed out.

'So you're still up to your old tricks then Uncle?' Steve stood at the edge of the sett. Jim stopped digging and glanced across at Steve's Uncle and waited to see his reaction.

Steve's Uncle's gruff voice called out to his nephew, 'What you doing up here boy? You come to give your Uncle a hand eh?' he began laughing and looked across at terrier man, 'He's come to give his poor Uncle a hand! Sticking together like good family should. Ain't that right Steve?'

Terrier man laughed nervously wondering where it would lead. He knew Steve had fallen out with his Uncle after standing up to him a while back when Steve had told him he didn't want any more part in his dodgy dealings. It hadn't gone down too well.

'Jim? You coming back with me?' Steve called across, daring to cross his Uncle even more, 'Suz rang me, she's worried about you man! Come on, we can sort this.'

'Susie worried about her poor Daddy is she?' Steve's Uncle taunted Jim as he laughed manically.

Jim threw down the shovel, 'I've had enough of this!' he raged, 'Fuck you! I'm off.'

He jumped down and went to make his way across the ditch but Steve's Uncle grabbed at the spade and marched over to Jim and blocked his way. He stood, eyeball to eyeball with Jim and this time the laughter was replaced with menace.

'Well Susie won't be able to pay off your debts will she Jimbo? How you going deal with that if you piss off half way through the job. Eh?' he poked the handle of the spade into Jim's stomach, 'You owe me mate!' he screamed, 'Now get digging, or else you will have to face the consequences!'

'What consequences is that then?' a calm voice came from the edge of the woods, 'Am I to arrest you for threatening behaviour as well as badger baiting?'

Steve's Uncle turned towards the voice, 'You can't prove anything,' he said as Roger made his way out through the trees.

'Well it looks very much to me like you are digging out the sett,' Roger said and then indicated to Jim to move away, 'Get out of my sight Jim! I'd have thought better of you.'

'He forced my hand Roger,' Jim pleaded, 'I had no choice.'

'Keep your explanations for the station,' Roger said dismissively and headed towards Steve's Uncle.

The terrier man began to walk towards them, 'We were just trying to dig my dog out, that's all. He went down the hole after a rabbit and has got stuck.'

'Leave your porkies for the Wildlife Crime officer. Anyhow, if what you say is true we'll have to wait for a licence from DEFRA before you can start digging again. It's the law I'm afraid,' Roger grinned.

Roger spoke into his radio, 'Assistance required at the hill fort off Monkton Lane. Suspected contravention of the Badgers Act 1991.'

Steve's Uncle realised he had a moment where Roger wasn't giving him his full attention. He began to kick at the straw they had pushed down one of the entrances and then started to scrape it out with the spade.

Roger turned and shouted, 'Leave it!' and put his foot across the hole to stop any tampering with the evidence but he didn't react in time as the spade came down hard. Roger shut his eyes, swirls of red and black danced across his eyelids as he tried to hold back a cry. Searing pain screamed up his leg as the sharp edge of the shovel cut deep into his foot.

'You bastard!' Jim screamed at the top of his voice and ran over and pushed at Steve's Uncle who lost his balance and fell to the ground, rolling down into the ditch. A stump of a broken elder bush, jagged and sharp caught his face and rammed into his cheek. He held a hand over the cut and staggered to his feet, blood pouring through his fingers.

'You'll pay for this Jimbo!'

The terrier man stood like a frightened rabbit caught in the headlights. He glanced at the sett, giving his terrier a moments thought and then turned tail and ran with his remaining dog at his heels towards the trees.

Jim leant across to Roger who rolled around in agony as he held onto to his leg. His ankle, red with blood where the spade had cut deep into his foot.

'Rog, Rog - come on mate, try to stay still.'

Steve shouted to them, 'I've called for help.' he then called out to his Uncle who was beginning to make his way into the wood, 'They'll find you! You can't hide for long! The police will find you.'

Steve dashed across and knelt down beside Roger and put his arm around his shoulder. Roger gently rocked back and fro, his hands clasped tightly around his calf as he tried to handle the excruciating pain.

'Ambulance is on its way,' Steve said and turned and looked at Jim, 'You're a fucking idiot!'

Jim nodded, 'I know,' he whispered as the sirens sounded, heading towards Monkton Lane.

The lights in the ward flickered as he walked along past the sleeping patients. He stopped by her bed and watched her. Her face looked serene. Her dark hair fanned out on the pillow. He longed to touch her, feel the silky strands fall through his fingers, taste her skin, hold her body tightly to his. He ached for her. But it wouldn't be fair. She had been through so much and she had survived. It was all over. She deserved to be happy now. Her lips were parted slightly as she slept. He leant over and softly brushed across her mouth with a whisper of a kiss.

When Al awoke she could still taste the peppermint on her lips. Her eyes fluttered open and she smiled. She expected to see him sitting beside the bed but there was no one. Just a nurse pushing a trolley, handing out tablets and remedies to cure the patient's ills. Could they fix a broken heart? She turned on her side and pulled the cover over her head and shut out the world.

The rain pounded against the window. Al lay on her back, the cover over her face, as she hid from the world, hid from the truth. She would find out soon enough. She savoured her ignorance but knew she'd have to come up for air soon. The chair scraped on the hard floor and Al reluctantly pushed the covers aside.

Tom was now sitting by her bed, a look of concern on his face.

'Al? How are you feeling now? '

She pulled herself up and sat back against the hard metal backrest.

'Hello Tom. I'm fine. They've stitched up the gash in my thigh, given me a tetanus,' she told him and subconsciously rubbed at her arm, 'They wanted me to stay in over night, just in case,' she shrugged before twisting round and struggled to move one of the pillows higher, to protect her back from the utilitarian backrest.

'Here let me,' Tom stood up and pulled the pillow up behind her head. He smiled, his face inches away from hers.

'How about you?' she asked as he sat down again, 'Is your head okay?' Polite conversation. She held back asking the one question she really needed to know the answer to but didn't want to know…just in case.

He nodded, 'I'll live...Al…I'm really sorry I got you caught up with all this badger stuff. I didn't mean for you to get hurt.'

'I know. So tell me Tom, what happened? Did I miss much action after I went off in the ambulance? Did you manage to catch them?'

Tom became animated at once, 'Yes. Yes we did. Roger had got to them first. Apparently he'd been out looking for you.'

Her stomach tightened, 'Roger had been looking?'

'Yes, he'd been searching for you. I went up to the sett with some of the officers who had found us in the cave and the baiters ran straight into us as they were heading off into the woods. But Al…'

She stopped adjusting her bedclothes and looked up expectantly.

'Al, I'm afraid Roger was injured.'

'Oh God no! Is he alright? Is it serious?'

Tom nodded, 'It was his foot. It's been very badly damaged, the bone smashed.'

'Where is he? Is he here?'

'He's in the next ward.'

She started to get up, 'Maybe I should go and see him.'

'Not now Al, he's going for surgery today,' he looked at his watch, 'Probably on his way to theatre now.'

Al slumped back in the bed, 'Poor Roger. That doesn't sound good at all.'

The door to the ward suddenly banged open and Amy came galloping in. 'Alison! Alison!' she ran over to Al and leant across the bed and put her arms around her neck and kissed her, 'I dreamt about the sad lady last night. She said she's not sad anymore!'

'That's good news Amy,' Al said and continued to hug her as the pain of the past few days edged its way to the surface.

Tom looked back towards the door and saw Kit slowly making her way in. Her eyes were bloodshot, with heavy dark lines sweeping underneath where she had been crying. Tom jumped up and went over to speak to her while Amy continued to hug Al.

'Kit. How is he?' Tom asked as they stood by the ward door out of earshot.

'Yeah, Okay. A bit woozy. Should be going down soon for the op. How's Al? How much does she know?'

'Only about Roger and catching the baiters. I thought best to break it all slowly. But we'll have to tell her soon, the Police want to talk to her. They want to try and find out what happened down there.'

Al put the last few bits of clothing in the case and zipped it shut. She stood and looked around the bedroom. She'd waited so long to move into the cottage and now she couldn't wait to get away. She checked her watch, she had an hour before her Aunt was due to collect her. Al sighed and picked up her case and headed down the stairs. As she walked through to the kitchen she hesitated for a moment, she had to dare herself to walk past the heavy wooden door. The memories of being trapped down there had haunted her every night since she'd been back from the hospital. She'd been staying at Kit's, couldn't bear to be alone. Couldn't cope with the dark.

The police had finished up at the cottage now. They had been there for days on end. Forensics checking and doubling checking that there hadn't been any foul play. She had told them all she knew. They didn't believe her. Things she told them didn't add up in their logical minds. They didn't believe that the evil of the villagers had stayed trapped in the fog for centuries and had finally been eradicated by Tom's echo detector. She didn't blame them. She probably wouldn't have believed it either. Chas and Kit believed her. They knew.

As for Roger? He was still adjusting to the fact that the hospital couldn't save his foot. He wasn't open to conversation with anyone at the moment.

Al checked the front window. There had been swarms of reporters out there for days, but now the lane was empty. Another news story had obviously caught their eye. She was fish and chip wrapper now. She left the suitcase in the kitchen and opened the back door. She'd have one last walk amongst the ruins before she headed off to her Aunt's.

It was a cold day but the sky was blue and framed the golden leaves of autumn. She skirted around the ruins, disturbing a blackbird that began to call out in alarm causing her to jump. Would she ever feel at ease again? Would she always be looking over her shoulder? Her counsellor told her it would take time; she had to take it slowly. She'd had a very traumatic time, the adrenaline was permanently switched on even though she knew Ken and Mick were not longer a threat. Knew they were gone for good.

She'd been asked to identify Ken's body. She had hesitated, wasn't sure if she could, with so many emotions raging in her head. There had once been love bursting through her heart for the man who laid still and cold in the morgue. He'd looked innocent again, like the boy she had first fallen for all those years ago. But the love had been replaced with fear.

Al stopped at the well and leant for a moment against its edge thinking back to her living nightmare of climbing up across the skeletons. She shuddered. Experts were now examining the monk's remains up at Dundee University. They had been promised a Christian burial back in the village once they had been probed and poked. Then they would be able to rest in peace at last.

Al headed for the river. The water level was high and it flowed strongly. A gust of wind caught her off guard and she pulled her coat around her to keep the icy wind at bay. Too cold for skinny-dipping today. She smiled, thinking back to the day she had caught Mark in the river, as he jumped and yelled and splashed about, with the sun shimmering on the beads of water on his tanned skin. He knew how to live life to the full.

Al sat down on the bank and let her thoughts wander back to that day, savouring the memories but it hurt so much. She wiped away the first tear as it slid down her cheek and hugged her knees to her chest as she spoke his name out loud.

'Mark, Mark…I love you so much,' There was a constant ache in the pit of her stomach, a longing to see him again, feel him touch her, hold her. But she knew that was impossible.

She knew. Knew that the day he had come to see her to say goodbye had been final. She now knew that as he had said goodbye to her and she had watched him walk away into the ivy tunnel, his sick and suffering body had actually been lying in a hospital bed taking its last breath. He'd had a massive internal bleed and fallen into a coma. He'd told her the big boss wanted to move him on but he hadn't been talking about his police boss, he'd meant the big Boss in the sky.

The night he had come to warn her about Mick and Ken, he had been dead. That's what had been niggling at her, she had sensed something wasn't quite right. He had looked healthy again; his hair had been long and wavy. The painfully thin body from his previous visit had been replaced with the firm muscular form of the Mark she had known and loved.

They hadn't had long together in this life, but she now knew for certain that the bond between them had been strong and it bound them in this world and the next. The salt of her tears touched her lips as she sat and gazed at the river that gurgled and rippled over the rocks, heading away from her, out towards the sea.

Another gust of wind blew across Al's face, bringing with it the aroma of peppermint. Her lips parted into a gentle smile and she looked up at the sky. What was it he had said? 'This time next month I will living another life, have another name' As another tear fell slowly down her cheek she wondered who he would be?

She knew one day, when they both lived different lives, were different people, their paths would cross again. She leant forward and tugged at a plant by the river's edge and held the stalk to her lips, breathing in the fresh smell of the water mint. She smiled. One thing was certain in her mind that when it did happen she would know.

Eighteen months later

A stiff breeze filled the air with the sweet smell of daffodils as their yellow bonnets bobbed happily in the sunshine. Al hopped up the step and pushed open the door as a huge flock of rooks circled overhead, twisting, dipping and diving as they enjoyed their acrobatics amongst the scudding clouds. Al stopped a moment to enjoy the display and smiled at their cries of joy.

She dashed up the stairs and quickly slipped out of her dark suit and pulled on old jeans and a shirt, ready to start preparing the food for the lunchtime rush. It was always a busy time feeding the hordes.

As Al threw her handbag down, the order of service fell out onto the bed. She allowed herself a few moments to sit and read again the words of the hymns she had sung. Reverend Mahoney's service had been very beautiful and she had found it hard to keep her emotions in check.

One hymn in particular had touched her deeply and Al scanned the page to re read the words.

In this world, the Isle of Dreams

While we sit by sorrows streams

Tears and terrors are our themes

Al didn't know why the Vicar had chosen this particular hymn but it had felt as if he had some access to her mind, as if he knew what she has suffered. Friends had never been sure if Mark really had come to see her that night, most had dismissed it as wild imaginings during a time of intense stress. She had let it lie and let the wounds slowly heal.

Al continued to read the hymn. A single tear fell as she absorbed the last few lines of the poem

Me immortalized, and you;

And fresh joys, as never to have ending

Rev Mahoney had clasped her hand tightly as she left the Church and smiled at her warmly, 'I hope you have been able to find closure today my dear.'

She could tell in his eyes that he knew she was ready to finally let go.

'It was a beautiful service, yes. Thank you.'

It had been very moving. A memorial service for Greysmead Village to remember those that had lost their lives. Al had looked at Roger as she stood next to him in Church. She was so proud of him, how he'd managed to put everything behind him now.

He'd been a rock to Dorothy when she had come back to the village for her Mother's funeral. Poor Mrs Blackman. Wrong place, wrong time. Al realised that now but it had taken a long time to accept she wasn't to blame. She had felt so guilty, for it had been because of her that Kenny and Mick had been in the village that night.

It had been hard so soon after his injury, but Roger had testified in court against the Woodhurst baiters. It had certainly not been their first offence so they were given the maximum 6 months sentence. Steve's Uncle was also charged with GBH and was sent down for five years. Not long enough in Al's eyes.

Jim was given a fine, more debts to add to his money woes but Roger came to the rescue. He had been looking for something else to do with his life now he'd left the police force so he decided to buy the Jolly Abbot. It had given him a new lease of life and he was thriving on running the business and trade was on the up.

Jim had headed off with his tail between his legs to live in Somerset with Susie and Steve who were now expecting a baby.

During the service the vicar had said a few words about all who had lost their lives on that terrible night. He spoke of Mrs Blackman and how her friends and neighbours at Greysmead had loved her and that she was sorely missed. He talked about the brothers of the Abbey and how they had lost their lives in such a brutal way. Their remains had finally been returned to Greysmead a few months previous and had been given a Christian burial and now lay at rest with their Abbot at the side of the churchyard.

The Vicar also said a few words about Desmond and the villagers and even spoke of Kenny and Mick. He preached to the congregation of God's love and forgiveness of sin. Al had glanced at some of the faces in the pews, she knew no one there could find any love in their hearts for the evil-doers of either this century or the past.

The forensic team had also returned the remains of Desmond and his angry mob. But no mourners had stood at their graveside as the jumble of bones and dust had been lowered in one casket, deep into the ground in an unmarked grave under an elder tree in the field at the back of the churchyard.

Al had half expected Mark to be mentioned at the service, but why should he have been? He hadn't died at Orchard Cottage or at Greysmead. He had lost his life alone in a hospital bed in London. As far as most of the village knew he played no part of the events of that night.

A male voice called from downstairs and brought Al away from her thoughts.

'Come on Al, we've got a lot of hungry guests to feed down here!'

Al put the service sheet on the bedside cabinet and headed down to start on the preparations for the lunches.

As she stood at the worktop cutting up vegetables Amy put her head around the door.

'Hello Alison. I've come to see if I can help?'

'Hi Amy love,' Al smiled and handed Amy a knife, 'Is your Mum and Dad with you?'

'Yes, we couldn't resist coming to see the babies again.'

Al laughed and put her knife down, 'Okay! I should have guessed it wasn't me you wanted to see! Come on then, they are due for a feed about now.'

Amy followed Al to the nursery. Kit and Chas were already in there looking down at the sleeping bundles.

Al's heart felt full to bursting when she looked down at them, so fragile and small.

'Hello little ones.'

'Have you decided on names yet?' said Kit, 'Any ideas?'

Al nodded, 'Yep, I think Mary and John would be good names, don't you?'

'That's a lovely idea,' Chas said, 'But what about that bruiser?' he asked Al as she picked up the third badger cub that Tom had rescued from a sett over in Surrey.'

'She's made up her mind on that one,' said Tom, his face full of smiles as he walked into the room, 'She's decided to call it Mark.'

Al held onto the cub as it wriggled with delight, its paws clawed at the bottle as it took its milk, 'You don't mind do you Tom?'

Tom put his arm round her waist and gave her a little squeeze, 'You know I don't mind! I think it's a good name.' Tom kissed her lightly on the tip of her nose, 'Sorry folks I've got quite a few other creatures to deal with, they all seem to know when its lunchtime. See you abit later.'

'Oh can I come Tom? Can I come and see the fox again?' Amy looked at Tom pleadingly and then to her Mum, 'Can I?'

Kit laughed and nodded, 'Yes, off you go, but don't forget Roger and Dorothy are expecting us all up at the Abbot later. And be good girl for Tom!'

Amy whooped with delight and dashed out the back of Orchard cottage with Tom. The large expanse of grass and shrubs now gave way to wooden sheds, stables, shelters and cages where Tom and Alison ran their wildlife rescue centre.

Back in the nursery, Kit and Chas helped Al feed the young badgers who hopefully would be able to be set free again once they were older and stronger.

'I'm so glad Aunt Betty feels happy to visit the village again. It'll be so nice to have a big family get together down at the pub later this afternoon,' Kit said.

'Yes, we're looking forward to it and I'm honoured to be classed as a family member even though it's a very distant claim!' Al laughed.

'Betty always thought that you and Roger would end up together you know. To be honest so did we.'

Al shook her head, 'It wouldn't have worked, he'd have always been jealous of a dead man. No, it turned out just fine, he and Dorothy are made for each other. They both looked so happy at their wedding.'

Still holding the hungry cub in her arms Al went over to the window to look outside and watched Tom as he showed Amy how to mix the feed for the young fawn he'd found injured. He was so good with Amy, so patient. He was a good man. She was so lucky.

Al gazed out at the view, her eyes traced the line of bushes that followed the river before it disappeared into the wood. It was then she spotted two figures standing by the old ruins. She strained her eyes to see who it was. A sudden feeling of peace overwhelmed her as she realised it was her Father and he had someone with him. She watched as they turned to head towards the woods and she heard their voices in her head as they walked away.

'Come on Mark, it's time to go. She'll be okay now.'

A voice with a hint of fun replied, 'But a badger? Jeez! She's actually naming a badger after me?'

Mark's laughter echoed in her mind and she smiled.

The faint smell of peppermint and wood slowly faded and then was gone.

Epilogue

The Buzzard stretched his wings and alighted his post at the edge of the wood. He took to the air, lifted by the thermals high above the fields across from Orchard Cottage.

He made his way towards the village and circled above the churchyard. His keen eyesight focused amongst the long grass at the rear of the church in hope of catching a vole. His razor sharp vision spotted a hint of movement. The bird held his gaze. He could see a disturbance just under the old elder tree at the farthest edge of the burial ground.

Down in the darkness, deep below the sunshine and swaying flowers the soil shifted. The jumble of bones and dust lay in wait, confined and imprisoned within the bowels of the earth. As the spade had shovelled the soil over the mass grave one tiny atom of life force had remained. It knew the day would come that one small spark would ignite it again into a flame of energy and evil.

It would wait. It was patient.

The buzzard called out in alarm and flew away.

After word

When I first began Echoes at the Abbey I had set the location of the village of Greysmead close to a real town in Sussex. It was only after writing the first three or four chapters that I delved a little deeper into the lives of the lay brothers and Cistercian Abbeys in Sussex. I was amazed to discover that there had been only one Cistercian Abbey in the county and spookily it had been located close to the town I had chosen. I therefore changed the town name to the fictional town of Lunsford. Further research revealed that was not where the strange co-incidences ended. The Abbey ruins do still sit in the grounds of a now lived in home - a house that was once the Abbots house complete with undercroft and stone angel!

The banishment of Brother John to Coggeshall Abbey was partly based on a true story of a monk, also named John from 1403. A John Holmborn, a monk of the only Cistercian Abbey in Sussex, was discovered in a wood with an unmarried woman. He was beaten and then sent by his abbot to Coggeshall Abbey, in Essex.

The excerpts of the hymn sung at the memorial service was taken from The Place of the Blest by Robert Herrick

Printed in Poland
by Amazon Fulfillment
Poland Sp. z o.o., Wrocław